The BOY with the Latchkey

Cathy Sharp is happily married and lives with her husband in a small Cambridgeshire village. They like visiting Spain together and enjoy the benefits of sunshine and pleasant walks, while at home they love their garden and visiting the Norfolk seaside.

Cathy loves writing because it gives pleasure to others, she finds writing an extension of herself and it gives her great satisfaction. Cathy says, 'There is nothing like seeing your book in print, because so much loving care has been given to bringing that book into being.'

Also by Cathy Sharp

The Orphans of Halfpenny Street
The Little Runaways
Christmas for the Halfpenny Orphans

The Boy with the Latchkey

CATHY SHARP

HARPER

Harper
An imprint of HarperCollins*Publishers*
The News Building,
1 London Bridge Street,
London SE1 9GF

A Paperback Original 2017
1

www.harpercollins.co.uk

A catalogue record for this book is available from the British Library

ISBN: 978-0-00-821160-8

Set in Sabon LT Std 11.5/14.5 pt by
Palimpsest Book Production Limited, Falkirk, Stirlingshire

Printed and bound in Great Britain by Clays Ltd, St Ives plc

MIX
**Paper from
responsible sources**

FSC™ C007454

CHAPTER 1

'Here's the money for some bread, Archie,' Sandra Miller said. 'There are eggs and bacon in the pantry so you can get yourselves a meal when you come home.'

The old-fashioned wireless behind her was playing one of the biggest hits of the music charts the previous year – 'Oh Mein Papa' sung by Edie Calvert and one of Sandra's favourites, but she snapped it off impatiently as her son fiddled with his football boots and pushed the ten-shilling note at him.

'Yeah, all right.' Archie shoved the money into his pocket and looked bored. He knew the routine: let yourselves in with the key that hung on a string through the letterbox, make a meal for himself and his younger sister June, and leave the washing-up in the sink for when she got back. It wasn't ideal and Sandra hated the fact that her kids were one of a growing number of latchkey kids whose mothers worked and didn't get home until later in the evening.

Sandra hadn't planned this kind of life when she'd married Tim Miller. He'd been a soldier then and the war that had devastated Europe and much of the world

1

had been raging fiercely. They'd anticipated their wedding night because Tim had been going back to the Front and Sandra had feared she might not see him again. However, they'd been some of the lucky ones. Tim had come through the war unscathed. He'd landed a good job as the manager of a grocery store and until one foggy night in January 1950, Sandra's life had been perfect . . . until the ring at the door and a young constable's stuttering announcement that her husband had been killed cycling home from work in thick fog.

She'd been carrying Archie when Tim got leave from the Army in November 1941 and came home to marry her, but Sandra's parents had stood by her and she'd appreciated their loving kindness. Her throat caught with grief as she recalled the night when their house had been blown apart with them still inside. They'd had no warning, because it was one of those terrifying rockets they called the V2; it came out of the night and suddenly a home and the people in it were gone just like that, leaving a gaping hole in Sandra's life and that of her kids.

If her parents had lived she would have had someone to look after her children when she was working late, but unfortunately Tim had been an orphan and the kids had only her to feed, clothe and teach them about life, and sometimes Sandra felt it was a heavy burden, even though Archie did all he could to help her.

'What time will you be home then?' Archie asked, a little resentful now. Sandra knew he didn't mind doing little jobs down the Docks or even washing windows for elderly neighbours to bring in a few shillings, but he hated it that she was hardly ever home before it was time for cocoa and bed.

'I'm not sure,' she said. 'I'll come straight home from the office, I promise. I'm not working at the pub tonight.'

Twice a week she did a few hours in the evening at the Dog & Gun in Bethnal Green, to earn extra money, because growing kids needed so much, and Sandra hated the idea that hers might have to go short.

'I'm sorry, Archie,' Sandra apologised, the reproach in his eyes pricking her. 'I know I expect a lot of you, but I can't help it . . .'

'Yeah, I know, Mum,' he said and grinned at her. When Archie smiled it was as if the sun had come out. With his dark-red hair and his green eyes, he was the image of his father and her heart turned over with love. 'We'll be all right.'

'I know I can rely on you to take care of June . . .'

'Yeah, I'll look out for the brat.' From the lofty position of his thirteen years, Archie saw his nine-year-old sister as a troublesome kid, but despite their constant bickering, Sandra knew that he would care for her as best he could. Yet he shouldn't have so much responsibility and it hurt Sandra because she couldn't provide the loving, stable home her children were entitled to.

Leaving the house, Sandra ran to the end of the dingy lane to catch her bus because she didn't want to be late for the office; she was so used to the boarded-up houses on either side that she no longer noticed. This slum area was all she could afford since Tim died, although she was always looking for something better. She worked in a biscuit factory in the accounts department, keeping track of invoices and making up the wages. It was hard work but she didn't mind that – in fact the only thing she disliked about her job was Reg Prentice. Reg was the office manager and a menace to anything in a skirt. None of the girls liked him, but most of them had the courage to stand up to him and tell him to get lost when he touched their bottoms and squeezed up against them in the corridor.

Sandra had asked him to leave her alone several times. In fact, he'd been such a nuisance that the previous evening, when he'd pushed her up against the wall, she'd slapped his face and told him that if he didn't stop harassing her she was going to Mr Jenkins, the overall manager of the factory.

'Do that and you're out of a job,' Reg hissed against her ear. 'Besides, I'm your manager. He's hardly going to believe a little scrubber like you. We all know what you widows are like; you can't do without a man. I know you don't say no to some others.'

'I'm not interested in men, just in doing my job . . .' Sandra protested.

'I've seen you givin' Mr Jenkins the eye,' Reg sneered. 'Well, he's the sort that doesn't stray and he doesn't like loose women . . . By the time I finish tellin' what I know you'll be lookin' for work without a reference.'

'I don't give in to bullies,' Sandra retorted. 'He wouldn't believe you. I know Martha Jenkins and she will vouch for me.'

'Not by the time I've done,' he muttered beneath his breath.

Sandra had walked out on him, but a lingering doubt nagged at her mind. If Reg really had it in for her, she might be in serious trouble. He was a vindictive man and she wouldn't be the first woman to lose her job because of wicked lies . . .

Her bus was stopping. She got off and walked quickly towards the factory, noticing the headlines on the newspaper stand. Anthony Eden had taken over from Mr Churchill when he resigned and now he was talking about calling a general election – as if that would make any difference to women like her! Reaching her workplace at the corner of Brick Lane, Sandra hung her jacket in the small dark cloakroom and entered the office. Here it was lighter, because of the large window at the back, and there were several desks, some equipped with typewriters, others like her own, piled high with folders and an overflowing in-tray. Reg smirked at her as she passed him and she saw two of the other girls whispering and giving her odd glances.

'Don't sit down, Mrs Miller,' Mrs Landsbury said from the doorway into her office. 'Mr Jenkins would like to see you immediately.'

Sandra looked at the manager's secretary and saw frosty disapproval in her eyes. She glanced at Reg and knew at once that he was gloating. Obviously she was in trouble and she had no idea why . . .

'I want to play with Mimi,' June said that evening, pulling at Archie's hand as he dragged her into the baker's at the end of Whitechapel Road. 'I don't see why I shouldn't go round her house. Her dad got her some skates and she says I can borrow them . . .'

'You can go round there on Saturday,' Archie said as he paid for the crusty cottage loaf from the baker. 'It's no use you sulking, June. Mum told me to look after you. I've got to get some tea for us both and then I've got schoolwork to catch up on. I have to do twenty sums tonight and they're hard ones.'

'I hate sums,' June said, making a rude face at him as they walked together towards the row of dilapidated houses where they lived. The entire street was scheduled for demolition, some of the terraced houses already derelict, and the gutters choked with rubbish. Archie had heard the landlord telling his mother that she would have to find somewhere else to live, but she said everywhere was too expensive and she was staying put until she was forced to quit.

'If you don't do your schoolwork you'll never get on . . .' Archie muttered and put his hand through the letterbox to fish out the key on a string.

'I'm going to be a famous model and wear lovely clothes when I leave school. I don't need sums to look pretty.' She kicked at the scarred front door, with its peeling green paint. 'I hate comin' back to an empty house.'

With her pale-blonde hair and her blue eyes, June took after their mother. She looked so sweet that butter wouldn't melt in her mouth, but she could be a real pain as far as Archie was concerned. He would've liked to let her go with her friend so that he could have some peace, but there was no chance of that, because Mum would create if June wasn't home when she got back.

'Mum said she would be home earlier tonight,' Archie lied, trying not to notice that there was a faint smell of drains in the kitchen again. Mum had poured loads of strong disinfectant down the sink but the stink always came back. 'Maybe she'll let us listen to Dick Barton on the radio—'

'I don't like Dick Barton,' June said and flung herself down on the lumpy old settee. 'I don't like *Journey into Space* either. It frightens me when you listen to that, Archie . . .'

'What do you want to do then?'

'I want a comic. Can I have *School Friend*?' She sprang up eagerly.

Archie fingered the change from the loaf and sighed. Sometimes his mother would let them spend a few pennies on comics. He would have liked one about Rock 'n' Roll, because he was a big fan of Bill Haley & the Comets, and he was saving up because he wanted to go and see James Dean in *East of Eden*. He'd seen it once already, but he admired the rebellious American teenager who drove fast motorbikes, even though Archie wasn't old enough to see his films really; his friend down the local flea pit let him in with a wink and a nudge sometimes. However, June wouldn't stop moaning unless she had her own way. She would create all night and he would never get his homework done.

He gave her a florin. 'Here, go and get it from the corner shop but come straight back. If you run off, I'll come after you and you'll be sorry!'

June stuck her tongue out, grabbed the money and ran.

Archie saved most of what his mother let him keep from the odd jobs he did on Saturdays and in the evenings in summer. He'd dodged school for a while to find work down on the Docks, but the inspector had come after his mother and threatened to fine her if he didn't go regularly, so he'd had to give that up, which annoyed him, because he desperately wanted a gramophone. He listened to the popular songs on the radio, but it wasn't the same as having your own records. Some of his friends at school had record players and they bought the latest hits with their birthday money. Archie usually had clothes for his birthday from the nearly-new shop down near Petticoat Lane. His mother didn't buy from the market stalls, because she said a lot of the stuff was worn out.

'Some people buy new clothes and then sell the ones their kids have grown out of,' Sandra had told Archie when she'd bought him his first pair of long trousers the previous Christmas. 'These have hardly been worn, love. I wanted to buy new, but I just couldn't manage it – even with the money you earned from delivering papers.'

'They're all right, Mum,' Archie had smiled at her. 'At least they're long trousers and people won't think I'm still a kid.'

'I'm going to save up for some new ones for your birthday next year,' she'd promised. 'I did knit you a new jumper . . .'

'It's great,' Archie said, because the stripes were his school colours, which meant he could probably get away with wearing it there. The uniform was supposed to be grey trousers and a navy pullover or blazer and a white shirt. Archie's shirts were frayed at the cuffs but he pulled them up inside his sweater and hoped that no one noticed.

He was still investigating the contents of the pantry when his sister returned clutching her comic and a tube of wine gums.

'Hey, I said you could have a comic, not spend all of it,' Archie said.

'I'm hungry,' June said as she dragged her coat off and flopped down on the old sofa.

'What do you want – fried bacon and egg, or would you prefer scrambled eggs on toast?'

'Can I have bacon and egg with toast . . . in the middle like a sandwich, and I'd like some brown sauce.'

'What did your last servant die of?' Archie demanded. 'Set the table while I get it ready then . . . and I'm having some cocoa with mine . . .'

Archie looked at the clock. It was already half past eight in the evening and his mother still hadn't got back from work. June had gone up to bed and taken her comic to read on the promise that Mum would bring her some more cocoa when she came home.

Having finished the homework he'd been given, Archie eyed the dirty plates, cups and saucepans he'd used to cook their tea. He hated washing up and Mum seldom expected him to do it, but he knew she was going to be really tired when she got in, and he felt guilty. Sighing, he filled a kettle with water and set it on the range to boil; Mum always said you should pour boiling water over the soda and then add the cold, because it got the grease off better. He wished she would buy some of the washing-up powder that made things easier, but she said soda had always been good enough for her. It was because she couldn't afford newfangled things like washing powder, but it didn't help him when he was stuck with a chore that he hated.

He remembered the old days when his father was alive. They hadn't been rich but there had been money for new clothes, good food, trips to the zoo or a Disney film, and

birthday presents that weren't second-hand. He remembered his dad coming home with fish and chips wrapped
in newspaper on Saturday lunchtime. Normally, he'd have
sweets in his pockets for Archie and June and he'd given
them threepence pocket money a week that they could
save in their moneyboxes for whatever they wanted.
Archie missed those things, but most of all he missed the
way his dad smiled and swung him round or tossed him
in the air, the games of football they'd played in the park,
and the feeling of love in the house. His mother still
loved them both, Archie knew that, but she was so tired
all the time and so seldom around.

He listened to Dick Barton and then switched the radio
off because it was music he didn't like much. Sometimes,
he listened to country music but mostly he liked Rock
'n' Roll, because it was exciting. It made him realise that
he was a teenager, and teenagers were different these
days. The old dark days after the war had begun to
change and life was easier, even here in the East End,
though Archie's family couldn't afford to do all the things
that other families did – those that had both a mother
and father working were better off these days. The news-
papers talked about a time of new prosperity and
opportunities for everyone, and even here in the scruffy
East End things were improving in some places. One of
his best friends, Jamie Rawlings, had told him only that
morning that his dad was getting a car soon.

'We'll be going to the sea on Sundays in the summer,'
he'd told Archie. 'I'll ask Dad if he'll let you come with
us. I'm sure he will, because he likes you – he says
you've got a raw deal . . .'

Archie hadn't liked the idea that his friends pitied

him. His mother did what she could for him and June, and he wouldn't have changed her for the world. He just wished things could be as they were when his dad was alive.

Glancing at the clock again, Archie saw it was half past nine; it wasn't like Mum to be this late. He hoped she hadn't had an accident! A cold shiver went right through him as he remembered the terrible day his father had been killed. Mum had cried for days and so had he. June had wept too, but she hadn't really understood, and she didn't remember Dad the way Archie did.

Sighing, he decided to make their suppertime cocoa and take one up to June before he went to bed. She might be asleep, but she was probably still reading that comic . . .

Archie felt the panic surge as he realised that his mother hadn't been in all night. Her bed was just the same; everything was exactly as he'd left it in the kitchen, all the plates and cups on the scrubbed pine table, because he hadn't bothered to put them back on the painted dresser at the end of the room. Besides, he knew that Mum wouldn't come home and not let him know. She wasn't the sort to just stay out all night. Archie's mum didn't go with men. He knew for certain she wasn't like that, and he trusted her implicitly, therefore, something had happened. She must have had an accident . . .

Archie felt sick with apprehension as he chivvied June into getting ready for school. She moaned and whined and kept asking where Mum was. He told her that Mum had had to go out and been back very late.

'It's not fair,' June said and tears rolled down her

11

cheeks. 'I want her – why isn't she here? Mimi's mum doesn't work all hours like ours . . .'

'She has a husband to help her. Mum has to pay the rent on this dump and buy the food and clothes, everything. She can't help it, June. Come on and get ready. I'm going to take you to school . . .'

'What about my dinner money?'

'Didn't you pay that yesterday?'

'Mum said she would give it to me and then she forgot. If I don't pay today I shan't get any dinner . . .'

'I'll see if there's any in the pot.' Archie looked in the old silver-plated teapot that had belonged to Mum's granny and found there was just ten shillings. 'How much is it for this week?'

'Three ninepences,' June said and frowned, her tongue coming out of the corner of her mouth. 'I don't know how much that is . . .'

'It is two shillings and three pennies,' her brother said. 'Blimey, June, you ought to know how to add that much up.'

'I can add up if I've got a pencil and paper. I do it on my fingers and write it down.'

Archie had too much on his mind to argue with her. Once he had June in school, he was going to look for Mum. He wasn't sure where to start, but thought perhaps the best place would be the biscuit factory. If she'd had an accident they would probably know.

June lagged behind all the way to school. He practically had to push her in the gate and made her promise to wait for him after school.

'I'll walk you home so just wait in the playground until I get here.'

12

June reluctantly promised and ran off to join Mimi and her other friends. Archie sighed. He'd got football today, if only he could get there, but first he had to find Mum . . .

CHAPTER 2

'Angela, how lovely to see you,' Sister Beatrice said, welcoming the woman who had been their Administrator at St Saviour's for several years, and whom she sadly missed. 'It seems ages since you visited us . . .'

'Not for want of trying,' Angela Adderbury said and smiled. 'The twins had whooping cough last month, and then I had to pop down and see my father. I told you he hadn't been well, didn't I?' Sister Beatrice nodded. 'He had a few days in the nursing home and seems much better – and the lady he intends to marry had just taken him in a lovely bowl of fruit.'

'Your father is getting married again?'

'Yes, at last. He and Margaret have been friends for years. After my mother divorced him, he waited for a while before asking her, but I think his illness made his mind up for him. It's happening next month . . .'

'Spring is a lovely time for weddings,' Sister Beatrice said. 'Are the twins quite well now?'

'Yes, and into everything,' Angela said. 'One day I'm going to get time to organise some more fundraising events for you, but at the moment my hands are full.

Mark is always offering to help, but although he plays with them in the garden, he's not good when they're screaming and acting up. He lectures them about proper behaviour when all they need is a smack on the bottom and they behave. His intentions are good, but he isn't really into childcare.'

'Mark is a busy man, and children need a lot of patience,' Sister Beatrice said. 'I do miss your exciting projects, Angela, but I know Mark and your sons must come first.'

'Things have changed a great deal since we worked together, Sister.'

'Yes, and I'm not convinced they are entirely for the better. I'm sure the government's intentions were good when they brought us all under the state umbrella, but an institution is only as good as those that run it.' She paused for thought, and then, 'It sometimes seems to me that all they've given us is miles of red tape. Naturally, we must abide by the government's new rules, but St Saviour's was always run with the same principles of love and care as the law provides. We have never given our children cold showers or sent them to bed hungry night after night, or treated them as if they were prisoners in a place of correction. I know that in the past many orphanages did these things, but I should never have been a party to such practices . . .'

'Nor I,' Angela agreed, 'but St Saviour's was always the gold-standard and the government needed to protect children from the harsh acts of those less caring than you and your staff, Sister Beatrice.'

'Perhaps they ought to remember that when they descend on us for an inspection with scarcely an hour's warning. So far we've had nothing but praise for our care, though they criticise the state of the toilets sometimes, because we've had a leak no one seems to be able to fix. They warned us last time that water on cloakroom floors can make them slippery. As if we needed to be told! I have no patience with all this mealy-mouthed nonsense!'

Her disapproval when speaking of the state supervision was obvious, but since the Children's Act some years earlier the Children's Department was taking over more and more and dictated a great many rules and regulations, against which Sister Beatrice had railed bitterly for some time. She, like everyone else, had grown used to the fact that they had to defer to the Children's Department, who had taken over the new wing for their own purposes, and although Sister Beatrice was given a free hand with the day-to-day running she now had to report anything of importance to the Superintendent next door – a young, and in her oft-spoken opinion, pert woman who was far too inexperienced for the post.

'Well, I'll find time to organise a dance this summer, I promise – and one day soon the twins will be back at school. Mark says he doesn't mind looking after them sometimes, but he's so busy and . . . actually, I find I enjoy looking after them myself. I suppose we could employ someone to help but just for a while I want to be a full-time mother and wife. I have left them with a friend today; Janni is fond of them and always enjoys having them for a few hours, but I'll go back on the evening train, because I hate leaving them for too long.'

'I think you're entirely right,' Sister Beatrice said. 'Nothing is more important in my opinion. Have you seen Nan at all?'

'Not since her wedding to Eddie I'm ashamed to say,' Angela admitted. 'I sent her a birthday card and we always exchange Christmas cards, but I must try and see her while I'm in town for a couple of days.'

'I know she would be delighted to see you,' Sister Beatrice said. 'Nan visits me every week, to have a chat and a cup of tea. I'm partial to her cakes and she is very good to me.'

'You've been friends for such a long time,' Angela said. 'You must miss her terribly?'

'I was always confident that St Saviour's was in good hands when Nan and you were here,' Beatrice confided. 'I still have good people here but it isn't the same next door – especially in certain regards . . .'

'Do you have trouble from the girls?' Angela frowned, because it had caused great controversy when the Children's Welfare Department had taken over part of St Saviour's for their disturbed girls. Beatrice herself had resisted the change, but the Board had been told it was necessary to use all facilities to the full and forced to agree.

'I was against it from the start,' Beatrice said, looking over the gold-rimmed glasses she'd recently started to wear more often. 'I cannot say that I like this new woman they've put in charge either. Her predecessor seemed a sensible woman but this girl is too full of herself . . .'

'She respects you, doesn't she?' Angela looked concerned. 'You are in charge here, Sister Beatrice. Miss Saunders runs her department but in day-to-day matters, you are still responsible for our children. Although under the supervision of the state, we are still an independently run charity. Of course as an employee of the Children's Welfare Department Miss Saunders does have the authority to override us if she thinks we're doing something wrong . . .'

'She would like to take charge of the whole place if she could,' Beatrice sniffed. 'She is a very modern young woman, Angela. Not your sort at all, brash and abrasive in my opinion. She may keep good discipline with her girls, and I dare say they need it – but I do not care for all the things she says. She came from a working-class background, as I did myself – but I never was radical in my ideas. Compassion mixed with sense, and morality, is my motto, as you know.'

'Yes, I do,' Angela agreed and Beatrice laughed as she recalled their disagreement over using the cane on children. Angela had been totally against it and Beatrice had come round to her way of thinking.

'You taught me a lot, my dear, and perhaps I shall learn from Ruby Saunders, but at this moment I do not think it.'

Angela drank her tea and looked thoughtful. 'If you are really uneasy about her I could have a word with Mark? The Board has some influence with the Welfare Department. It is still early days for them in all honesty. It would be impossible for them to take over every orphanage in the country and run them. They are overwhelmed by sheer numbers and rely on private institutions like ours and Barnardo's to take some of the strain . . . and therefore open to a little gentle persuasion now and then.'

'Say nothing at this stage; Miss Saunders has only been in the job a few weeks and I don't want to undermine her position. I dare say we shall get used to one another in time.'

'I'm sure you will,' Angela agreed. 'I bumped into Wendy on my way up. She seems happy here?'

'Yes, she is my only staff nurse at present and a good one. I thought she might marry but when Andre died she seemed to accept that her life was here and, although she has friends, I do not think she will marry.' Beatrice paused. 'You must see Muriel while you're here, Angela. She is always asking after you. I fear she may retire after Christmas so you should take the opportunity to see her.'

'You'll be sorry to lose her, and the children enjoy her cooking,' Angela said. 'You've kept several of the staff, haven't you? Once upon a time we were always having them leave us, but Tilly and Kelly are still here, although I understand Tilly got married last year and works just three days a week?'

'Yes, but that is sufficient most of the time. Nurse Michelle still does a shift two mornings a week, and Nurse Paula comes in as relief when Wendy has her holiday. I'm trying to secure the services of another nurse full-time, but it isn't easy. You did know that Wendy's friend in France died of his war wounds in 1950?'

'It was just about five years ago, before I left to have the twins, so yes, I did know,' Angela said. 'I think she lost two men to the war and is now a dedicated career nurse.'

'Wendy is my rock,' Beatrice confirmed. 'She takes a month's holiday in France once a year to visit the May twins and her friends there, but the rest of her time is devoted to St Saviour's so we are very lucky.'

'Extremely,' Angela agreed. 'Well, I think I've taken

up enough of your time, Sister Beatrice. I'll go and see Muriel and then I'm meeting Mark for lunch.'

'Give him my best regards,' Beatrice said.

She took her glasses off and rubbed the bridge of her nose as Angela went out. It was good to talk with old friends and she didn't see enough of either Angela or Mark, because they lived in the country and were more closely involved with Halfpenny House, which was nearer for Angela to pop in when she had an hour to spare.

Glancing at the paperwork in front of her, Beatrice sighed. Reports had never been her strong point and Angela had helped her so much with that kind of thing, but life moved on and the years seemed to fly by. However, she had a part-time secretary who came in once a week to keep the accounts straight. She was efficient, and would type up the report that Beatrice had written out, but she just wasn't Angela. Oh, well, there was no point in trying to hold on to the past.

'Sister Beatrice, may I have a word?' Sergeant Sallis tapped the door as he put his head round. 'I just passed Mrs Adderbury on the stairs. She said she thought you might have time to speak to me?'

'Certainly,' Beatrice said. She'd known him from the time he'd first joined the force and he was still as helpful and polite as he'd been as a constable. 'What can I do for you, Sergeant?'

'More of the usual,' he said ruefully. 'A couple of children in trouble, I'm afraid. The mother is in our cells awaiting trial for embezzling from her firm. She seems a decent woman and I can't believe she did it, but the evidence is damning and that means the kids are on their own. I spoke to the Children's Department and they advised bringing them here until something can be sorted out, otherwise they'll have to leave London. All their resources are stretched to the limit . . .'

'You want to know if we have a place for the children?'

'Yes, I'm afraid I do,' he said regretfully. 'I know you're full to bursting – but the boy is rebellious and if we don't keep them together I think he will get into serious mischief. He went round to the factory where his mother worked in the office and when they told him she'd been arrested he lost his temper. Threw things about and yelled at the manager – called him a liar. Mind you, I don't like that Reg Prentice myself.'

'Oh dear, the rebellious ones usually end up next door, at least, if they're girls.'

'Archie is a decent lad. His neighbours all say he's done his best to help his mother since his father died, but she was having a hard time of it . . . They live in a row of slum houses that are hardly fit for habitation, but she kept hers like a new pin inside.'

'Do you think she took the money out of desperation?'

'I've spoken to her and I believe she's innocent, but she's been committed for trial. The evidence seems to prove her guilt, and money has definitely been taken from the firm – stolen cheques as well as cash from the safe . . .'

'What will happen to her if she's convicted?'

'She is previously of good character and if we can get someone to speak up for her, she might get off lightly – but it depends who is taking the case.'

'So the children have no home . . .'

'Literally,' Sergeant Sallis agreed. 'Their house was in any case on the list for demolition and now that the rent hasn't been paid for a couple of weeks, the landlord intends to board it up ready for the bulldozers.'

'In that case they must come here,' Beatrice said. 'You know we are mostly a halfway house these days. The majority of our children are passed on to Halfpenny House in Essex. The Board think the air is better there for them and I dare say they're right – though we've had two or three run away from the home there. Some London kids just can't settle anywhere else.'

'I'm a Londoner myself,' Sergeant Sallis said and nodded. 'Right then, I'll bring them round later. I thought I'd better ask first, because I know you don't always have room these days. I hoped when they opened that new wing our worries were over, Sister.'

'Yes, so did I, and for a while we managed well,' Beatrice agreed with a wry smile. 'However, the local authority needed somewhere to put their disturbed girls and they decided to take over that wing of St Saviour's, leaving us to carry on here as best we can. I think they should have taken them elsewhere, but the Children's Department have the power to do as they want these days.'

'You don't get any trouble from them, do you?'

'From the girls you mean? They can be a bit cheeky, but we haven't had any real upsets. I think they must be disciplined before they get here. I'm not happy about them being there, because I need the rooms for my orphans, but I was not given an option.'

'I dare say they thought this side of the home was enough for you to manage . . .'

'I may not be a young woman, Sergeant, but I'm not old,' Beatrice fixed him with a hard stare. 'I've hardly had a day's illness for years . . .' It wasn't quite true, but she didn't like it to be thought that she was too old to do her duty. She had no intention of being retired to the convent while she had breath in her body.

'No, Sister, not at all,' he said apologetically. 'I don't think it would be the same here without you . . .'

'Well, I have things to do,' Beatrice said. 'Bring the children when you're ready.'

'Yes, I shall – and thank you for your help as always . . .'

Beatrice sighed as the door closed behind him. Her visitors had put her off her stride. She would leave the report for later. It was time for her to check on the sick wards and talk to Wendy about the cases of tummy bug they currently had on their hands.

'Well, Billy,' Staff Nurse Wendy said to the tall, well-built young man who had just fixed her medicine trolley for her. 'You certainly know what you're doing with machinery. That wheel has been wonky for weeks. Mr Morris said it was past fixing, but it looks sturdy enough now.'

'I've put a steel pin right through and fixed it with a bolt,' Billy Baggins said and grinned at her. The evidence of his work was spread on the floor, metal shavings, tools and drill, and in his greasy hands, which he was wiping on a much-used cloth. 'You only have to ask, Nurse, and I'll see you right. 'Sides, the caretaker has more than enough to do. They make a lot of work next door . . .' He jerked his head at the wing used for disturbed girls. 'He told me he's had to mend the window at the back three times this month. I reckon they deliberately break the lock so they can get in later at night . . .'

'And to think you were the rebel of St Saviour's,' Wendy said and smiled at him approvingly, as he cleared the mess and packed his tools away in the battered old bag he kept them in. 'Always running everywhere and getting into trouble with Sister Beatrice.'

'Me and her are mates now,' Billy said cheekily, 'at least, most of the time. I doubt she'd feel like taking a cane to me now, even if I upset her – and I shan't do that. She's all right, she is . . .'

'She's one in a million and don't you forget it, Billy. No one else would let a great hulking lad like you have the run of the place at your age . . .'

'I'm looking for a room I can afford,' Billy said ruefully. 'You don't earn much as an apprentice mechanic, you know. I'm saving up for driving lessons, and to get married as well . . .'

'You're still set on Mary Ellen then?' Wendy twinkled at him. 'I remember seeing you at the Christmas party last year . . . under the mistletoe . . .'

'Yeah.' Billy's cheeks were slightly pink. 'We're promised to each other, but Mary Ellen's sister won't let her marry me until I'm doing a proper job – and it will be years before I'm through my apprenticeship.'

'Well, you're too young to marry yet, either of you,' Wendy said. 'I haven't seen Mary Ellen for a long time. Is she still working at Parker's clothing factory in Stepney? I was surprised when she went there; I thought she was set on being a teacher.'

'Rose made her leave school and be apprenticed in the rag trade,' Billy said. 'When she took her to live with her in that posh council flat . . . Gone up in the

world now she's Sister O'Hanran, has our Rose . . .'
His eyes flashed with mischief.

'Well, that is something to be proud of,' Wendy said.
'Rose worked very hard, and she always promised that
she would have Mary Ellen to live with her when she
could afford her own place.'

'Mary Ellen wanted to stay here with me.'

'It's only because Sister Beatrice likes you that you
can stay,' Wendy reminded him. 'Most of the boys leave
at fifteen and you're eighteen now.'

'Yeah and I ought to be earning more money,' Billy
grumbled. 'Well, I'll get out of your way then . . .'

Wendy smiled as the good-looking lad left the ward.
Billy was like one of her family now. She'd come to the
home a year or so after he did and she'd stopped on,
just as Billy had. He was a part of the place and helped
out with little jobs that needed doing. Mr Morris was
the caretaker, but in an ancient building like this there
was always something that needed doing: washers on
taps, cracked basins, stained ceilings when there was a
leak in the bathroom, which Billy had found and fixed
without them needing to call in a plumber. Sister Beatrice
said Billy was useful, and as he had no family around
she'd let him stay on, even though he was working.
Wendy suspected the stern nun had a soft spot for the
rebellious boy who'd done so well since he joined them
at St Saviour's. He ate sandwiches at work during the
day but had his breakfast and supper with the older
boys at the home, many of whom still looked up to
him. Billy had gained quite a reputation for winning
cups for running and football, and he still acted as a

monitor at times, keeping some of the wilder ones in order and taking them to football practice in a battered old shooting brake he and a friend borrowed sometimes. Once he'd passed his driving test and could drive without supervision, he hoped to get a small van of his own. It would help with the football team he'd organised for the local youth club, to which most of the lads belonged.

Sister Beatrice had been given the discretion to choose when her children were ready to move on. It was the one clause she'd stipulated when the contracts had been drawn up and the local authority moved in.

'I must be allowed to decide when my children are sufficiently settled to move on,' she'd said, fighting tooth and nail for the principles she believed in. 'Moving a disturbed or vulnerable child out to a place where he or she feels isolated or uneasy can set them back years. While I agree that the fresh air and better facilities at Halfpenny House are so much better for them, their mental state and ability to accept that move is paramount. If everything is to be done in a matter of days I am not the person for the job.'

Mark and Angela had done battle on her behalf, both with the Board of St Saviour's charity, and the local authorities, who had wanted to impose their own ideas. However, such was the esteem she was held in by the local police, community bigwigs and general population, that her terms were accepted, and even Miss Ruth Sampson, who was still in overall charge of the local Children's Department, had agreed that they needed Sister Beatrice if the swell of public feeling was to be appeased. Over the years of hardship she'd become firmly entrenched in the hearts and minds of the people of the area and was known as the Angel of 'Alfpenny Street to everyone. Women who slammed their doors in the faces of the council busybodies opened them to Sister Beatrice with a smile and the offer of a cup of tea.

St Saviour's wasn't quite the same as it had been in Angela's time. She'd started up all kinds of schemes to keep the children busy and formed a team spirit amongst the orphans, most of whom had known poverty and tragedy. These days the children were brought here for a while to get over their bereavement and to learn to cope with life again without the parents they'd lost, but then most were moved out to Halfpenny House in Essex, unless they were considered to need a more specialised home. Billy was different. He would never have settled anywhere but the East End of London, and because she knew that, Sister Beatrice had provided him with a home until he could find his own.

Wendy knew how difficult it was to find somewhere decent to live. She'd stayed on in the nurses' home for a while and taken her time before getting herself a nice little maisonette in one of the renovated buildings within walking distance of St Saviour's, but she hadn't done that until after she knew St Saviour's was going to be her life. At one time she'd hoped that she might marry Andre and live in France, but the shrapnel in his head had moved sharply and entered his brain. Wendy had been horrified when she'd received the telephone call asking her to come at once. It had been too late when she got there. Mercifully, Andre had felt little pain, because it had happened so quickly. Wendy had understood that he'd been badly wounded in the war, but he'd seemed to be well and the shock of his death had devastated her, destroying her last hopes of marriage and a family.

If it hadn't been for the twins, Sarah and Samantha May, who had some years previously come to them near to starving after their father abandoned them, she wasn't sure what she would've done. Wendy had been instrumental in rescuing them when their uncaring aunt had tried to separate them and she'd accompanied them to their new home in France when their mother's sister had claimed them, seeing them settled and happy before returning to London. When a couple of years or so later, Andre died and Wendy had wept bitter tears, Sarah had wound loving arms about her and sung her a lullaby in French, and, in remembering all the young girl had suffered, loving her and promising her that she wouldn't be sad and she would always be her friend, Wendy had found solace.

Eventually, she'd made a nice home for herself above a sweet shop just off Commercial Road, but she knew Billy wouldn't be able to afford anything like her flat on his wages; it was hard for youngsters with no family to find anywhere decent to live, even though a lot of new building had been going on since the war. If you didn't dwell on the loss of life, Hitler had done them a favour really, bombing the slums, because there were better homes to be had now; flats and council houses further out in the suburbs. Yet Wendy hated the war and everything to do with it; she'd lost two men she loved to that awful war, and she knew she would never risk her heart again.

She was a nurse and that would be her life, just as it had been Sister Beatrice's, even though she wasn't thinking of becoming a nun. Wendy sensed that something terrible had happened to Sister Beatrice when she was a young woman. It wasn't just that she'd lost a man she loved – no, it was more than that, because it had gone too deep for her ever to recover. Sister never spoke of her past and Wendy wouldn't dream of asking her. They were friends and relied on one another in their work, but it didn't go further than that . . . she couldn't ask personal details.

Wendy was thoughtful as she started writing up her report for the day. Nurse Paula would be coming to take over in another twenty minutes. Wendy was visiting Nan and Eddie that evening; they'd asked her to supper to celebrate Eddie's birthday. He was seventy-two and as forgetful as ever, but he and Nan were like family to Wendy. Alice and her husband Bob would be there too; they had three children now and Alice had given up her part-time work as a carer at St Saviour's. She didn't need to work now that her husband had a nice little business of his own. He was in partnership with Alice's cousin Eric, and was married to Michelle, who had worked with Wendy as a nurse when she first arrived. Michelle had one child but had confided to Wendy that she was expecting her second, and so would be leaving, because with two children she wouldn't be able to manage to work, at least until they started school – and that meant they would be short-staffed again. They had temporary nurses in to cover holidays, and Paula helped out when she could, but they really did need another full-time nurse.

Wendy had just finished her report when Paula came in. She looked cold and was rubbing her hands.

'The wind is bitter this evening,' she told Wendy. 'You want to wrap up well because you'll feel it when you get out.'

'It's supposed to be spring,' Wendy said and pulled a

wry face. 'Billy came and fixed the trolley for us. He's very good at it but he wants a better job so he can get married.'

'He's far too young to think about it yet,' Paula said and shook her head. 'I'm sure Mary Ellen will tell him she's not ready to marry yet anyway.'

'Have you seen her recently?'

'Yes. I met her in the market just this morning. She was on a break from her job at that factory. She'd popped out to do some shopping for her boss. Apparently, he's a widower and lives alone now that his kids are grown up . . .'

Paula broke off as they heard a commotion and then someone burst into the ward. The boy was angry and looked as if he'd been fighting the harassed police sergeant who followed him.

'Get off me,' the lad said. 'I ain't going to let her wash me. I can look after myself.'

'I'm sorry, Staff Nurse,' Sergeant Sallis said. 'Your carer was just trying to tell them they needed to be bathed and looked at and he broke away from her . . . Come on, Archie lad, let the young lady look after you. She's only doing her job.'

'I've told you, we can wash ourselves. We're not dirty and we've not got nits or fleas. Mum kept us proper and I've made sure June washes every morning and night. If you'd left us alone, we could've looked after ourselves at home . . .'

'How were you goin' to do that, lad?' Sergeant Sallis asked mildly. 'You're still at school. You couldn't earn enough to feed yourselves, let alone pay the rent and the gas. Besides, the landlord wanted you out of the house, because it's coming down. Sister Beatrice says you can stay here until we sort your mum out . . .'

'She didn't do it,' Archie said, glaring at him and then at the nurses. 'Mum ain't a thief. She'd belt me round the ear if I pinched anything. I know she didn't do what they say she did . . .'

'I believe you, lad,' Sergeant Sallis said, 'but there's evidence that says she did . . .'

'It's false,' Archie said and looked angry. 'She told me someone had set her up, made it look as if she was guilty, but I know Mum wouldn't do anything like that. She just wouldn't, however hard-up she was . . .'

'We'll get to the bottom of it,' Sergeant Sallis promised, but looking at his face Wendy could tell he was worried. 'Do you know anyone who has it in for your mother, lad? Give me a hint and I'll do what I can, I give you my word.'

'She didn't tell me, but I know she was bothered about something,' Archie said. 'She wouldn't let on, because she wouldn't want to upset us – and we don't need to be taken into care. Mum will be home soon and she'll look after us.'

'Well, until she is, you're lucky to be brought here,' Wendy told him. 'Look, I'll tell Tilly that you can wash yourselves – but I need to examine you to make sure you don't have anything infectious, measles or something like that, all right?'

Archie thought for a moment and then inclined his head reluctantly. 'As long as you don't start washing our hair with that horrible stuff like the school nurse does to the kids with nits.'

'I promise,' Wendy said, smiled at Archie and went

out into the hall with him. 'You don't need to stop any longer, Sergeant. Archie is going to be sensible now. We have to look after June, don't we?' She looked at the truculent lad and saw him nod. 'At least here you will have decent food and you don't have to worry about the rent until your mother comes back.'

'What will happen to all our things? The landlord says we have to get out and they're going to pull our row down – but I don't know what to do with our things.'

'I'll talk to Sister Beatrice. She's the Warden here. I can't promise anything, but someone ought to be responsible. Perhaps we can find storage for you. Sister knows lots of people and she may be able to arrange it.'

Wendy was thinking it was a job for Angela Adderbury. If she'd been here she would have known someone who could store the family's possessions, but all Wendy could do was ask Sister for advice.

'All right . . .' Archie said grudgingly. 'But we shan't be here long. Mum will be home soon and she'll find us somewhere to live. I know she didn't take that money and they can't keep her in jail if she's innocent, can they?'

Wendy murmured something appropriate, but she knew life wasn't that simple or that fair. It wouldn't be the first time an innocent woman, or man, come to that, had been jailed for a crime they didn't commit. If life turned out the way it should, Wendy would have a husband and children, but she hadn't and wouldn't, and she'd had to learn to accept that – as Archie would accept this in time.

She felt for his bewilderment and his hurt, but for the moment there was nothing she could do to help him, except ensure that he was warm, comfortable and safe.

'Are you hungry?' she asked.

Archie hesitated and then inclined his head. 'We had a sandwich at the police station, but that was ages ago.'

'As soon as you've bathed, changed into our clothes and I've made sure you're healthy, which won't take a minute, because I can see you're fine, you can have your supper. I'll ask Cook to make you some eggs on toast – how about that?'

'I'd rather have beans,' Archie said. 'June likes scrambled eggs though.'

'One beans on toast, one scrambled eggs,' Wendy said. 'Tell you what, I'll make them myself and have my supper with you in the dining room – what do you think?'

'Yeah, all right,' Archie said and grinned at her.

Wendy blinked, because the change in him was amazing. This one was a real charmer, she thought and laughed inside, because there was something infectious about that grin. She found herself drawn to the young lad; he'd been like a tiger in defence of his mother's honesty and she liked that – found it admirable.

Wendy would talk to Nan and Eddie about the family's possessions that evening, she decided. Eddie was an old soldier and resourceful. He might know somewhere they could store Mrs Miller's things so that they wouldn't be looted or destroyed when the demolition people moved in – and if Eddie could help she would oversee the move herself that weekend . . .

CHAPTER 3

'Where are you going?' Rose O'Hanran asked her younger sister as she saw her putting on her boxy red jacket with the swing pleats at the back. 'Not to meet that Billy Baggins I hope?'

'Yes, I'm meeting Billy this evening. We're going to the church social hall. It's Rock 'n' Roll night on Fridays. You know we go every week for that . . .'

Rose snorted her disapproval. She'd done her best to break the bond that had formed between Billy Baggins and Mary Ellen in the years they'd lived at St Saviour's together. Sometimes, she wished that she'd never taken her sister there, but at the time she'd seemed to have little option. With their mother dying of consumption, Rose had needed to make a choice between staying in the slums to look after her young sister and never achieving her ambition, and putting Mary Ellen in the orphanage so that she could train as a nurse. She'd chosen the latter and it had been a good decision in every way but one.

'I know that boy will never amount to anything,' Rose grumbled at her. 'I've told you, Mary Ellen, you could do a lot better.'

'I love Billy,' Mary Ellen said and looked rebellious. 'You made me leave school and go to work as a seamstress and I did as you asked, but I'm not giving Billy up, whatever you say. He's my friend and one day we'll get married.'

'And end up back in some grotty little terrace slum house?' Rose was scornful. 'Remember what happened to his brother . . .'

'I'm not likely to forget, and nor is Billy,' Mary Ellen retorted. Arthur Baggins was currently in prison serving the first of twenty years' hard labour for armed robbery. He'd been released from prison six months previously, fallen in with a gang of rough types and ended up back in jail before he'd had time to catch his breath. 'You're wrong to think Billy is like his father or his brother. He works hard and he will get on, I know he will. He's not going to be just a mechanic forever. One day he'll drive the coaches as well and maybe he'll own a garage . . .'

'If ifs and ands were pots and pans, there'd be no need for tinker mans,' Rose chanted, feeling irritated by Mary Ellen's blind faith in the boy she'd befriended years ago. 'If he ever amounts to anything I'll go to China and back.'

'Be careful, I might keep you to that,' Mary Ellen laughed and swung her long brown hair back as she picked up her purse and slipped the loop over her wrist. She was dressed in a grey felt full skirt with several layers of net petticoats underneath, the waist nipped in tight with a wide red belt. Her flat shoes were red, and matched her jacket, and she had a red hairband holding her hair back from her face. Her hair wasn't permed but had a natural bend and she had it cut every three months at the hairdresser near the market. Her lipstick was pale peach and she had a dusting of powder on her nose and cheeks, but didn't wear a foundation. Because her complexion was so clear, Mary Ellen hardly needed make-up at all, as Rose was always telling her, but she couldn't stop her because at seventeen she was old enough to know her own mind in most things. 'I shan't be later than half past ten.' She popped a kiss on Rose's cheek and picked up her scarf, going towards the door.

One good thing about Mary Ellen's job was that she got a decent discount on all she bought from the factory. Of course she was capable of making her own clothes, and quite often made up a skirt or a shift dress in a night for Rose. There were sometimes offcuts of material left over at the factory, not enough to make a whole garment, but with a bit of skill Mary Ellen turned them into rather fetching and original outfits. Sam, her boss at the factory, had told her she could have these scraps of material cheap, sometimes for nothing, but offcuts were popular with all the seamstresses so Mary Ellen had to take her turn with the others. It meant she had several pretty dresses and skirts to wear, and she'd made sure Rose benefitted too.

'I'll give you something for them,' Rose had offered when Mary Ellen made her a summer skirt and matching bolero jacket, but she refused, saying that Rose had done plenty for her. Her generosity made Rose feel uneasy at times, because she'd always treated Mary Ellen as a duty. For years she'd begrudged the time she'd had to give up to visit her sister and she hadn't bothered about finding a place to rent where she could have her sister to live with her until it suited her. When the new high-rise flats went up, Rose had known they were for her. Situated a short bus ride from the hospital, where she was now Sister O'Hanran, at reasonable rent and with three bedrooms, it was perfect for them. Although, if she could've got a smaller flat she would have taken that; they didn't need the extra room and Mary Ellen had plagued her to let Billy have it for weeks, until she'd finally given up.

'I shall be out myself this evening,' Rose said, capitulating, because she couldn't forbid Mary Ellen to go to the club when she herself was meeting some friends from work – and one friend in particular. 'I'll be home by eleven, so make sure you're back by then or there will be trouble.'

''Course, Rose,' Mary Ellen's eyes twinkled with laughter, and Rose was struck by how pretty she looked. For years she'd thought of her as a kid, but she was very definitely a young woman with thoughts and ideas of her own now. 'I shan't do anything you wouldn't . . .'

She danced off laughing and Rose frowned as she returned to the bedroom to continue dressing. As she fetched the new dress her sister had recently made for her, Rose was feeling excited. Mike Bonner was the registrar for one of the senior consultants at the London Hospital. Rose had admired him from afar for some time now, but although he always smiled when he came to her ward, she hadn't thought he was interested. This evening he'd asked her to be one of the crowd he'd invited to share his birthday celebrations at a rather smart restaurant that had just opened up West. She would have to catch a bus to get there and that meant coming home alone late at night, which she wasn't keen on, but it would be worth it if Mike Bonner finally noticed her . . .

'Ellie, you look gorgeous,' Billy said and kissed Mary Ellen softly on the lips as they met at the bus stop. He'd waited outside the youth club for her bus to arrive and it was still chilly in the evenings yet, even though it was April. 'And you smell delicious – I could eat every bit of you.'

Mary Ellen smiled and touched his hair. Thankfully, Billy didn't smother his hair with Brylcreem, as some men did, but allowed it to spring up in the same unruly style it always had. The colour was still a riotous red and she was glad, because she didn't want him to be any other way than the way he was. Without Billy, Mary Ellen knew she would never have made it through the dark days after Rose abandoned her in the orphanage eight years previously.

'Have you found anywhere to live yet?' Mary Ellen asked as they joined the queue for the Rock 'n' Roll club, which was held in St Mary's church hall and supervised by the man who ran the youth club. The youth club had been started three years earlier by Father Joe, the Catholic priest who had organised so many events for St Saviour's Orphanage and other kids. After he'd left London to go and work in a mission in Africa for two years, another clergyman had come to take over. He told the kids to call him Peter, and he was an Anglican curate in his first post in Spitalfields. Peter Simmons was involved with many activities for children, and popular with the teenagers who visited the club, because of his easy-going nature. He was keen on rugby and rowing and a member of the same athletics club that Billy frequented at least twice a week and together they'd organised a football team for the local kids, both those from St Saviour's and any other kids who loved to play. There was no shortage of volunteers, because belonging to a club that played matches was better than kicking a ball about the streets.

'I went to see a couple of rooms near Assembly Lane yesterday evening,' Billy said, looking rueful. 'They were awful and the whole place stank of old cabbage. You would've hated it, love. I'm still looking . . .'

'I know you are,' Mary Ellen said and squeezed his hand. 'I got a rise today – another five bob a week. If we were married we might get a flat somewhere, because with my money we could afford it.'

'Rose would never let you, not unless I could prove I can keep you, Mary Ellen. You know what she thinks of me . . . a waster like my brother.'

'You're nothing like Arthur,' Mary Ellen fired up. 'I've told her so many times but she doesn't listen. She thinks I'm still a kid but I'm not . . . I'll be eighteen this September and you'll soon be nineteen; neither of us is a kid now.'

'No, you're a real woman, my woman,' Billy said and slid his arm about her waist, 'but unfortunately, Rose can stop us gettin' married until you're twenty-one. It ain't fair, because we can drive at seventeen, fight for our country and drink in the pub at eighteen – but we can't marry until we're twenty-one without permission. The bloomin' government should change the law, but what do they know? I'd have to get round Sister B –

but that's a doddle . . .' He grinned. 'Shall I get us a coffee while you take your coat off?'

'Yes, all right – listen, I love this one. It's Bill Haley . . .'

'Yeah, one of my favourites,' Billy agreed. He shrugged off his old and much-worn leather bomber jacket, which he'd bought from Petticoat Lane and believed to have belonged to a fighter pilot in the war, and gave it to her. 'Stick this with yours, love?'

''Course,' Mary Ellen said and took the two jackets through to the cloakroom to hang on a peg. She paused for a moment to fluff her hair up in front of the mirror and then jumped as someone grabbed her arm. Turning, she looked at the girl who'd caught hold of her and smiled in pleasure. 'Marion! I haven't seen you for weeks. Where have you been?'

'My boss at Woolworth's sent me away for training. I'm a senior adviser on the counters, and windows, supervising how they look, and the girls on them; I'm getting six pounds a week now . . .'

'Lucky you,' Mary Ellen said, half envious. She still wasn't earning that much, even after she'd been given her rise. 'I think I'm going to pack in my job and start on at Woolworth's.'

'You wouldn't get as much as me,' Marion said. 'It's about three pounds ten shillings or even less for newcomers.'

'Oh . . . that wouldn't be as much as what I'm getting now,' Mary Ellen said, feeling disappointed. If she could have earned as much as Marion, she might have been able to afford her own house with Billy, always supposing Rose would let her get married.

'Six pounds sounds a lot,' Marion said, 'but I'm struggling to find a decent room I can afford. If I go out a few times a week and eat three meals a day it doesn't leave anything much over for clothes – at least you get discount on yours, Mary Ellen.'

'Yes, I do,' she agreed. 'How much are you paying for your room then?'

'Three quid with breakfast and evening meal,' Marion said. 'You're lucky you've got a sister. When I left St Saviour's I had to stay in a hostel for girls like me; it was much cheaper but it was awful, worse than being an orphan. All the rules . . . and the beds were hard and the toilets were filthy . . .'

'I bet Rose would let you move in with us for less than you're paying,' Mary Ellen said. 'She charges me twenty-five bob a week for board and all my food . . .'

'But you're her sister,' Marion pointed out. 'I wouldn't mind giving her two pounds a week if she would have me.'

'I'll ask her,' Mary Ellen promised. 'I think she would be glad for you to share the rent. It makes it easier for her, and we can help with the chores and cooking. Rose gets tired sometimes when she's on late shifts. If they're short of nurses she sometimes has to do longer hours.'

'Is Billy with you?' Marion asked as they left the cloakroom together. 'I came with Jill from work. She's on the cosmetic counter and gets a lot of free samples when the salesmen come round. They think she can influence the buyers, but of course our stuff is all ordered from head office. Jill only gives advice as to what is selling and what isn't . . .'

'I like that Tangee lipstick,' Mary Ellen said. 'They've got some lovely colours and it stays on well.'

'Do you like this scent?' Marion leaned nearer for her to smell. 'It's Lily of the Valley and Jill gave it to me – the last of the bottle. She's got a new one . . . Evening in Paris . . .'

'Yes, it's all right,' Mary Ellen said, not liking it but not wanting to offend her. 'Billy got me some Elizabeth Arden perfume for last Christmas; it's lovely . . .'

'I can smell it,' Marion agreed, looking a bit envious. 'Did that skirt come from your workshop?'

'Yes, but I made the net petticoats myself. If you come round one night I'll show you some of my stuff, Marion. We could get some material cheap on the market and I'll make a skirt and petticoats for you, too.'

'Will you really?' Marion looked pleased. 'If Jill gets any of those lipsticks you like free, I'll ask her for one for you . . .'

Billy stood up as the girls approached. 'I've got a coffee for us, Ellie. Marion, I can get one for you if you like?'

'No, thanks, Billy,' Marion said, giving him a flirtatious look. 'I'm with a friend – but you can ask me for a dance later, if you like?'

'Maybe,' he said. 'I expect you'll be busy all night once you start . . .'

Billy shrugged apologetically as Marion swayed off, her hips moving enticingly. You'd never know now that as a child her leg had been badly broken and for a while she'd walked with a limp. 'We were all mates at St Saviour's,' he said. 'I suppose she thinks she can say things like that . . . but she knows we're together . . .'

'Marion fancies you,' Mary Ellen said, feeling a twinge

of jealousy, which she instantly quashed. Billy was good looking – not handsome, but rugged because of all the sport – and he had a nice open face. She knew there were plenty of other girls who fancied Billy but she also knew that he loved her.

Mary Ellen hadn't wanted to work in the clothing manufacturers' workshops. She still wanted to teach children, but Rose had put paid to her dreams when she'd made her leave school at fifteen and start on as an apprentice. She was well aware that life didn't always give you what you wanted; she'd learned that when she was very young and her mother died, but she'd got more of the good things than most, because she had a steady job working for a boss she liked, and she'd got Billy – and when she was twenty-one they would marry, no matter what Rose thought, but that was such a long time to wait . . .

'Feel like a shuffle round the floor?' Billy asked as she finished her coffee.

Mary Ellen was on her feet straight away. They'd both learned to jive at the youth club, and Billy was really good. Because he was tall and strong, he could toss her over his shoulder and round his waist with ease, and the way he pulled her through his legs and then threw her in the air and caught her usually drew a crowd of watchers, who often applauded when they'd finished. Billy was unusual in that he'd learned the steps properly; his kicks and flicks were sharp and fast and he bounced high in time to the music. Mary Ellen was always out of breath by the time they finished, but Billy never seemed to turn a hair. It wasn't surprising that he had a following of young women who eyed him longingly.

'Listen,' she said as they sat down again. 'They've put a Guy Mitchell record on now – "My Heart Cries for You". Oh, I love that, Billy. Come on, dance this one with me please.'

'It's not Rock 'n' Roll,' Billy objected, but Mary Ellen was on her feet, offering him her hand, and he couldn't refuse. She moved into his arms and they did a slow rhythmic shuffle around the floor, her face pressed against his shoulder and his touching her hair. 'You smell lovely. I really love you, Ellie – you know that, don't you?'

Mary Ellen looked up at him and smiled, feeling the warmth of her happiness spread through her as she saw the expression on his face. 'Yes, I know. I love you too, Billy.'

'I want us to be married soon,' Billy said. 'If I could afford a place of our own, would you say yes?'

'You know I want to,' she said, the happy feeling fading. 'Rose just won't let us. You know what she is like.'

'Yes, she hates me . . .'

'She doesn't hate you,' Mary Ellen denied quickly. 'She just thinks I'm too young, Billy, and perhaps I am – but in a year or so she'll get fed up saying no. I'll keep on at her until she just wants to get rid of me . . .'

Billy laughed, bent his head and kissed her. 'This is almost like making love in public,' he remarked softly as she responded by pressing herself against him. 'We'd better be careful or Peter will throw us out . . .'

Mary Ellen laughed, because they weren't the only ones smooching, and many of the couples would be going outside for a kiss and maybe more before the evening was over. A lot of the girls had difficulty in fighting off their boyfriends' eager hands, but she'd never had that trouble. Billy sometimes told her he wanted her and kissed her passionately, but he didn't try to persuade her into doing anything silly.

'I don't want us ending up in a slum tenement,' he'd told her once when she'd been reluctant to break up their embrace. 'I love you, and I want you – you don't know how much, Mary Ellen – but I want us to be married properly, because we want to, not because we have to get married in a rush. If you have a baby at seventeen, you'll never have any fun . . .'

'Oh, I don't know, it might not be such a bad idea. Rose couldn't say no then, could she?'

'She would never forgive us,' he said shaking his head. 'No, your sister has some daft ways, but she's respectable and I want her to know I am too. I'm not going to get you into trouble, Ellie love.'

When he called her Ellie like that Mary Ellen's stomach went all funny and she felt like melting. Several of the girls she'd known at school were already married and had a child, and sometimes she envied them – and yet somewhere buried deep inside her was the determination to make something of herself, to be more than just a girl who worked in the rag trade.

'I'm going to night school,' she announced when they sat down at their table again with the fresh coffees Billy had bought. 'I'm going to try and sit my GCEs so that I can train as a teacher . . .'

Billy looked stunned for a moment, then, 'Is that what you really want? To be a teacher? You know it will take ages doing it that way, don't you?'

Mary Ellen nodded, the doubts already beginning to

crowd in on her. She wasn't sure why she'd suddenly made up her mind to do it, though she'd been thinking perhaps she might for ages.

'I might not be good enough, but I think I should try – don't you?'

For a moment he didn't answer and her heart sank. Rose was going to be against her, and if Billy also said it was daft she didn't think she would be strong enough to proceed on her own.

'I think if it's what you really want you should try,' Billy said a little reluctantly. 'It means I shan't see so much of you . . .'

'I'll only go twice a week,' Mary Ellen offered, but she knew it wasn't just the evening classes. She would have to study hard if she wanted to pass the exams she needed to for teaching college. If Billy had objected she would probably have given in immediately, but he nodded and looked sad.

'I wish I could get the sort of job that would support us both through you going to college and all of it,' he said. 'If I'd got that job with the railways . . .'

'Sister Beatrice said you had to take an apprenticeship, and the railway wouldn't offer you anything, because you were too young,' Mary Ellen reminded him. 'Rose was the same with me. They think they know best and they make us do what they want . . . and it isn't fair . . .'

'No, it isn't,' Billy agreed. 'This is 1955 and we're young. We're the future, Mary Ellen. I may not get to be a train driver, but I don't see why you shouldn't train as a teacher if you want.'

'Really?' She looked at him earnestly. 'You won't get

46

angry and throw me over if I can't always do what you want?'

'I'd never do that, Ellie. Surely you know there's never been anyone else for me?'

'Yes, of course I do,' she said and clasped his hand, her fingers entwining with his. 'I love you so much, Billy. I just feel we have to do something with our lives. Do you remember what Miss Angela used to tell us about looking up and reaching for what seemed beyond our reach? We were so eager when we had our teams and earned stars for a trip to the zoo or the flicks. I felt as if I'd lost something when I had to start working in the factory. Oh, I like Sam; he's a dear and almost like a father to us girls, but I want something better for us – and our children.'

Billy's eyes were fixed on her face. Their colour seemed intensely green rather than the greenish hazel they usually were; she'd noticed before that they changed colour when he was passionate about something. He had so much life, so much eagerness in him, that she knew he must be frustrated in his job too.

'I want it too, Mary Ellen,' he said and his voice sounded guttural as if emotion caught at his throat. 'I get so mad at times because I can't do the things I want – can't give you the life you deserve . . .'

'I don't want things,' she tried to explain, but knew he didn't really understand. Mary Ellen didn't want to better herself because of the money; it was for self-respect, for making life fuller and richer. 'It's just that . . . oh, I suppose it's a better world for everyone . . .'

Billy nodded, but she knew he still didn't see it the way she did. A better world to Billy meant a decent house, good wages and kids that didn't have to go to school in bare feet and trousers with their backsides hanging out. For Mary Ellen it was more, but she couldn't explain the mixed-up feelings inside her. She laughed suddenly. What was she thinking? She already had a better life than her mother's, but there was something inside her that questioned. Surely after the terrible war they'd all endured there should be something more . . .

After seeing her safely home, Billy was thoughtful as he left Mary Ellen. He kicked at an abandoned pop bottle, feeling moody and unsettled. It was all his fault for letting himself be pushed into a dead-end job. Mary Ellen was right when she said she wanted a better life for them and their kids. He wanted it too, but he didn't know how to achieve it.

'Where yer goin' then, Billy?'

The voice made him pause and then turn reluctantly, because he recognised Stevie Baker from school. He wasn't one of St Saviour's kids; his father worked on the Docks and his mother was a waitress in a greasy spoon café. Stevie had left school at fourteen and started work as a labourer for the council. Yet as he looked at his one-time school friend, he saw that Stevie was wearing clothes that proclaimed him as a Teddy boy and, by the look of his jacket, smart drainpipe trousers and thick-soled suede shoes, he'd paid a small fortune for what he was wearing. His jacket was blue, the trousers black and the shoes dark blue. The thin tie he wore with his frilled shirt was also black; like a girl's hair ribbon but held by a silver clip. His hair had been brushed together at the back in a DA and he could've passed for one of Billy's Rock 'n' Roll heroes if he hadn't known him.

'Home,' he said in answer to Stevie's question. 'I've been down the club and now I'm going home.'

'You still livin' at that dump?' Stevie sneered. 'I should've thought you couldn't wait to get out of that place. It gives me the creeps just to look at it – more like a prison than a home. Mum says it used to be the old fever 'ospital, where they sent folks to die . . .'

'It's all right inside,' Billy said, defending the home that had given him sanctuary. 'I can't afford a room on what I earn as an apprentice – not if I want to save for the future.'

'More fool you then,' Stevie crowed. 'You want ter come down the Blue Angel if you want to see life – and they're always after blokes to help chuck out the rough element. Ask for Tony and he'll give yer a job, mate.'

Billy knew about the nightclub and its unsavoury reputation. He'd always steered clear of places like that, but now he was curious. 'Is that where you earn your money then?'

'Yeah, that and other places,' Stevie said, avoiding his eyes. 'Think about it, mate. I can help yer get some money if you're willin' ter work fer it and keep yer mouth shut.'

'I'm not my brother, and I don't steal,' Billy said. 'I wouldn't mind an honest job, though.'

'Plenty of stuff goin' if you're not too fussy – I don't mean thievin' either.' Stevie grinned at him. 'I'll see yer around then, Billy. One of these days you'll realise the bastards grind us all down unless we stand up for ourselves . . .'

Billy stared after him as he walked away. He might

envy Stevie his smart clothes and wish he could afford something similar, but he wasn't willing to do anything dishonest. Arthur had gone down that road, and Billy had vowed he never would. No, he just had to find himself a better job . . . and soon . . .

CHAPTER 4

'What's up, young 'un?' Billy asked the next morning when he saw Archie Miller disconsolately kicking a tin can in the street outside St Saviour's and recognised him as one of the recent arrivals. 'Shouldn't yer be at school?'

'We got a day orf,' Archie said. 'I was goin' down the nick ter see me mother but Sergeant Sallis ain't there and the other old misery guts wouldn't let me in.'

'Does Sergeant Sallis let you visit her?'

'Yeah, he's all right,' Archie said and Billy nodded.

'I get on good with him,' he said and grinned. 'Supposing we nip in the phone box on the corner and give him a ring – ask him to phone the station and tell them to let you in for a few minutes?'

'Would yer? Thanks, mate, that's great,' Archie said. 'I've heard about yer – playin' football and runnin' fast an' all . . .'

'Come on then,' Billy said. 'I'll come with yer down the nick if he agrees and back you up . . .'

Billy opened the door of the phone box and they squeezed in together, Billy asking for a number and putting the coins in when the police officer answered.

They chatted for a bit, Archie watching anxiously all the while and then smiling as Billy gave him the thumbs up.

'Thanks Sergeant, I'll do the same for you one day.'

'Just keep your nose clean so I don't have to arrest you . . .'

Billy grinned even more as he replaced the receiver and turned to Archie. 'He's goin' to meet us there in ten minutes. He says you can have five minutes and that's all. He ain't supposed to do it, but he likes you, Archie – and he don't think yer mum should be there . . .'

'Thanks, Billy. You're a real mate . . .'

'Play football, do you?' Billy asked as they walked the short distance to the police station. 'Only, I help Peter to run the football club and we keep it goin' even in the summer – keeps everyone fit and interested.'

'Can I join?'

'Why shouldn't you?' Billy nodded and held Archie's arm. 'We'll wait out here until Sergeant Sallis gets here – he's the best of them, believe me . . .'

As they stood outside in the rather fitful sunshine, which kept disappearing as clouds scudded across the sky, a rather unkempt-looking man walked out of the side door of the police station and glanced their way. For a moment his eyes dwelled on them thoughtfully, and he half smiled to Archie before moving off. Billy noticed that his walk changed from a brisk stride to a careless shuffle, and his whole demeanour seemed to change as he disappeared down an alley. It struck him as a bit odd, as if the man wanted to be thought something other than he was, but he forgot it as Sergeant Sallis arrived and smiled at them in his friendly manner.

'Right, I'll take you in, lad. Billy, why don't you wait

across the road in case Archie needs a hand when he comes out . . . ?'

'Yeah, all right.' Billy watched as the two went inside the police station, the sergeant's hand on the boy's shoulder. It was rotten for Archie having his mother locked up – especially when even Sergeant Sallis didn't believe she was guilty.

It was wrong and he felt upset for his new young friend, but there was nothing he could do. Billy couldn't even find himself a decent room or earn enough to support a wife . . .

'Mum . . . how are yer?' Archie said as she was ushered in and he saw she was wearing the same dress he'd brought in for her the day after she was arrested. 'When are they goin' to let yer out?'

'It's *you*, not *yer*, Archie,' she reminded him gently and moved towards him, holding her arms out.

Not usually one for hugs, Archie moved towards her and threw his arms about her, close to tears. He struggled to hold them back because he knew she would cry if he did. This was the second visit since she'd been in here and the first time she hadn't been able to hold back her tears.

'I miss you, Mum,' he said, automatically correcting his speech for her. 'June is miserable. She wants you home – we both do. I would've brought her but Sergeant Sallis says he can't allow it. He shouldn't have let us meet, but he's all right.'

'Yes, he has been kind,' she said and smiled through hovering tears. 'As kind as he can be in the circumstances . . .'

'Have they told you when you can come home?'

Her bottom lip trembled. 'It may not be for a while, Archie,' she whispered. 'They got me a solicitor and he says the case will go for trial – but I know he thinks I'm guilty . . .'

'Mum! They can't think that,' Archie said loudly. 'You would never do anything bad. I know you wouldn't . . .'

'Keep on believing in me, my love,' she said in a choking voice. 'And promise me you will look after your sister. Please, Archie. You have to take care of her until I can get home to look after you both . . .'

'Oh, Mum, it isn't fair. June hates being at St Saviour's – and I don't much like it, though it's better than bein' on the streets . . .'

'You'll be safe with Sister Beatrice,' his mother said and stroked his hair back. 'I wish this hadn't happened, Archie. Someone hates me – I think Reg Prentice is behind all this, but I can't prove it . . . and no one but Sergeant Sallis believes me . . .'

'The judge will, Mum,' Archie said fiercely and hugged her again. 'I wish I could make him pay for what he's done – that rotten manager of yours . . .'

'Promise me not to do anything stupid,' she said and kissed the top of his head. 'You're like your dad, Archie, and I know you'll be all right at St Saviour's. Don't let them split you up and ask Sister to keep you here in London until I get home – but if they don't I'll find you. I promise . . .'

'I'm sorry, Archie, but you'll have to go,' a voice said from the door. 'If my chief constable finds you here I'm for the chop. It's back to your cell, Mrs Miller . . .'

'Yes, of course,' she said. 'And thank you so much for this . . .'

Archie stared rebelliously as she was led away, but he followed the police constable who beckoned him and showed him out of the side door.

'You're a lucky lad,' he told him. 'I wouldn't have risked my job like the Sarge has . . . Get off with you now and behave yourself . . .'

Archie shot him a resentful look and left. He became aware that tears were trickling down his face and brushed them off angrily as he went to join Billy in the café opposite.

'All right now?' Billy asked and got up to join him. 'I'll take you to meet some of the football team. You'll be fine with Sister Beatrice and if there's any justice your mum will be out afore you know it . . .'

'Ah, Nancy,' Beatrice said as the girl knocked and then entered her office. 'Is everything all right?'

'Yes, thank you,' Nancy replied. Her soft fair hair was pulled back into a neat plait at the back of her head and she wore the pink gingham dress that was the uniform of all the carers. She was an attractive girl who could have made more of her looks if she'd tried. Since Nan had left them, she'd unofficially taken over her duties, liaising with Beatrice over the rotas and doing extra duty when needed. 'I just wanted to let you know that I shall be visiting Terry this weekend.'

'How is your brother?' Beatrice felt the tiny prick of guilt she always felt when Nancy mentioned Terry. He was now living in a special home in Cambridgeshire for the mentally retarded, where Nancy said he was happy and content to spend his days. 'Any change?'

'Not really,' Nancy said and sighed. 'Last time I was down he didn't know me for the first hour or so and then he came out of his trance and was pleased to see me. I never know for certain whether he will recognise me or not.'

'That is so sad for you, my dear. I had hoped he might make a complete recovery.'

'Mr Adderbury explained it to me,' Nancy said. 'Terry is blocking the past out of his mind. He isn't violent these days. Everyone says he's easy to look after, and he helps the gardeners, but he doesn't remember much about what happened before they took him to the clinic, and sometimes he doesn't seem to know me. I think it's the treatment they gave him when he was first taken in . . .'

'Well, perhaps it is better for him, Nancy. If the past hurts too much . . . not all of us are as strong as you, my dear.'

'I don't think about it; it's over and gone and I've put it behind me,' Nancy said, though something in her eyes told Beatrice that wasn't quite true. 'Well, I'll get on. Tilly is in this morning but she can't do everything on her own. We're changing the linen today.'

'I'm sure you're very busy,' Beatrice said. 'Thank you for reminding me that you will be away this weekend.'

'Jean said she would come in on Sunday if we need her.'

'Yes, that would be most helpful, but I doubt we shall need her,' Beatrice said. 'Wendy will be on duty and I'm sure we can manage for once.'

Returning to her paperwork after Nancy had gone,

Beatrice sighed. Jean Marsh had worked for them as a carer before her marriage, and had two young children at school. She sometimes worked a few hours in the mornings if they were short-handed, but it was a case of balancing the budget. Beatrice was fortunate in her staff, she knew, because they were all dedicated to their jobs and willing to work extra hours, often for no extra money. Wendy would sometimes do the work of the carers if necessary, even though her training meant she should not be asked to do menial work, but she never objected in a case of emergency.

Beatrice's longest-serving carers were Tilly and Kelly, both of whom seemed devoted to St Saviour's, and although Tilly had married she hadn't left them, nor did she intend to until she had children. Kelly had a long-standing boyfriend, but no plans for marriage as far as Beatrice was aware. She supposed it was because both she and her friend had families to look after at home, but neither of them confided in her as Nancy and Wendy did. Nurse Michelle had recently given her a month's notice, because she was having another child, and that meant Beatrice would have to try and find a replacement. It was so difficult to find a good staff nurse willing to work at the home. These days they were all busy at the hospitals, perhaps because nursing wasn't as popular an occupation with young girls as it had once been. Beatrice had read something about nurses from overseas wanting to come to Britain and she wondered if perhaps she might be luckier if she took on a nurse from another country – and yet there might be difficulty in getting permission for them to work here for more than a few months.

If Angela were here she would know exactly what to do about that sort of thing. Beatrice had resented it when she'd first been appointed as Administrator for the orphanage but she certainly felt the lack of Angela's organising skills . . .

A knock at her door made Beatrice look up. Most of her staff simply knocked once and put their head round the door, but this person had knocked twice and was obviously waiting for an invitation to enter.

'Come in then,' Beatrice said impatiently. She wasn't really surprised when Ruby Saunders entered. The young woman was wearing a brown pleated skirt and a fawn jacket over a brown jumper. Her dark-brown hair was dragged back into a tight knot and she'd clipped it firmly back with brown slides. Her complexion was pale and she wore only the faintest smear of pale-pink lipstick. She certainly wasn't vain about her appearance, that much was apparent, because underneath those dowdy clothes and awful hairstyle there might have been an attractive woman.

'Ah, Miss Saunders, what may I do for you?'

'I wondered if you'd heard about Mrs Miller.'

'Mrs Miller?' Sister Beatrice frowned as she sought for clarification. 'Ah, I believe you mean the mother of those children we had brought in last month . . . Archie and June? No, I don't believe I've heard anything – why?'

'She's been committed for trial next week, which means she will almost certainly be given a prison sentence.'

'You can't be sure the woman is guilty . . .'

'They wouldn't have brought a trial if they weren't pretty sure of a conviction,' Ruby said. 'It means those children will be without a mother for some time – what shall you do if she's sent to prison for a long term?'

'I hadn't considered it,' Beatrice said. 'They will stay here until I'm certain of the outcome and then . . . well, we may have to send them on to Halfpenny House.'

'Did you know the Miller girl has been in a lot of trouble at school? She broke a window yesterday by throwing a stone at it and she hit a teacher with a ruler when she was disciplined for bad behaviour.'

'That was unfortunate,' Beatrice frowned. 'I dare say she is very unhappy at what has happened to her. Her mother has been forcibly taken from her and she must wonder what is happening to her life. My carers haven't reported bad behaviour here at St Saviour's.'

'Well, I thought you should know,' Ruby said. 'If such behaviour isn't stopped immediately she may become uncontrollable and once they start down the slippery slope they end up before the courts. Perhaps you should have a quiet word, unless you would prefer me to speak to her?'

'I believe I am capable of looking after the children in my charge, Miss Saunders. Leave it to me if you please.'

Ruby shrugged her shoulders. 'Well, you've been warned. Some of these girls are devious, Sister Beatrice. I saw June talking with Betty Goodge yesterday morning and it made me wonder; Betty is a troublemaker and a bad influence on others – I've never been in favour of mixing your children and my offenders. Some of my girls are not a good influence. You might be well advised to move the girl before she gets into real trouble.'

'Thank you for your advice, which will be considered,' Beatrice said coldly. Did the woman think she'd been born yesterday? 'Is there anything more you wish to discuss concerning my children?'

'No. I just feel you would be better advised to move her or to think about fostering. June needs parents to keep her in order and her mother clearly cannot cope. She's been allowed to get out of hand and . . .' Ruby was silenced as Sister Beatrice rose to her feet. 'Well, it's just my advice, for what it's worth . . .'

'Quite.' The one word was quelling.

Ruby's cheeks turned dark pink and she turned and left without another word. Beatrice fought for calm. She didn't know when she'd felt angrier. These people just couldn't help interfering, making difficulties where none existed. Anyone would think she'd never dealt with a difficult child in her life! No one could have been a bigger rebel than Billy Baggins when he first arrived, and look at him now . . . He'd certainly repaid the care he'd been given in many ways, and that was why she was disinclined to ask him to move on, even though he ought to have gone long ago. However, he helped out with the older boys, getting them interested in football and athletics and keeping them out of trouble.

Still, there was no sense in ignoring the warning. She would speak to Wendy and Nancy about June and her brother. It was at times like these when she missed Nan. Her old friend had a wise head and they'd often discussed the difficult children, but like Angela, Nan had her own life these days . . .

Leaving the paperwork on her desk, Beatrice decided to take a walk round the home. It was by quietly observing the children at their work and play that she made her own decisions. Obviously Archie and June

Miller would not be able to stay here if their mother was sent to prison long term, because few of the children did these days. St Saviour's did a very necessary job of taking in frightened, anxious children, reassuring them, making them understand that a new life awaited them at Halfpenny House and then sending them on. However, Beatrice would do her utmost to make certain that the brother and sister stayed together . . .

Ruby made herself a coffee in her office and glared at the dividing wall between her and the orphanage next door. Sometimes it made her as mad as fire to see the way that lot went on, heads in the clouds as if all children were little angels who must be treated like fine china. Talk about a dinosaur! Sister Beatrice should have been shipped back off to her convent years ago in Ruby's opinion. Stuffy old trout! Ruby had only been trying to give her good advice, to prevent a girl on the edge from slipping over into the abyss, from which it was very hard to climb back. Once the girl had a reputation for being trouble she would find life a lot harder than simply being moved to an orphanage in a pleasant location.

Ruby knew a bit about hardship herself, but she hadn't gone to the bad, even though she'd had every provocation. She'd had to fight for what she'd got and that didn't give her much patience with those that had it easy. By the look of her, Sister Beatrice had never done a proper day's work in her life. Oh, she'd trained as a nurse, but she hadn't had to struggle every step to claw her way through high school and pass her grades. With Ruby's home life, she could've been forgiven for leaving school at fifteen and taking a job – anything to get away! She hadn't lain down and wept and felt sorry for herself. She'd passed her exams despite all the stuff she'd had to cope with and, after some years of hard graft, she'd landed a good job with the Children's Department. An orphan herself, Ruby had lived with an uncle and aunt for four years, until she'd won a scholarship to college. After that, she'd made her own way. Nothing would ever persuade her to live under *his* roof again. She didn't even visit her buttoned-up Aunt Joan and she wouldn't go near *him* if she were starving! Her uncle was a grubby-minded little man who couldn't keep his hands to himself – and Ruby should know! She'd had to fight him off since she was twelve.

When she'd taken the first lowly position in the Children's Department, Ruby had had to struggle for recognition and the chance to realise her ambition. It was only when she'd helped Ruth Sampson out with a difficult case on a couple of occasions that she'd started to move up. It was important to Ruby that her superior should appreciate her; she wasn't sure, but she had the feeling that Ruth didn't like men any more than she did – it was why she'd never married and dedicated herself to her job. What Ruby didn't know for sure was whether she felt more than liking for her.

It was something she had to keep hidden, this passion for another woman. Sex and love between two women wasn't seen as correct, either politically or lawfully, and although the voices raised against the old-fashioned laws were growing in number, at this time it didn't look as if things would ever change. Ruby saw that as unfair and discrimination against someone like her; she couldn't help it if she wanted to love a woman and not a man. The very thought of a man touching her made her shudder – so why shouldn't she find happiness with someone of her own persuasion? Yet she knew she had to be careful. If she offended Ruth, she would be out of the Department and looking for another job – and she might find herself in worse trouble . . .

Ruby's job paid quite well. She had her own tiny flat, just a bedroom, tiny bathroom, kitchen and that was it; there was no space for anything much but it was hers, her sanctuary. Her bed folded away during the day and she had a battered old sofa she sat on; a single wardrobe, a chest of drawers, a chair and a table that let down and could be stood against the wall at night. It was all she needed. She'd got where she was by working hard and keeping her emotions tightly under control.

She was in charge of this side of St Saviour's, but her bit wasn't called that now. It was a centre for girls on probation, girls who could end up in an institution that had bars on the windows and cells rather than dormitories if they didn't behave. Ruby had twenty girls in her care at the Halfpenny Probationary Centre, and two assistant female workers under her supervision as well as a male orderly; his strength was needed occasionally if one of the worst offenders became violent. One girl had been strange whenever there was a full moon and they'd had to restrain her a few times, but she'd now been removed to a secure unit. There wasn't a sick ward here, and in the case of illness Ruby called in the doctor or asked one of the nurses from next door to pop in, but if the girls were ill they went to hospital. She wasn't a nurse and wouldn't allow herself to be drawn into caring for her girls in that way; they were here because they needed to be disciplined and she was here to see they behaved. Ruby wasn't soft, she'd been trained in a hard school, and she was up to the tricks of the girls who landed themselves in her charge.

At twenty-seven she'd finally got the kind of job she'd been after for years and she was proud of herself. She wrote regular reports on the behaviour of the girls in her charge and she prided herself that she'd had nothing significant to report for months. Ruby had made certain that her girls knew they must live by her rules; she considered herself as being fair but strict and she'd told them that if they made trouble or ran away the next step was a remand home and then prison. So far not one girl had run away, and that was more than they could say next door. Ruby happened to know that one of the boys they'd sent to Halfpenny House had absconded recently. She'd heard that they'd had trouble keeping staff there and that some of the kids were rebellious. Of course the boy who'd run off wasn't an offender and at fourteen he was probably old enough to find himself a job, but that old trout next door shouldn't be too proud to take some advice when it was given in good faith . . .

An altercation outside her door interrupted her thoughts and then a girl burst in, shouting at the top of her voice, followed by one of the carers. Ruby dismissed the carer with a wave of her hand and looked at the girl. She was Betty Goodge and she was wearing lipstick again, something expressly forbidden.

'Be quiet, Betty,' Ruby said sternly. 'Why are you wearing lipstick? You are far too young, even if we allowed it – and you know the rules. Even the older girls are not permitted any make-up during their stay here.'

'Rotten ole rules,' Betty sneered at her. 'I didn't ask to come 'ere – what do I care what yer say?'

'Would you prefer to be sent to the remand home?' Ruby asked sternly. 'This is your last chance, Betty. If I have any further nonsense from you, you will be sent somewhere you will learn discipline.'

'See if I care . . .' Betty stuck her tongue out at her. 'Rotten ole cow!'

Ruby went round the desk and slapped her across the face just once. 'You will care if I send you away. What I just did is nothing. You'll be restrained and drugged if you're violent and kept in a padded cell . . .'

Betty stared, shocked into listening. 'Sorry,' she mumbled, eyes filling with tears. 'Didn't mean it . . .'

'You have one last chance,' Ruby repeated and held out her hand. 'Give me the lipstick and don't let me see you wearing it again . . .'

Betty handed it over reluctantly but raised her head in defiance. She held her tongue, still stunned by the slap and the threat of what would happen to her in a remand home, but Ruby guessed it wouldn't last long. Because she knew what the girl had been through at home, she would give her one last chance, but she didn't regret the slap. Betty had to learn discipline and if she didn't she would deserve all she got . . .

'How are the Miller children settling in?' Beatrice asked Wendy when she saw her later that afternoon. 'Do you think they're ready to be moved on yet?'

'In my opinion no,' Wendy said, looking thoughtful. 'Archie is set on visiting his mother at the police station and wants to prove her innocence. I don't think he has much chance of doing either, even if Mrs Miller is innocent – but I believe he would resent being sent away or being separated from his sister. She is a little truculent at times, but does what the carers ask her, so both Tilly and Kelly say . . .'

'That is exactly my own opinion,' Beatrice nodded her agreement. 'I shall wait until we hear what happens to their mother. If she is sent to prison, of course, they must both be moved to Halfpenny House.'

'Yes, I suppose so. It's a pity we can't just keep them here.'

'We only have so much room. I spoke against handing over the new wing to the Children's Department, but we had little choice in the matter. I'm afraid that in the case of a prison sentence for Mrs Miller I shall have no alternative but to send them on. However, I shall keep them together.'

'Oh yes, they must stay together,' Wendy agreed.

'Well, that has settled my mind,' Beatrice said. 'You are off this evening I believe?'

'Yes, I'm looking forward to it,' Wendy said. 'I've arranged to go to the pictures with Kelly. Her boyfriend is working and her father said she should have a night out for once, and as her sister is old enough to help about the house now she asked me if I wanted to see *Annie Get Your Gun* with her.'

'Is that a new film?'

'No, it came out in 1950 but somehow I never got to see it and neither did Kelly. It's on again at the Odeon and we thought it would make a nice change; it's a musical.'

'Ah yes, you will enjoy that,' Beatrice said. 'How is young Dick this evening? He has as nasty a case of the measles as I've seen . . .'

'He has been feeling very sorry for himself,' Wendy smiled in sympathy, 'but I've seen an improvement today, and fortunately we haven't had any further cases presenting themselves.'

'Good. Well I shan't hinder you; I'm sure you have things to do . . .'

Beatrice smiled as she walked back to her office. Thank goodness she didn't have to work with Ruby Saunders!

CHAPTER 5

'Can I see my mother?' Archie asked the following Saturday morning at the police station. 'I've brought her some fudge. She likes fudge and I got it special for her.'

'I'm sorry, lad,' Sergeant Sallis said from behind the counter. 'She was found guilty at her trial yesterday and she's been moved to Holloway . . . they gave her an eighteen-month sentence . . .'

'They can't have . . .' Archie was stunned. 'She's innocent. Why doesn't anyone believe us? If she took that money where is it?'

'She said she was innocent but the stolen cheques were found in her desk and a sheet of paper on which she'd been practising the manager's signature – and there was ten pounds missing from the cash box too. Only she and Reg Prentice had the key . . . and he was the one that drew attention to the missing money.'

'Then he took the money and he put those things in Mum's desk, I know he did,' Archie said belligerently. 'It ain't fair. Mum ain't a thief . . .'

'If it were up to me I'd give her the benefit of the

doubt,' Sergeant Sallis said. 'I'm truly sorry, lad. I wish there was something I could do, but the evidence went against her. She got a light sentence because of her previously good record and with good behaviour she might be out in a year or less.'

Archie felt the rage building inside him, but he wasn't going to rage at Sergeant Sallis. Twice, he'd let him see his mum for a few minutes, and he wasn't supposed to do that, Archie knew.

'How can I see her?'

'I'm not sure they will let you visit at the prison,' Sergeant Sallis said doubtfully. 'You're still a child in the eyes of the law – but I'll find out for you, and if there's a way I'll get you a visiting order, and if not I'll get you the proper address so you can write to her and send her a little parcel.'

Archie swallowed his anger and bewilderment and thanked him. He shoved his hands in his pockets as he walked away, shoulders hunched defensively. It was hell being a kid with no parents. If he'd been older he could've stood up to those people who'd labelled his mum a thief; she'd told Archie she was innocent and believed she'd been set up and she'd whispered a name. For some reason Reg Prentice had had it in for his mum, but she hadn't told him why; instead she'd told him to keep it to himself and not make trouble.

'If you go round there and accuse him it will only make them think you're a troublemaker, Archie. You have to stay strong, look after June for me, and I'll come back and find you when I can . . .'

Tears were burning the back of Archie's throat. He wished there was something he could do to comfort his mother, picturing her sitting in a cell, either alone or with other women – women who were thieves and worse. How she would hate it! Sandra Miller had always done her best to keep her children honest, clean and decent, and she'd been that way herself. Archie didn't believe for one moment that his mother had stolen those cheques or any money either. Someone had wanted to punish her and one day Archie was going to find out why and when he knew for certain . . . Reg Prentice had just better look out, that's all.

For the moment he had to take care of his sister. Archie was well aware June had been in trouble at school. He'd taken her to task over it, telling her what a fool she was to let others provoke her. He knew she was getting a lot of bullying at school, other girls jeering at her because her mother was locked up for theft and calling her names. Archie had endured some of the jeering himself, but he'd ignored it, squaring up to one of the boys and asking him if he wanted to make something of it. Because Archie was older and stronger than his sister, he'd succeeded in quietening the bullies, but June was different. She didn't like to be the object of scorn, and she was upset because their mother had gone away. Archie had tried to tell her it wasn't Mum's fault, but he didn't know whether she believed him or not.

He kicked angrily at a discarded can, lingering at the edge of the market. He didn't want to go back to his room at the orphanage; he hadn't made many friends there and he missed the life he'd known before his mother was arrested.

'Hey there, young 'un,' a voice said and he saw Billy Baggins coming towards him. 'Got nothing to do?'

'I went to visit Mum,' Archie said. 'They've moved her to prison . . .'

'I'm sorry about that,' Billy said. 'My brother is in prison, you know. I felt ashamed the first time, but he's no good – it's different for you. Sergeant Sallis told me he doesn't think your mum got justice.'

'She's not a thief. I know she's not . . .' Archie shuffled his feet moodily. 'I'm going to try and visit her in prison, but I might need an adult to go with me – if they'll let me at all . . .'

'I'll go with you if they'll give us a visiting order,' Billy offered. 'Just keep believin' in her, mate. It doesn't matter what the world says, as long as you know the truth . . .'

'Thanks, Billy,' Archie said. 'I wish I could run as fast as you.'

'I don't run as much as I used to. I'm too busy working these days,' Billy told him. 'Look, do you want to earn a few bob?'

'Yeah – what do I have to do?'

'See that man at the fruit and veg stall?' Archie nodded. 'You tell him Billy Baggins sent you and he'll give you a job trimming stuff and clearing up the rubbish. I used to work for him, but I've got other things to do these days. He's a fair man is Ted Hastings; he'll treat you right. I've got to go now. I'm takin' a mate to help clear his house and move him into a new council place . . .'

Archie thanked him and watched as he strode off, looking for all the world as if he were king of all he surveyed. He thought he'd like to be like Billy one day, but he didn't think he could win cups in running or football. He hesitated, and then approached the man on the stall Billy had pointed out. Archie hadn't anything else to do with himself for a few hours, and a few extra shillings would come in useful if he did get to visit his mother . . .

It was the stuff of nightmares, but even in her worst dreams Sandra had never seen herself in prison; she wasn't the sort who broke the law and one of the worst things of all was being labelled a thief in the eyes of the world, even though she knew she hadn't touched that money. There was no doubt whatsoever in Sandra's mind that Reg Prentice had set her up because she'd threatened to go to the boss with her complaints. How he must be laughing now and how she hated him for doing this to her; it was her anger against him and the others who had turned against her, people she'd thought her friends, that made it possible for her to bear the humiliation.

Sandra wasn't sure which part of the nightmare had been the worst: her arrest and the look in the eyes of people who believed her guilty; the time she'd spent in the police cells, her trial or her arrival at the women's prison. The sound of that metal door clanging shut behind her, the stench, and the knowledge that she was shut in this foul place for months on end would've broken her if she hadn't been so angry. She'd always believed in British justice and until sentence was pronounced she'd believed she would be declared innocent and set free.

Sandra had still been in a state of shock when they took her down from the dock and put her in a van with other women – women who were hardened to crime and laughed, jeering at the guards and swearing in a way that made Sandra wince. She could hardly believe that it had really happened, and because of that she'd endured the strip search, the showers during which the women huddled together, watched over by a warden who looked as if she'd never smiled in her life. She'd seen her things taken away and put in a box for which she'd had to sign, and she'd been given a shapeless grey sack that, belted in the middle with a tie, might just look like a dress.

All of that was bearable because she was angry. It was only when they'd pushed her into a cell and locked the door on her that Sandra began to tremble and the useless anger became a nameless fear that made her want to scream and scream, shouting her innocence out loud, and yet she didn't because some inner instinct told her that the only way to endure this was to keep her thoughts to herself – to live for the day when she was released. Shouting abuse as some of the others did wouldn't help, nothing would alter what was happening to her and being abusive would only make things worse.

'So what did you do then?' the only other occupant of her cell asked. 'I'm in 'ere fer sellin' it on the streets – wot 'ave you done, ducks?'

Sandra had hardly noticed the woman, or girl as she now saw, because she couldn't have been more than seventeen surely. She had bleached blonde hair, dark eyebrows and lashes and pale skin, which was blotched in a few places with red patches.

'They say I stole money and cheques from work,' Sandra said. 'I was set up by a man who hates me because I told him to get lost.'

'Yeah, I know that sort,' the girl said and pulled a face. 'It were one of them that got me started on the game. I 'ated him and got away from him when I found Dicky; he's a pet and saw me right . . . 'Ere, you ain't got a fag, 'ave yer? I'm gaspin' fer one and the buggers don't give us enough ter last the week . . .'

'I'm sorry, I don't smoke . . .'

'Don't let the buggers know that,' the girl said. 'Or you won't get yer ration. Fags are bloody gold dust in 'ere, love. If you don't want 'em there's plenty do, and you can trade 'em for privileges, see . . . There's women in 'ere that can make yer life 'ell if they want, or if they take to yer, they can make it easier.'

Sandra nodded, warming to the girl despite her unkempt appearance. She probably looked much the same herself now, because she hadn't been able to dry her hair properly after the shower, and she hadn't brought anything in the way of cosmetics into the prison with her. Archie had brought her a comb and toothbrush to the police cells, but apart from those and a bar of prison-issue soap she had nothing of her own.

'Is this your first time inside?'

'Nah, third, but I'm only in fer six months this time – four if I keep me nose clean . . .'

'I'm Sandra.' She offered her hand and after a moment the girl took it and grinned. 'I'm glad I'm sharing with you . . .'

'Mo, they call me, but me name's Maureen,' the girl said and laughed. 'Tell the truth, I don't care what they call me. I do what I'm told and keep out of trouble. If I were you I'd do the same. It's no use complaining, whether it's the screws or the other lot. You just have to put up with it until they put you out of the front gate and tell you not to come back.'

'I shan't be back,' Sandra said. She wanted to say that she would soon be released and that her friends would prove her innocence, but she didn't know who her friends were any more or even if she had any . . .

'I didn't think to say last time so I thought I'd better come round and tell you,' Sergeant Sallis said to Sister Beatrice later that day. 'Archie Miller came to the station and asked to see his mother, brought her a bag of fudge – and I had to tell him that she'd been sent down for eighteen months. I've told him I'll try to get a visiting order, but I doubt they will let him see her; he'll have to be accompanied, even if they'll allow it.'

'That would be no problem, one of my carers could go,' Beatrice said and frowned. 'However, this means I shall have to move him and his sister to Halfpenny House, because I can't keep them here for that length of time.'

'Archie isn't going to like that,' Sergeant Sallis said. 'I'd take the lad to visit myself and I'm prepared to vouch for him – but I can't promise anything . . .'

'Well, I'll delay it for a week or two but if we get more children needing to be admitted, Archie will have to be moved, and his sister . . .'

'Now that's the other thing . . .' Sergeant Sallis looked grave. 'We've had a complaint about June Miller. Apparently, she and an older girl . . .' he consulted his notebook, 'Betty Goodge, currently residing next door, were seen stealing lipstick from Woolworth's this morning . . .'

'Are you certain it was June Miller?' Beatrice frowned. 'I know Betty Goodge is a convicted thief. If she was older she would be in prison – and that is probably where she belongs. I understand she is a bad influence on the other girls next door . . .'

'Sometimes you get a bad one,' Sergeant Sallis sighed heavily. 'It seems to be bred in them and no matter how many chances you give them they won't change. I've told Miss Saunders and she said that Betty was already on a warning so I dare say she may find herself on the way to the remand centre before she knows what has happened.'

'Will you leave June to me, Sergeant?'

'Yes, of course. It's why I've told you. We don't have any proof she actually stole something. She was with Betty Goodge and that was enough to bring me here, but perhaps if you talk to her she will see the error of her ways.'

'I think I may have to send the children away after all, for June's sake,' Beatrice said. 'I shall tell Archie that if he wishes to visit his mother he may do so and St Saviour's will fund his fares to the prison and back to Halfpenny House. It is not ideal, but if the girl is in danger of being corrupted the sooner she is moved the better, and I do not think separating them would be the right thing.'

'No, I am certain it would not,' he agreed. 'Well, I'll get off home then. I know I can leave it to you to sort things out . . .'

'Here, shove it in your pocket, June,' Betty hissed as she handed her a fistful of lipsticks she'd snatched off the counter in Woolies. 'We'd better make a run fer it or they'll nab us . . .'

June giggled nervously. She was in awe of Betty, who

was bold and daring and didn't seem to fear anyone. She felt flattered that the older girl had noticed her and chosen her as her special friend. Betty was already leaving the shop when June felt the hand on her shoulder and was suddenly stopped in her tracks.

'Betty . . .' she cried piteously, but her friend looked back and grinned as she ran off, leaving June to face the anger of the shop manager by herself.

'You're in trouble now, girl,' he said gruffly. 'I'm holding you responsible for the theft of those lipsticks and you'll sit quietly in my office until the police come . . . and it will be better for you if you tell me who the girl was that actually snatched them.' He paused and frowned at her. 'I saw what she did and I'll tell Sergeant Sallis who was to blame – but you're in serious trouble, girl, and she's run off and left you to take the blame . . .'

June looked at him, tears hovering. 'I want my mum,' she whispered miserably. 'I want to go home to my mum . . .'

'Oh no, not again,' Sister Beatrice groaned as Sergeant Sallis pushed June forward and told the sorry tale. It was his second visit of the day and by far the most serious. 'June, what have you got to say for yourself?'

June hung her head but didn't speak. Sister Beatrice sighed and looked at her sadly.

'Don't you know what kind of a girl she is, June? She isn't your friend or she would've stayed with you and helped you – she got you into this trouble and you're very lucky not to be sent to a remand home. If it happens again, I shan't be able to stop the police bringing a case against you . . .'

'I'm sorry. It was just a lipstick . . .'

'At least four,' Sister Beatrice shook her head. 'Go along and have your tea, but remember this is your last chance . . .'

She stared at the police officer in exasperation as the door closed behind June. 'She isn't a bad child – it's that Betty Goodge.'

'I've spoken to Miss Saunders about her and she's having her sent on to the remand centre. Apparently, she gave her one last chance – and now she'll have time to repent at leisure . . .'

'Do some of them ever learn? I don't think even we could have helped that girl – and she's certainly had no understanding or love next door . . .'

'Miss Saunders doesn't see things the way you do, Sister. It will be a sorry day if her kind ever takes over completely – they don't seem to know the meaning of compassion; it's all morals and rules with that lot.'

'Yes, I believe you may be right,' Beatrice said. She was thoughtful as Sergeant Sallis took his leave. June would soon be leaving for Halfpenny House and out of the way of the bad influence from next door, but did she ought to visit the prison and tell June's mother any of this? Mrs Miller surely had a right to know whatever she'd done . . . Perhaps she would wait until she had better news to pass on, when June was settled in Essex and doing better. Surely, it couldn't help to give Mrs Miller bad news, because she must be worried enough as it was . . .

Ruby replaced her telephone receiver and smiled in satisfaction. After what had happened today, Sister Beatrice wouldn't have a leg to stand on if she tried to hang on to June Miller. Ruby had rung the Children's Department as soon as she'd heard and told them she was moving Betty into secure care. Her call to Miss Sampson had turned out to be more worthwhile than she'd hoped, because her supervisor from when she worked in the Children's Welfare Department had agreed with everything she said; they were alike in more ways than one, though Ruth was a few years older, but neither of them was interested in marriage or men. Ruby suspected that Miss Sampson's reasons might be different from hers, but it did mean that they got on well, and Ruby took care to consult her about important decisions, even though she was in charge of her girls, within the Department rules.

'I know that strictly speaking it isn't my affair, but I felt in the interests of the child I should consult you. In my opinion she has been allowed to run wild for years and even if the mother were not in prison I believe she would be better with a decent family. Otherwise she will end in a remand home like so many others.'

'You were very sensible to contact me,' Miss Sampson said primly. 'I have always thought that St Saviour's would be better run by someone like you, Ruby – especially now that Angela Adderbury has retired. Sister Beatrice was kept there because a lot of influential people refused to move her, despite my advice. Sister Beatrice is well-meaning, I have no doubt, and I believe she is strict – but I think I shall look into this matter and quite possibly make an order for fostering.'

'I'm so glad I rang you. I thought you might reprimand me for interfering?'

'Not at all, Ruby. Did you have anyone in mind for foster parents?'

'Well, I do know of a couple who have asked about fostering one of my girls. Mr and Mrs Bailey said they wanted to give a child a good home. I explained that my girls are here to be disciplined and could not be considered for fostering or adoption, but then I thought of June . . .'

'What kind of people are they?'

'She is a school teacher and he owns a grocery business; he helps to run a youth club in the evenings. They are both in their thirties and childless – and willing to foster older children, but they did ask for a girl.'

'They sound ideal,' Miss Sampson said. 'Yes, give me their details in writing and I'll make some inquiries. We are a little short of available foster parents at the moment, so they might very well be suitable.'

'I am so pleased I rang you now. I was afraid you might think I was interfering in St Saviour's business.'

'Not at all, Ruby. You are a woman after my own heart and I trust your judgement. Please keep me informed of anything that attracts your notice.'

Ruby glowed under her superior's praise. It was exactly what she wanted – for Ruth to notice her and approve. Perhaps it was the first step to a relationship between them . . . but she still needed to be very careful; she must be sure her affection was returned before she made a suggestion. 'I'm so glad you agree, because I am sure Sister Beatrice will not . . .'

'Well you know my opinion there. Leave it with me, but as soon as I've verified this couple, I shall make an order for June Miller to be taken into custody . . .'

Ruby was feeling elated when she finished her call;

Ruth Sampson had thought she'd behaved properly, though Sister Beatrice would almost certainly be furious. She would believe that Ruby had gone beyond her remit and would no doubt be angry to receive an order for one of her children to be taken into care and then fostered. Ruby pushed the thought from her mind. She'd acted in the best interests of the child, which any by-stander was entitled to do . . .

Archie was pleased as he fingered the half-crown in his pocket. Ted Hastings had praised him for his work and rewarded him generously. He'd been so pleased that he'd told Archie he could have the job every Saturday morning if he wanted it.

'I've been lookin' for a likely lad to work on the stalls,' he'd said as he handed Archie a plastic mug of tea and a sticky bun. 'If you keep up the good work I could take you on when you leave school. In time you could be running a stall yourself and you might even own one in time . . .'

Archie knew that Ted Hastings owned several market stalls. His daughter Maggie ran a stall selling material and she'd been busy the whole morning. Ted had sent Archie over with a cup of tea for her and Maggie had been just as friendly as her father.

'Thanks, Archie,' she'd said after he'd told her his name. 'That's just what I could do with. I hope you're going to work for us every week?'

'Mr Hastings said I can work for him when I leave school,' Archie said. 'I could leave next term, but Mum wanted me to stay at school and learn to be something proper – in an office or a mechanic or somethin' . . .'

'Dad says you never get anywhere as a wage-slave,' Maggie told him. 'I think you should come and work for us as soon as you leave. You'll do all right for yourself with us. When Dad takes to someone he looks after them . . .'

Archie wondered what Mr Hastings would think if he knew his mum was in prison for theft . . . a theft she hadn't committed. Perhaps he should have told him, but it wasn't something he was proud of. He might have believed Archie, but if he didn't he probably wouldn't have let him help on the stall.

Archie was just going to have to prove himself, before he told his new friend.

'Where did you get to all day?'

June's sulky tones made him turn to look at her. He'd been sitting in the little garden behind St Saviour's because it was quiet and he wanted to think but now he was suddenly angry.

'I should think you're the one who should be telling me that,' Archie said and stood up. 'Why did you take those lipsticks? You know Mum would be furious if she thought you'd pinched anything.'

'I didn't,' June said truculently. 'Betty gave them to me . . .'

'But she stole them and you knew what she'd done,' Archie said. 'It was stupid, June. Do you want to end up in a remand home like her?'

'No . . .' June looked fit to burst into tears. 'I want to be at home with Mum but she's in prison . . .'

'Because someone lied about her,' Archie said. 'You've still got your freedom and it's not too bad here. Sister

Beatrice looks stern but she's fair – and Wendy is lovely, so are Sally and Nancy. All of them are . . . We could be in a lot worse places, June.'

'I know . . .' June hung her head. 'It was Betty. She kept taunting me and I wanted her to like me.'

'If you want me to like you, just behave. I don't want you sent off to some remand home. Mum would kill me when she got home. We've got to stick together, love – don't you see?'

'I'm sorry,' June said. 'I wish Mum was here . . .'

As the tears slipped down her cheeks Archie relented and put his arms about her. 'It's all right, June. I'll look after you. You'll always have me. I promise . . .'

CHAPTER 6

'Was it a good film last night?' Tilly asked as she met Kelly coming into work that evening. 'My sister Mags wants to see it and I've told her she can go with her friends, but I've been thinking I'd like to see it myself.' Tilly's brother had joined the Army the minute he was old enough and intended it to be his career, but Mags had come to live with Tilly and her husband Terry after their mother had died the previous year. Mrs Mallens had been too fond of the drink and when she caught pneumonia, she hadn't had the strength to fight it.

'It was *Seven Brides for Seven Brothers*. It came out last year but I hadn't seen it and I loved it,' Kelly said. 'I don't get to the flicks often, because I work most nights and I'm usually busy at home even if I'm not at work . . .'

Tilly nodded her understanding. She knew how ill Kelly's mother was and sympathised with her, because although hers was a happier home than Tilly's had been, there were several younger children for whom Kelly had been responsible until they were old enough to leave school, and there was still the youngest boy and her sick mother to care for. Until her death, Tilly's own mother had often been moody, sometimes drunk, and always irritable since her second husband was sent to prison for attacking a young woman. She'd blamed Tilly for everything, but she'd got used to it over the years, ignoring her tantrums until the last. Mags had started working on the counters at Boots the chemist and contributed to the household income, which made it easier on Tilly because she couldn't do a full-time job now she was married. Mags was a pretty girl and Tilly thought it wouldn't be long before she was thinking of getting married and settling down.

Tilly was pretty too, or she had been when she was younger. She sometimes thought that she was looking older, perhaps because she'd had to struggle to keep a roof over her family's head all these years. Sometimes she went out with Terry for a drink, but mostly she just went home so that Mags could go off with her friends. Even after her mother died and she'd married, Tilly didn't get out much. She and Terry had moved into a nice council house in the suburbs, which meant she had to get the train to come to work and that didn't leave an awful lot out of her wage. Terry said it was a waste of time and wanted her to take a job in the corner shop near their home, but Tilly liked her work and she was staying put until she got pregnant and she had a feeling that might not be too far away. She was going to have to see a doctor very soon if her suspicions were correct . . .

Kelly's situation was different. Her home was filled with love. They weren't much better off than Tilly's family had been, because Mr Mason was sometimes on shift work at the Docks and didn't have a big wage.

Yet he loved his sickly wife and all his children, and he made sure that Kelly was rewarded for her hard work now and then – and Kelly was courting. She'd been going with Steve Jarvis for seven years, but both of them had commitments and seemed content with their lives as they were. At least, Kelly never said any different, even if she thought it.

'Well, I'd better get my coat off and start,' Kelly said cheerfully and Tilly let her go. She was thoughtful as she left St Saviour's. It was milder that evening and still quite light. For some reason she was restless and the thought of going home to an empty house wasn't pleasing. She decided that she wouldn't catch her bus; instead, she would walk home by the river, give herself time to sort out her thoughts. She'd been stuck in a rut for years and she was getting pretty fed up with it . . .

'How is your mother?' Wendy asked when Kelly popped into the sick ward with a tray of tea and sandwiches for her. 'Is she any better?'

Kelly shook her head sorrowfully. 'No, if anything she's a little worse. The doctor came this morning and he told us he thinks she won't last much longer.'

'It's such a shame,' Wendy sympathised. 'You've done everything you can to help her but sometimes there just is nothing more you can do – it was like that for me when my mum died. I still miss her so much even though she died years ago.'

'I don't know what Dad will do,' Kelly said and swallowed hard. 'I haven't told him yet, though I shall have to, because he has to know . . .' She sighed. 'We thought she would be better when we moved into our new house, and she was for a few years, but since last winter when she had that chest infection she's just got worse.'

'Oh, Kelly, don't cry,' Wendy said as a sob escaped the younger woman. 'You know if there's anything I can do to help, you've only to ask . . .'

'Thanks, Wendy, you're a good friend, but there isn't anything. If the doctor says there's nothing, we just have to accept it and make her last months as happy as we can.'

'If you need time off work I'm sure Sister Beatrice would understand. She would take you back when you were ready . . .'

'Yes, she told me that the other day,' Kelly said and gave her a watery smile. 'When I first started here in the kitchen I had more warnings than Billy Baggins, but I worked hard and I've made a place for myself here. I might have to stay off towards the end, but at the moment Dad and Cate are managing at night – and my younger brother is wonderful. The older one is off with his mates all the time, but he pays his share at home so I don't try to force him.'

'Well, I hope Mrs Mason will be better soon,' Wendy said. She knew the words sounded foolish given that Kelly had just told her that her mother was dying – but what else could she say?

Wendy poured herself a cup of tea and settled down to look at Paula's reports for the day. No new cases had been admitted and they just had one case of measles and another had been treated for a tummy upset. Paula had done a check for nits and treated six of their children, who had picked it up at school. It was a constant battle against reinfection. Now and then the children presented with fleabites, caught when visiting their friends in slum properties infested with rats. The rats harboured the fleas and no matter how much the women scrubbed their homes, they couldn't get rid of them.

Wendy sometimes thought that the kids sent on to Halfpenny House were the lucky ones. Conditions were better in the country, because there was often better housing and fresher food. Although, Angela had told her they still had a few fleabites to deal with now and then, and apparently it wasn't all honey down there. Angela said they'd had some trouble with the older boys, who'd been playing truant from school. Because of it they'd taken on a new carer who'd retired from his job as a headmaster and claimed he could soon sort their problems out. In Wendy's opinion what they needed was to send for Sister Beatrice and let her talk some sense into the lads.

'We're quiet at the moment, Staff Nurse . . .'

Wendy looked up as Sister Beatrice entered the ward. 'Yes, I can't remember when we had so few children presenting sick – but then, we used to have many more than we normally have now.'

'Yes, although I believe we may have two brothers coming tomorrow.' Sister Beatrice glanced at the report. 'I think we have enough beds for them if they arrive – and I've decided that June Miller and her brother will be moved to Halfpenny House next week. James Benton is due to go too and Philip Manse. So we'll send them all together.'

'Yes, I think it's better if several go together,' Wendy agreed. 'Are you going to send Susan Marsh too? She's been here three months and seems quite well and happy now.'

'That would mean sending more than one car,' Sister Beatrice frowned. 'I'll see how many new admittances we have in the next week. I like to keep them here until I'm sure they can cope with another change in their lives . . . If only we had more resources so that we could keep them all here . . .'

'I think we just don't have enough staff to look after larger numbers, as we used to.'

'Staff is a part of the problem,' Sister Beatrice agreed.

'Talking of staff – Kelly was telling me how ill her mother is . . .'

'Yes, I feel most concerned for her,' Sister Beatrice said. 'I shall take on a temporary replacement if she feels she needs time off to be with her mother, but I would like her to return when she can.'

'Oh, I think she will. Kelly has worked hard for her place here.'

'Indeed she has. Well, I'm going home. You don't need me this evening. We can only hope that things stay quiet for a while . . . though I shouldn't tempt fate, should I?'

'Oh dear, let's hope she didn't hear,' Wendy said and laughed.

Whether it was Sister Beatrice tempting fate or just the way things happen, they had a steady influx of children in need over the next ten days. First the two brothers, Ben and Malcolm, who had been picked up wandering the streets and were both suffering from malnutrition and the cold. They were admitted into the sick ward, because Sister Beatrice was horrified by the way their ribs were showing through their emaciated bodies. Neither of them would tell her, but she suspected they'd been on the streets for weeks. Their parents had apparently abandoned them and the boys had been wandering around London trying to find them and to beg for food.

After they'd been dealt with, a girl of seven was admitted; Maggie Ryan had been sent on from the hospital that had treated her for a broken arm and severe bruising to her body. Her brutal father had been arrested and her mother was dead, so she would now be in the care of the orphanage until the Children's Department decided where her future lay. Another three children were brought in from the streets, two having been found with evidence of severe beatings and another in a confused state – he didn't know his name and needed special supervision from the nurses.

Beatrice had decided that she would bring the date of the transfer of several children forward to the next day. She knew that she had to explain to Archie what was happening and to reassure him that he would be able to visit his mother, if a visiting permit was granted. Though so far no such permission had been forthcoming, as Sergeant Sallis told her when he visited that morning.

'I've phoned them three times and they say they will let me know, but I understand it is irregular for an underage lad to visit a prisoner and I've said I'll go with him. However, if they refuse I'll visit myself and then let him know how she is . . .'

'I'm afraid he won't be here,' Beatrice said. 'I don't like to make him leave London when I know how important he feels it to be near his mum, but we're bursting at the seams. I just have to send them on.'

'Would you like me to explain for you?'

'No, I'm going to talk to him this afternoon when he gets in from school,' Beatrice said. It was her decision and her responsibility.

However, she found it harder than she'd imagined to look into Archie's eyes and explain he was being sent to the country, not because it was better for him, but because she didn't have the room to keep him and his sister indefinitely.

'I am truly sorry, Archie,' she said, 'and I want you to know that we shall pay for your fares to visit your mother when an order becomes available. Sergeant Sallis won't give up trying, and if a permit comes through he will contact you. I shall make sure you have the fares – and I think you will like it at Halfpenny House. They have playing fields and more facilities for sport than we have here . . .'

'I don't want to go. I've got to stay here,' Archie said. 'I've got a job on the market on Saturdays and I'm savin' for when Mum gets home. She'll need some money to get started . . .'

'I'm sorry, Archie. You have to go. I really don't have a choice – but my promise to you is that you will be able to see your mother if that permit comes. And it might be better for your sister to get away, don't you think?'

Archie looked rebellious and she thought he was going to refuse. She was wondering if she could possibly manage to keep them on when she saw his slight nod of acceptance.

'It would be better if June wasn't here,' Archie admitted. 'She hates it at her school, because they bully

91

her, and she won't listen to what I tell her. If we're away from here she might settle down and not run wild . . .'

'I'm glad that you are so caring towards your sister,' Beatrice gave him an approving nod. 'You will be leaving tomorrow, both of you – and please feel free to write to me if you have any worries. I am always here for you; do you understand?'

'Yes, Sister,' Archie said. 'May I go now? I have to talk to June, make sure she understands . . .'

'Of course,' Beatrice said. 'I'm very pleased you've behaved so responsibly and I shall do whatever I can for you in future – should you wish to return to London, as I'm sure you will once your mother is home. After all, yours is only a temporary situation, is it not?'

'Yes, Sister . . .'

Archie inclined his head and went out. Beatrice looked at the closed door and wondered. Had she done what was best for the boy and his sister? She didn't really have much choice given the situation at St Saviour's. True, she would have two free beds when they'd gone, but she needed them for emergency admissions.

If only the new wing hadn't been leased to the Children's Welfare Department. She'd never had this worry once the new wing was built, because it provided a lot of much-needed extra space for her children, but the Board had decided that the future lay in moving the children out of the East End, nearer to the country where the conditions were better and the air was fresher, and Beatrice was only one voice. It meant that once again she was often short of beds for emergencies and had to pass her charges on sooner than she would like. Was she the only one who saw that some of these children could never belong anywhere but the streets where they were born and bred? At least here she'd been able to help many of them into good jobs and better lives than their parents had known.

She had an uneasy feeling about sending Archie and his sister to Halfpenny House, but the decision was made and perhaps it was for the best . . .

'We've got to go, June,' Archie told his sister. He gave her a penny lollipop and tried not to notice the tears in her eyes. 'I'll write to Mum and let her know where we're goin'. She said if they move us, she'll come and find us when she gets out and we'll all be together again.'

'When?' June demanded truculently. 'I don't want to go to this rotten old place. I want to stay here with my friends . . .' Two tears slid down her cheeks and she glared at him. 'I hate Sister Beatrice for sendin' us away – and if you let her I'll hate you too.'

'It's not my fault and it ain't hers either,' Archie said, though in his heart he was blaming everyone. They were all equally to blame. Why hadn't anyone stood up for his mum and stopped them sending her to prison?

'I hate you,' June said stubbornly. 'I hate everybody . . .'

Archie put his arms about her. Just at this moment he felt very much the same . . .

CHAPTER 7

Sandra stood in line with the bucket, waiting to empty the slops from the previous night down the toilet. Some of the women had already spilled urine on the floor and the smell from the buckets was appalling. Listening to the other inmates swear and curse as they yawned and scratched themselves, Sandra shuddered inwardly. Prison was torture for her and not just because of the primitive conditions.

Where were her children? Were they still with Sister Beatrice in St Saviour's or had they been moved on? Was Archie managing to look after June and do his schoolwork properly? She wished she'd remembered to tell him where his father's watch, a few bits of hers, and a couple of pounds were hidden in the old house. When he'd visited she'd been too emotional to think of such things and realised that her precious memories were probably lost along with the house. She felt torn in bits because she was stuck in here and no one seemed to care that she was innocent. Sandra had no one to turn to, no one who would fight for her and her kids and the injustice of it burned in her like a fire.

'Bloody freezing this mornin',' one of the inmates observed. 'Got a fag, Sandra, love? I'd do anythin' for a fag . . .'

Bella was a lesbian and the look she gave Sandra was one of unconcealed lust. Sandra shuddered inwardly, though she tried not to show it, because Bella had been one of the few to treat her decently, and she'd protected her from some of the other wildcats in here. Sandra had hardly known what the word 'lesbian' meant before she got sent here, but she'd soon discovered what it was once she'd been manhandled in the showers a few times. Sandra had given Bella half her first packet of cigarettes and after that she'd protected her, even though she'd made a few hints about what she'd like herself. However, she was usually satisfied with a couple of fags, which Sandra passed to her when the screw's back was turned. Bella grinned and tucked them into her bra.

'What's up, luv?'

'I was thinking about my kids, wondering how they are – if they're still in London.'

'You should ask to see the Governor,' Bella whispered as the female warder turned her pale mean eyes on them. 'She'll find out fer yer – or write to someone and I'll get it sent out fer yer . . .'

'There's no one I can write to,' Sandra said, her throat tight. 'I don't have any relatives and that's why I'm so worried . . . unless I wrote to Sister Beatrice . . .'

'Got a sister, 'ave yer?'

'She's the nun in charge of St Saviour's orphanage.'

'Never 'eard of it,' Bella said. 'I'm from Bermondsey, ain't I? Bloody nosy Social lot runs things there . . . always bleedin' interferin' . . .'

'That's what I'm afraid of . . . in case they get fostered out . . .'

'We'll be gettin' letters today,' Bella said. 'Mebbe your son will send a letter or visit you . . .'

'No talking,' the warder snapped. 'Move up the line, Bella, or I'll have you on latrine duties . . .'

Sandra nodded at her and Bella moved on. The woman winked at her and, despite the horror of it all, Sandra felt a little better. Perhaps she would get a letter from Archie today. She'd had one but it was weeks ago and she couldn't stop worrying, especially about June, who was so sulky and inclined to get into trouble if she didn't watch out for her . . . If anything happened to her kids she didn't know what she would do, because they were her reason for living . . .

Ruby replaced the receiver and smiled. It was all in place. Miss Sampson would be here at eight thirty in the morning to take June Miller into custody. She'd decided to come in person in case Sister Beatrice tried to stop her officers taking the child.

'I'll leave it to you to notify her,' Miss Sampson said. 'I'm sure you've made her aware that it's happening so it shouldn't be too much of a surprise.'

'I didn't actually say, because I wasn't sure,' Ruby confessed. 'I'll go and tell her this evening.'

'Make sure you do. I would've written to inform her myself, but I thought we'd arranged it would be best coming from you.'

'Yes, of course,' Ruby agreed hastily. 'I'll make sure she knows.'

She felt a bit apprehensive as she went next door to

inform Sister Beatrice of the arrangements. Knocking twice at her office door, she opened it gingerly and saw no one was there. It was past six so perhaps Sister had gone home. Ruby felt it wasn't appropriate for her to wander about St Saviour's looking for its Warden. She would write a note and leave it on Sister Beatrice's desk, she decided. Yes, that was a good idea. Obviously, she would have to face up to Sister Beatrice at some point in the future, but once the child was in the custody of the Children's Welfare officers, it wouldn't be worth arguing over. Surely Sister would see that? Of course she would, because Ruby knew she was right . . .

Hastily scribbling a note, she folded it and left it on the desk, then left. Sister Beatrice would find it in the morning when she arrived. She was sure to be in early and she could tell the children what was happening. It was far better that June should be fostered, because she was still running wild and her mother had obviously never taught her how to behave . . .

'Have you got all your things, Archie?' Beatrice asked as she went to wish him well and remind him of her promise. The small group of children were gathered in the hall with their bundles of personal possessions and suitcases, some of them laughing and chattering, but Archie was standing silently on his own looking serious. 'You are going to the station with the others and Jean. She is taking the boys down to Halfpenny House, where you will be met by one of the carers there. June is coming down by car with Nancy. She's driving all the girls down and will take them directly to Halfpenny House herself.'

'Why can't June come on the train with us?'

'For one thing you have too much to carry on the train. Some of your things have to travel in the car; it isn't just you, Archie. There are seven children leaving us today.'

Archie nodded, looking rebellious. 'June won't like it. She'll scream and kick up a fuss if I'm not with her . . .'

'There isn't room in the car for you as well. Now go with Jean. She's taking you all on the bus to the station . . .'

Archie went down to the hall and spoke to his sister. June shook her head violently and clung to him, but Archie pushed her away and walked off with the other boys. Satisfied, Beatrice returned to her office. She had that wretched report to write this morning, and then . . . Seeing a folded piece of paper lying on her desk, she picked it up and stared at it, hardly taking in what she was reading. This was impossible, ridiculous! It couldn't be right?

At first she was too stunned with disbelief to react and then the anger rippled through her. How dare Ruby Saunders behave in such a cavalier fashion – leaving a scribbled note as if a child were a mere commodity to be disposed of on a whim?

. Oh no! June and Archie! Sister Beatrice realised what this news would do to the children. She'd given her word to Archie that his sister would meet him at Halfpenny House and now she had to tell him that it wouldn't happen – but it might be too late to let him know before they left. She walked swiftly down the stairs and out of the front door. A bus was just leaving from the stop and there was no sign of Jean or of the children so they must be on it. Her heart sank, because she had no way of stopping them from leaving, even if she dashed off to the station. Besides, what could she do?

Even as she hesitated a car drew up and Miss Ruth Sampson got out, looking very officious in her dark-grey suit and sensible black shoes. She was clutching her cardboard folder and clearly in no mood to brook an argument.

'You know why I've come?' she said and handed Beatrice an envelope. 'These are all the relevant documents. I believe Miss Saunders informed you of our decision?'

'I received a scribbled note when it was too late to tell Archie. His sister is in the hall waiting for Nancy to take her and the others to Halfpenny House.' She was opening the envelope, scanning the documents inside, but she'd known it would all be official; Miss Sampson wouldn't leave anything to chance. 'I consider that both you and Miss Saunders have acted in a high-handed manner, going behind my back and interfering in the work of St Saviour's. I shall be speaking to the Board about this and I intend to lodge an official complaint.'

Miss Sampson frowned. 'I understood Miss Saunders had discussed the girl with you?'

'She spoke of fostering but I disagreed. In my opinion the sister and brother should have been kept together. I shall be protesting in the strongest terms about the way both of you have acted – and it is my intention to have your order overturned if at all possible . . .'

'Come now,' Miss Sampson argued mildly. 'We have proceeded in the best interests of the girl. Under your care she has been getting into more and more trouble. She needs a loving family and it is my opinion that her mother had no control over her – and she is clearly not fit to have the care of her children . . .'

'Because Mrs Miller was found guilty of stealing it doesn't necessarily mean she is a bad mother,' Sister Beatrice argued. 'I think you have been hasty, Miss Sampson. You should have consulted me, asked for my opinion before applying for this order.'

'Miss Saunders contacted us, Sister Beatrice, and I trust her judgement. She was concerned about the moral welfare of June Miller, and I agreed with her. While you have the day-to-day care of St Saviour's, you now come under our jurisdiction at the Children's Department, and my decision is final. Therefore, I have acted properly in asking for an order to take her into our care. However, she will be fostered and not sent to the remand centre for bad girls . . .'

Beatrice felt the frustration building inside her, because she hated the bureaucracy that had overtaken the Children's Welfare services these days, but she was bound by red tape and a stone wall that she could only rail against. Miss Sampson was just one of many officials who believed they knew best in all situations and refused to take the advice of someone with years of experience. However, Beatrice wasn't going to give in without a fight.

'So I should hope. I do not believe either you or Miss Saunders has acted well. I should have been consulted from the beginning and I think this is all highly improper, if not to say illegal. As June's temporary guardian I should have had the opportunity to put my point of view before this order was sought or granted and I would not have agreed to such ill-thought-out action. June believes she is going to join her brother. When she learns she is not she will naturally be very upset . . .'

'Well, I shall not tell her the details just yet. Mr and Mrs Bailey are coming to my office this morning and will sign the papers for the charge of June.'

'Who are these people? Are you certain they are proper persons to have the charge of a young girl?'

'They have been checked and verified as respectable people,' Miss Sampson said. 'While I should perhaps have written to you earlier apprising you of our intention, I believed Miss Saunders was keeping you in touch with our plans and that you were broadly in agreement. I have the authority to act when I believe it in the best interests of a child and I am at fault only in not informing you myself.' Beatrice shook her head grimly. 'I shall reprimand Miss Saunders for her neglect in keeping you informed and you have my apologies for the oversight on my part – but surely as a caring woman, you must believe the girl will be all the better for a family to look after her?'

Beatrice hesitated, knowing that Miss Sampson had reason on her side – calm, cold reason – while Beatrice's own feelings were compassion and sadness for June's distress.

'She has been getting into bad company – but if your department hadn't taken over our wing, she would never have met that girl . . .'

'Yes, well, that has been taken care of,' Miss Sampson shrugged. 'I have a busy day ahead. I should like to take the girl with me now . . .'

Beatrice felt trapped, knowing that she couldn't prevent her from taking June. The paperwork was in order and she had the legal authority to remove the girl from St Saviour's care.

'Very well, since I cannot stop you, but allow me a moment to speak to the child.'

She went ahead of Miss Sampson and saw June sitting on her case, a teddy bear clutched close, apart from the others and desperately lonely. Clearly she had no friends here. Perhaps after all it would be better for her to make a new life with a new family.

'Come along, June dear,' she said. 'Miss Sampson is waiting to take you.'

Some of the others stepped forward but Beatrice shook her head and took June by the hand. The girl pulled back and looked tearful, but Beatrice clasped her hand and led her to Miss Sampson.

'I'm sorry, this wasn't my idea,' she said. 'You've been taken into care, June, and you will be meeting your new family later this morning . . .'

'I want Archie – will he be there?'

'No, Archie has gone somewhere else,' Beatrice said. 'You will no doubt be allowed to see him sometimes. Go along now . . .'

'No! I'm not going,' June screamed and kicked out at Beatrice, catching her ankle and making her let go of her arm. June ran towards the door, but Miss Sampson grabbed her by her arms, holding her in a tight grasp. June screamed again and kicked at her, but Miss Sampson shook her, looking angry. 'Let me go. I want my mum. I want to go home . . .'

'This behaviour will result in your being disciplined,'

Miss Sampson told her. 'Be silent or you will feel the back of my hand – and I shall shut you in a dark cupboard until you calm down.'

June looked back at Beatrice, accusation in her eyes. 'I hate you for doing this . . .' she cried, and struggled as she was propelled towards the open door and then out into the street, still struggling and screaming.

Drawn by a compelling need to watch, Beatrice went back outside and saw another woman get out of the car. She took hold of June's arm and thrust her into the back seat of the Morris car and then got in beside her. Coldness settled at Beatrice's nape and she felt distressed. She disliked both Miss Sampson and the large woman who had handled June so expertly and yet so harshly. The child must be frightened and in great distress and Beatrice was consumed with guilt that she hadn't been able to stop them taking her.

Ruby would not escape lightly from this! She should have kept Beatrice informed of every step. She might then have tried to prevent the order being granted or at the very least warned the brother and sister of what had been decided.

Beatrice was so very angry. She would certainly complain of the way this affair had been handled, because it was irregular to say the least, and in her view improper. Yet once the order had been obtained, it would be difficult to overturn it. Beatrice needed help – and the only people she could think of who might know what they could do were Angela and Mark. She would telephone immediately, and then she would be paying Miss Ruby Saunders a visit that she would not soon forget.

Yet even as she battled with her own indignation over

the way she'd been overruled and ignored in this matter, she knew that it would affect Archie so much worse – and she dreaded to think what poor little June was feeling now. Even if the Baileys were perfect parent material, she had been torn away from her mother and now her brother and she must be terrified.

Archie would think she had lied to him deliberately. She would have to telephone Halfpenny House later and try to apologise to him in person . . . though whatever she did he would be angry and distressed . . .

'Welcome to Halfpenny House,' Gerald Smith said as he opened the door of his battered old shooting brake for the boys to emerge, after fetching them from the railway station. 'It's a bit different to what you're used to, I know, but you'll soon settle down and find it comfortable and better too. I'm here for you boys to come to when you need help, and I supervise games. We've got our own playing fields behind us and there is a large gymnasium, where you can play in the evenings, climbing and stuff . . .'

Archie listened to the man's bluff, hearty talk about becoming part of a family and enjoying life in a better environment. He couldn't see what was better about this place, except that it was set adjacent to playing fields and had bigger gardens, which smelled strongly of the horse manure dug in round the rose beds.

The home itself, a long and square-looking building with a flat roof, was unlike the crumbling grandeur of St Saviour's; it had started life some fifty years ago as a grammar school and had undergone extensive renovations to turn it into what it now was. The local authority had handed the building over to the Board of St Saviour's charity to run as a children's home, being partly funded by the state and under their control.

Archie noticed that it smelled different, a strong odour of disinfectant coming from the toilets mixing with new paint. Immediately, he missed the comfortable shabbiness of St Saviour's, the imposing staircase with its mahogany banisters and the shining wood floors. Here it was all metal and stone, tiles on the floor, lacking the feeling of permanence and age that St Saviour's had. He could hear voices from somewhere overhead and it sounded hollow, making him feel awkward and ill at ease.

The boys' dormitories were at the back of the home, he discovered as Gerald Smith led the way inside, and faced the playing fields and a magnificent oak tree that must have been there for hundreds of years. The rooms at the front of the ground floor had big, wide windows and were set up as the gymnasium, another recreation room for the children, and various offices, toilets and the dining room. At the back was what looked like a sitting room for the staff, a kitchen and the caretaker's office. On the first floor was the nurse's room, but there was no sick or isolation ward here.

One of the children asked about it and was told that the nurse was there for emergencies and to dispense an aspirin if needed, but if any of the children were really unwell they were taken to the doctor and to hospital if required. The Superintendent was called Mrs Mellors and she had her office on the ground floor.

The dormitories were smaller than at St Saviour's, with no more than three beds, and each child had a

105

bedside cabinet, which he could lock, and also part of a wardrobe at the end of the room, each section divided by a thin metal sheet. Archie found himself put in with two other boys, neither of whom had been sent down with him that day. Keith Jones was a lanky boy with a shock of light-brown hair that stood up in tufts on his crown, and Harry Wade had fair hair and blue eyes that looked slightly vacant behind his thick spectacles. Neither of them seemed inclined to talk much and Archie sat on the edge of his bed and stared at the clean bare walls, wishing he was anywhere else but here. At St Saviour's the boys had stuck charts and pictures cut out of magazines on all the walls around their beds, and that had made for a comfortable atmosphere. Archie's first impression here was that everything was new and too clean. He hadn't been used to living like this and he didn't feel at home. It hadn't been too bad at St Saviour's, where he knew all the streets and could find his way to the market, school and wherever else he wanted to go. Here it was strange and he felt like a fish out of water, struggling to survive.

Looking out of the window all he could see was the playing fields and a line of houses at the far end. He felt a wave of homesickness for the dirty old streets of the East End and his throat tightened.

'It's all right once you get used to it,' Keith Jones said and, turning his head, Archie saw that he'd joined him at the window. 'I felt lost when I first came but I don't mind it now. The town isn't bad and I've applied for an apprenticeship in an engineering works when I leave school next year – the only thing is, look out for Mr Smith.'

'What do you mean?'

'Just don't cross him or you'll find out . . .' Keith showed his right hand and the red scar that was almost healed across it.

'He did that?'

'Yeah, but it was me own fault 'cos I was fightin' him . . . so don't say nuthin' or I'll be in worse trouble.'

'Why don't you run away?'

'Got nowhere to go except the streets . . . What about you?'

'I had a job on the market back home promised me when I leave,' Archie said gloomily and felt angry. Why had he been sent to this dump, where he didn't fit in, when he might have stayed in London and worked on Saturdays to earn money for his mother?

He realised that Ted Hastings would wonder why he didn't turn up for work on Saturday. He would think he'd simply decided not to bother and was just another kid wasting time. A loud bell intruded into his thoughts, making Archie jump.

'That's the bell for supper,' Keith said. 'We have breakfast, tea and supper here, but we don't come back for lunch because it's too far to walk from school. We're on the outskirts here and that means we need a bus if we want to go into the flicks or the youth club.'

'It's different to St Saviour's,' Archie said. 'We didn't need a bell there, we just knew when supper was and went down if we were hungry.'

'I didn't come from St Saviour's,' Keith said. 'I've heard some of the kids say they liked it more – but this is no worse than where I was . . . except for Smithy . . .'

Archie nodded. He wasn't hungry but Keith and Harry

Wade were obviously going down so he might as well tag along. He vaguely remembered being told where the dining room was but he couldn't be certain. Following the stream of children moving towards the ground floor, girls mixing with the boys as they reached the stairs, giggling, pushing and arguing, Archie felt out of it. He would just as soon have stayed up in the dormitory but he knew he had to find June. If his sister was feeling as bad as he did, she would be either sulking or crying.

He filed into the dining room, looking round all the tables with blue and white Formica tops, where condiments were set waiting; several children were sitting on light-coloured wooden chairs, with seats that matched the table tops, but June wasn't one of the first to arrive. At least here the routine was the same. Everyone helped themselves from the food set out on a long table and then took it to sit with friends. Archie selected a slice of bread and butter and a spoonful of strawberry jam. He looked for scones or slices of cake, but instead there were individual jam tarts or small dishes of cold rice pudding and tinned apricots. That was another bad mark against this place, Archie thought. He didn't think the supper looked as good as it did at St Saviour's; the food there was more like his mum cooked.

'Sit with us,' Keith invited so Archie did as he suggested. He ate his bread and jam but hadn't bothered with the rice pudding or the jam tarts. His cocoa was all right though and he drank it with relish, constantly looking for June to enter the room. She didn't come and, after a while, Archie left his place and went to speak to one of the St Saviour's girls who had come down in the car with his sister.

'Have you seen June, Lucy?' he asked. 'Is she upstairs sulking?'

'June didn't come with us,' the girl said. 'Sister Beatrice brought a woman to her and she took her off in a car. I watched out of the window and June didn't want to go . . .'

'What do you mean, this woman took her off?' Archie felt chilled. 'Sister Beatrice told me June was coming in the car with you.'

'We thought so too but then the woman came and took her away . . .'

The girl next to Lucy swallowed a mouthful of bread and jam and said, 'I know who the woman was – she's Miss Sampson from the council. She took a kid down our lane away once and her mother tried to stop her but the police restrained her. She was cryin' and the kid was screamin', but they still took her . . .'

Archie felt the rage building inside. He could hardly believe what he was hearing was true, because Sister Beatrice had promised him June was coming by car and would join him at Halfpenny House. If he'd known what they were planning, he would never have come here!

That was it, of course. They'd deliberately deceived him, lied to him so that he would do as he was told without making a fuss. If he'd guessed what they meant to do he would've taken June and run away. Archie wasn't sure how they would've lived, but perhaps Ted Hastings might have helped; Archie could've left school and worked on the market, even though he wasn't old enough to leave school . . . but now his sister had been stolen from him. There was no other word for it! His rage was near to boiling point. He was going to ask that man who'd driven them here how to get to the station, because he needed to get back to London immediately. He had to force Sister Beatrice to tell him where June was and then he would just go there and fetch her back again.

He saw Mr Smith leaving the dining room and went after him. Catching up with him on the stairs, he grabbed his arm, causing him to turn round and frown at him.

'You're one of the new boys, aren't you? You must learn some discipline, lad. You do not attack the carers just to attract attention.'

'I've got to get back to London right now,' Archie said. 'My sister has been kidnapped and I have to get her back or Mum will kill me.'

'Calm down, lad,' Gerald said, seeming unperturbed. 'I think it very unlikely that your sister has been kidnapped – first of all, who are you?'

'Archie Miller. My sister June was supposed to come down with the girls. Sister Beatrice lied to me and now that woman from the council has got June and I have to go after her.'

'Ah, I get you now,' Gerald said and shook his head sorrowfully. 'Been getting into a bit of trouble, had she? Yes, well, I know it's upsetting for you, Archie, but no doubt they will let her write to you in time and she'll be much better off with a new family . . .'

'No, she won't. You don't know my sister. Please, Mr Smith, can you take me to the station and buy me a ticket back home? I'll pay you back as soon as I can. I promise.'

'No, certainly not. St Saviour's cannot keep you

indefinitely, lad. It is only intended as a receiving centre these days. You have to make a new life here – and besides, your sister will be a ward of court and you wouldn't be allowed to take her from the family that has fostered her.'

'You don't understand. June will be cryin' and screamin' and I promised her I would look after her. I have to go back and find her, I have to!' Archie was desperate. Why wouldn't this man listen to him? It seemed as if the whole world had turned against him and his family, and he was burning with the injustice of it all.

'I know it seems desperate now,' Gerald said in a manner that was meant to be calming, but Archie found infuriating. Didn't he understand that June wouldn't be able to bear this further upset? If Mum discovered what had happened she would blame him for not taking better care of his sister!

'Please help me, sir. I'll earn the money and send it back to you as soon as I can . . .' Archie swallowed his pride as he begged, the tears choking him as he fought for understanding.

'I would give you the money for your fare and welcome,' Gerald said, 'but it isn't possible. Now be a sensible lad and accept what has happened. Your sister is much better off with a family and I'm sure she will be fine as soon as she comes to her—'

'Stupid old fool!' Archie said as the frustration boiled over and he kicked at his ankles. 'You haven't understood a word that I'm saying. I've got to get June back or Mum will never forgive me . . .'

'Kicking people's ankles isn't going to help you,' Gerald said and took hold of Archie's arm firmly, his

111

grip painful as he propelled him along. 'I can see you need a lesson, my boy. I was a headmaster for twenty years and I don't believe in allowing boys to run wild. I believe in discipline for troublesome boys and once you understand that we shall get along very well . . .'

He began to propel Archie towards the back of the building. 'Where are you taking me?' Archie demanded, trying to pull away but unable to break his hold. 'Let go! I have to go back to St Saviour's and find June . . .'

'You'll feel differently in a while,' Gerald said, opening a door and thrusting Archie inside. 'You can cool your heels for an hour or two and then we'll see if you've learned your lesson . . . if not we'll see if you like a taste of the cane . . .'

Archie blinked in the sudden darkness. There was no light in here at all and he realised it was some sort of cupboard. He pushed at the door but there was no handle and it wouldn't give. He was locked in this dark hole as a punishment and for a moment he panicked, screaming and kicking against the door. No one answered and he realised that Gerald Smith had just gone off and left him here.

When the screaming fit wore off, Archie sat down on a box and tried to make out shapes in the darkness. He thought it was a store cupboard and big enough so that he could move about, but it was stuffy and he felt hot and for a few moments he was frightened. Supposing that rotten devil just left him here? Supposing no one found him until he'd died of thirst and starvation?

Common sense reasserted itself. Mr Smith just wanted to scare him. He wasn't the sort that would actually try to kill a child. No, he would come back and expect to find Archie remorseful and apologetic. His anger was cooling, but it wasn't going away; instead it had formed into an icy knot in his chest. He would apologise and pretend to accept what he was told, but he was going to leave this hateful place and he would find June. He didn't care how long it took him, he would find her, Archie vowed – and he'd get even with that Sister Beatrice for lying to him. He'd thought she was all right, but she was an evil woman and she'd conspired with that Miss Sampson to steal June from her family . . .

CHAPTER 8

'I'm going along to help the driver and make sure the kids are kept in order,' Billy told Mary Ellen that Friday evening. 'It's what I always promised we'd do, though I'd hoped to have a little car of my own before this . . .'

'Come with you and a party of St Saviour's kids to Southend?' Mary Ellen's eyes sparkled with excitement. 'I'd really love that, Billy. It's just like the trips we went on years ago, before Angela left and they changed things . . .'

'Some of the kids are from the preparatory school. There will be three teachers, Nancy and Tilly, as well as us so it should be a lot of fun. I managed to get the last seat for you. You will come, won't you?'

'Try keeping me away,' she said and laughed up at him. 'I think I deserve a treat after all the hard work we're doing, at the workshop and at night school. I thought I was good at English, Billy, but you should see the list of books Mr Harvey has said I need to read if I'm going to have a hope of passing my exams.'

'Textbooks are expensive. How will you find the money?'

'Mr Harvey said most of them are available through the library and he has some I can borrow. Getting hold of them isn't the problem; I'm not sure when I'll ever have the time to read them . . .'

'You will if you really want to,' Billy said, hiding his doubts. He was sure Mary Ellen was up to the task, but he didn't much like the idea of her being stuck at home reading every night, because that meant he wouldn't see her so often. 'It's what you want, Ellie love, so don't give up at the first hurdle.'

'I wish there was somewhere we could be together,' she said wistfully. 'If we had our own place I could sit and study until supper and then we'd share our bedtime cocoa and a biscuit . . .'

Billy placed a comforting arm about her shoulders. 'We will one day, I promise. This studying to be a teacher is going to take years. Before then I'll have earned enough money to pay for a flat or maybe a small house where we can be together.'

'Rose still wouldn't let us get married and it's ages until I'm twenty-one . . .' Mary Ellen frowned. 'She's been in an odd mood lately. I don't know what's wrong with her. One minute she's rushing around, singing and in a hurry to go off and meet someone, and the next she's miserable, walking around as if she had all the troubles of the world on her shoulders.'

'She's got man trouble,' Billy said. 'Why don't you ask her what the matter is?'

'I wouldn't dare. She bites my head off every time I speak these days.'

'Don't let her upset you. She can't prevent us getting together in the end.'

'I know . . .' Mary Ellen's smile was back in an instant. 'I'm really looking forward to the trip to Southend, Billy. I'm so glad you got me a ticket on the coach.'

'It's going to be lovely,' Billy promised and drew her into his arms for a kiss.

Billy had been right, Mary Ellen thought on the bus travelling home at the end of a day filled with sunshine and fun. She'd enjoyed herself from the moment she helped shepherd the excited children on to the coach, sharing out white cardboard boxes of packed lunches. Everyone had the same, including Billy, the driver and Mary Ellen. Inside were a sausage roll, cheese-and-tomato sandwiches, a jam tart, a few grapes and a two-finger chocolate biscuit, also a small bottle of lemonade each for the children and flasks of tea for the adults.

Mary Ellen thought she would have preferred the lemonade, because tea out of a flask always had an odd taste, but Billy had brought some orange squash in a bottle and she had a drink of that before the rest of it disappeared down the throats of thirsty kids.

On arrival at Southend the driver had taken them to the seafront before going off to park the coach. Despite the packed lunch everyone was hungry and they all lined up to eat fish and chips from newspaper as they trooped down to the sands. Once the kids were settled on blankets and towels, and the adults had found striped canvas deckchairs to sit in, Billy had flopped down on the sand beside Mary Ellen and grinned at her.

'This is all right, isn't it?'

'Lovely,' she had agreed, squinting into the sun. 'You should put some calamine lotion on your skin, Billy.

With your hair you'll have the sort that burns and get sore if you're not careful.'

Billy took the lotion and smeared it on his arms, neck, forehead and nose. Mary Ellen laughed because it looked as if he'd painted whitish stripes on his face. He grabbed at her and dabbed it on her nose and tried to smear it all over her face, but she got up and ran towards the sea laughing and shrieking, Billy following after.

Most of the kids were already paddling at the sea edge and Billy pulled off his socks and shoes, joining them and splashing the nearest. That resulted in a fierce battle that ended with Billy getting the worst of it and his clothes becoming soaked. Mary Ellen watched for a bit, paddling just at the edge but staying clear of the kids and her boyfriend, who was acting like a kid again himself.

She went back to the chairs, dried her feet and sat down to relax in the sun, enjoying the feeling of having nothing to do for once. The workshops had been at it flat out for weeks, and trying to fit in her studies at the same time was tiring. This had been a wonderful idea of Billy's.

Billy returned after a while and took off his soaking wet shirt and trousers, revealing his swimming trunks underneath. Mary Ellen made him turn round so that she could spread calamine over his back.

'Your clothes will be stiff with salt when you put them on,' she said but he just laughed and lay back in his chair enjoying the warm sunshine.

Later on that afternoon, they'd taken the children for a tea of tomatoes on toast or toasted teacakes, soft drinks and a pot of tea for the adults. Nancy had sat next to Mary Ellen and they'd talked like old friends, which they were because they'd met when Nancy first arrived at St Saviour's as an orphan herself.

'You and Billy get on well, don't you?' Nancy had asked.

'We always have, even before we went to St Saviour's. I was miserable at first there and so was Billy underneath, but he told me we'd stick together and we always have.'

'Will you marry him?'

'Rose is against it, but yes, we'll marry one day. I'm trying to pass the exams I should've taken at school, but it is hard work with a job to do and other things . . .' Mary Ellen sighed. 'I'll just have to keep at it until I get there . . .'

'I wish I felt as confident as you,' Nancy had told her. 'I don't think I'll ever have a boyfriend or get married . . .'

''Course you will, if you want,' Mary Ellen had said. 'You just haven't met the right person yet.'

Nancy had shaken her head and turned her attention to her tomatoes on toast. She'd looked so sad that Mary Ellen wondered what was wrong. What was the secret grief that made her so sure she would never find anyone to love? Mary Ellen remembered that Nancy's brother had been in lots of trouble when they first came to St Saviour's; he was mentally ill and Nancy visited him regularly, so perhaps that was why she didn't want to get involved with anyone – though just because her brother wasn't as he should be, it didn't mean any children she had would be the same.

They were later leaving Southend than had been planned, because the children wanted to go on the pier to buy presents and to try out some of the penny slot machines. The driver didn't seem to mind, nor did he object when they had to stop on the way home so the kids could go to the toilets. It had been such a lovely day and everyone had enjoyed themselves so it didn't matter that they were late getting the children back to their homes.

'I'll see you on Wednesday,' Billy said as he left her at the door of the flat she shared with her sister after all the kids had been delivered. 'I enjoyed myself today.'

'It was lovely, really lovely,' Mary Ellen said and kissed him softly on the lips. 'You're a special man, Billy Baggins. I love you very much . . .'

'And you're a special woman,' he responded, hugging her to him just as the door opened and Rose stood there in her dressing gown, her hair in soft curls held by grips under a pink hairnet and a sour look on her face.

'Where the hell do you think you've been until this hour?' she demanded of Mary Ellen. 'It's nearly eleven o'clock – don't tell me you've been at the sea until this hour!'

'We were late leaving Southend and the traffic was heavy for a while,' Mary Ellen said, feeling sick inside as she saw the anger in her sister's face. Why couldn't Rose be pleasant for once?

'Get in then,' Rose muttered and glared at Billy. 'Haven't you got to be back at St Saviour's by a certain hour?'

'Sister Beatrice lets me have a key to the side door,' he said and grinned at her. 'Thanks for your concern, Rose. It's nice to know you care about what happens to me . . .'

Rose pushed Mary Ellen inside and slammed the door on him.

'Why did you do that?' Mary Ellen demanded. 'Billy has been brilliant with the kids all day. He's a caring man – and we haven't been doing anything wrong so you can just put that right out of your mind. Me and Billy are going to wait until we're married. Billy knows I want to teach and he's helping me.'

'I wouldn't trust that Billy Baggins as far as I could throw him,' Rose snapped. 'His family were all wastrels and he'll be no better, you mark my words. I'm telling you now that I won't put up with this, Mary Ellen. I don't want you to see him again . . . and don't look at me like that. He's no good to you. If you don't care about your life, I do. It would be much better if you broke with him altogether. I don't want to see you stuck in a slum with half a dozen kids tugging at your skirts . . .'

'It wouldn't be like that!'

'You've got more faith in him than I have . . .'

'You've always been unfair to him,' Mary Ellen protested in dismay. 'I don't know what's happening to you, Rose. Sometimes, I think you don't deserve that I should care . . .'

'I haven't noticed you caring about my feelings much . . .'

"Course I do, but I love Billy. I'm going to marry him one day.'

'Not if I can prevent it . . .'

'That's so unfair – and you won't be able to prevent it forever. I'm eighteen later this year and then there's only three years until we can marry without your permission.'

Rose looked angry, but shook her head, changing the subject abruptly. 'Your friend Marion came round today. She wanted to know if I would let her have the spare room and I told her yes. She stopped and helped me change the beds and make up the parcel for the laundry. I suppose I can rely on you to take it in tomorrow before you go to work?'

'Certainly, I will,' Mary Ellen said and sighed. 'Don't begrudge me my lovely day, Rose. I help you as much as I can, you know I do . . .'

'Yes . . .' Rose bit her lip. 'Yes, I know you do. I'm sorry. I'm in a bad mood, but it isn't your fault. Go to bed. I have to be up early. I'm on first shift . . . but I meant what I said. If you can't get home at a proper time, I shall stop you seeing him altogether.'

Mary Ellen stared at her in resentment and then went through to her own room, feeling close to tears. Her sister couldn't really mean that she would stop her seeing Billy. She wouldn't, no matter what Rose said! She'd brought a box of fudge for Rose but she would give it to her tomorrow. Something was eating at her sister, but she wouldn't tell Mary Ellen even if she asked. Perhaps Billy was right and she was having trouble with a man, but Mary Ellen had never heard her mention anyone . . . except that doctor at work . . .

Rose crawled into bed feeling downright miserable. She'd fallen out with Mary Ellen over a silly incident and the problem was nothing to do with her sister or that Baggins boy. Rose didn't like him and she didn't want Mary Ellen to marry him, but he wasn't what was causing her to feel as if her life wasn't worth tuppence. No, that was entirely her own fault, because she'd known the first time she'd let Mike Bonner take her out that she was a fool.

She'd guessed the registrar liked to play the field long before he even noticed her. She'd seen the way Nurse Simmons had draped herself all over him at his party, and she'd vowed she wouldn't be as big a fool, especially when she'd discovered the nurse in the linen room crying her eyes out a few weeks later. Her inquiries had met with stony silence, but when Nurse Simmons left two days later the rumours had soon been flying round the hospital. She was having a baby and she'd refused to tell Matron who the father was – and no, he wasn't going to marry her.

Rose had heard the whispers. They were saying Mike Bonner was the father of Nurse Simmons' child, but he hadn't been dismissed and he showed no sign of guilt when he asked Rose out for a drink alone. She'd refused twice but in the end she couldn't resist. She'd asked him straight out if the stories were true that evening and he'd denied it, putting his hand on his heart and smiling at her.

'I doubt if Nurse Simmons knows for certain who the father is,' he'd said and rolled his eyes heavenward. 'She really wasn't my type. I prefer women with a little more pride in themselves . . . someone like you, Rose.'

Rose had tried not to be flattered; she'd tried to keep her head, because for years she'd hardly bothered about men at all, but perhaps that was why she'd fallen so hard. Now she was head over heels with Mike and on Saturday night they'd kissed in the back of his car. He'd demanded much more but she'd pushed him away, even though she was tempted to give him what he wanted.

122

'I really enjoyed myself this evening,' she said. 'I do love you, Mike, and of course I want you, but I'm not that kind of girl. I'm saving myself for marriage . . .'

And that of course was her mistake. As soon as she'd said the words Rose knew that she'd spoken out of turn. Mike wasn't looking for a long-term commitment and now he would back off and she would lose him . . . and the knowledge of her folly had left an aching hollow inside her that she couldn't cope with . . . except that she had to, because she'd known as he drove away that he wouldn't ask her out again.

As her eyes closed, she felt the sense of loneliness sweep over her. She was devoted to her nursing, but there was a part of her that longed to be loved . . . a yearning for the children she knew she might never have.

CHAPTER 9

Archie was biding his time. Mr Smith hadn't left him in the cupboard for long, no more than an hour at most. He'd given him a stern look and a lecture about the behaviour proper to a lad of his age and then told him he would be a fool if he allowed his distress at what had happened to his sister to ruin his life here. Archie had nodded, not saying a word. He didn't want to be locked in that stuffy cupboard again, and he had to be careful if he was going to escape and return to London.

He needed money, but the few coins he had left from his earnings on the market would hardly pay for his fare to London or his food when he got there. Archie didn't mind sleeping rough for a while but he would need food and money if he was going to find June and steal her away from her foster parents. Maybe he could earn some money for the future. Ted Hastings might even let him work for him on the market, unless he'd finished with him because he hadn't turned up on Saturday. Surely, he'd understand when Archie told him why; it wasn't his fault. He'd never wanted to come here, but he would've made the most of it if they'd kept their word and let June come with him.

Sister Beatrice was the one that had lied to him. She was rotten, because it was cowardly to lie just to get him to go without a struggle. Archie burned with hatred for all the people that had harmed him and June – lying about his mum, getting her put in prison out of spite, and then letting June be taken into care when there was no need. Yes, June had been a bit silly, but away from that girl – that Betty Goodge – Archie could have made sure his sister behaved. Why hadn't Sister Beatrice trusted him to do that?

It was on the following Monday that Archie accidentally learned what he needed to know. The petty cash box was kept in the room that all the staff used to have coffee and relax. He heard one of the carers saying that they needed some more coffee and telling her colleague that there was ten pounds in the petty cash.

It was what Archie needed to take him to London. Perhaps he wouldn't take all of it, just enough to cover his fare – and a bit over. He would leave an IOU so it wouldn't be stealing, and he would pay it back as soon as he earned enough money. Anyway, Sister Beatrice had promised him the money to visit his mother so he was only taking what was rightfully his, so he argued. His mum would be furious, he knew, because she'd brought him up to be honest, but she'd half kill him if June was lost forever . . .

Archie hung around when the other kids had gone out to play after afternoon tea. He was regretful because it was a lovely evening and he wouldn't have minded having a go at tennis or cricket with the others, but he knew he mustn't get settled here. He had to borrow what money he could from the cash box and return to London as soon as possible. Sister Beatrice must tell him where his sister was because she had no right to hide it from him – and those foster parents had no right to take June over without consent from Mum.

It was so easy. The cash box was in the drawer of the side table where the coffee cups stood; it was just left there, unlocked, waiting for someone to take advantage. Archie saw there were several pound notes as well as some silver and coppers. He took three pound notes and several half-crowns and shoved them in his pocket, leaving the IOU in the box, but signing it just with scribbled initials. At least they couldn't say he was a thief, because he'd only borrowed the money – and Sister Beatrice had promised it to him anyway.

Archie knew he couldn't take all his clothes with him, but he would take a couple of shirts and a pullover, because he needed a change of clothes in case he discovered where his sister had been taken. He had to look clean, like Mum told him, or people wouldn't take him seriously.

With the money burning a hole in his pocket, guilt all over his face and wearing an extra shirt and pullover, Archie sneaked out while everyone else was on the playing fields. He knew it wasn't far to the bus stop, which would take him to the railway station; once there he would buy a ticket to the next station for a few bob and then hide in the toilets all the way to London . . .

It was so simple that Archie couldn't believe his luck. He'd managed to avoid the ticket inspector by going in and out of the toilets every time he saw the man coming. Then, when he got off, he saw a party of children just ahead of him; they were with an adult who seemed to be fussing around, trying to keep order without much success. Archie walked quickly to catch up with them and managed to get through as the ticket collector was count-ing tickets and trying to match them to heads. He ran off seconds before the man realised there was one too many and though he heard the shout, he just kept running.

In the comparatively rural setting of Halfpenny House, he'd felt lost and found it difficult to get his bearings, but here in the noisy dirty streets of London he felt safe. Now all he had to do was to talk to Sister Beatrice and demand that she told him where his sister had been taken. He hopped on a bus, sat right at the back at the door and got off a couple of stops later before the conductor had time to ask for his fare.

Gaining in confidence with each success, Archie did the same thing several times and only had to pay tuppence for one stage of his journey. It was dusk by the time the last bus had got to its destination and he thought it must be nearly eleven o'clock in the evening by the time he managed to get within walking distance of St Saviour's. The main entrance would be locked for the night, but Archie knew the secrets of the old house and he scaled the gate into the garden at the back and tried the back door. That too was locked but he knew the pantry window had a loose catch and by wiggling the blade of his penknife up and down he managed to get it open and crawled through the small space. For a moment he thought he might get stuck but after some effort and a painful scratch on his arm, he was through.

Pausing to get his breath and listen for any sudden noises, Archie caught the unmistakable smell of Cook's sausage rolls; they smelled fresh and he knew they must have been cooked that very day. His mouth watered and he risked snapping the light on to find them, cramming one into his mouth in three bites and stuffing two more in his pockets. He'd missed tea and he was hungry; besides, the food wasn't as good at Halfpenny House as it was here, and discovering a plate of small rock cakes, he took one of those too.

That digested, he went into the kitchen and filled a glass with water and drank it. No one was around, but he knew there would be staff here somewhere: Kelly and one of the nurses – and Sister Beatrice too perhaps, if he was lucky. Archie knew that she was here quite a lot during the night, but if she'd gone home, he'd find somewhere to rest for a few hours until she came back on duty.

There was no point in putting it off. Archie knew Sister would either be in her office or in one of the sick wards. He found his way to the stairs without switching a light on and walked quietly up them, trying not to make a noise and bring someone out to investigate. As he approached the sick ward the door opened, the hall light was switched on and Archie shrank back against the wall as he saw Nurse Wendy walk towards Sister's office. She didn't look back but knocked at the door and went in. Archie ran quickly to the stairs at the end of the hall and up two of them, sitting there in the dark as he waited for the nurse to leave. He was tempted to eat another sausage roll but decided to keep it because he might need it more another day.

After what seemed ages Sister's door opened again and he heard the steady tread of the nurse walking back down the hall. He waited another few seconds and then went to Sister's door and opened it. She was sitting at her desk sipping a glass of some dark liquid he thought might be sherry and looked up in alarm as he entered.

'Archie! What are you doing here? When I rang Halfpenny House a few hours ago and asked to speak to you they told me you'd run away . . . where have you been all this time?'

'You know why I'm here,' he said accusingly. 'What have you done with my June? You had no right to let them take her. You lied to me. Why did you tell me she was coming in the car? Did you think I'd refuse to go if I knew the truth?'

'Archie, listen to me, please.' Sister Beatrice stood up and walked towards him. 'I didn't intend to lie to you. There was a mix-up in the paperwork and I didn't receive it until after you'd left. I was not informed that your sister was to be fostered until the last moment . . .'

'You're lying again,' Archie said fiercely. 'Don't lie to me! I'm not a child. I'll be old enough to leave school and find a job soon. My sister isn't up for adoption and Mum will want her back when she gets out . . .'

'Yes, I'm sure she will. Unfortunately, the Welfare people have a say in what happens to your sister, Archie. They have the backing of the courts in this and it doesn't always matter what the family wants . . .' She put a hand out towards him. 'I did not agree with the decision made by Miss Sampson and I am challenging the way this affair was conducted. I intend to discover just why they considered it necessary to take June away from us – but at the moment I know no more than you . . .'

'They've got no right to take her!' Archie shouted, too upset to listen to the calm voice. 'How do I know I can trust you? You lied to me and you lied to June . . . and you sent me to that horrid place where they shut you in a cupboard if you ask for help to find your sister . . .'

'What are you talking about?' Sister Beatrice shook her head. 'Don't be silly, Archie. I know the people at Halfpenny House and they would never do such a thing . . .'

'I ain't lyin'! You wouldn't care what he did – and you tell lies anyway . . .'

'Believe me, I am not in the habit of lying. Had I known of Miss Sampson's intentions I should've tried to prevent it, but I was not told officially – that in itself may be sufficient cause to have this order overturned but I cannot promise anything . . .'

Archie was confused, too upset and angry to take in what she was saying. What order? What did she mean by the backing of the courts? Were they the same courts that had convicted his mum of stealing just on the word of someone who had it in for her? Archie saw a red mist before his eyes and he lost his temper, running at her and hitting at her as she raised her arms to defend herself.

'This is foolish,' Sister said. 'Calm down, Archie, and let me get you some food. You can sleep here tonight in one of the spare beds in the isolation ward and then I'll talk to you in the morning . . .'

'No! I hate you. I hate all of you,' Archie shouted, no longer in control of himself or his thoughts. 'I'm not going to let you send me back to that other place. I'm staying here until I find out where June is and then I'm going to get her back . . .'

'Archie please, listen to me. I want to help you and June . . .'

He was too far gone in the whirlpool of his emotions to listen as he turned round, fled down the stairs and through the house; he paused to unlock the back door and went out into the garden, scaling the gate and falling to the uneven ground the other side. He'd grazed his knees on sharp stones through the cloth of his trousers and the scratch on his arm was sore, but Archie was aware only of anger as he started to run.

He had to get away from this place before Sister called the police and had Archie arrested. They would put him in prison for taking that money and the food and he would never find his sister or see his mother again . . . but he knew the East End streets like the back of his hand and he could find places to stay.

They were all against him but somehow he would discover where June had been taken and he would go there and get her away from the people who had no right to have her. June was his sister and she belonged with him and Mum and he was going to get her back, and then he would look after her until Mum got out of prison.

Beatrice was tired. She'd been having a quiet drink before retiring when Archie had burst in on her and after that she hadn't been able to think of going to bed. Instead, she'd sat in a chair all night and pondered the problem. Archie blamed her for what had happened, just as she'd known he would; he believed she'd lied to him and refused to trust her, even though she was as angry about the way June's fostering had been handled as he was himself.

Perhaps she ought to telephone the police and let them know Archie had run away from his home, but she felt disinclined to do that, because in his eyes it would be another instance of her betrayal. No, she must give him time, time to come to terms with what she'd told him. Perhaps if he understood that she was telling the truth and came to her they could talk sensibly. After all, he was in his opinion nearly an adult, old enough to start work if it weren't for a stupid law that said he had to be fifteen and he should be able to understand the way the courts worked. All Beatrice could do was to demand to know where June was now and try to get the decision of the courts reversed.

It might help if she visited Archie's mother in prison. Beatrice shrank from entering such a terrible place, but when she gave the matter sufficient thought she realised it was her duty to make the visit. Indeed, she ought to have done so before this. If Sandra Miller was innocent, as her son insisted, there had been a terrible miscarriage of justice and something must be done about it.

Glancing at the clock, Beatrice saw that it was nearly six in the morning. She got wearily to her feet, deciding that she must go to her room, wash and change into clean clothes and make herself a cup of tea while she decided whom to consult.

It was as she was halfway across the garden that the idea came to her. She would enlist Angela's father's help. Mr Hendry had retired from his profession some years back, but he was a solicitor and, from what she'd heard from Angela, a good one. If he felt able, he might handle the case himself, and if not he would know of someone who could help her.

She would telephone Angela after breakfast and ask her for his telephone number. And she would also ask if it was possible that someone at Halfpenny House was in the habit of locking boys in a cupboard to punish them, because Archie had never been the sort of boy that lied. The decision made her feel very much better. She'd been anxious and undecided for days, but now she knew exactly what she was doing . . .

'Mr Hendry, it's Sister Beatrice of St Saviour's,' she said into the telephone later that morning. 'I do hope you don't mind my telephoning you?'

'Angela gave me a quick ring and told me you have a problem,' Edward Hendry said with a smile in his voice. 'I should be very happy to help in whatever way I can . . .'

'It's two problems really,' Beatrice said and went on to explain about the high-handed manner in which both she and the Miller children had been treated. 'I want to discover just where she is and to have the order overturned, if I can – and I should also like someone to make inquiries about Mrs Miller's case. If she was falsely accused something should be done . . .'

'I couldn't agree more,' Edward Hendry said. 'I will undertake to look into the matter of the girl myself, Sister Beatrice. However, you need a specialist to poke about and discover what he can in Mrs Miller's case. I know of someone who owes me a favour or two. I'll ask him to call on you in the next day or so. He's in the police force and his name is Jonathan Carter – and he is based in London so it will be easier for him to make inquiries. And I'll contact a solicitor friend as well and ask him to discover what the legal position is, both for the mother and the daughter.'

'Would his services cost a great deal?' Beatrice asked hesitantly.

'Consider any fees a gift from me,' Edward Hendry said. 'As I said, I'm owed a few favours and I'm calling them in now . . .' He chuckled. 'I was feeling my age, but this has given me an interest. I'll be in touch as soon as I've started the ball rolling, Sister.'

Replacing her receiver, Beatrice smiled. It was good to have friends at times like these. She wished that either Nan or Angela had been here to help settle her mind, because she was uneasy about Archie. Was she doing the right thing in letting him run free – or should she call the police and risk losing his trust forever?

Sighing, she got to her feet. It was time for her to begin her rounds. She could not make such a huge decision feeling as tired as she did; there was no doubting that time was catching up with her. Like Angela's father, she was feeling her age, though he, poor man, had had a couple of small heart attacks. Fortunately, he'd recovered and was planning to marry the woman he'd loved in secret for years. Like so many before him, he'd suffered an unhappy marriage for the sake of his daughter, keeping his unhappiness to himself.

She was pleased she'd asked him for help. For too many years she'd refused help from anyone, standing firmly on her own two feet, but the years had mellowed her.

She knew nostalgia for the past, when she'd been a

girl, before life had disillusioned her, before it all happened; the loss of her lover to the first big war, her unhappy marriage and then the tragic death of her son. It had taken her years to come to terms with the despair that had caused her to enter the convent . . . Sighing, she thrust the foolish thoughts from her mind. Beatrice had lived fully, devoting her time and her energy to helping others, and if God approved she would go on doing that for a few years yet . . .

Angela waited until Mark had settled down with a glass of wine before telling him what was on her mind. After Sister Beatrice's phone call she'd paid a visit to Halfpenny House and had a long chat with Mrs Mellors, the Superintendent, and what she'd discovered had bothered her.

'What do you know about Gerald Smith's background?' she asked, curling up in the deep armchair opposite him. This was what they called the Den and they used it because it was comfortable for quiet evenings when they were alone and looked out on to their pleasant but rather large garden at the back.

'I know that look,' Mark said, frowning over his glass. 'When we interviewed him his references were excellent . . . more than thirty years as a school teacher and twenty as the headmaster of a private school for boys.'

'Yes, but what do you know of the man himself? His methods of discipline for instance?'

'Ah, now we're coming to it,' Mark smiled at his wife, both love and laughter in his eyes. 'What has happened?'

'You know that Archie Miller ran away a few days after he was brought here?' Mark nodded. 'Well, Sister

Beatrice seems to think Mr Smith may have locked him in a cupboard . . .'

Mark frowned. 'Was he being violent? We brought Gerald in because we felt the older boys needed a man to discipline them, but I'm not sure I approve of that sort of thing. It can have severe mental consequences in some cases. How long was he there and why?'

'Sister Beatrice wasn't able to discover. Archie paid her a fleeting visit but, according to him, he was asking Mr Smith for help and got locked in a cupboard – that's all she knew.'

'He may have been lying . . .'

'Yes, but Sister says he's a very honest boy and he was angry. I'm wondering, Mark. Mrs Mellors told me she doesn't like Gerald – and although the boys have quietened down a bit, she said one of them had a cut hand a few weeks back. One of the carers took him to the doctor and they were told he'd cut himself on broken glass, but he wouldn't tell them how he did it – and there have been a couple of other incidents . . . nothing she could put her finger on but she thinks Mr Smith doesn't fit in at Halfpenny House.'

'Right.' Mark finished his drink. 'I'm glad you told me, Angela. We did need a man to keep some kind of discipline, but I'd hoped a headmaster would not need to resort to either violence or petty vengeance, which is how I would describe shutting a lad in the cupboard. Leave it with me. I'll talk to Mrs Mellors myself and make a few inquiries.' He got up and refilled their glasses. 'Now tell me what kind of a day you've had – and what the terrible twins have been up to . . .'

136

CHAPTER 10

'I'm so mad at her,' Mary Ellen said to Billy as they sat drinking coffee at their favourite table, the noise and chatter of the Rock 'n' Roll club flowing round them. 'She's been like a bear with a sore head for weeks, snapping at me every time I open my mouth and threatening to stop me meeting you. She even had the cheek to tell Marion to keep an eye on me tonight – as if I needed that . . .'

'Rose is Rose,' Billy said smiling gently as he tried to soothe her. 'Don't let her upset you, love. She knows she can't stop you meeting me. You would just ignore her; besides, we only get to see each other twice a week these days.'

'I know,' she sighed. 'I'm sorry, Billy. It's rotten for you when I'm studying, but I've got a big exam coming up in the autumn. If I pass that I can apply for teacher training college . . .'

'How do you feel about the work you're doing?' Billy asked. 'I mean the stuff you have to read and that . . . is it harder than you thought?'

'Not really, now I've got used to it and sorted the

proper reading list. I never knew there were so many books out there, Billy. They don't teach us half of it in school . . .'

'That's because they do those books in the last year and we neither of us stayed on.' Billy looked sad. 'I suppose it was never meant for me – but you deserved your chance, Mary Ellen.'

'Well, I've got it now, if you can put up with me working most nights?'

'I'll have to, won't I?' he replied as Marion sashayed up to them. 'Hi, how yer doin'?' he greeted her.

'I'm OK,' she said and took a packet of Sobranje cigarettes out of her pocket, offering them to him and then Mary Ellen.

'What are these then?' Billy asked, raising his brows at the bright colours in the smart black box.

'Cocktail cigarettes,' Marion said. 'They were a present from someone – a man I met at a coffee bar the other night. He said I was a special girl and deserved something special and then he bought me these cigarettes tonight.'

'Watch him,' Mary Ellen said. 'He sounds a bit dodgy, Marion. You be careful of strangers . . .'

'We can't all be as lucky as you are,' Marion said and pouted as they both refused her offering. 'Don't know what you're missing. See you later, I've got to see my friend . . .'

They watched her walk off and join a man dressed in a blue Teddy boy jacket and black drainpipes, with a pale-blue shirt and a shoestring tie, and dark-blue suede shoes. The strains of 'Unchained Melody' sung by Al Hibbler were coming from the record player and Mary Ellen watched the dancers drifting by in each other's arms.

'She wants to be careful of him,' Billy said and looked concerned. 'That's Stevie Baker. I knew him at school. He's a show-off and he's into all sorts. I wouldn't trust him as far as I could throw him – though he did put me on to my job at the nightclub . . .'

'You didn't tell me about a job at the nightclub. You haven't given up your apprenticeship?'

'Not me,' Billy said. 'It's just a few hours at night. I throw people out if they get rowdy. They pay me more than I get working days and they want me to go full time, but I've told them I can't do every night and I shan't leave my proper job.'

'No, you mustn't,' Mary Ellen urged. 'I'm not sure I like you doing that sort of work, Billy. You might get hurt . . .'

'Nah, I'm all right,' he said, grinning. 'I'm just doing my job. Mostly they go quietly when I ask and if they don't I simply pick them up and carry them out gently.'

Mary Ellen shook her head. She didn't believe it was that easy, but she couldn't blame Billy for wanting to earn more money. With her latest rise he got less than she did, but she hadn't told him that because she knew it would make him feel small. Billy wanted to be the provider, the one who looked after her and gave her nice presents. She knew how hard he had to save every time he bought her something, but she just thanked him and kissed him; Billy had his pride and Mary Ellen would never make him feel any less satisfied with life than he did already. One day he would earn more and then perhaps they could marry, but in the meantime they had to put up with only seeing each other twice a week.

'Rose wouldn't approve of you being a bouncer,' she

said. 'I shan't tell her – and don't let on to Marion, because she might let it out. Billy, I don't much like it either . . .'

'I need the money,' he said and she noticed he looked a bit impatient. 'Besides, I want something to do – you're working all the time and I want to get on, make something better of my life.'

Mary Ellen didn't answer. It was the first time Billy had got annoyed with her and she knew it wasn't much fun when she was working. It was only to be expected even though he'd encouraged her to start the course – but there had been something in the way Marion looked at him that made her a little uneasy. Billy had just been himself, but Mary Ellen couldn't help feeling a pang of jealousy when he'd seemed concerned for her over Stevie.

Marion had been their friend for years and he didn't understand that things had changed. Marion was jealous of their special relationship and, if she guessed that Rose would stop them meeting if she knew of Billy's job, she would let it slip somehow . . .

Billy didn't go straight back to St Saviour's after seeing Mary Ellen home. He'd offered to make sure that Marion got back safely too, but she said Stevie was taking her. They didn't see anything of the other pair as they walked home, but Billy knew that Stevie sometimes drove a car belonging to one of the nightclub owners.

He was feeling a bit gloomy, because Mary Ellen had made it clear she didn't like him working at the nightclub, but she didn't understand that he felt trapped in his job. He wouldn't get a rise until he'd reached a certain stage in his training and he was fed up living at St Saviour's and never having the money to get a decent place of his own. It was all right for her, she had a bright future when she passed all the stuff she needed, whereas he'd still be doing a job he didn't much like . . . and he didn't intend to give up this nightclub work even for Mary Ellen.

He'd arranged to go in from half past ten to four in the morning, which was when the last punters were politely – or not so politely – asked to leave. Sister Beatrice knew where he was working. She'd put him through a stiff interrogation before she agreed to him staying out late, but in the end she'd agreed that the extra money would come in useful.

'You will give me your word that you will not get mixed up with anything illegal or underhand, Billy?'

'Yes, Sister, I promise I shan't let you down. It's a way to earn some money for my own home – and the future, that's all . . .'

'Very well, I shall trust you, young man. You haven't let me down yet.'

Billy promised he wouldn't and she'd given her permission. In the old days Sister Beatrice would simply have refused to listen; he would have been forbidden to work at the nightclub and told that if he disobeyed he must find himself another room. However, the last seven years or so had mellowed her, and they had a sort of understanding. He liked the nun far more than he would ever admit to anyone but Mary Ellen, and did what he could at St Saviour's to repay her kindness.

Billy checked in at the club, was told it was a quiet night and was asked to stand at the door to prevent any drunks trying to force their way in after the public

141

houses had finally shut their doors. A couple of men he'd never seen before tried to bluff their way in, but they weren't members and Billy stood his ground, refusing them entrance, even though they offered him five pounds as a bribe. It was a lot of money, but if he took it that would be the end of his job.

At a quarter past four the last customer left. He was an older man that Billy had seen at the club several times. He saluted as the man paused to take his bearings.

'Goodnight, sir.'

'Goodnight, Billy. Nearly finished, have you?'

'Yes, sir; Mr Marshall will be locking up at any minute now . . .'

Billy watched as the other man walked off down the street rather unsteadily. It was still dark and some of the lights had gone out, which made the streets a little eerie somehow, as if monsters lurked in the shadows.

'Right, off you go then, Billy. We'll see you tomorrow?'

'Yes, Mr Marshall. I'll be here at the same time. Do you think Mr Connolly was all right this evening?'

'Probably had one too many whiskies,' his boss said. 'He'll be all right.'

Billy nodded and wished him goodnight and set off in the same direction as Mr Connolly had taken earlier. He was thoughtful, his mind dwelling on how soon the extra money he was saving would amount to enough to pay for a decent place for him and Mary Ellen to live in, when he heard the shouts and a cry for help.

Dashing forward, Billy saw the fight going on. One man was being attacked by three rough types and he was getting a beating. Without hesitation, Billy charged in and started throwing punches. He knocked the first ruffian down and had the second one on his knees before they knew what had happened. He was just about to go for the third when they heard the police whistle and the thugs turned tail and ran, leaving the man Billy had knocked out lying on the ground.

'Are you all right, sir?' Billy turned to the man who'd been attacked. 'Mr Connolly, sir. I didn't know it was you—'

Before he could say more three policemen arrived on the scene, truncheons at the ready. One of them grabbed Billy by the arm, apparently believing he'd been one of the rogues who had attacked Mr Connolly. Another bent over the man on the ground, who was just stirring, while the third inquired after the victim.

'Are you hurt, Mr Connolly?' he asked. 'We'll see that these two pay for what they've done. Take him away.'

'It wasn't me,' Billy protested. 'I was trying to help—'

'Leave Billy,' Mr Connolly said as he began to breathe more easily. 'They would've finished me if it hadn't been for his timely arrival – the one on the ground is a thief. I dismissed him for stealing from me and this is what he did to get his own back.'

The police constable reluctantly let go of Billy, still looking at him suspiciously. He would clearly have been in trouble if Mr Connolly hadn't spoken up for him.

'Shall we call for an ambulance?' one of them asked.

'No, I don't think so . . .' Mr Connolly began but then swayed and Billy caught him, propping him up.

'You'd better take him in,' he said. 'I think he's been cut; he's bleeding . . .' He looked at himself and saw that his own hand was bleeding. 'It's all right, Mr Connolly, I'll come with you. You need treatment, and so do I, sir.'

'Yes, all right, thank you,' he said and clung to Billy's arm. 'I don't know what would have happened if you hadn't . . .' He gave a little moan and passed out, Billy supporting him to the ground and then quickly folding his jacket to put under Mr Connolly's head.

He saw the blood seeping through Mr Connolly's jacket halfway up his arm and thought quickly, removing his tie and tying it tightly over the wound to prevent him losing too much blood. Busy with his act of mercy, Billy wasn't aware of what was going on until the ambulance drew up, and then both he and Mr Connolly were taken in and were on their way to the London Hospital in minutes.

Billy knew that he was covered in blood, his shirt soaked and smears over his face and hands, though most of it was Mr Connolly's. Once they got to the hospital the man he'd tried to help was swiftly wheeled away and Billy was taken into a cubicle and patched up. His own wounds were slight, even though one eye felt sore and his hand needed a bandage round it.

'Take a few days off from work,' the nurse told him. 'I'm sure if you explain your boss will understand.'

'Perhaps,' Billy said. 'Sister Beatrice isn't going to be pleased. She's the Warden of St Saviour's and doesn't approve of fighting.'

'If it hadn't been for you a man would almost certainly have died tonight,' the nurse said. 'The police told our men about your quick actions – protecting him and then that bandage to stop the blood. You're a brave man, Mr Baggins.'

'Yeah?' Billy grinned at her as he got ready to leave. 'Can I see him – Mr Connolly?'

'I'm sorry. He will have been in surgery, but I'm sure he will be fine now. You can visit tomorrow if you wish.'

'Thanks,' Billy said and left, trying hard to look as brave and nonchalant as she thought him, even though his eye hurt like hell and so did his hand.

As he left the hospital he saw a nurse walking towards him and groaned. Rose O'Hanran! Why did she have to see him leaving in this condition at this hour? She would be sure to get the wrong idea.

Rose didn't speak but the look she gave him spoke volumes and he knew what she was going to say to Mary Ellen when she got home.

'Billy! How could you?' Sister Beatrice said as she saw him the next morning after he'd been into breakfast. 'What have you been doing with yourself? I knew I shouldn't have permitted you to work at that place – brawling like a prize fighter!'

'It wasn't like that, Sister,' Billy protested. 'Believe me, it happened after I left work . . .'

'That makes it even worse. No, Billy, I don't think I want to know what happened. I cannot condone fighting wherever it took place . . .'

Billy stared after her in exasperation. She'd jumped to conclusions just as Rose had. Goodness knows what Rose would have said to her sister. He'd better go round there and try to explain, even though his head felt as if a thousand drums were beating inside.

Mary Ellen worked every day apart from Saturday and Sunday, so that meant she would be at home. It would've been better if she'd been at work, because then he might have been allowed to see her and explain properly, but he could just imagine what Rose was going to say when she saw him. If anything, he looked worse than he had the previous night when Rose had spotted him leaving the London.

It was Rose who opened the door of her flat. She stood there barring his way and looking furious. 'If you think you're coming in here looking like that, Billy Baggins, you've got another thing coming. I don't hold with fighting . . .'

'It wasn't my fault,' Billy said. 'I don't have to come in, can I just see Mary Ellen and explain to her please?'

'She's gone to the shops,' Rose said. 'I've told her what you are enough times. When she sees you like this she might take notice of me. You'll find her down the market – if she wants to be seen with the likes of you . . .'

Billy backed away from her fury. Rose was getting worse. He'd hoped that she would come round and begin to understand that he was really trying to make something of himself. If she would just let him explain – but she probably wouldn't believe him anyway. He headed down to the market, determined to tell at least one person the truth.

Mary Ellen was shopping with Marion. She gave a little scream when she saw Billy and ran to him instantly.

'I didn't believe Rose when she said she saw you leaving hospital after you'd been fighting, but I can see she was telling the truth. How could you, Billy? I wish you wouldn't go to that horrid place . . .'

'Why does everyone think I got into a fight at the club?' Billy asked, exasperated.

'You must have, unless you had an accident?'

'I stopped a man being beaten up and killed,' Billy

said. 'He'd been drinking at the club and left just before I finished. When I saw those thugs attacking him I had to stop them – didn't I?'

''Course you did,' Marion said and looked at him flirtatiously under her lashes. 'I think you're ever so brave, Billy. You shouldn't nag him, Mary Ellen . . .'

Mary Ellen hesitated and then inclined her head. 'Yes, you did right,' she agreed, 'but if you hadn't been there you wouldn't have been involved . . .'

'In which case Mr Connolly might have died; he probably would have, because they were after more than money . . .'

'What do you mean?'

'I'm not sure why they were intent on killing him,' Billy said, 'but the vicious way they went at him was more than just a robbery – I'm sure of it . . .'

'Oh, Billy . . .' Mary Ellen gave a little sob. 'You did the right thing; it's just that I don't want you to be hurt like this.'

'It isn't likely to happen again,' Billy replied and shrugged. 'Besides, I'm only working extra hours because I want to earn money for us, Mary Ellen. If we had our own home, I could support you while you go to college . . .'

'Perhaps I shouldn't even be thinking of it,' she said doubtfully. 'I'm doing well at work and Sam is really good to me. I think we could manage on what we both earn if I gave up my idea of being a teacher . . .'

'It's your dream,' Billy said and smiled as she reached up to place a tender kiss on his cheek. 'I don't want you to give it up, Ellie love. I want you to be happy, and when we do have children of our own you'll be ready and you won't feel that you missed out . . .'

'I'll see you later,' Marion said, turning away in disgust from the tender scene. 'See you, Billy . . .' She winked at him and walked off, her hips swaying. Billy laughed and shook his head.

Mary Ellen put her arm through his possessively. 'No one else is like you, Billy,' she said. 'You're so good to me and I love you.'

'I love you, too,' Billy said. 'Shall I see you this afternoon? We could go to the early house at the flicks if you like? It's James Dean in *East of Eden*; I've seen it twice already but I want to see it again.'

'Yes, all right,' she smiled, knowing he was a big fan of James Dean. 'Are you working tonight? Surely you'd be better in bed?'

'I shall go in, but if Mr Marshall sends me home I'll go,' he promised. 'Now what about the flicks?'

'We'll go to the matinee,' Mary Ellen said. 'I've got some reading to do but I can do that later.'

'All right. I'll meet you at two outside the Odeon and we'll have a fish and chip tea afterwards.'

'Lovely.' Mary Ellen's smile lit up her face and Billy felt the familiar lurch in his stomach. He'd loved her for so long now and he didn't know what he'd do if he lost her. He'd be an idiot if he didn't know Marion was making a play for him, but why would he look at anyone else when he'd got his own Mary Ellen?

Billy got in at around half past seven that evening. He intended to wash and change and get ready for his stint at the club. Mr Marshall wanted him on at ten that evening so he had plenty of time. Just as he was about to mount the stairs, Sister Beatrice came out into the hall.

'Ah, Billy,' she said. 'I'm glad I caught you. I wanted to talk to you in private. Would you come to my office please?'

Billy's heart sank. Was she going to tell him he either had to give up the job at the nightclub or move? He wasn't ready to move out yet and Mr Marshall paid him decent money for a few hours' work; he wouldn't find another job like that easily.

However, he followed obediently and was asked to sit down. Sister sat behind her desk, removed her glasses and looked at him. 'Well, Billy, it seems I owe you an apology. I had a visit from Sergeant Sallis today. He told me that you're quite a hero. Apparently, you saved a man's life . . .'

'I stopped him getting a worse beating,' Billy said. 'He's all right, the nurse said when I asked this morning, but they're keeping him in for another day or so to make sure . . .'

'Yes, well, I'm glad to hear that. If I misjudged you this morning, I'm sorry, but you must admit you looked terrible.'

'Yeah, I know,' Billy grinned at her. 'I was in trouble with Mary Ellen too until I told her what happened – and her sister thinks I'm like my brother.'

'No, I can safely say you're not in the least like Arthur – and nor are you one of those dreadful Teddy boys that keep smashing up cinemas and making trouble,' Sister Beatrice said and smiled slightly. 'I can't say that I approve of your working at that nightclub but I do understand that you need to earn more money . . .'

'I shan't do it any longer than I need,' Billy said. He was about to get up and leave when he saw that she hadn't finished. 'Is there something I can do for you, Sister Beatrice?'

'There may be,' she said hesitantly. 'I dare say you remember Archie Miller?'

'Yes, of course. I thought he'd been moved to the new home?'

'He was but he ran away and came here. His sister was taken into care and he blames us at St Saviour's. I told him I would try to help him and his family, and I shall. Indeed, I've already taken steps to find out as much as I can about the foster family – and it is my intention to visit Sandra Miller in prison as soon as Sergeant Sallis manages to get me a visiting order . . .'

'But you want me to do something?'

'Archie ran off again and I'm worried about him. I don't want to report it to the police just yet, because I know that would alienate him immediately – but I wondered if you might make a few inquiries. He mentioned a Saturday job on the market. Could you make inquiries for me please?'

'I know the man he worked for,' Billy said, his frown lifting. 'Yes, I'll ask around and I'll take a look down the Docks. A lot of kids and vagrants hang about there, and under the arches.'

'I know you're busy, but if you do discover something it could help us to find him. If he doesn't turn up I shall have to report it to the police officially. Sergeant Sallis knows but I've asked him to keep it to himself for the moment . . .'

Billy nodded and promised to do what he could. He

150

was thoughtful as he went to his room. Once upon a time Sister Beatrice would have reported the boy's absence immediately, but she was being careful, and Billy wasn't sure why. No one knew better than he did how cold and dangerous the streets of London were for a young lad like Archie Miller. He was big enough to stand up for himself these days, but against a couple of thugs like those he'd found beating Mr Connolly, the boy wouldn't stand a chance . . .

CHAPTER 11

Archie shivered and pulled his jacket collar up about his ears. He wished he'd brought a big coat with him when he'd run away from Halfpenny House, but it had been early summer and the evening warm. It was summer now but you wouldn't think so that night, because the wind was cool and it was damp with the rain that had been drizzling all day, wetting the grimy pavements so they were slippery beneath his feet. He'd huddled up in this shop doorway once the streets had gone quiet, hugging his knees to try and keep out the chill that seemed to seep into his bones. All he'd got to sit on was a newspaper he'd picked up earlier and he envied some of the tramps he'd seen on the streets, with their layers of old coats and blankets, and their cardboard boxes that kept off some of the wind and rain.

He'd only been on the streets a few nights, because after leaving Halfpenny House he'd gone back to his old home, only to find that the doors and windows had been boarded up. He'd managed to wrench the wooden slats from a window and had broken in, but the house was empty and cold, as cold as the streets. Archie had searched the house in case anything was left behind, but all their belongings had been removed. He felt resentful of the way his family had been treated and wondered where all his mum's stuff had gone; she'd had one or two nice things his dad had bought her.

Remembering that his mother had a secret place for her valuables, Archie felt his way upstairs in the dark. On the landing it was a bit lighter, because one small window hadn't been boarded over. He entered his mother's room and waited until his eyes became adjusted to the gloom, then started to pace it out until he came to the loose board next to where her wardrobe had stood. She'd kept a rug over the loose board, but that had gone with all the rest. Kneeling down, Archie felt around and then tipped the loose board up. He thrust his hand into the space beneath it and came up with a couple of objects and what felt like a little drawstring purse. He felt all round the opening and then replaced the board, thrusting the objects he'd found into his jacket pocket.

On the landing, he sought the faint light of the window and looked at what he'd found – a pocket watch he knew had belonged to his father, a pretty silver brooch that his mother loved and the purse. Opening the drawstrings, he tipped the money into his hand and discovered that he had several half-crowns, a few florins and a couple of shillings, but also two pound notes. Tears stung his eyes as he thought of his mother painstakingly saving her few coins for something she thought her family needed. If she'd stolen those cheques and the ten pounds from the cash box the money would be here and it wasn't. Archie hadn't needed proof, but felt that

153

he had it, because his mum would definitely have put the money here if she'd got it.

Archie had spent four nights in the house, leaving it only to purchase a few chips or a bottle of drink during the day, hoarding his money carefully, knowing it had to last if he was going to save enough to go in search of June. On the fifth day he went out to buy something to eat and when he got back, he saw two men replacing the boards he'd torn down. This time they'd made a proper job of it and Archie knew he wouldn't be able to tear them off with his bare hands. Since then he'd been on the streets and already he was dreading the onset of darkness, because on his first night sleeping rough, he'd tried to take shelter with some other vagrants and they'd told him to clear off, threatening him with their fists. Archie had been eyeing their fire in an old oil can with envy, wondering if he could creep closer and perhaps beg a cup of tea from their billycan, but they'd made it clear he wasn't welcome. Since then he'd been looking for shop doorways to shelter in, but quite a few of them were already in use and Archie just wandered from street to street, looking for somewhere he could camp until he worked out what to do.

His money was running low, because he'd bought drinks and buns from cafés at the start, but today he'd joined a queue of vagrants at a stall giving out cardboard cups of hot soup and bread, because he dared not spend any more of his precious hoard, which was fastened inside his shirt. The man serving behind the stall was a vicar; he wore his back-to-front collar and a dark vest under his jacket and dispensed the free drinks with a smile, but when he saw Archie he'd looked concerned.

'What are you doing here, lad?' he'd asked. 'You shouldn't be on the streets at your age. I'll give you the address of a hostel you can go to if you wait a moment . . .'

Archie had taken his soup and walked off. He didn't want people like that interfering in his life. No doubt the vicar meant well and would try to help him if he let him, but Archie knew what would happen the moment he entered the hostel. The police would be called and he'd be taken back to St Saviour's or that other place . . . unless they arrested him for theft and put him in a remand home for bad boys.

Archie felt a surge of anger against the people who had ruined his life, sending his mother to prison when she was innocent and then taking his sister away, just because she'd got into bad company. He hunched his knees to his chest as he pondered what to do for the best. He'd been counting on help from Sister Beatrice, but she'd denied her involvement in what happened to June, and that meant she was a liar and not to be trusted. If he got sent back to Halfpenny House, he would be shut in that cupboard again . . . and he might end up being sent to a remand home.

Archie sat with his knees hunched and his head bent forward. For a moment tears wetted his cheeks, because he was hungry, cold and tired and felt defeated. How could he get June back when he didn't even have the money for shelter and food? Where would they go even if he did? No doubt as soon as the authorities learned that she'd run away from her foster home they would put them both in a secure place where punishment was handed out for the merest infringement – like that rotten

155

cupboard Archie had been shut in just for speaking up for his rights.

'Something the matter, lad?' The soft voice startled Archie and he looked up in alarm. He'd thought he was safe here, because no one had bothered him for two consecutive nights. 'Want to tell me about it? Perhaps I can help?'

Archie rose warily to his feet. The man didn't look like a tramp that wanted his spot back, nor was he a do-gooder like the vicar who had been handing out soup earlier. In the light of the street lamp it was possible to see that he was slightly balding, plump in the face and wearing a good suit and shoes.

'I'm not doing any harm,' Archie said defensively. 'If this is your shop I can move on . . .'

'No, this isn't my business,' the man said softly, his voice rather like the purring of a cat. 'I just thought perhaps you were in trouble. I should like to help you if I can. Would you like to come back to my place and tell me what happened to you? I could get you something hot to eat and you can stay the night if you want . . .'

Archie was tempted, but something told him not to trust the man. He wasn't sure what it was, but he didn't like the way he was looking at him . . . as if expectant, eager; his narrow-set eyes unnaturally bright.

'Nah, I'm all right,' he muttered. 'I was just restin'. I'm goin' home now . . .'

'You don't have to lie to me.' The man's voice had become insistent as his fingers curled round Archie's wrist. 'I've helped a lot of boys like you find a better life. How would you like a soft bed to sleep in at night, good food and money in your pocket? You just have to do a few favours for people like me. You know what I mean, lad. I'll bet you've done it scores of times before now, but I'll introduce you to the right people and they pay well . . .'

It suddenly dawned on Archie what the man was after. He'd heard vague things about men like that; he'd never taken much notice, but now he recoiled in disgust.

'You bloody pervert,' he yelled and wrenched away from the man, who caught at his arm and held on to him, beginning to drag him towards a car parked just down the street. Archie kicked out, catching him on the shin and as he yelped and let go, he took to his heels and ran.

'You little bugger,' the man called after him. 'Wait until you've been on the streets for a few months. You'll come crawling to me then . . .'

Archie neither replied nor looked back. He just kept running until he was out of breath and had to lean against a wall to get it back. His chest hurt and he was scared, because he didn't know where to go next. He needed to find a group of vagrants that would accept him, people who would share their fire and sometimes perhaps their food; he wouldn't mind working to earn a few coppers, but he wasn't doin' what that rotten bugger wanted, however much he paid him.

Archie lingered outside a cinema, looking at the posters for a new film called *The Dam Busters* and wishing he could be in there in the warm watching the picture on the big screen, but he didn't have the price of a cup of coffee in his pocket and he was afraid to spend the two pounds that belonged to his mum, because he would need that to find June, so he couldn't go to an all-night café to get warm. He would just have to keep walking until he found somewhere to stay where it was safe. He thought regretfully of St Saviour's and wished he dare return, because it was warm there and he had found food in the pantry, but he'd hit Sister Beatrice and if she caught him she would be sure to hand him over to the police. No, he couldn't trust anyone at the home; he just had to find someone to give him a job . . . Perhaps he would ask Ted Hastings on Saturday . . . but that meant he had nearly another week to wait . . .

Beatrice began her rounds of the dormitories, glancing in at the sleeping faces and feeling the sense of peace that always came when she knew these children at least were safe from the perils of the streets. Yet even as she returned to her office, satisfied that all was well, little niggles of guilt and anxiety played on her mind.

'Sister, can I get you anything?' Nancy asked as she came from the sick room and saw her just about to enter her office. 'Are you all right?'

'Perfectly. What should be the matter with me?'

'I just wondered, because it's late and I thought you might have gone home, Sister. I was about to make some tea for Nurse Paula, perhaps you would care for some?'

'That is very kind of you, Nancy,' Beatrice said, aware that she'd been sharp. 'I've just been making my rounds of the dormitories. I shall be going home in half an hour or so, unless we have an emergency.'

'It seems very quiet tonight,' Nancy said and laughed. 'I hope I'm not tempting fate, Sister. Shall I bring you some tea?'

'Yes, please, and then you may talk to me for a while.'

Nancy nodded and went off, returning some twenty minutes later with a tray of tea, two cups and some biscuits. She placed them on the desk, poured the tea and sat down, waiting.

'It seems cooler tonight,' Sister Beatrice said and sipped her tea. 'Oh yes, just how I like it. How long have you been here now, Nancy?'

'Seven years, Sister.'

'Yes, the years fly, don't they?' She took another sip of her drink. 'Are you visiting your brother this Sunday?'

'Not this week. I'm going to the zoo with Wendy and some of the children. It's a while since we had any outings and Wendy asked if I would like to go. We're going to take a packed lunch with us . . .'

'Let's hope we have better weather tomorrow then,' Sister said and replaced her cup in the saucer. 'Are you happy here, Nancy? You're not thinking of leaving us?'

'No, Sister. I hope you're satisfied with my work?'

'Yes, I am, quite satisfied. I just wanted to be sure, that's all – for the future. I shan't always be here and I want to know that our children will be in good hands. It has occurred to me that you might be ideally placed to take over my position in a few years . . .'

'Me?' Nancy stared at her in amazement. 'I'm not a nurse and I don't have your experience . . .'

'I am not thinking of retiring for a while,' Beatrice replied with a smile. 'It may be that in future the Board would appoint a Warden who did not have a nursing background; she would have the backing of a senior nurse, of course, but that may not be so necessary by then. We have our nurses and carers but things have changed over the years. More and more of the children are being sent on to Halfpenny House and we are merely a reception centre, a temporary refuge before they go on to better things. You've lived here for some years and you know our routines as well as anyone. We've been lucky in our staff, but it isn't as easy as it once was to find girls who want to work in a place like this, especially someone who would dedicate herself to the children; but this is merely a thought for the future, Nancy.'

'Thank you for considering me,' Nancy said, looking slightly dazed. 'I never expected it, but I do like my job and . . . well, if I were asked I suppose I might consider it . . .'

'Well, give the idea some thought, as I shall . . .' Sister began as the phone suddenly shrilled on her desk. She picked it up, answering automatically, 'Yes, Sister Beatrice of St Saviour's. How may I help you?'

'It's Sergeant Sallis, Sister. We've just had three children under the age of seven brought in. Their father is drunk in the cells and was arrested for brawling and causing a nuisance, and the mother died last year. Can you take them in for us until we decide what to do about the father?'

'Yes, of course,' Sister Beatrice said. 'I'll alert my staff. Will you bring them round yourself?'

'Yes. I'm on my way home. We've had a busy night here, Sister. Thank you for responding as always. I don't know what we would do if you closed up shop . . .'

'Well, you heard that,' Beatrice said as she replaced the receiver. 'We have three young children on the way. It looks as if we shall be busy for the rest of the night . . .'

Beatrice sighed as Nancy departed with the tea things. For a moment she'd thought it would be news of Archie

Miller, but she would have a word with Sergeant Sallis when he came in, ask him if he'd heard any news concerning the boy . . .

Nancy was thoughtful as she bathed the new arrivals and got them into clean clothes before feeding them and putting them to bed. Nurse Paula had examined them all in turn and pronounced them fit, apart from severe bruising, some of it fresh, and a tendency to be underweight for their ages. Since the majority of the children admitted had similar problems, Nancy was able to look after them without taking too much of Paula's or Sister Beatrice's time. They'd had much worse cases over the years and she thought it likely that the children's father would be allowed to claim them once he'd sobered up.

After they were all tucked up in the isolation ward, which had no other occupants at present, Nancy went down to the kitchen and washed the various dishes. She could have left them for the kitchen staff, but Muriel hated to start by washing up and her help didn't always arrive promptly in the mornings. Sister was right when she said it wasn't easy to find reliable staff for menial jobs. These days the girls wanted more glamorous jobs, like working in the perfume or fashion departments of the big stores or even modelling clothes for the customers. Of course there weren't enough of those jobs to go round, but that didn't stop girls who had no hope of ever getting that sort of job dreaming about it.

At one time Nancy had thought she might like to work in a Lyons teashop, but after Terry's breakdown she'd settled here at St Saviour's and by the time she was old enough to apply for a job at Lyons, she'd forgotten it was ever in her mind. Her life was here in the busy children's home where she never had time to just stand and stare; there was always a job to do and someone to talk to. Sister Beatrice, the nurses, Muriel – their long-suffering cook – and the other carers had become her friends. Tilly and Kelly were like her; they'd chosen to stay here rather than go off to more glamorous jobs. Kelly's mother had always been fragile and she was getting worse. For years Kelly had helped support her family, but her elder brother had left home, her sister was courting and her little brother was doing well at school and would soon be leaving to become a mechanic. If Kelly's mother died she would be free, although she might feel it her duty to stay and care for her father . . . Tilly was married and her sister lived with her and her husband now that their mother was dead. Their step-father had gone to prison for years and when he came out he'd disappeared.

'Good riddance as far as I'm concerned,' Tilly had told Nancy once. 'Ma would have had him back, but I told her, if he comes in I'll take Mags and leave her to fend for herself.'

'I don't blame you, but he won't bother you now.'

'My husband would give him a black eye if he did,' Tilly said and grinned. 'Ma was weak where men were concerned, but she used her weakness to make the rest of us do what she wanted.'

People who used emotional blackmail were perhaps worse than bullies, Nancy thought as she stacked the cups back on the old wooden dresser. Nancy's mother had been weak, taking to the bottle as her comforter, just as Tilly's mother had, ignoring what was happening under her nose and failing to protect her children. If her mother had looked out for them instead of feeling sorry for herself, things might have been so different.

Nancy sighed as she prepared to take one more look round the dorms. She'd tried to forget it all, what her father had done to her, and all the rest, but even though she sometimes didn't think of it for weeks, it was still there at the back of her mind. Nancy knew it was unlikely she would ever be able to trust a man or bear him touching her. What Pa had done had scarred her in her mind, making her reject the act of sexual loving as something unpleasant and evil.

She'd seen enough girls of her age falling in love to know that it needn't always be that way, but there was something inside her that rejected every man that made a friendly gesture towards her. She'd been asked to dances and to the flicks several times over the years; the plumber's mate who'd repaired their pipes one icy winter had asked her to go for a fish and chip meal but she'd said no, even though she'd liked his smile, but he wasn't the only one. It was just that his smile was the one Nancy remembered.

She hadn't given him a chance, any more than she gave the fish porter she'd met in the market, the bus conductor who flirted with her whenever she got on his bus or the market traders where she did her shopping or the hospital orderly who told her where to go when she was visiting one of their children. It wasn't that Nancy couldn't feel; she felt love for the children, friendship and concern for her friends, and she felt lonely – especially after visiting her brother Terry in his home.

Sometimes, that made her feel so upset that she wanted to break down and cry, especially when he didn't know her. Nancy had long ago given up hope that Terry would ever be normal again. The doctors said that his mind had been so badly damaged by his father's brutality and whatever had happened the night of the fire that he just couldn't face it.

'If he did it might send him right over the edge,' a doctor had told her. 'No, I think you must accept that your brother will always live here with us, Nancy. He is as happy as he can be in the circumstances . . .'

Nancy wondered if Terry would ever have been right, even if his father had treated him better. There had always been something strange about him, even as a small boy. Perhaps that was another reason why she didn't think she would ever marry and have children; she couldn't bear to give birth to a child who turned out like her brother . . .

Nancy finished her rounds of the home. Sister had gone to rest after the three children were admitted and she and Paula were the only ones left awake, though a quick call would have brought Sister hurrying back if necessary.

Apart from that one little flurry, it had been a quiet night. Nancy decided to have a chat with Staff Nurse Paula. In another hour the day staff would come on and they could go home to their beds . . .

CHAPTER 12

It was Monday morning when Billy walked into the coach depot whistling cheerfully. His eye was sore and had developed a beautiful purple colour over the weekend, and his arm was still in its sling. He didn't feel like working for nine hours under a coach engine, but he'd come in because he couldn't let his boss down.

'What happened to you?' Tom asked, brows rising as he paused in his work of polishing the bodywork of one of the coaches. 'You look as if you've been five rounds with a prize fighter!'

'You should see the other bloke,' Billy bragged, unaware that his boss was standing at the office door listening. 'This is nothing to what I gave him—'

'Baggins, I want to see you in my office.'

Billy turned, heart sinking as he saw the angry look on the manager's face. 'Yes, sir . . .' He followed him inside and went cold as he saw what looked like a wage packet and his cards on the desk. 'I was just joshing Tom, sir. It wasn't my fault . . .'

'The fight is neither here nor there,' his boss said, 'nor the fact that you obviously can't work with one arm in a sling. I thought I made it clear when you started here that we don't allow second jobs. Even if you hadn't been embroiled in a disgraceful fight I should've had to let you go once Mr Heston knew that you were working at that nightclub . . .'

'But it doesn't affect my work,' Billy protested. 'I thought you meant I couldn't work as a mechanic for anyone else . . . it's just keeping order when folks get rowdy. Surely you're not lettin' me go for that?'

'If it were up to me I would let you off with a warning,' the manager told him. 'However, Mr Heston saw a piece in the paper about you on Saturday night in the *Chronicle* and he didn't like it. They're doing a series about people doing the right thing and standing up to the bullies, and they made you a hero, but I'm afraid Mr Heston didn't see it that way. He doesn't approve of nightclubs or anything to do with strong drink – and I took you on only because Sister Beatrice spoke up for you. I'm afraid this is your final notice, Baggins – two weeks' wages and no reference. I'm sorry, lad. I don't like to be so harsh, but I've no choice . . .'

Billy accepted the envelope and put it in his breast pocket. He wanted to yell and hit out with his fists, but he knew that wouldn't do him any good, not that he could hit anyone with his right hand in a sling.

'It's not your fault, Mr Simkins,' he acknowledged. 'I'm sorry I let you down . . .'

Billy walked out of the office. Tom gave him a sympathetic look and shook his head, but could offer no help. Billy wasn't experienced enough to get a job as a qualified mechanic, and he wasn't likely to be offered another apprenticeship after being thrown off this one without a reference. They usually cost money and it had been a favour to Sister Beatrice that had got him his place here – and now he'd lost it . . .

Feeling sick at heart, Billy walked away from the coach depot. Mary Ellen would stand by him; she would be angry at the way he'd been treated and tell him he'd find a better job soon, but he knew it wouldn't be that easy. He might find odd jobs down the Docks or sweeping up at one of the factories, but he wasn't trained for anything and no one would set him on at a decent job without a reference. He would have to start at the bottom, earning next to nothing – and that meant it might be years before he could afford to get married.

'The rotten devil, to do that to you – and after you were a hero!' Mary Ellen said angrily when he told her later that day. 'Never mind, Billy, you'll show them. You'll soon find something else . . .'

'Yes, I'll find a job. I can do a few hours for Ted sometimes, but it isn't leading anywhere, Mary Ellen. I can't ask you to marry me on what I shall be earning now.'

'You've still got that job at the club, haven't you?'

'Yes, but . . .' Billy sighed because it wasn't what he was looking for. 'Don't worry, love. I never wanted to work at the coach depot and this is my chance to better myself.'

Her smile lit up her face and he felt cheered to know that at least she believed in him. He would have to inform Sister Beatrice, but she would be upset and Billy didn't feel like telling her his news until he'd found something else to put in place of his steady job.

He hoped to avoid seeing her and headed straight up to his room, but she came round the corner and saw him before he could make good his escape.

'Ah, Billy,' she said. 'Mr Connolly was here earlier. He wishes to thank you in person and wants you to go and see him on Saturday afternoon at his warehouses. He seemed to think you would know where they are?'

'Yes, Sister. They're adjacent to the East India Docks. He trades in a lot of foreign goods, I think, and they store the stock in the warehouses until it is taken to the various shops and market stalls . . .'

'Ah yes, a market trader,' Sister mused, a questioning look in her eyes. 'One imagines he is rich these days, but you can still catch a trace of the East End lad in his speech at times . . .'

'You can take us out of the East End, but you can't take the East End out of us,' Billy quipped and to his surprise she nodded her agreement.

'Perfectly right, Billy. It is my opinion that if born in the East End you never truly belong elsewhere, however high you rise. That is why I was always against the move to the country, but unfortunately I was overruled . . .'

'Me and Mary Ellen was lucky to be your kids, Sister Beatrice, before they started the new ways. I 'spect it's all right, but I wouldn't want to be sent there. I'm glad we never had to go away . . .'

'I do not think you would've stayed there any more than Archie Miller did – you are somewhat alike, Billy. I suppose you haven't heard anything yet?'

'Sorry, Sister. I had a look round the Docks yesterday and again earlier today, but no one seems to have seen him.'

'Oh well, we must keep trying,' she said. 'Off you go, I'm sure you have things to do . . .'

'Yes, Sister. I have to get to work soon.'

'At that horrid club, I suppose?' She walked off shaking her head in disapproval.

Billy hardly dared think what she would say when he told her it was the only job he had now . . .

He set his mouth firmly. In the morning he was going to start looking for work. He'd tried a few places already, taking his sling off so he didn't look so much like a prize fighter, but without any luck. Once he'd been told a job as a barman had just gone; Billy had no experience of bar work but was willing to learn. It had given him more hope and he'd tried a few more pubs and restaurants. He'd been offered two hours in the evenings washing dishes, but that was at the same time as his work at the club so he had to refuse.

It was going to be difficult to find anything worthwhile – something Rose would approve of, because once she discovered that Billy had lost his job at the coach depot she would forbid Mary Ellen to see him . . .

'I told you he was a waster,' Rose was saying to Mary Ellen as she and Marion washed the cocoa mugs that evening. 'He's lost the apprenticeship Sister Beatrice got for him and he'll lose every other job he ever gets. He'll end up thieving like his brother. You listen to me, Mary Ellen, and stop seeing him now before it's too late.'

'I love Billy and I believe in him,' Mary Ellen said, turning her nails into the palms of her hands to stop herself getting into a temper. It was no good getting angry with Rose, because she would always have the last word, but whatever she said, Mary Ellen wasn't going to give up on Billy. 'He'll find another job soon, a good job. I know he will. It isn't as if he did anything wrong. He saved a man's life . . .'

'That's his story,' Rose said. 'I shouldn't believe everything he says if I were you. You'll end up with a brood of children you can't feed and in debt – and he will probably be behind bars . . .'

'You've no right to say such things about Billy.' Mary Ellen's eyes stung with angry tears. 'You can be so unkind, Rose. Billy's never done anything to you, never been rude or aggressive or hurt you. Why can't you think about me, about how I feel?'

'Rose didn't mean to be nasty,' Marion put in and got a glare for her pains.

Rose hesitated, then in a softer tone, 'It's you I'm thinking of, Mary Ellen. I just don't want you to get hurt – and you will be if you marry him.'

'I don't want to listen to any more of this,' Mary Ellen said and went into her own room, slamming the door behind her.

'They're looking for a porter in the stockroom at Woolworth's where I work,' Marion said to Rose after Mary Ellen had gone. 'I'll tell her. He might get it if he's got a reference . . .'

'They wouldn't take him,' Rose scowled. 'But tell her if you want. I suppose he might be lucky . . .'

Marion knocked at the door and went into Mary Ellen's room. She'd been crying and she was wiping her face with a pad of cotton wool and a pot of Pond's face cream, but she put on a smile when Marion entered.

'Sorry, I don't mean to quarrel with Rose, but she's so mean about Billy at times.'

'Rose don't know him like we do.' Marion perched on the side of the bed. 'I wanted to tell you about a job where I work. I know it's coming up but it hasn't been advertised so if you tell Billy he might stand a chance.'

'Thanks, Marion,' Mary Ellen laughed. 'It's almost like old times havin' you livin' here with us . . .'

Marion looked sad and turned away. 'I wish I was back there sometimes . . .'

'What's wrong?' Mary Ellen looked at her intently but she shook her head and got up, then winced. 'Something is the matter . . .' Mary Ellen caught her arm as she would've left the room and she gave a little scream. 'Your arm . . . you've hurt it . . .' She pushed up the short sleeve of Marion's jumper and stared at the dark bruise. 'What happened?'

'Oh, I banged into something at work,' Marion said and shrugged it away. 'It's just a bit sore, that's all . . . anyway, I only came to tell you about the job. I'm going to bed. I want to put my hair in pins . . .'

Mary Ellen let her go; puzzled because she was certain her friend was lying. Marion hadn't hurt herself at work and she seemed nervous . . . so what was she hiding and why?

Over the next few days, Billy tried for the job at Woolworth's and one for a night watchman at the boot factory, but they both wanted references and said the letter from Sister Beatrice wasn't enough. It had to be from his last place of work. Billy tried explaining but they just shook their heads and told him to come back when he had proper references and some work experience.

Billy found a few hours unloading at the Docks. He earned fifteen shillings and was able to pay for his food for the week at St Saviour's and a bit over, but even with his pay from the club he knew it wouldn't be enough to cover everything and let him save for the future. He still had some savings, but they wouldn't last long and he wanted to get Mary Ellen a ring for her birthday.

He wouldn't be able to manage for long without spending what he'd saved, and that meant he was going to have to make a choice, but he could always ask Ted Hastings if there was any work going on the markets – and he'd tell Ted about Archie at the same time . . .

'So that's the story,' Billy said to the market trader. 'I thought I'd come and explain why we're lookin' for Archie Miller. He's bound to be searching for a way to earn money, and if he's had as much luck as I have, he'll be pretty desperate. If he does come to see you, can you let me know please?'

'Yes, I'll do that,' Ted Hastings said, nodding his head and looking concerned. 'I don't like to think of a lad like that running the streets; he's not streetwise like some of them. I thought he was a nice lad when he asked me for work.'

'Archie is convinced his mother is innocent of the charge against her. I don't think he would be so insistent if he wasn't sure of his facts. I offered to visit her with him, but I think Sister Beatrice is going to visit her and find out what she can.'

'It's not justice when an innocent woman is convicted

because someone has it in for her,' Ted said. 'If the lad had confided in me I would have had a talk to a few people, see what we could find out about the circumstances. I must admit I feel sorry for the whole family.'

'Sister asked me to look for him, but I'm damned if I know where,' Billy said. 'I suppose he wouldn't have gone back to his home, would he?'

'Do you know where that was?'

'No, but Sister may . . .' Billy shook his head. 'Thanks, Ted, you're a good mate. I knew Archie would be all right with you.'

'Well, if I could put up wiv a tearaway like you, Billy Baggins, he were a doddle . . .' Ted grinned at him and Billy laughed. He went off whistling and smiling to himself. He'd done what he could for the moment as far as Archie was concerned, though Ted had regretfully told him he didn't have much to offer Billy at the moment. 'A couple of hours on Saturday mornings is no good to you, Billy – but I'll keep an eye out and let you know if I hear of anything, and I'll give you a reference if that will do?'

Billy thanked him, walking across the busy market square, which was littered with debris between the colourful stalls and thronged with shoppers looking for a bargain. Ted was a good mate, but Billy knew that a reference for a few hours' work on a market stall wasn't what he needed for the kind of job he preferred. A sigh escaped him, because he hadn't thought it would be this difficult to get work. However, he had an appointment this afternoon. Mr Connolly had left a message for him at St Saviour's that he wanted to see him at his warehouse. It was only a short distance away, thirty minutes' walk or so, but he hopped on a bus, because he didn't want to be late, and Billy was curious why the man he'd helped wanted to see him. Of course it was probably just to say thank you. He might offer him a couple of quid as a reward, but Billy was determined not to take it; it wouldn't be right for doing what was the duty of any decent bloke.

The smell of the Docks was unmistakable; oil and grease and a faint whiff of smoke, also tar and wood, and exotic scents that came from a shipment of spices being unloaded into one of the warehouses. Out on the river there were the stacks of boats that plied their trade, a crane unloading on the quayside and the dark shadows of warehouses that clustered the water's edge.

The door of Mr Connolly's warehouse stood open and there were two large vans parked outside. Stock in boxes was being carried out to the vans and Billy stopped one of the men to ask where he could find Mr Connolly.

'His office is in there, mate,' the man said. 'If you're lookin' fer a job yer outta luck. He's in a right old mood . . .'

Billy thanked him and walked to the office. A week had passed since he was injured and his arm was no longer in a sling and his eye had stopped being sore, though the flesh was still dark around it. He knocked at the closed door and was told to come in. Opening it, he looked round and saw Mr Connolly at his desk going through a pile of receipts; he did look angry but his expression changed as he glanced up and saw Billy. He got to his feet and came round the desk, offering his hand to him and shaking it warmly.

'I'm glad you came, Billy. I know I didn't thank you

properly for what you did that night. If you hadn't stepped in I should've likely died and I'm very grateful for what you did.'

'I'm glad I was there, sir,' Billy replied. 'I'm sorry I couldn't have stopped them sooner – did they steal much?'

'Steal? Ah yes, my wallet,' Mr Connolly said, his eyes veering away. 'Luckily, I wasn't carrying much that day, but sometimes I might carry a thousand pounds or more in cash – and that is why I wanted to see you, Billy . . .'

'Me? I'm not sure I understand.'

'I'm offering you a job as my bodyguard,' Mr Connolly said and smiled. 'The way you reacted the other night is exactly what I'm looking for, Billy. I've never needed anyone before, but after what happened . . . I want a young strong lad like you to protect me from my enemies, people who attempt to rob me . . .'

'Bodyguard?' Billy was stunned. His idea of a bodyguard was what he'd seen in American gangster movies; men in dark suits with sunglasses and trilby hats, and only gangster bosses and rich foreigners had them. 'Are you sure I'm the right one, sir? I don't carry a gun or a knife.'

'From what I saw you didn't need them,' Mr Connolly said and smiled. 'I don't like guns and knives are too messy. We have to keep in with the law, don't we? No, I want a strong lad who is handy with his fists and can protect me without getting us into trouble with the law. I'm not a gangster, Billy, just a hard-working trader who needs help. So what do you say? Your wage will be seven pounds ten shillings a week and you'll get bonuses sometimes . . . a present from our stock for your girl-friend, perhaps . . .'

'Seven pound ten, a week?' Billy was astounded. It was the sort of wage top managers earned at the Co-op and fancy stores, and nearly three times what he'd earned as an apprentice. 'I can't thank you enough, sir. What do you want me to do?'

'You will come with me when I need you, at nights when I visit clubs and during the day if I have to carry large sums of money. Also you can collect the rent money for the market stalls I own – and you can run one of your own on Saturday mornings if you want. I'll supply the goods and what you make above their cost to me is your own.'

'The job alone is more than I could ask for,' Billy said. It would mean giving up the job he did at night, but that wouldn't matter. Regular work minding Mr Connolly and his market stalls was a far better option. As far as Billy knew, Mr Connolly was a respected man who owned property up West as well as in the East End.

'Well, there's a place with me for an enterprising young man,' his new employer said. 'I'll give you my home address and you can meet me there on Monday morning. We'll go on a tour of my property because once you've got used to the way things work you can collect the money due to me yourself and save me the problem. Get off and see your young lady, treat her to the pictures . . .' He took ten shillings from his wallet. 'Here, think of it as an advance on your wage if you like.'

Billy hesitated and then took the money. 'Thank you, sir. I've been a bit short this week, but I'll be able to save for my own home now and to get married.'

'That's what I like to hear,' his new boss said. 'A good family life is what it's all about, Billy. You'll meet my good lady and my daughters. They're all decent girls but I'm sorry I didn't have a son to take over after me – but we don't get everything in this life, as I'm sure you know, and I've got a young grandson. He will take over my business one day, but I need you to protect it in the meantime.'

Billy thanked him again and set off to find Mary Ellen. He couldn't wait to tell her his good news. Seven pounds ten bob a week! He would soon have enough to buy a pretty ring for Mary Ellen and he could afford a nice little council flat for them to live in, or perhaps a house with a garden if they could get it. Suddenly the future looked brighter and it was all due to the good turn he'd done for Mr Connolly. It seemed now that losing his apprenticeship was all part of the plan, because he'd been ready to start somewhere new and he couldn't wait to get going.

Billy didn't consider that the fight he'd entered into might have cost him his own life, nor did he delve into the reasons why his new boss had been attacked in the first place, accepting it was purely theft. The rogues that had attacked Mr Connolly had taken advantage of a vulnerable man in his sixties; when the rogues and thieves got used to seeing Billy with him they would think twice about attacking him in future. If Mr Connolly had wanted him to carry a gun or a knife he'd have had to turn him down, but using his fists to protect his employer was perfectly justified in his mind and the police had seemed to think he'd done well, so they weren't likely to warn him off.

He was smiling as he hurried to Rose's flat to give them the good news . . . Billy could afford to take Mary

Ellen out for a nice meal as well as the pictures and he was feeling very pleased with himself.

'So you'll be earning more than you were with your apprenticeship and your work at the club,' Mary Ellen said when he told her his news over a cup of coffee. She'd invited him in because Rose was working and so was Marion and she had the place to herself. 'That's really good, Billy.'

'It's not much more, but I've got the chance to sell stuff on the market on Saturdays as well; I don't know much about it yet, but he said there will be bonuses . . . it sounds too good to be true, Ellie love. If things go well, we might get married when you're nineteen. It's only next September and that will soon go round . . .'

'Rose might let us if we can show her we have money saved, but if I pass my exams I'll have to go to college two or three days a week and that means I'll be earning less, because Sam won't pay if I'm not working.'

'That doesn't matter, if it's what you want?'

Mary Ellen sighed, and then smiled oddly. 'I can't be certain, Billy. I love what I do and Sam is a good boss, but I've always wanted to be a teacher and if I don't do it now . . .'

'You might regret it,' Billy said. 'I promised you I would support you through it and I shall, even if you have to leave London for a while . . .'

'Oh no, I shan't do that,' she said. 'The college I want to try for is right here in London, and I should be able to sign on as a pupil teacher for a while and do my college work as I train.'

'What you've learned at Sam's will help if you take needlework as one of your subjects.'

'Yes, I've put that down as one of them, with English literature and art,' Mary Ellen said. 'It seems daft but I've still got to pass my maths and other subjects that I'll never need, but I was always good at art, reading and needlework so I should get a job in one of those areas.'

'What if the jobs are outside London?'

Mary Ellen frowned and shook her head. 'I think it's harder for them to find people who want to teach here in the East End amongst deprived kids. Most teachers want a new modern school in a small town or the country, so they've been telling us at night school, but I want to help kids like us, Billy – kids who know what it's like to be hungry and have holes in their shoes . . .'

'You'll be good with them,' Billy said and got up to draw her into his arms. He held her close, kissing her and pressing her hard against him so that she could feel the arousal of his body and her breath came faster. 'I love you so much, Ellie. I can't wait to be with you . . . really with you . . .'

'I love you, Billy.' She glanced at the clock on the shelf. 'Marion gets back in half an hour but I'm not sure when Rose is finished . . .'

'No, love,' Billy smiled as he ran his hands down the arch of her back, looking at her hungrily. The scent of her inflamed his senses, making him aware of the hot need inside, but he tamped it down, denying the desire that threatened to overwhelm him. 'I want to, you know I want to as much as you, but we can't. Rose would kill us if she caught us – and, besides, I promised I'd wait. When we're married I'm still going to be careful so you can be a teacher. We'll get something to use, but not until you're ready.'

'I'd be ready now if I thought it would be safe,' Mary Ellen said and caught her breath as she heard the key in the lock. 'Rose is back. Sit down and drink your coffee while I tell her the good news.'

Billy arched his brows. If they'd given into temptation and gone on Mary Ellen's bed, Rose would've come in and caught them, and even if they'd only been petting she would've raised the roof.

'What is he doing here?' Rose demanded as she put her nursing bag and her cloak on the nearest chair.

'Billy has found a good job with Mr Connolly, the man he helped that night,' Mary Ellen said. 'He'll be giving up his work at the club nights – and we'll be looking for a place to rent so we can get married when I'm nineteen.'

'You still need my permission, don't forget,' Rose said, glaring at Billy. 'I've yet to see him showing signs of being able to afford a wife . . .'

'I shall now, Rose,' Billy said and stood up once more. 'I'll see you tomorrow afternoon, Mary Ellen. We'll go somewhere for an hour or two and then you can study in the evening.'

She nodded and walked to the door with him, whispering as he left, 'She can't stop us forever, Billy. Once you've got your own place she'll come round, I promise . . .'

Billy leaned in and kissed her softly. Rose had turned her back on them, clearly annoyed to find him here, but unable to forbid it since Mary Ellen ignored her when she told her to give him up.

Leaving them to sort out their problems themselves, Billy walked home via the river. He saw some boys playing tag but after a moment's scrutiny decided that Archie wasn't amongst them. His problems seemed to be sorting themselves out, but he was no nearer to solving the question of what had happened to Archie Miller . . .

CHAPTER 13

Archie ate the bag of chips he'd bought with the few pence he'd earned cleaning the back of a lorry that had transported stinking bones to the glue factory. Maggots had been crawling all over it and he'd had to use bucketfuls of water to rinse it down. For that he'd earned two shillings and sixpence, which had paid for a big bag of chips, leaving enough over for a bread roll and a cup of tea. The man behind the counter had topped the packet up with crispy bits off the fish batter for him and he devoured them with relish. Finding work wasn't easy for a lad of his age; he was only ever given the worst jobs but he didn't care, because he'd learned to get by on very little. Water from the public toilets was the only drink he'd had for nearly a week, though he'd been given a bun and a cup of milky coffee at the Italian café where he'd earned two bob for cleaning all the windows.

Archie had been going to ask Ted Hastings if he would give him a permanent job, but when he reached the marketplace on the Saturday morning he'd seen Billy Baggins talking to the market trader. They'd both looked serious, though obviously on the best of terms, and Archie suspected they'd been talking about him. Perhaps Sister had asked Billy to look out for him – but why? He'd thought she would've set the police on him but he hadn't seen any signs that they were looking for him in particular. If he passed a police officer on the street he was careful to keep his eyes down and avoid confrontation, but no one had stopped him and asked his name.

Perhaps he wasn't in trouble with Sister – or not as much trouble as he'd feared. He threw his empty chip paper to the ground, because there wasn't anywhere else to put it. Mum would clip his ear if she saw him do that, but she wouldn't be pleased with a lot of the things that Archie had been obliged to get used to, like not brushing his teeth and only washing his face and hands in the basin in the public toilets if he had a penny to get into them.

Archie didn't like living on the streets; he didn't like the constant moving from one place to another and the feeling that he had to keep looking over his shoulder the whole time. Even in summer it got cold at night when you didn't even have a blanket to cover yourself, and he dreaded the onset of colder nights when the ground was icy. Fortunately, that wouldn't be for some months. In the meantime, he had to find a proper job and somewhere he could safely take his sister when he found her.

It was past seven and in a few hours the blackness of night would descend and Archie still hadn't found a place to sleep. He'd given up shop doors after the approach from the man with the soft voice and creepy eyes, and he headed towards the railway bridges most nights. Usually other homeless men were already settled for the night, some with fires to warm themselves by and make a can of tea. Archie had learned not to ask for anything and was usually allowed to stay as long as he kept his distance.

He saw the arches ahead of him, his steps slowing uncertainly, because he was never quite certain of his reception. The stench of oil, tar and other less pleasant odours wafted in from the river, but Archie was used to them and took little notice. Perhaps if he was lucky he would find a sheltered spot where he would be out of the wind. Once or twice one of the less surly tramps had allowed him to creep near to his fire, but at other times he'd been ordered to get away. He was developing an instinct that told him whether he dare approach or not and he usually hesitated on the fringes until someone either yelled at him to clear off or shrugged to indicate a vacant spot.

That night he saw there were a couple of fires burning and both men were brewing tea in billycans. Archie edged as close to the fires as he could, but didn't ask for a drink. He sat down on the sheet of newspaper he carried, because he still hadn't found an old cardboard box for himself, which was what most of the men used to shelter them from the damp ground.

'What you starin' at, kid?' one of the men muttered.

He was a tall thin man with a ragged dark beard and long straggly hair. In his hand he held a bottle of something Archie thought was some kind of alcohol; he'd seen other men drinking from similar bottles, but it wasn't beer or any recognisable brand and he thought it might be something called 'meths', but wasn't sure because he'd only heard the word in passing when two men were quarrelling over a bottle they shared.

'Nuthin',' Archie said, averting his gaze instantly. It was too late, because the man had got to his feet and lurched unsteadily towards him, clearly drunk and quarrelsome. Archie was instantly afraid of him because he'd seen fights erupt over nothing under the arches.

'I asked yer what yer were starin' at, boy!'

'Nuthin',' Archie repeated, quaking inside as he saw the man's bleary eyes. 'Honest, I just came for a sit down. If I'm in your way, I'll go . . .'

'Copper's nark, are yer? Run to 'em and tell 'em what we're doin'? Boy like yer don't belong 'ere I reckon . . .'

'I ain't a nark,' Archie said desperately. He rose gingerly to his feet and prepared to flee, but the tramp grabbed him, holding him by his throat and peering into his face. Archie could smell the foul odour of his breath and felt the gorge rise in his throat; he couldn't stop himself vomiting onto the man's body. Its taste was bitter and it smelled almost as bad as the breath that had made him bring up his supper. 'Sorry. I didn't mean to do that . . .' he gabbled as he tried to wipe the vomit from his mouth.

'Yer soddin' filth,' the man said and started to shake Archie. 'I'll teach yer to spew yer guts over me . . .'

He punched Archie in the mouth, sending him reeling. He fell to the ground and struck his head hard, feeling the pain where he'd connected with something metal. Unable to rise, he heard the man's voice coming to him through a dark mist.

'I'll teach yer to mess with me. By the time I've had yer arse yer won't forget it . . .' His hoarse laughter

185

sounded in Archie's ears and he felt the man's hands clawing at his trousers, dragging them down round his ankles, and he gave a shout of rage, trying to kick out at the devil attacking him.

'Leave the kid alone,' a calm voice reached through the mist.

'Bugger off, Ikey. Ain't yer business what I do . . .'

'I told you to leave him alone. He did nothing wrong . . .'

Archie heard the sounds of a scuffle. He felt his trousers dragged up to cover his backside, and then he was hauled to his feet and thrown over someone's shoulder. Fearing the worst, he struggled feebly for a moment, but his head was aching and when the calm voice told him to be quiet because it was all right he subsided. The mist in his head made him hardly aware what was going on and he drifted in and out of consciousness until he realised he was being placed down on something soft and the smell of fresh linen alerted him to the fact that it must be a bed.

'What are you doin'?' he demanded, attempting to sit up and failing.

'I'm going to let a doctor take a look at you,' the calm voice said. 'It's all right, lad. No one is going to hurt you. We're safe here. Doctor Kingsley is a mate of mine . . .'

Archie felt something cool on his face. His head seemed to be clearing and he managed to focus on the men's faces; one was that of a down-and-out he'd noticed sitting by one of the fires under the arches, and the other belonged to an elderly man with grey hair and a white coat.

186

'I banged my head,' he offered by way of explanation. 'When he knocked me down and . . .' Sitting up hastily, Archie groaned as he felt a wave of nausea sweep over him, but retched on an empty stomach. 'He never done nuthin', did he?'

'No, lad, it's all right,' the calm voice said. 'I stopped him in time. He's a drunken idiot, but he can be handled if you know how. He won't touch you again now he knows you're under my protection.'

Archie attempted to sit up but his head was going round and round and the doctor told him to lie still. He was asked to look at him and to follow his finger and then a light was shone into his eyes.

'Been on the streets long?' the doctor's voice asked.

'Nah, just a couple of weeks or so . . .' Archie said and at last managed to sit up. 'I'm all right, Doc. Thanks for helping me, sir, but I've got to go now . . .'

'Hold your horses, lad,' the calm voice said and as his vision cleared Archie saw smiling eyes looking at him. Eyes as blue as his mum's were. Somehow the thought eased his panic. 'We're not going to hurt you or hand you into the police, but you might as well have some soup and bread, and a cup of tea now you're here.'

'Ain't hungry . . .' Archie said but his stomach grumbled.

'Well I'm going to eat so you may as well have something, because I can't let you go back to the arches alone. We can get a bed here for tonight and then tomorrow maybe we can find some work . . .'

'Work, are you kiddin' me?' Archie looked at him in disbelief.

'I'm sure that's what you want, isn't it?' Ikey grinned

at him. There was something at the back of Archie's mind then, a feeling that he'd seen this man once before briefly, but he couldn't recall when or where. 'You can tell me your story while we eat, if you like . . . You don't have to if you'd rather not, but sometimes it helps to share a problem.'

'What kind of work?' Archie said and got up off what he now saw was a doctor's couch. 'Thanks, I'm all right now.'

'Yes, lad, I'm sure you are,' Doctor Kingsley said. 'Ikey will show you the ropes. You're not the first he's brought here by any means.'

Ikey led the way from the small consulting room through a hall into a large dining room. About twenty tables covered in oilcloth were set out in lines and men were sitting at most of them eating chunks of bread and bowls of soup, and they all had mugs of tea on the table. A few curious stares followed them as Ikey led the way to the counter where food and tea was being dispensed. Archie's stomach rumbled again when he smelled the delicious soup.

'It's fresh vegetables and it will be good,' Ikey said as he asked for their food. Archie saw that no money changed hands and looked at him curiously as they walked to the nearest table.

'You didn't pay for the soup?'

'No, it is free. The mission is run by Doctor Kingsley and some of his friends. You can get a meal here twice a week and a bed if you need it. They open every day but the rule is you only come twice in a week. They can't serve everyone every night and there are only so many beds . . .'

'I didn't know there was a place like this . . .'

'Actually, there are several, but some of them charge a few pence for a meal and a bed, some only take sailors or servicemen. You have to get to know them and stick to a routine. I only use this place if I have to, because others are in more need. I've got regular work in a lumber yard so I can pay for my bed if I want.'

'Why were you down the arches tonight then?'

'Because it suits me to remember what happens if you let the demon drink take over,' Ikey said. 'Lucky thing for you I was, young 'un. What's your name by the way?'

'Archie . . .' Archie hesitated, then, 'I ran away from the home in Essex because I've got to find my sister June – and they locked me in a cupboard. I weren't in there long, but I thought if I asked about June they might shut me in there again so I came back to London . . .'

'Why don't you start at the beginning?'

Archie was silent, then, 'You're a man that's been educated proper. Why are you on the streets?'

'I lost everything I cared for in life and then took to drink,' Ikey said. 'Why were you in a home? Have you no parents?'

'My father died and they put Mum in prison for stealing – and she's innocent,' Archie said, giving him a belligerent stare. 'They said she pinched some cheques and money but Mum wouldn't do that. She told me Reg Prentice had it in for her . . .'

'Who is he?'

'He was her manager at the biscuit works. She wouldn't tell me why he'd set her up but I reckon he was after her. She wouldn't let him near her and he didn't like it so he made up lies and they believed him . . .' Archie glared as Ikey remained thoughtful. 'You think I'm making it up . . .'

'No, Archie, I'm thinking that it's a story I've heard all too often.' He looked at his soup. 'You can tell me it all as we eat, but don't let your soup go cold . . .'

Archie put a spoonful in his mouth. It was the best thing he'd eaten in ages and he could hardly stop himself shovelling it in, but saw that Ikey ate his slowly with relish and decided to do the same.

Ikey nodded approvingly, pushing his empty bowl away. 'The food is good here, that's why I come sometimes, but I try not to abuse their kindness. Tomorrow, I'll see if you can work at the lumber yard with me – that's if you want?'

'Yes, please,' Archie said. 'I have to save enough money to get tickets for the train.'

'Where do you want to go?'

'I don't know where June has been taken. Sister Beatrice said she didn't know about it until it was too late, but she must have the information in her files – don't you think?'

'Yes, I would think so . . .' Ikey nodded. 'I think I've heard of her – she runs St Saviour's in Halfpenny Street, doesn't she? I've heard it's a decent place for kids . . .'

'Yeah, it was all right,' Archie acknowledged. 'Only, they wanted to send me and June off to Essex – to Harlow; Halfpenny House is on the outskirts I reckon, 'cos there's fields and trees all round and it's quiet. We drove through the town to get there; bits of it looked all right, but the buildings all looked square and ugly, not like here in London. I went by train and June was

190

supposed to follow in the car but the council people took her to be fostered. Mum will kill me if she gets home and finds that June has gone. She should be with us . . .'

Ikey looked thoughtful again. 'You want to get her back, is that it?'

'She belongs with me and Mum.'

'Yes, but the law may not see it that way, Archie. It may be that because your mum went to prison they will say that she isn't fit to have the care of your sister. You're nearly old enough to choose for yourself, but June is still young – unless I've got that wrong?'

'She's nine, ten next spring,' Archie said and worried at his bottom lip with his teeth. 'I've got to see her, talk to her – find out if she's all right . . .'

'Yes, I see how it would be upsetting for you, but you have nowhere to live and June is too young to be on the streets. You wouldn't want what happened to you to happen to her?'

'No!' Archie shook his head vigorously. 'No, not that – but I have to know she's all right so I can tell Mum. She won't let them adopt her and then she can get her back when she has a house for us . . .'

'Perhaps . . . no, don't flare up at me, Archie. Your mum has fallen foul of injustice. That needs to be put right. If we could prove she was innocent, they would have to let her out – and she would get June back then . . .'

'How do we do that?'

'We need a lawyer . . .'

'Lawyers cost money, don't they?'

'A lot of money . . . unless you know someone,' Ikey

191

agreed. 'Finish your meal and then we'll go to the baths. We could both do with one before we go to bed . . .' He grinned as he saw Archie's scowl. 'Yeah, I know. It's a pain in the backside, but one of the rules. Besides, it's good to feel clean. You don't want nits, do you?'

'Mum would kill me,' Archie said, resigned to his fate. He hung back for a moment. 'Why are you helpin' me like this?'

'No particular reason, except that I happen to hate bullies and injustice,' Ikey said. 'Stick with me, Archie and I'll see what I can do to get you through this . . . Do you trust me?'

'Yeah . . .' Archie nodded as he looked long and hard. Ikey's clothes were much the same as every other down-and-out's, but there was something different about him, something he couldn't define, but liked. 'You remind me of my dad . . .'

'Your dad was a good man?'

'Yeah, the best! We were all right until he died.'

'Well, we'll see what we can do to make things right again.'

'I can't afford a lawyer though . . .'

'Maybe I can find one who doesn't want money,' Ikey said and smiled. 'No promises, mind. Just wait and see what comes . . .'

CHAPTER 14

'Have you finished those skirts I asked you to do?' Sam asked as he walked into the workshop and discovered Mary Ellen still at her machine. 'I need to pair them with the jackets and get them on the rack. I've got an important customer coming to buy this afternoon.'

They were using a lot of Indian cotton now that the government had removed purchase tax from non-woollen materials and India had slashed the high tariffs they'd previously charged. Sam had decided to take full advantage and there were bales of cotton piled everywhere.

'Yes, this is the last one,' Mary Ellen said and snipped the cotton. 'Lily checked that pile before she went to lunch. If you'd like to check this last one, I can start pairing them with the jackets . . . lovely summer suits . . .'

'Let's have a look,' Sam said and took the skirt, examining the seams thoroughly and turning it inside out. 'Yes, it's perfect, but your stuff always is, Mary Ellen. You should be out to lunch now you've finished.'

'Yolande isn't back yet,' Mary Ellen said. 'I'll help you put the suits together and then I'll eat my sandwiches. I don't need to go anywhere – unless you'd like me to shop for you?'

'No, that's fine; I don't need any errands today. Let's get these suits on the rack. Thank goodness none of them ended up on the cabbage rail. I can't afford for the good material to be wasted too often.'

Mary Ellen thought Sam looked a bit worried and wondered why. They'd had plenty of work recently, some of it on spec but mostly orders for firms who came back to them time after time. The garments they made with their own label were stacked on the racks in the showroom, but those made for firms had to have their label sewn into them, and should something be spoiled by a crooked seam or a little cut in the material, the label then had to be cut out and the offending article placed on the cabbage rail. That didn't mean it was worthless, of course, because market traders bought their waste, but for far less money, sometimes less than cost price if the fault was very noticeable.

Mary Ellen often bought something off the cabbage rail for herself or Rose, but she bought it in a size larger and then unpicked it and made it up perfectly. Sometimes it just meant unpicking one bad seam and taking it in a little bit so the old stitches didn't show. That was the trouble with thin or delicate material of course, because if you unpicked it there were tiny holes left – unless like Mary Ellen, you completely re-shaped it. She'd suggested it to Sam a couple of times when an expensive article had been spoiled by bad seaming, but he'd shaken his head.

'We have to allow for some spoiled goods, Mary Ellen. I don't want to risk sending a faulty garment to one of my regular retailers. It could cost me far more than the loss of a dress.'

'We've had a few spoiled garments this week,' she said. 'I think it's that new girl, Sam. Twice I've caught her setting the machine up wrong, and she got her thread tangled this morning. Do you want me to take her off the machines until I have time to show her what we need?'

'I'm not too worried about a few mistakes,' Sam said and sighed. 'I may as well tell you, Mary Ellen. One of my best customers has complained that she was short of garments in her delivery . . .'

'How could that be?' Mary Ellen was puzzled, because Yolande checked the orders personally, and Herbie Clarke did the cutting and she always checked that they had the right amount of pieces before she gave them out to the machinists. 'I always check them right through to when they're put on the ordered goods rails ready for packing in boxes . . .'

'Yes, and Herbie ticks each one off his list when he packs them,' Sam said. 'It must happen either during the packing or after . . . before the boxes are taken out for delivery.'

'Do you trust Bert?' Bert Higgins was their delivery driver. He loaded the packed and sealed cardboard boxes into the small van they used and drove it to the various shops in the East End and also the West End of London; the few orders for outside London were sealed and then taken to the sorting office either by Bert or Sam himself.

'Bert has been with me since the beginning,' Sam said. 'Besides, he's as honest as the day is long. No, it has to be here, either in the workshops or the showroom . . .'

'I don't think any of the workshop girls take anything other than the offcuts. We all check that with Yolande,' Mary Ellen said. 'Anything we purchase in the showroom has to go through Mrs Baxter. Jilly bought a tweed suit yesterday, but it came off the cabbage rail . . .'

'Did you look at it properly?' Sam asked.

'She just showed me in the bag. I didn't take it out and look – why?'

'Two of those lilac tweed suits went missing. Pretty Patricia Modes were most upset that two of those suits were unaccounted for. They ordered fifty and got forty-eight and there was enough material to make fifty-five initially. Surely we didn't have that large a wastage?'

'Have you checked the cabbage rail?'

'They aren't there, but we sold two dozen garments from the rail yesterday afternoon . . .'

Mary Ellen frowned, because there was no way of knowing what had been sold from the cabbage rail. They were mostly priced between fifteen bob and a pound, to cover the cost of the material with perhaps a shilling or two profit, unless the garment was very badly damaged; they were just invoiced as damaged and not itemised.

'I didn't look through the rail yesterday, because I had that big order to get out for Hobbs,' she said. 'I'm sorry, Sam. I had no idea garments were going missing. What can I do?'

'You already do more than your fair share round here,' Sam said, 'but could you make it a rule to check the cabbage rail at least twice a day? Just in case some-thing perfect has been slipped on to the wrong rail by mistake . . .'

Or on purpose perhaps? Mary Ellen thought the

question was in Sam's mind as well as hers, and it was an uncomfortable thought. She'd believed all the girls in the machinists' room were honest; they were her friends and she enjoyed working with them. Yet if one of them was slipping perfect goods on to the cabbage rail in order to purchase something cheap herself – or to please one of their customers – then they were letting Sam down. No, she couldn't think Lily or Yolande or Jilly would be so dishonest, but Herbie and Bert and Mrs Baxter from the showroom were above suspicion. So that left one possibility, the new girl Anna, who had only recently been taken on as a seamstress.

Anna was the first to return after her lunch break. Mary Ellen watched her take her place behind her sewing machine and start stitching the bodice of a new line in silk blouses. Mary Ellen went to watch over her shoulder because the material was very fine and needed careful work, but Anna seemed to have learned her lessons and was having no trouble with the machine now.

One by one the girls returned to their work. Mary Ellen had a pile of cotton dresses to machine, but she found herself watching every time a girl went out of the room to take a toilet break and timing her. None of them exceeded the time they were allowed.

When everyone stopped for a mug of tea mid-afternoon, Mary Ellen took her mug and went through to the showroom. She checked the cabbage rail and made sure that everything was genuinely passed as faulty and then looked round the other rails to make sure that the missing lilac tweed suits had not been slipped in with their own label. Everything seemed in order and Mary Ellen turned to go back to her own bench, but just as she was on the point of leaving the showroom door opened and Mrs Baxter moved forward eagerly in order to greet their customer.

'How nice to see you, sir,' she said. 'We have some lovely suits with our own label fresh in today . . .'

'That's good,' he responded with a pleasant smile. Mary Ellen thought he looked nice, though obviously an older man, but well dressed and respectable. 'Yes, I do need some stock for the shops in the West End – but I should also like to see what you have on the cabbage rail please. My vendors sell your stuff well on the market, and I may take a larger than normal order today, if you can tempt me?'

'Yes, of course, sir. You know we always find you a few bargains . . .'

Mary Ellen frowned as she went through to the workshops. What did Mrs Baxter mean by a few bargains? It was true that some of the spoiled goods were almost perfect . . . She bit her lip, because she mustn't jump to conclusions. Sam would never believe the thief could be Mrs Baxter and in her heart Mary Ellen didn't either . . .

Mr Connolly owned fifteen market stalls in various parts of London. That morning Billy had been to Bermondsey to collect the money owed from three stalls in the market there. One was selling fresh vegetables; the second had a variety of second-hand bits and pieces, including some nice silver jewellery; and the third had a selection of suits, blouses, skirts and dresses. The first two just paid rent for their stalls but the clothing stall also sold stock belonging to Mr Connolly. Looking at the suits and skirts hanging on the rails, Billy thought he'd seen something similar at Mary Ellen's workplace, because their stuff had a bit of style about it and some of the garments looked too good to be sold on the market. He looked at a lovely lilac tweed suit, which he thought would suit Mary Ellen and inquired the price.

'That's three pounds ten bob, mate,' the stallholder, Joe, said. 'Cost yer double up the West End that would . . .'

'What's wrong with it?' Billy asked, because there always had to be something, given it was selling at half price on the market to what it would be in the shops.

'Nuthin' far as I can see,' the man replied. 'I reckon some of this cabbage stuff is fiddled, but I only sell it . . .'

'Yes, I know. I've come to collect Mr Connolly's money.'

'Yeah, I remember yer comin' wiv 'im,' the trader replied, looking sourly at Billy as he handed over a small bag of money. 'Be careful wiv that – and I want yer mark 'ere 'cos I ain't responsible if it goes astray.'

Billy looked inside the bag and saw the bundle of notes. 'How much do you reckon's here then?'

'Twenty quid . . . do you want to count it?'

'Nah, I'll take your word for it,' Billy said. 'If it doesn't tally I'll come back and knock your head off!'

The trader hesitated for a moment then scowled. 'All right, there's sixteen quid, ten shillings and thruppence halfpenny. Give us the book and I'll make the figure right . . .'

'Yeah, I think Mr Connolly would appreciate that; he doesn't take kindly to being cheated and neither do I . . .'

The market trader looked at him oddly, as if he didn't

know if Billy was for real. 'OK, mate, 'old yer 'air on, I was just testin' yer . . .'

'That's fine, just don't try it on again, right?'

'Nah, I'm straight, me. It ain't me yer want ter look out fer, mate.'

'What do you mean?'

'You're bloody honest Joe, ain't yer? Still wet behind the ears I reckon, but yer'll 'ave ter find out fer yerself. It's more than me life's worfth ter tell yer,' Joe said and grinned again. 'Just watch yer back that's all. Things ain't always the way they seem – and don't cross the old man, that's my advice.'

'Why should I want to cross Mr Connolly?' Billy asked. 'He's given me a good job and I'm grateful.'

'Yeah, I'll just bet you are,' Joe said. 'Well, good luck, mate. I wouldn't be in your shoes . . .'

Billy walked away feeling puzzled. He went into the gentlemen's conveniences at the edge of the market, entered a cubicle and counted the money. It was exactly what Joe had told him, which meant that he probably was honest – as honest as most traders. He'd tried to trick Billy, but maybe he *was* testing him. Some of the traders he'd visited had paid either rent or the previous day's takings without comment; one or two had been reluctant to part with the money, making out they weren't sure he had the authority to collect it, although Mr Connolly had been everywhere with him the first time. Maybe that was what Joe meant, and yet there had been an odd look in his eyes that puzzled Billy – and what did he mean about some of the stuff being fiddled?

Mr Connolly was an honest man, a rich, respectable man. He wouldn't have pinched stuff on his stalls, Billy was certain about that, because the last thing he wanted was to break the law and end up in prison like his brother, but Joe didn't get all his stuff through Mr Connolly so if he had some things he thought weren't honestly gained, they might have come from anywhere . . .

Feeling thoughtful, Billy tucked the money from Joe into the money belt he wore and left the toilets. He needed to visit three more markets that morning and he had to be back to escort Mr Connolly on a visit to the club that evening.

He was going to earn every penny of his generous wages, and it was a good thing Mary Ellen was too busy to expect him to take her out most nights, because he wouldn't have much time . . . but if he did well, he would have his own stall that he could work on Saturday mornings. He just had to decide what he wanted to sell, and he thought he might go in for cabbage; he could buy it from Sam, like others did . . . unless Mr Connolly insisted that he take stock from him exclusively.

Billy didn't much care one way or the other. He wouldn't even have thought of running his own stall if it hadn't been for his employer. The stalls themselves were difficult to get hold of, because most stayed in families and got passed down from father to son, just the way Ted Hastings' stalls would, except that he only had a daughter.

No, Billy wouldn't mind where his stock came from, as long as it was bought honest. He was pleased with his new job and the Saturday morning stall would just be an extra bonus. Soon he would have enough money put by to rent a place of his own, and once he had that Rose would have to admit that he was doing a steady job and perhaps Mary Ellen could persuade her to let them get married on her eighteenth birthday in September . . .

Mary Ellen was in the showroom when Billy entered that evening. She was surprised, because although he sometimes came to walk her home after work, he normally waited outside.

'What are you doin' here, Billy?' she asked.

'I wanted to have a look at the cabbage rail,' he said. 'I think I might sell clothes on the market when I get my stall, Mary Ellen. What sort of price are those suits? I saw something similar today but that was a lilac tweedy thing . . . very much like those on that rail . . .'

'They aren't cabbage,' Mary Ellen frowned. 'That's our own label stuff and we sell them for three pounds and five shillings.'

'The one I saw looked similar but the material was grey with lilac bits and the bloke was selling it for three pounds ten shillings.'

'Where did you see it?'

'On the market,' Billy looked at her. 'What's wrong?'

'We've had some of those lilac tweed suits go missing – about four I think. It was a special order we made for a firm with their own label and they expected fifty out of the material they ordered and bought, but when they got them there were only forty-eight. I've been checking and Yolande says we made fifty-two but we didn't do the fancy velvet collars on the extra two and they went on our own label rail; they aren't here now and they haven't been listed as sold . . .'

'Pinched you reckon?'

'Yes,' Mary Ellen looked over her shoulder. 'Keep

your voice down, Billy. Sam wants me to keep a check on the stock rails in future and that's why I stayed after Mrs Baxter left and decided to check – and I'm sure we've lost at least four suits in that material.'

'None of them went on the cabbage rail?'

'Yolande checked them all as perfect and so did I . . .' Mary Ellen bit her lip. 'We can't afford to lose stuff like that, Billy. It's worse that two of a customer's suits went missing, because Sam had to buy more cloth and we've made up the missing suits and sent them off, but if we're losing our own stuff too . . .'

'It's odd, but one of the market traders I spoke to today said there wasn't anything wrong with the suit he was selling. Do you think some of the suits were put on the cabbage rail by mistake? Could they have been sold to a market trader as cabbage?'

'Ah, still here, Mary Ellen?' Sam greeted them with an odd look instead of his usual beaming smile. 'How are you, Billy? Mary Ellen tells me you've started working for Mr Connolly – sort of his minder?'

'Yeah, I was lucky he gave me a job,' Billy said. 'Ellie was just tellin' me you've lost some stuff, Sam? I saw a suit that was similar to one you made selling on a stall in Bermondsey market for three pounds ten shillings. Didn't look as if there was anything wrong with it . . .'

'It could have been the lilac tweed, Sam,' Mary Ellen said. 'Yolande told me she'd made two suits out of the remainder of the cloth and put them on our rails, but they aren't here – and they aren't in Mrs Baxter's receipt books either . . .'

Sam nodded and looked grim. 'So we know for sure

that pilfering is going on,' he said, a flicker of anger in his voice. 'I hoped it was just a one-off mistake, but I'll be keepin' a sharp eye out in future . . .'

'I'll look every day,' Mary Ellen said. 'It's not right that any of our staff would cheat you – and I can't work out how they do it.'

'The stock must be switched to the cabbage rail somehow,' Sam said. 'Either one of the staff knows when someone is coming in and they do the switch when Mrs Baxter's back is turned, or—' He broke off, looking concerned.

'I'll keep an eye out when I'm on my rounds of the stalls,' Billy offered. 'I know what your stuff looks like, Sam, because Mary Ellen shows me sometimes and I've seen her wearing things.'

'We have to find a way to stop the pilfering,' Sam said. 'Can't think how though . . . Mind you, that's the least of my problems at the moment . . .'

'What's wrong, Sam?' Mary Ellen asked.

'It's nothing you can help with, Mary Ellen,' Sam said and broke off as someone walked in behind her. His mouth thinned and he looked angry. 'You'd better go. I've got some business to take care of . . .'

Billy and Mary Ellen looked at the man who'd walked in and then at each other, because it was Stevie Baker and they wondered what business he could possibly have with Sam.

'What yer, Billy,' Stevie said. 'Just leavin', were yer – only me and Sam have got private business . . .'

'You need any help, Sam?' Billy asked, lingering because he sensed things weren't right. 'If you want to stop the pilferin', why don't you put some mirrors up so you can see behind the rails? I'll come and help yer one evenin' if you like . . .'

Sam's face split in a smile of pleasure. 'You're a clever lad, Billy. I'll do as you've suggested. We'll have a stock take, Mary Ellen and I'll get some mirrors up – and I'll move the rails round – and now you two can get off. I'm going to stop here and sort things out a bit . . .'

'We could help if you want?' Mary Ellen offered and he shook his head.

'No, you've done extra today as it is. Get off, both of you. I know you don't get much time together – and I want to talk to this person in private.'

Again, Billy sensed something in Sam's manner. He was upset and angry for some reason. He took Mary Ellen's arm and steered her out of the showroom into the sewing room, closing the door behind them, but the sound of raised voices reached them.

'I'm not going to pay,' Sam was shouting angrily. 'If I gave in to you I might as well shut up shop – so you can run back to your boss and tell him to keep his fingers out of my business . . .'

Stevie replied in a quiet voice they couldn't hear properly but Mary Ellen thought he sounded menacing.

'Do you think Sam is all right?' she asked, looking anxious.

'He can handle himself,' Billy said. 'I wouldn't trust Stevie as far as I could throw him, but I don't think he could knock Sam down – he'll be all right, and he didn't want us there . . .'

'All right, I'll get my coat,' she said. 'But I don't like that friend of yours, Billy.'

'He ain't a friend, not really,' Billy said. 'Somethin' is

goin' on, I know that – but unless Sam wants to tell us we can't help him sort it out . . .'

Billy was thoughtful as he walked Mary Ellen home. He hoped he was mistaken, but it looked to him as if Sam was being threatened into paying protection money. It would be the reason behind the pilfering and if he refused to pay, that would only be the start of his problems . . . and Billy's, because he'd heard Stevie use a name and if he'd heard correctly that meant he too was in trouble. He remembered the market trader who'd told him he was wet behind the ears and wondered. Yet the police had treated Mr Connolly with respect . . .

Shaking his head, Billy dismissed his suspicions, because if his new boss was mixed up in a protection racket it probably meant that the rents and other money Billy had been collecting were really payments extorted from the market traders by force. And that made Billy feel sick to his guts . . .

CHAPTER 15

'Ah, Wendy,' Beatrice said as she entered the sick room. 'I'm glad I caught you before you left. Nancy told me that you've had three cases of chicken pox today. Did you have the doctor see them to make sure?'

'Yes, Sister Beatrice,' Wendy confirmed. 'I came to your office but Tilly told me you'd gone to the monthly Board meeting so I rang the doctor and he came out as soon as he could. Doctor Symonds confirmed that they are the latest victims. Apparently, there is quite an epidemic at the school the boys go to.'

'Exactly who has gone down with it?'

'Alfie Jones, his brother Freddie and Peter Jackson . . .'

'Ah yes, they are all in the same dorm,' Sister Beatrice said. 'Hopefully, we may contain it to those three, but let me know immediately if you get a fresh case please.'

'Yes, of course, Sister.'

'You have them in the isolation ward – and you gown up when you enter?' Beatrice looked round and saw that the only occupant of the sick ward was a girl called Margaret, who had recently suffered a nasty bout of tonsillitis and was almost recovered. 'Of course you couldn't put them in with Margaret. She is almost ready to return to the dorm I think?'

'I thought tomorrow,' Wendy said. 'I would've let her go this afternoon but she had a headache and I thought it better to keep her one more night to be sure. We don't want her to get the chicken pox.'

'No. I'll gown up and take a look at our sufferers,' Beatrice said and went to the cupboard for the necessary aprons and gloves, before going through to the isolation ward where the three sick boys were feeling very sorry for themselves.

After supplying them with cool drinks, taking their temperatures and observing them for a moment, she discarded her soiled apron and gloves. The last thing they needed was for the disease to spread to other children at the home, because many of the children here were the ones who needed more individual care before being sent on and they were the vulnerable ones, the children who might be at risk.

Satisfied that they were not particularly at risk at the moment, Beatrice returned to her office and sat down at her desk. She was about to pour herself a small sherry when someone knocked at the door and then Nancy walked in carrying a tray of tea and a plate of biscuits.

'How thoughtful of you, Nancy,' Beatrice said. 'Those biscuits look tempting – did you make them yourself?'

'Yes, I did,' Nancy admitted and laughed. 'Muriel was so busy she didn't have time to do much baking and I'd caught up with all my chores so I offered to do them. There are almond shortbread and some coconut ones too . . . I remembered you liked coconut . . .'

'It's such a treat to have biscuits like these instead of

those things out of a packet,' Beatrice said. 'For years we had to be grateful for whatever we could find. It's such a luxury now that the rationing is over . . .'

'Yes, very much so. I always take Terry a big bag of sweets when I visit him.'

'I'm sure you do,' Beatrice nodded, about to say more when someone knocked at the door.

'I'd better go,' Nancy said. 'I'll fetch the tray later.'

'Yes, thank you – Come in . . .'

She rose uncertainly to her feet as the door opened and a man entered. To her knowledge she'd never seen him before, and the suit he was wearing, while not exactly in rags, had certainly seen better days.

'Shall I stay, Sister?' Nancy asked, looking shocked.

Beatrice studied her visitor for a moment and then shook her head. 'I don't think this gentleman means me any harm, Nancy. You may leave.'

Nancy picked up her tray and went out, looking doubt-fully at the stranger as he opened the door for her to exit.

'To what do I owe this visit, sir?' Beatrice asked as he returned to stand in front of her desk.

'I came for a special reason, Sister Beatrice,' he said in a voice she recognised as cultured. Despite his appear-ance this man had been well educated. 'I mean no harm to you or anyone in this building . . .'

'Indeed?' Her gaze narrowed. 'Perhaps you will tell me your purpose in coming here at this hour?'

'I work all day,' he replied. 'I know you feel I've imposed by coming here without an invitation, but I couldn't be sure you would see me if I tried to make an appointment.'

'It is highly irregular. I'm not sure how you got in.'

'One of your children opened the door and let me enter when I rang the bell – and he kindly told me where your office could be found.'

'Did he now?' She fixed him with a hard stare. 'Perhaps you could tell me what you intend? I am rather busy.'

'And you wish me gone,' he said and smiled. 'I've come on behalf of a young friend of mine – Archie Miller. He wants to know where his sister has been taken so that he can visit her. I suppose you do know where she is?'

'I have managed to discover her whereabouts,' Beatrice frowned. 'If you know where Archie is, please ask him to come here to me. I need to see him and to know he is safe . . .'

'I assure you he is perfectly safe now, although he wasn't when I found him. I'm sorry, but I fear Archie doesn't trust you, Sister. He feels you betrayed him and if he knew I'd come here this evening he would think that was my intention too . . .'

'Who are you? What have you done with Archie? If you've harmed him . . . have him locked in somewhere for your own wicked purposes . . .'

'You wrong me, Sister. I found Archie on the streets and saved him from the kind of thing you suspect. I assure you that he has nothing to fear from me. My intention is to help him . . .'

'Then bring him here. I will do what I can to secure visiting rights, but June's foster parents may refuse if they think he would be a bad influence.'

'Will you tell me where the child has been taken?'

'I am not at liberty to give privileged information to

210

someone I don't know . . .' Her eyes went over him, conveying her disapproval in a way she stopped short of speaking.

'Someone like me, I think you meant to say,' he spoke calmly with a smile on his lips. 'Well, you have the right to think it, Sister, though you are wrong. My appearance is not what it once was, but my integrity remains and if you were willing to trust me I might be able to help both Archie and you – if, as you claim, you did not approve of the way the child was taken into custody without your knowledge or consent . . .'

'And who are you to make such claims? How do you know so much?'

'I am no one,' he smiled. 'Once I was someone you would have approved of, Sister, but misfortune brought me to the place I stand now. Will you not trust in my intentions, if not my person?'

Beatrice hesitated; there was something about him that seemed to say he might be trusted, but she could not go by her instincts in such a case. Archie was a vulnerable child and should be in her care.

'I cannot give you the information you seek,' she said. 'Even if I did trust you, it would be highly improper for me to tell you anything about the child's foster parents. I will ask you again to bring the boy to me and leave him in my hands. I shall do all that I can to reunite the children . . .'

'I fear Archie would run away again and then he would be vulnerable for he would no longer trust me,' he said. 'Forgive me, Sister. I should not have presumed on your time or your good nature . . .'

Beatrice watched in frustration as he turned and

walked to the door. 'I don't even know your name or what you do,' she protested. 'How can you expect me to trust you when you haven't even told me . . . ?' She was talking to herself as the door closed behind him.

Sitting down sharply, Beatrice's hands trembled as she reached for the teapot and poured the golden liquid into a cup. She felt sick and shaken and filled with self-doubt. The man had come to her and despite his appearance she believed he was honest and to be trusted, so why hadn't she? She wished she'd acted or spoken differently, but what else could she have done? The information he'd asked for was privileged and she did not have the authority to release it to a man she'd never seen before. Yet she had the feeling that she'd missed an opportunity to help Archie and make sure of his safety. She should have found a way to negotiate with the man . . . a man she sensed had not always been a man of the streets, but someone she might have looked up to.

Getting to her feet, she left her office and on the spur of the moment went to the head of the stairs, but the front door had just closed behind him, and even if she ran after him and caught him, what could she say that would make him see things her way?

Returning to her office, Beatrice went to her metal filing cabinet, unlocked it and took out the details she had concerning the Baileys' fostering of June Miller. She read them through, frowning as her sense of unease increased. Something about these people worried her, but she couldn't quite place it – had she seen their photograph somewhere, read something about them in a newspaper?

It was no use, she could not place the source of her unease, but there was something – it was the man's eyes. She was almost certain she'd spoken to him at some time in the past and yet the name didn't sound familiar . . . and yet alarm bells had begun to ring in her head and she had the strangest feeling that June might be in terrible danger.

Perhaps she should ring Miss Sampson in the morning, ask who had recommended the Baileys as foster parents and whether all the necessary checks had been done. She thought the checks might have been skimmed over, because it had all happened so quickly – as if they'd wanted to get the child fostered at any cost.

She decided that she would telephone Miss Sampson the next day and raise her concerns, though the woman would probably accuse her of making waves for no good reason – but in all her years dealing with abused children, Beatrice had always trusted her gut instinct and it was telling her now that a terrible mistake had been made . . .

Archie looked up as Ikey entered the room they were sharing at the hostel with six other vagrants. He'd been anxious because Ikey had been gone a long time and he didn't fancy sleeping in a room with these men if his friend wasn't here to protect him. The incident under the arches had made him nervous of men like these, even though he knew that most of them were all right; they greeted him with a smile and seemed friendly enough when Ikey was around, but Archie couldn't quite conquer his fear that one of them might attack him again.

'You're late,' he said half-accusingly as Ikey sat down

on the bed next to him. 'I thought something might have happened to you?'

'Thank you for caring,' Ikey said. 'I went to see Sister Beatrice and ask if she would let us have June's address but she rightly says she can't – so I'll have to go in at night and find it.'

'You didn't tell her where to find me?'

'Certainly not. I think she means well, lad, but her hands are tied. I'd hoped she might see sense, but no joy – so I'll have to resort to other means . . .'

'I know how we can get in,' Archie said. 'At least I can – and I could unlock the back door for you . . .'

'I was thinking of going on my own. I don't want you to get caught. It doesn't matter about me, but you would end up in a remand home and that's the last thing we need.'

'We can be careful. The window I got in last time isn't big enough for you. Unless I squeeze through and let you in, you'd have to break a bigger window or force the lock and there's mostly someone about at night – a nurse or a carer or Sister herself.'

Ikey was silent for a moment, clearly thoughtful. 'You realise that we're preparing to commit a criminal act?'

'It's her fault for lettin' them take my sister away. She lied to me and I trusted her – but she's like all the rest . . . those fools that put my ma in prison and that man who shut me in a cupboard. They talk about what's right and proper but they don't treat people fair.'

'No, Archie, they don't,' Ikey said. 'I've been on the receiving end of the kind of injustice you're talking about, lad, and I didn't like it any more than you do. I'm going to help you get your sister's address and we'll go and see her. It depends on what we find whether or not we can do more – and I'm going to visit your mother myself after we've paid your sister a little visit . . .'

'Is it because you had bad things happen to you?' Archie asked in a hoarse voice. 'Is that why you're helping me?'

'Yes, partly,' Ikey said and smiled, 'but I like you, lad. You're a plucky young 'un and I think you deserve a break . . . I'll be talking to a friend of mine that may be able to help us – but I'm not promising I can make everything right, Archie. We'll find June, talk to her and see how she feels about her foster home – and then we'll see what we can do . . .'

Archie's throat felt tight and tears stung behind his eyes. Until Ikey dragged the tramp off him, he'd been feeling desperate, at the end of his tether, hating the world and almost everyone in it – even his mother sometimes for leaving him and June. Ikey reminded him of his father. There was something about him that made him think he was a decent man, honest and straightforward. He wondered what had happened in Ikey's life to put him on the streets. Ikey worked hard on the Docks in the wood yard there, hard physical labour, and he seemed to enjoy it, but Archie was sure it wasn't what he'd done before whatever had happened to bring him down. He was curious but he wouldn't ask, because it was Ikey's business and he didn't have the right to poke his nose in. He just felt grateful that Ikey was around when he needed him . . .

Ruby looked up startled as Sister Beatrice entered her office. It was the first time the nun had sought her out in her office and relations had been strained between them since the incident over June Miller. She was pretty certain that if Sister Beatrice had the opportunity she would have put her out on the street without a reference.

She rose to her feet uncertainly. 'Yes, what can I do for you, Sister?'

'I have spoken to Miss Sampson and she told me that you recommended the Baileys as foster parents. I wanted to know about the people you thought suitable to be June Miller's foster parents. How well do you know them?'

'Why?'

Ruby felt a trickle of unease. Had something happened to the child?

'Because I have a feeling I've seen the man before – but he wasn't going under the name of Bailey at the time . . .'

'They made inquiries about taking one of our girls, but they're here for punishment and there was no question of it – I gave their details to Miss Sampson and everything was properly checked. Why do you ask? What are you implying? I know you're angry because I forgot to tell you about the Miller fostering, but . . . this is rather petty . . .'

'My feelings over the matter have nothing to do with this. I think something may not be quite right about them . . .'

'Like what?' Ruby's hackles rose. 'Are you suggesting I did something wrong deliberately?'

'Did you?'

'No, I did not!' Ruby was indignant. 'What reason do you have for your suspicions?'

'I'm not sure,' Sister Beatrice replied. 'I just have an odd feeling . . . it may be my conscience, because of the way the children were deceived, but I did not approve of your actions in this matter, and Miss Sampson was very high-handed in her manner when she collected the girl.'

Ruby remembered Miss Sampson's comments regarding the nun and her sense of unease deepened. 'Well, I suppose she has to be firm, considering some of the cases she deals with; the mothers and fathers are often common and abusive in their language and manner when children are removed into care . . .'

'That did not apply in this case. Besides, I think this case should be reviewed and further checks made on the foster parents chosen.' Sister Beatrice looked angry and Ruby went cold all over, just as though someone had walked over her grave. 'I think I should inform you that I have consulted a lawyer over this business and he considers that I may very well have cause to overturn the decision. I shall not hesitate to do so if that is the case – and I should warn you that I shall not stand by and let you interfere in the same way again. Good morning, Miss Saunders.'

Ruby watched as the nun turned and walked out, leaving her feeling distinctly anxious. She felt a prickling sensation at her nape, because it was odd that Sister Beatrice should say she was uneasy. Ruby had wondered a couple of times if she'd done the right thing. Had her zeal to protect the girl from a feckless mother and a woman she'd thought too soft made her reckless? After all, what did she know of June Miller's foster parents apart from the fact that he ran a grocer's business and helped run a youth club in the evenings?

217

Ruby's own childhood and young adulthood had been far from happy and she'd decided to devote her life to this job, because she understood how easy it was for a girl to go wrong. Ruby had been in trouble with the law herself at one stage of her life, but she'd been lucky enough to be put on probation and her officer had been a woman she admired. She'd helped her to conquer her hatred of her uncle and to face the future. It was because of Francine that she'd gone on to pass her exams and now had this job. She'd wanted to be like her, but at the back of her mind the horror of her life at home still lingered and perhaps it was that that had made her act so rashly. Or perhaps it was just that she'd hoped Ruth Sampson might notice her and think of her as more than a colleague – and that part of it had failed, because if anything Ruth had been more formal in her speech since then. She'd actually reprimanded Ruby for failing to keep Sister Beatrice informed.

Supposing Ruby had been wrong to recommend that June was fostered by the Baileys? No, it was just that silly old trout making waves, she told herself stoutly, and yet she couldn't quite get rid of the niggling doubts that had crept into her mind . . .

CHAPTER 16

Rose looked at herself in the mirror, straightening her uniform before leaving the nurses' rest room. There were dark shadows beneath her eyes, because she hadn't been sleeping well recently. It was her own fault for being such a fool over Mike Bonner. He wasn't worth her tears because all he'd wanted was a brief affair and when she'd refused he'd dropped her.

'Nurse O'Hanran . . .' Hearing his voice in the corridor behind her, she hesitated, a tingle of anticipation running through her as she waited for him to catch up to her. 'You've been avoiding me, Rose,' he said in a teasing voice. 'I was hoping we might have a nice weekend away somewhere at the sea – are you on duty this weekend?'

Rose felt her pulse quicken and her knees seemed suddenly as if they'd turned to jelly. A part of Rose longed to say that she was free, and would love the chance of a weekend at the sea with him, but her natural caution held her back.

'Sorry, I'm working Saturday night,' she managed to say, even though she knew she could have changed with one of the other nurses.

'Surely you could change duty for once?' Mike asked, looking annoyed. 'It isn't often I get a chance to go right away for a couple of days and I like company.'

Rose took a deep breath, because there was only one way to end the torture she'd been putting herself through. 'I'm sure you have plenty of other strings to your bow,' she said. 'Why don't you ask Nurse Simmons? Excuse me please; I'm due on the ward . . .'

Rose could feel his eyes on her as she walked away and she felt sick. In his position Mike could make things awkward for her, even though she knew she was a good nurse. She wasn't sure what had prompted her to cut at him like that, but it was surely best to finish it for good. Mike Bonner wasn't the sort of man who would marry a girl like her; he came from a different class and if he married he'd choose a girl with money and background. He was merely fooling around with girls who were daft enough to fall for his charm and his good looks, with no thought of marriage or settling down. Rose was ashamed that she'd been one of those foolish girls, but she wasn't going to spend the rest of her life feeling the way she had when Mike had just ignored her for weeks on end. No, it was better to end it now, even if she might have to change her job.

It was a lovely sunny afternoon when Rose finished her shift. She didn't feel like going straight home and decided to have a look round the market; perhaps she would buy herself something new to wear. She hadn't splashed out for ages, because Mary Ellen made her quite a few things, which were always smart – but Rose felt in the mood to indulge. Since Marion had come to lodge with them, she'd had more money in her purse, money she didn't have to spend on food or rent or paying the bills. When she thought of all the years she'd spent saving and scrimping to put herself through her training and provide a few treats for her sister, she considered herself lucky these days.

After browsing the market stalls for a while Rose decided to try a small dress shop on Commercial Street. The busy street was thronged with shoppers, noisy with passing traffic that passed up and down the wide thoroughfare, the air heavy with the odours of exhaust fumes, horse manure that a pair of shire horses pulling a dray cart had left, and spices from a grocer's shop. Some of the best shops in Spitalfields were here. She saw the lilac tweed suit immediately she stepped inside the dress shop and knew that it was her size and a style she liked. Looking inside the jacket, she saw it bore the label of Mary Ellen's firm and smiled, because it was priced at four pounds and ten shillings. She could just about afford it, and she took it into the changing cubicle to try it on. The mirror told her that it looked really good on her and she decided to buy it. No doubt Mary Ellen would say she could have made it cheaper, but just for once Rose wanted to buy something from a shop rather than the market or cabbage from Sam's workshops.

She paid her money and went back out into the sunshine, feeling pleased with herself. Not knowing why, she turned her steps in the direction of St Saviour's. She would see if Sister Beatrice had time for a chat, because she'd once mentioned to Rose that she might welcome her there if she ever felt like changing her job . . .

*

'Rose, are you there?' Mary Ellen called out as she let herself into the flat and dumped her shopping on the kitchen table. 'I bought the stuff you asked me to get . . . cheese and bread and some ham and tomatoes. I fancy a ham sandwich, what about you?'

'Yes, but I'd like some mustard in mine,' Rose said and came out of the bedroom wearing the new suit she'd purchased that afternoon. 'What do you think?'

'It looks lovely on you,' Mary Ellen said and then frowned, moving closer to look at it properly. 'Where did you buy it?'

'A shop called Polly Anne Fashions on Commercial Street,' Rose said. 'I know it's one of yours but I fancied it so I bought it . . . and it wasn't expensive really.'

'How much did they charge you?'

'Four pounds ten shillings,' Rose said. 'I thought it might be more and I shouldn't have bought it if it had been . . .'

'It ought to retail at over seven pounds,' Mary Ellen said. 'It's our own label and that tweed is good material – unless it has a cut label, of course?'

'No, it isn't cabbage,' Rose said. 'If I'd wanted that I should have gone to the market. I fancied something posh for a change . . . I know you make me lovely things, Mary Ellen, but I was feeling fed up and wanted to splash out.'

'It's up to you where you buy your clothes,' Mary Ellen said. She could've told her sister that she'd made the suit herself. It wasn't one that had gone missing from their client's box, but one of the two made from the extra material without the velvet collar that made the Pretty Patricia Modes version so stylish. It was still stolen goods and the sight of her sister wearing it and looking so pleased with herself made her feel sick to her stomach. 'If I were you I should return it and ask for your money back – tell them you didn't like it after all . . .'

'That's mean of you,' Rose said, looking cross. 'I don't often spend money on myself. I don't know why you would grudge it to me.'

'Of course I don't,' Mary Ellen said. 'That suit is one of four that were stolen from Sam's workshops. I didn't think you'd want to wear something that was stolen goods.'

Rose looked horrified. 'Pinched? How can you know that? I can show you the label; it hasn't been cut out or nicked to show its cabbage . . .'

'We made two like this one,' Mary Ellen told her, 'and several with velvet collars. The ones with velvet collars were meant for a special customer and had their label in the jacket but two were missing when the box arrived at the client's premises, and when I checked the two own label suits had gone as well, but they hadn't been listed as being sold.'

'Surely, that can't be right,' Rose said, not wanting to admit that the suit was stolen goods. 'This came from a respectable shop on Commercial Street. If I'd bought it from the market, I might have accepted it was stolen – but I'm sure they wouldn't steal . . .'

'I shall tell Sam about it in the morning,' Mary Ellen said. 'You can't keep it, Rose. Sam will go to the shop and ask where they bought it, but you should return it and get your money refunded.'

Rose glared at her, obviously reluctant to return the

suit she'd been so pleased with. 'How can you be sure it was stolen? It might be one that was bought and paid for in the proper way.'

'There were only two in this material,' Mary Ellen said. 'It's what we do when we have extra material left over from a special order. We make them look different, in this case a different shaped jacket and a collar made from the same material rather than velvet lapels . . . but they weren't part of a full range. Sam thought they were too good to go on the cabbage rail and so they went out on the rail with our own label and there's no record of the suits being sold. You can't keep it, Rose.'

'Oh, all right,' Rose was clearly annoyed. 'I'll take it back tomorrow.'

'Don't tell them it's because it was stolen. Sam will need to see it on the rails if he's to ask where it came from . . .'

'Why don't you take it with you tomorrow, give him my receipt and ask him to deal with it?' Rose snapped. 'But whatever happens, I want my money back or the suit.'

'All right, put it in their bag and I'll show it to Sam in the morning . . .'

Rose went off to the bedroom in a temper and Mary Ellen sighed. She knew her sister was upset over the incident but she'd had to speak up, because she couldn't let her walk round in a suit that had been stolen . . .

'I know that shop,' Sam said when Mary Ellen showed him the suit and the receipt Rose had reluctantly handed over. 'I'm surprised they would buy stolen stuff. They've bought from us in the past. I'd better check with Mrs

Baxter that she didn't sell them those suits and forget to put the sale down in the book . . .'

Mary Ellen nodded, biting her lip as she asked what he meant to do about the suit. Sam hesitated, frowning, 'Let me speak to Mrs Baxter about the missing suits and then I'll decide.'

Mary Ellen got on with her work, feeling uncomfortable as she remembered Rose's disappointment over her suit. She hadn't liked telling her that it was stolen, but it wasn't right that stuff was disappearing from the showroom.

She worked on machining a new line of dresses they were making for one of their regular customers and was just sewing the labels in when Sam came back carrying the bag containing Rose's suit.

'Mrs Baxter assures me she did not sell these suits,' Sam told her. 'She does vaguely remembering seeing them on the rail when you put them out but she hadn't realised they were gone.'

'So they were stolen, just as you thought . . . but who took them?'

'That's what I'd like to know. We've only had regular customers here in the last few days – no strangers . . .'

'So it has to be someone we know.' Mary Ellen felt sick. 'That makes it even worse, Sam. Are you going to take the suit to the shop and ask them where they got it?'

'No, because the sales girls wouldn't know where it had been bought; the stock will be given to them already priced up, all they have to do is sell it. I know the man who owns that shop, so I'll have a word with him about it . . . and you can give the suit back to Rose.'

Mary Ellen nodded. 'What do you want Rose to do? Should she take it back to the shop?'

'It's up to her, Mary Ellen. Your sister bought the suit in good faith so I shan't mind if she decides to keep it. I have to be very careful about this, you see, I can't just charge in and accuse a good customer of stealing. I have to make discreet inquiries . . . What we really need is to catch them in the act . . .'

'You've improved the visibility in the showroom,' Mary Ellen said. 'Mrs Baxter will be able to see what's going on behind her back . . . all those mirrors should make a thief think twice before stealing from you again, Sam.'

'Once a thief always a thief,' Sam said. 'If I stop the pilfering they may decide to break in. Trouble is I'm not a young man these days and neither is Bert. We could do with a bit of muscle about the place . . .'

Mary Ellen decided to pop home in her lunch break and leave the suit in Rose's bedroom with a note. If Sam didn't object to her keeping the suit it was really up to Rose what she did with it.

When Mary Ellen got home that evening Rose was standing at the sink peeling potatoes. Rose gave her a cross look and said, 'I took that suit back and told them I'd changed my mind. They were a bit sniffy about returning my money, but I got it in the end. One thing is certain, I shan't go there again.'

'You could've kept it, Rose. Sam didn't mind . . .'

'You spoiled it for me,' Rose retorted. 'I should have been conscious that it was stolen every time I wore it.'

Rose obviously wasn't going to forgive her lightly, but what else could she have done? Mary Ellen would've hated it if Sam had seen her wearing the suit and thought that she, Mary Ellen, was the thief.

'I'm sorry, but Sam's been losing quite a bit of stuff and we need to find out who is behind it . . .'

'If you ask me that Mrs Baxter is involved,' Rose sniffed. 'I've never liked her – she thinks she's above the rest of us with her airs and graces. If I were your boss, I should get myself a new manager to take care of things in that showroom.'

Mary Ellen was silent as she helped Rose to cook their tea and then did some tidying before settling down with her books. It was awful, having to suspect the people you worked with of stealing . . . and know that some of them were probably thinking it was you.

Mary Ellen thought about what Billy had said about seeing a lilac tweed suit on the market – was that where the other one had gone? He'd promised to keep an eye out on the markets for stuff that might have been pinched, and she was going to be vigilant at work, so perhaps they would discover who the villain was before long . . .

CHAPTER 17

'Shine the torch over here,' Ikey said softly as he examined the metal cabinet of drawers. 'Not locked – that's a bit of luck. She must trust her staff not to lock her files . . .'

'Sister Beatrice wouldn't think anyone would break in,' Archie said, feeling guilty at what they were doing, but Ikey had tried asking Sister for the information they needed, so it was her fault. 'Are they what you're looking for?' he asked as Ikey took an armful of files out and quickly went through them.

'Yes, this is it,' Ikey said and placed a file on the desk, before replacing the others in the drawer without looking inside them. He opened the relevant file and shone the torch on the first page. Archie saw that there were only a few pages and Ikey took his time reading them, which made Archie nervous. He kept listening, waiting for someone to throw open the door and demand to know what was going on.

Ikey took the top page, folded it and slipped it inside his jacket and then returned the file to its original place and closed the cabinet.

'Come on, let's go,' he said and switched off the torch.

Everything was quiet as he led the way along the landing, which had only one shaded light, and down the stairs. Archie heard the quiet murmur of voices from inside the sick room and then, as they walked down the stairs, a door opened and Sister Beatrice's voice could be clearly heard.

'It's a good thing you called me, Wendy. Dick has a nasty rash and I think we should have the doctor out to him. It isn't chicken pox, I'm fairly certain of that, so we'll be on the safe side . . .'

Ikey pulled Archie into the shadows of the hall as a light flicked on upstairs. They waited until they heard the door of Sister's office open and shut and then made their way swiftly to the scullery. Ikey went out of the back door and Archie locked it and then scrambled back out of the window that he'd entered through earlier.

Ikey took hold of his body and helped him down. He looked serious as they both scaled the side gate but he didn't speak until they were in the street and away from St Saviour's.

'Don't think that I approve of what we did this evening,' he said as they strode away. 'It was wrong, Archie, and we stole what didn't belong to us – but in this case I believe we had good cause. I want you to promise me that you won't make a habit of breaking into places.'

'I promise,' Archie said. 'When I did it the first time, I just wanted to talk to Sister and if she'd told us where June had gone we wouldn't have gone there tonight . . .'

'Yes, but even a good reason doesn't excuse what we did,' Ikey said. 'I did it only because your sister may not be in safe hands.'

'What do you mean?'

Ikey shook his head. 'It's just a feeling, a sixth sense – but I picked something up from Sister Beatrice when I spoke to her. She didn't actually put her concern into words, but I believe she is anxious about your sister, Archie. I think a woman like that has a great deal of experience and if she is uneasy about June's fostering then I believe we were justified in what we did – though she would undoubtedly be angry with us if she knew . . .' He was thoughtful, then, 'I'm going to show these details to someone I know and find out a bit more about Mr and Mrs Bailey.'

'We only just got away with it,' Archie said and frowned. 'You found their address – the people who've got June?'

'Yes, it was on the top of the file, almost as if it were waiting for us to find . . .'

'Where do they live?'

'It's a quiet place just outside Cambridge,' Ikey said. 'I went there once or twice some years back on business. We can take a train to Cambridge and then we'll have to get a bus . . . and walk some of the way I expect. Unless I can borrow a car from someone . . . that would be best, of course,' Ikey mused.

'Can you drive?' Archie asked, looking at him in surprise.

'Yes, but unfortunately my driving licence ran out a while back and I didn't renew it . . . but we mustn't allow such small things to put us off, must we?'

'You won't 'alf be in trouble if they catch you,' Archie said in some awe. 'Are you goin' to pinch a car too?'

'No, I don't think I need to be quite that desperate,'

Ikey said with a slight smile. 'I have a very good friend who will loan me his modest vehicle . . . and we shall trust to our luck that my driving will not draw the attention of the law . . .'

Beatrice frowned as she looked at her filing cabinet. Had she left the top drawer slightly open? She could not remember when she'd last been to it and pulled it out, flicking through the files inside. Everything was in its usual place and none of the files was missing. She closed the drawer properly but dismissed the small matter as she reached for her phone. She did not like disturbing the doctor at this hour, but she really needed a second opinion, because she hoped her own was wrong. Dick's rash might be nothing, of course, but it could be meningitis and that was a terrible disease for a young child. If not treated quickly it might result in all kinds of complications, and even if they were able to treat the child, he could still die.

Reaching for the phone, Beatrice prayed that she was wrong. Meningitis was a killer and she hoped the child she'd just examined just had some kind of a skin rash rather than the horrible disease that might lead in the worst cases to amputation of limbs or even death . . .

Every child that came to them was precious. Perhaps it was the tragic loss of her own child many years ago that had made her so determined not to lose any of her charges to illness or any other cause. Replacing the receiver after asking a very tired and slightly grumpy doctor to attend her patient, Beatrice frowned and returned to her file cabinet, opening the top drawer once more. She took out the file on June Miller and instantly saw that the letter she'd placed on top had gone. Closing the file with a grim little nod of satisfaction, she made no attempt to search for the missing letter. Beatrice was sure that she knew exactly where it was, and although it was quite disgraceful that it had been taken, she could not help feeling that in this case it might serve her purpose very well . . . She had a suspicion that the man who called himself Ikey and apparently had no fixed abode was someone – or something – very different. She'd met his kind before and her sixth sense told her that Ikey had his own reasons for championing Archie's cause . . .

Archie turned his head to look at the man driving the disreputable old Ford car they had borrowed from one of Ikey's friends. It made occasional popping noises every now and then and it rattled whenever they went over a bump in the road. Archie wasn't sure it was safe to be on the road, but he didn't care because it was exciting to be driven in any car. If you didn't count that awful time at Halfpenny House, it was his first time out of London, apart from one visit to Southend by train when his father was alive, he found the experience fascinating and watched avidly as the scenery changed and they left the dirty, smoky buildings of London behind and passed through smaller towns and villages, sometimes spending long periods on country roads with hardly anything but fields and the occasional barn to be seen.

'Are we lost?' he asked as Ikey pulled into a layby on the side of the road.

'No. We're not far from our destination now,' Ikey said. 'We'll take a break for a sandwich and have a talk about what we need to do when we get there . . .'

Archie opened the packet of sandwiches wrapped in greaseproof paper and bit into one. It was cheese and shop-bought pickle, and he ate hungrily.

'This is good,' he said, 'but not as good as the piccalilli my mum used to make . . .'

Ikey nodded and munched in silence for a while, then took out a flask and poured tea into two mugs, offering one to Archie.

'It's like a picnic,' Archie said, but his smile disappeared as Ikey spoke.

'You have to realise that they may not let us see June, Archie. We don't have an appointment, but I doubt if they would have let us visit her even if I'd written an official letter.'

'I'll see her somehow,' Archie said. 'I have to know she's all right so I can tell Mum when I visit her.'

'That's another thing,' Ikey said. 'I've made inquiries about visiting and they don't permit youngsters into the prison, but I've asked for a visiting order to see your mum and I'll take anything you want in with me . . . sweets, letters . . .'

Archie scowled. 'I'm not a kid. I've left school and I can work.'

'I know that but according to the law you should be at school for another two years, and you're considered a minor when it comes to prison visits,' Ikey said. 'However, you can't win even if you kick against it. What we've got to try and do is prove your mum isn't a thief, Archie, and then we can get her out – but that's for another day. Today we're here for June, to see if she's happy or – not . . .'

'What do we do if she isn't?' Archie asked. 'I know

233

June. She isn't easy to please, but whatever she is, I care what happens to her.'

'Yes, I know, that is why we're here,' Ikey nodded grimly. 'Let me do the talking at first, Archie. I'll tell them we've come from the Children's Department and have a permit to see June . . .'

'What do we do if they ask you to show them the permit?'

'I thought of that,' Ikey said. 'Keep quiet until we get to see her and leave everything to me. It's important that you don't do anything to arouse their suspicions or they'll just slam the door in our faces.'

'Is that why you're wearing that suit?'

Ikey had come dressed in a navy-blue pinstripe suit that looked to be a few years out of fashion but was made of good cloth and fitted him well, except that the waist on the trousers was a bit big and had to be pulled in tight with a leather belt; his shirt and tie looked respectable, as did the polished black leather shoes, and he was carrying a briefcase, which he'd put in the back of the car.

'Yes, I was loaned it for the occasion,' Ikey said. 'I look as if I might work in a council office, don't I? Respectable but not highly paid . . .'

'Yeah,' Archie said and grinned. 'You scrub up all right, Ikey.'

'Ah yes, my name is Mr Malvern for the purposes of our business today, Archie. Don't forget. I'm a probation officer and you're in my care and on an official visit to your sister. I'm not your friend and you probably resent me a bit – do you think you can manage that?'

'Yeah, I reckon,' Archie said. 'I'll think about that

rotten woman who took June away.' He scowled and Ikey laughed and nodded.

'Just right, but don't overdo it,' he said. 'We don't want to frighten them off . . .'

He brushed his hands, put the sandwiches away and switched the engine on again. It spluttered for a moment and Archie thought it wasn't going to start, but then the engine made a coughing sound and came to life.

The scenery once they left Cambridge behind was mostly fields and a few houses straggling along the sides of the road, with farm buildings on the horizon and what was left of an ancient windmill, its sails broken and hanging limply despite the breeze. When Ikey turned off the main road they passed a row of houses and came into a village with a sign proclaiming it to be Waterbeach, but there was no sign of a beach or any water, just a bit of a green surrounded by a few shops and houses, with roads and lanes leading off. Ikey seemed to know exactly where he was going and turned off into a small lane that had houses on one side faced with trees and fields. The semi-detached houses were flanked by a hedge, a dyke and then more trees and beyond that farmland and a barn.

'Number 19,' Ikey said and pulled up a couple of places back on the opposite side of the road. 'It's the house at the very end . . .'

Archie looked and saw a yellow-brick house with one window downstairs, a door and a glass panel, two windows upstairs; it was set back with a small garden, a lawn and a flower bed at one side, bushes and a wooden garage to the left side. A newish-looking Morris car sat on the drive in front. Somehow, its very ordinary look

235

was disconcerting. Archie had expected something different, a bigger house perhaps, though he wasn't sure why. He was fearful as Ikey got out of the car and took his briefcase from the back, signalling him to follow him.

Archie's stomach clenched with apprehension. Supposing June was happy here and liked her foster parents? Ikey would think he'd made a fuss over nothing, and his mum would be upset – and angry because he'd let his sister be taken away from them.

He lagged behind Ikey, feeling nervous, and had no difficulty in feigning unease as the door opened in answer to Ikey's knock. It was opened by a plain-looking woman in a print frock and apron, wearing velvet slippers on her feet and no make-up.

'Mrs Bailey? I am Nathaniel Malvern and I'm a colleague of Miss Ruth Sampson . . . Welfare Department?' He tipped his hat to her as she looked puzzled. 'You got my letter requesting a visit to June Miller of course . . .'

'Letter?' The woman shook her head. 'I'm sorry, I'm not Mrs Bailey. I'm her charwoman. I come in most days to cook and clean when she's at school . . . She didn't say nuthin' to me about a visit from the Social.'

'We've come down especially from London,' Ikey said and opened his briefcase, taking out a sheaf of papers. 'We have the right to see this boy's sister. Mrs Bailey must have been told that we would need to make inspections until we're quite satisfied that June is being properly looked after – and any attempt to stop us may result in the girl being taken away. I suppose she is here today?'

'Yes, 'cos she's off school with a cold,' the woman said. 'She's always off with somethin' if you ask me.

You'd better come through to the sitting room then . . . though I don't know what Mrs Bailey will say, and I don't hold with things like this . . .' She sniffed and stood back, allowing them to enter and directed them to the back room. 'I've got things to do; I ain't paid to stand around and watch you.'

'Yes, please get on with your work, ma'am – what was your name?'

'Mrs Jelly . . .' The woman shot a look at Archie and went off upstairs grumbling away to herself and scowling.

'That's a bit of luck,' Ikey said but Archie was already ahead of him and in the back room. It was square and furnished with old-fashioned stuff, a bit scruffy and not at all what he'd imagined. His sister was standing looking at the window and as soon as he saw her, Archie knew he'd been right to come; there was something defeated in her stance and, as she turned with a look of fright in her eyes, he felt a surge of anger against the people who had done this to his June.

'Archie?' She stared at him in disbelief, bursting into tears as she ran to him, clutching at him and sobbing as his arms closed around her. 'Have you come to take me away? Please take me away from them, please . . . I hate it here . . . I hate them both but him worse . . .'

'What have they done to you, June?' Archie asked but she shook her head, her face buried in his chest as she wept and mumbled something about it being horrible and wanting her mother. 'Look at me,' he insisted and turned her chin up so that he could see her eyes. 'Tell me what happened, June? Have they hurt you . . . hit you or beaten you?'

She nodded her head, her cheeks red. 'Not beaten . . .'

'What then? You can tell me, love . . .'

June looked beyond him to Ikey and shrank against Archie. 'Don't let him touch me. Don't let them do it again . . . it hurts and I hate it. I won't stay here, I won't . . .'

'Ikey is my friend,' Archie said. 'He won't hurt you; he's here to help us, June. What do you mean it hurts? Tell me . . .'

Her cheeks were flaming and she shook her head. 'It's dirty . . .' she whispered so that only he could hear. 'What he makes me do and she says I've got to please him . . . she holds me down sometimes if I struggle . . .'

'Did he touch you, interfere with you . . . under your knickers?' Archie said, because it was obvious June didn't know how to put what had happened to her into words. She nodded, lowering her voice to a whisper he could hardly hear.

'He comes when I'm in bed and pulls the sheets down and lifts my nighty and he does things . . . sometimes he pokes at me and it hurts . . .' Tears were rolling down her cheeks. 'Please let me come with you, Archie . . . don't leave me here . . .'

'Can we?' Archie said but before Ikey could answer someone entered the house and walked into the room. A smartly dressed woman in a grey suit with black shoes and a white blouse stood looking at them, her manner startled, shocked as she saw them. Her expression went from surprise to fear and then to anger.

'Who are you?' she demanded. 'How did you get into my house?'

'Your daily let us in,' Ikey said. 'You must have had

238

my letter, Mrs Bailey. You knew that we should want to visit June sometimes to make sure she is safe and properly looked after . . .'

'You're from the Children's Department . . .' For a moment the colour drained from her face. 'I didn't get a letter. Why are you here? Has someone been saying things? What did she tell you?' She shot a look of venomous dislike at June. 'That little devil would say anything to get her own way. We've done nothing but spend good money on her – look at that dress and those shoes; they didn't come from the market. I bought that dress in Roses' fashions in Cambridge – it cost me five pounds, but is she grateful? If she has been telling you lies, I'll give her a good smacking . . .'

'Don't leave me here,' June begged, clinging to Archie.

'Well, I think we shall have to investigate this further,' Ikey said. 'I shall be taking Miss Miller with me, Mrs Bailey, and you may apply to the department in writing to have her restored to you. I think we need to have her examined by a doctor . . .'

'No! You're making a big mistake. My husband is a respectable man and on the local council, and he has influential friends. This little liar is making it up, I tell you. She will do anything to get her own way . . . that is why she was taken into care. Miss Sampson told me . . .' She paused, her eyes narrowing in suspicion. 'Why isn't she here? Why hasn't she come herself? I don't believe you're who you say you are. Get out of my house before I call the police . . .' Her hand descended on June's shoulder, gripping her tightly. 'Go upstairs, girl, and stay there until I say you can come down. You will feel the back of my hand when I have time to deal with you . . .'

'Run for it, June,' Archie yelled and kicked the woman's shins. She gave a scream and let go of June, grabbing at her ankle and jumping out of the way as Archie aimed another kick at her other ankle.

June darted past her, through into the small kitchen and out into the back garden, Archie avoiding the woman's grasping hands followed her. She ran as fast as she could, across to the open ground, panic lending her speed. Archie had difficulty in catching up with her. At last he managed to grab her around the waist and she screamed.

'It's all right, June,' he said. 'It's me, it's Archie. Ikey's got a car waiting. Look, he's getting in it, he's reversing towards us. Come on, we have to get in before that witch comes after us . . .'

The woman had come down her path and was yelling at the top of her voice. She tried to throw herself at the car door, but Ikey just kept reversing at speed and she stumbled and fell back. Ikey reversed right over the garden at the side of the house; Archie pulled open the back door, shoved his sister inside and tumbled in after her. Ikey put the car into first gear and shot forward as Archie managed to pull the door shut. He saw Mrs Bailey loom up in front of the car as if to stop them but she must have realised that they weren't going to stop because she jumped back out of the way as Ikey brushed past her, just touching her and knocking her to her knees. Several people had come out on to the street and were looking at her, but Ikey had reached the corner and drove round it with all the speed he could muster, putting distance between them.

Archie sat back and looked at his sister. She was staring out of the back window as if frightened that they would be pursued, her eyes wide and scared. Archie felt scared himself. He knew Ikey was in a lot of trouble for what he'd done, knocking that woman down and snatching June from her legal guardians. He could easily go to prison for it if June's foster parents went to the police or made a complaint; the realisation made him feel sick and shaky. His friend had put himself in danger for their sakes.

'Will they come after me?' June asked at last. The look in her eyes made Archie angry and he reached for her hand, holding it tightly.

'You told us the truth, June? You didn't lie back there?'

'I told you the truth,' June said, tears welling in her eyes. 'They bought me things . . . sweets and clothes, but I hate them . . . they're bad, Archie. I'm not the first kid they've done things to . . .'

'Filthy beasts,' Archie said. 'How do you know?'

'I heard them talking one night,' June said and she was trembling from head to foot. 'She told him to be careful what he did, said he should remember what happened to the last one when he got too rough . . . She said something about she wasn't going to be a party to murder again . . .'

'Bloody hell! Did you hear that, Ikey?'

Ikey was on the main road heading back towards Cambridge. He didn't turn his head as he said, 'I'm not sure – can you repeat what June just said please?'

'She heard them talking. The woman said she wasn't going to be a party to murder again and warned him not to be too rough . . .'

'I'll want June to remember all she can when we get home,' Ikey said. 'Is she hungry? There are a few sand-wiches left. I daren't stop for a while, just in case Mrs

241

Bailey telephones the police and they come looking for us . . .'

'Do you think they will? If what June says is true they surely won't dare . . . ?' He gave his sister a stern look. 'You really are telling me the truth?'

June nodded, her face pale and her eyes dark as the tears trickled down her cheeks. 'I know I wouldn't listen to you and I did silly things and that's why they sent me away, but I promise I'll be good. I want Mum . . . she'll believe me; she won't let them take me away again . . .'

'No, she wouldn't,' Archie said and took her hand in his. 'I shan't let them take you again, June. I promise. I never thought anything like this could happen to you . . . you were supposed to go somewhere they would look after you and stop you gettin' into trouble . . .'

'They kept me off school when I had bruises on my face and arms,' June said. 'He told me if I ever said a word at school he would kill me . . .'

'Wicked devil,' Archie said fiercely. He put his arm about June's shoulders, feeling her tremble. He was certain she was telling the truth; there was nothing left of the defiant girl who had rebelled against Sister Beatrice's discipline. She'd been broken in spirit and bruised in body, and Archie wished he'd kicked that evil woman twice as hard. 'I'm sorry for what they did to you. I'm going to tell the police what you've told us and they'll be in lots of trouble.'

'Leave things to me,' Ikey said, still not looking back at them, though he was now driving at a more reasonable speed. 'I've got a few friends who know about these things and we'll need to move quickly and carefully, because people like that will be up and off if they

242

think June has told us what they did to her . . . We shall be lucky if they're brought to justice, but it won't be for lack of trying. I promise you that much.'

'You've done a lot for us,' Archie said. 'I hope you won't be in trouble for what happened back there . . .'

'I've been in trouble before,' Ikey said with a shrug. 'I dare say I can take it, whatever they do to me. It's you two I'm concerned about – and the others that pair might damage if they get the chance . . .'

Ikey entered the prison visiting room and took his allotted seat at the table indicated. His eyes swept over the prisoners filing in and he knew her at once. There was enough of her in June and Archie to tell him that she was Sandra Miller and he got to his feet as she approached, offering his hand.

'Mrs Miller,' he said, and something about the way she looked at him touched a chord inside him. 'You don't know me, but I know Sergeant Sallis very well indeed and he told me that he believes you were not treated fairly. I want you to trust me and tell me everything you remember about what happened that day you were arrested – and why you think it may have been Mr Reg Prentice who set you up.'

Ikey listened intently as she told him of the way Reg had pestered her relentlessly, and how she'd slapped his face and told him she would go to the overall manager if he didn't leave her alone.

'He threatened me but I hoped it would be enough to stop him touching me, but then the next morning I was questioned, sacked and then arrested for theft of several large cheques which had been made out to cash.

243

The evidence was in my drawer, but it wasn't me who practised those signatures. I told them so in court but no one believed me . . .'

'I believe you, Sandra,' Ikey said and smiled at her. He thought that her honesty shone out of her eyes and wondered at the fools who had allowed her to be so falsely accused and convicted of a crime he was quite certain she hadn't committed. 'I've been told that there is some evidence that it may indeed be Mr Prentice who forged those cheques. This is in confidence, but we've set up a trap and the next time one of those cheques is cashed, we shall have the proof we need . . .'

'How? I don't understand – what do you mean "we"?' Sandra stared at him, wanting to believe but not quite able to grasp it.

'I have friends in high places,' Ikey smiled at her. 'Please trust me when I tell you that I can't say more just yet. Certain cheques have been impregnated with a special chemical that will leave a blue dye on the hands of the person that handles them. He or she won't realise it is there, because it only shows up in a certain light. Mr Prentice should've stopped once he was ahead, but like all those who steal he got greedy – and one of the secretaries became suspicious. Apparently, she never believed it was you that took the money, and he'd been annoying her as well, so she watched him and then she came to us and told us she'd seen him take a blank cheque and put it in his pocket. It has since been confirmed that more money has gone astray . . .'

Tears rose in her eyes and trickled down her cheeks as she looked at him. 'I don't know how to thank you enough – and Sergeant Sallis . . .'

'Well, we don't have Reg's confession yet but it should happen soon, and when it does I'll do all I can to get you released as soon as it can be arranged.'

'Who are you?' she asked. 'Why have you done so much for me?'

'You could say I'm a friend of Archie's,' Ikey said. 'And before you ask, he's fine. I don't want you to worry, Mrs Miller. We're all working to get you out of here with your name cleared so that you can all be together again . . .'

Ikey had thought it his duty to tell her about her daughter, but something in her face told him that she had already suffered too much and he held back information that could well have destroyed her. She'd made quite an impression on him and he wasn't sure yet what that meant for either of them. Time enough for her to learn the truth when she was with her daughter and could hold her close . . . even though she might blame him for not telling her . . .

CHAPTER 18

'I thought I'd come and take a look at you,' Mary Ellen said and smiled at Billy standing behind the stall he'd set out with clothing. The stall itself was covered with jumpers in cellophane packets; dresses, skirts and a couple of suits hung on the rails at the side. Several customers were looking through the rails and the packets of jumpers, taking them out to examine them for any faults. 'Have you been busy?'

'On and off,' Billy told her. 'I've sold six jumpers, two skirts and a suit this morning so I think that's good enough for my first morning . . .'

'It sounds great to me,' Mary Ellen said, casting a practised eye over the goods on the rail. Most of it was cabbage, but not from Sam's firm. His wasn't the only clothing firm to sell their mistakes to market traders. Most things sold this way would have slight faults, though sometimes they were perfect, just made a bit on the skimpy side out of fabric left over from a customer's order. 'These jumpers look nice – what's wrong with them?'

'Nothing as far as I know. Mr Connolly told me they

246

were all end of lines he bought cheap. I've looked at a couple and they seem fine, but I tell people to take them out and have a good look before they buy.'

Mary Ellen took a soft pink wool jumper with short sleeves from the bag and spread it out, checking inside to see if the seams were straight and if there were any holes. She couldn't find anything and decided they were just surplus stock. Sam sold things off cheap at times, if something hadn't cleared after a couple of months on the rails. He always said it was money back to help things keep going.

'This is nice,' she said. 'How much is it?'

'Fifteen bob to anyone else, ten to you,' Billy said promptly.

'I'm not taking your profit,' she said and handed over the fifteen shillings. 'This is lovely and it will look nice on Rose – it's her birthday next week.'

'It's a pound for her,' Billy joked and Mary Ellen laughed, knowing he didn't mean it.

'She likes this colour,' she said. 'I was wondering what to get her, but there's a lovely pink tweed skirt we've got at work that would go with this – and make up for that suit she had to take back.'

'How are things at work now?' Billy asked. 'Has Sam noticed anything else missing?'

'No, not since he put those mirrors up. He was really pleased with the way that worked out, Billy. He keeps telling me you're a clever lad and he wants to talk to you.'

'I'll go round and see him one day,' Billy promised. 'I'm busy most of the time, keeping a look-out for Mr Connolly and collecting his rents and takings. He let me have all this stuff at cost, and I can pay him a bit every week instead of all at once.'

'You've got a good job,' Mary Ellen said. 'I'll see you later then . . .'

'We'll have a fish and chip tea if you like,' Billy said. 'I'll be finished here soon after two, and then I've got a job to do for my boss . . . so I'll be round to pick you up about five . . . if that's OK?'

'Yeah, I'll do some studying until you come,' she said and turned away. She walked through the market after she left Billy, glancing at the various stalls, but not really interested in buying anything. Just as she was about to leave to catch her bus, she saw a van pull up at the back of one of the stalls and a man opened the door, starting to unload armfuls of clothes. One blouse caught her eye in particular, because it was an exact copy of one she'd finished making only that morning. Yolande had checked it as perfect and put it out on their rails – now here it was being delivered to a market stall. Without really thinking what she was doing, Mary Ellen walked up to the man unloading. 'Excuse me, would you mind telling me where you got that yellow blouse please?'

The man glared at her, his eyes narrowed and wary. 'What's it to you?' he asked. 'Clear orf or I'll give you a thick ear . . .'

Mary Ellen saw that he meant what he said; there was something threatening about him that made her shudder inwardly. Obviously, he would win any argument between them. She took another long look at the blouse; it was the one she'd finished that morning, she was sure of it, because even if another manufacturer had got hold of the same material they wouldn't have used the same buttons or put the frill on the sleeve just above the cuffs as she had.

Instead of going home, Mary Ellen returned to Sam's workshops and went into the saleroom. Sam was there alone, looking at the book in which their sales were recorded. He looked surprised to see her.

'Did you sell that pretty yellow blouse I made this morning? It was yellow voile and I used those new pearl buttons and put a frill on above the long cuffs . . .'

'It was the first of our new line,' Sam said, frowning. 'Yolande showed it to me when she put it out this morning at eleven o'clock . . . why?'

'I just saw it being unloaded on a market stall,' Mary Ellen said. 'I asked where he'd got it and he told me to clear off or he'd hit me . . . and that blouse was perfect, too expensive for most market traders . . .'

'I haven't sold it . . . let's have a look,' Sam said and went to the rail that held their range of blouses. It took only a minute or so to discover that the blouse was gone . . . 'You're right, it isn't here – and it hasn't been sold. I'm the only one here this morning and I've had just one customer.'

Mary Ellen nodded, because most Saturdays were quiet in the showroom; the traders came in earlier in the week to buy because Saturdays were their busiest days on the markets.

'So someone took it . . .' Mary Ellen was puzzled. 'If you had only one customer . . . did anyone else come in here?'

'No . . .' Sam thought for a moment. 'Yes, that new girl was here when Mr Cameron's men came to collect his order.'

'Anna . . .' Mary Ellen hesitated, because she didn't want to lay the blame on a girl who was trying hard to keep her job. 'Who came to collect the goods?'

'A couple of men Mr Cameron sent to pick up the goods he bought the other day.'

'Mr Cameron – yes, I've seen him in here buying. He seemed nice . . .' Mary Ellen considered her next words carefully. 'Do you think one of his men could be doing the stealing on his own account?' It was unthinkable that a man like Mr Cameron would stoop to steal from another trader.

'I was thinking the same thing.' Sam looked worried. 'I've known Cameron for years and always thought him honest, but it is possible that he employs a crook to pick stuff up for him. I'll speak to him this weekend and ask him whether he thinks it is possible. If he vouches for his men I'm afraid that only leaves us with one alternative, Mary Ellen . . .'

'Yes,' she let out a sigh. 'She's been doing so much better and she really needs this job. Will you let me have a word with her, Sam, before you accuse her?'

He hesitated then nodded his head. 'I trust you and Billy more than anyone, Mary Ellen. It seems impossible that a young girl should be behind all this theft, but it can't go on. I have to find the thief . . .'

'I feel really angry about that blouse,' Mary Ellen said. 'I spent ages finishing it properly, because it was the first of a new line and now it's on the market for sale, probably at half the price it should be.'

'Well, there's not much we can do about that now, except change the styling of that line slightly. I thought I'd got things covered with those mirrors . . .' He broke off with an exclamation of annoyance as he noticed that one of the mirrors had been turned up to the ceiling. 'So that's how they did it – whoever it was.'

'It's no use having mirrors they can turn,' Mary Ellen said, following his gaze. 'You need to nail it to the wall somehow, Sam . . .'

'Yes, but what will they come up with next?'

Billy hesitated as he approached Mr Connolly's warehouse. He saw someone leaving and recognised his cocky strut. What was Stevie doing here? As far as Billy knew he worked for a nightclub behind the bar – so why was he coming from Mr Connolly's office?

'Stevie?' he said, making the other man aware of him. 'What are you doin' here? I didn't know you worked for Mr Connolly?'

Stevie grinned. 'Just shows yer don't know everythin', don't it? Didn't yer know Connolly owns them nightclubs? His name ain't over the door or anywhere you could find out, but he's the owner and he owns a lot more an' all . . . he's got his finger in a lot of pies round 'ere . . .'

'I thought he was an honest businessman . . .' Billy said lamely, though his suspicions had been growing recently.

'Yeah, you, me and the rest of 'em,' Stevie said with a grin. 'Ain't yer got no idea what yer doin', mate?'

'I'm minding Connolly and collecting some rents for him . . .'

'Yeah, if you say so . . .' Stevie burst out laughing and walked off shaking his head. Billy felt a cold shiver at his nape. What had he got himself into now?

He wanted to turn around and walk away, but then

251

he'd be looking for a job again, and he was enjoying his work – except for the sullen looks he got from some of the market traders. Had he been collecting protection money these past couple of weeks?

Billy was sick at the thought. Connolly had taken him for a right mug – and Stevie must have been laughing his head off after Billy's boast that he wasn't a thief.

He stuck his hands in his pockets and walked away, wondering what to do for the best. It was unlikely he would ever find a job that paid as much as this one and yet he didn't want to be a part of any filthy protection racket . . .

CHAPTER 19

'Now what are we going to do with you two?' Ikey said one morning after they'd snatched June from her foster parents. They'd spent two nights in a room Ikey had taken for the purpose, the brother and sister in a single bed and him in the armchair with a blanket thrown over him. 'It isn't fitting for you to stay here with me all the time so I think now that June is over the first shock of her escape, we'd best throw ourselves on Sister Beatrice's mercy . . .'

'You wouldn't?' Archie stared at him in horror. 'She'll only betray us – give June back to that awful woman and send me back to Halfpenny House . . .'

'Don't you trust me yet?' Ikey's eyes met his and his calming influence made Archie flush.

'Yeah, 'course I do,' he muttered. 'I don't trust her, that's all . . .'

'I admit that it may appear she let you down once, but I'm inclined to believe that when presented with the truth she will be on your side. You went to her at the start, Archie, but then you had no proof. Now we know what those people did to June . . . Besides, do you want her on the streets when we're working?'

Archie looked at his sister. She was sitting on the bed, her head bowed and he felt a wave of misery as he realised he didn't know how to cope with this new June. His sister had always been full of spirit, ready to fight him and the whole world, but now she looked pathetic, a frightened little girl. She'd cried all the first day and Ikey had left them alone to comfort each other, but now she was just quiet and unlike the sister he'd known. Surely Sister Beatrice wouldn't send her back once she'd seen what had happened to her at that place?

'No,' he said in answer to Ikey's question. 'I can't look after her and work and she can't cope with staying in the places we do . . .'

'If you promise not to run off I'll speak to Sister first,' Ikey said. 'I'll get her to promise that she will keep you safe while we sort out the people that hurt June – and if she insists on sending you back, I'll take you away from London for a while. I give you my word I shan't let them send June away again.'

'But what can you do if they insist?' Archie asked. 'They wouldn't listen to me and I'm her brother . . .'

'I'm asking you to take my word and just trust me for a bit longer,' Ikey said. 'I didn't always load wood on the Docks and I know a bit about what we need to do – and I know people who can help us.'

'All right,' Archie said. In his heart he knew that he had to trust the man who had befriended them, because there was no other choice. He couldn't look after June without Ikey's help and she wouldn't stand up to life on the streets; she'd been badly damaged and she needed help. Sister Beatrice would know what to do to help her – if she was willing. 'We'll stay here until you come back . . .'

'Good lad,' Ikey said. 'What the pair of you need is your mother home to look after you – and if you're sensible now, I'm going to get that for you as soon as I can manage it.'

Archie stared at him, a tingle at the back of his neck. 'Who are you really – or what were you, a bloomin' lawyer – or are you a copper workin' undercover?' His eyes narrowed in suspicion.

'Yes,' Ikey laughed and gripped his shoulder. 'I knew you were a bright lad, Archie. That's exactly what I used to be until I got drunk once too often and they threw me out . . .'

'Is that why you're called Ikey?'

'My middle name is Ezekiel; it's a Bible name and my mother liked her Bible stories. My friends called me Ikey as a joke and when I went on the streets I decided to use it – I didn't want anyone to trace me. Especially when I started to do important work . . .' He paused and then nodded to Archie. 'I've been after a criminal for a long time, lad. He runs a protection racket – do you know what that is?'

Archie nodded, 'Yeah. They ask for money to protect you and if you don't pay they smash your place up . . .'

'That's right,' Ikey said grimly. 'Well, a trader I knew who helped me when I was on the streets was beaten so badly that he died. He gave me a name before he died – but the man had an alibi. His thugs did the beating but he's the criminal behind it, and I vowed to get him. My friend at the station asked me to help them unofficially, because undercover I've been able to help them with a lot of unsolved crimes. My quarry has been too clever so far but I'll get him one of these days . . .'

'I bet you will,' Archie said. 'Can I help you?'

'We'll see,' Ikey promised with a smile. 'Now you know my story – are you going to believe I shan't let you down?'

Archie nodded, 'Yeah, thanks, Ikey. I knew you weren't a down-and-out all along; I reckon me and Billy saw you leave the nick once and you looked different until you turned into an alley and started to slouch as if you were drunk – I thought you were up to something but I just didn't know what you did . . .'

'Well, now you do, just keep it to yourself . . .'

Beatrice was at her desk when someone knocked at her door. She looked up impatiently from the report she was struggling with and invited whoever it was to enter. As the door opened and the man entered, she got to her feet a little warily.

'Yes, what do you want? Have you come to return what you took from me?'

Ikey smiled and removed a folded paper from his pocket, placing it on the table. 'It was very useful, Sister Beatrice. Borrowed is the word I would use. I always intended to return it, as I shall your errant children if you give me your word that you will not separate them or return the girl to those abominable people . . . I took her by force and Mrs Bailey may have been slightly injured as I drove away, but I would do it again in such a case . . .'

'So I was right?' Beatrice gasped. 'I was afraid of it . . . I don't know why because they were passed as foster parents and searches must have been made on their background, but something inside told me it was all wrong. It should never have happened and I've already set in motion an action to have the order overturned on the grounds of irregularity. I am their guardian and I was not informed.'

'If you wish for it, I can give you further grounds – evidence from June's own lips that is damning of the people who commit these foul acts and the flaws in our system, when half-trained women take the law in their own hands. I speak of Miss Ruby Saunders, Sister Beatrice, not you, of course . . . I believe you have the experience that is needed now to care for this sadly damaged child and her very angry brother. This man has been preying on vulnerable kids for a while. We had him once but the girl was retarded and her evidence didn't stand up. His name was Constable then – David Constable . . .'

'Of course! I knew the face but not the name. The child he abused was brought here until they transferred her to a home for the mentally unstable. I knew I'd seen that face . . . I remember being furious because he got off scot-free.'

'Will you take Archie and June back and try to understand if they are difficult at first? Archie resents you, unfortunately . . .'

'Yes, Archie will be very angry,' Beatrice agreed. 'Who can blame him in the circumstances? I am angry myself. Their mother was sent to prison on the flimsiest of evidence. You might like to tell Archie that a friend of mine has found evidence to suggest that Sandra Miller was innocent of the charges against her and the thief is very likely another person in her office . . .'

'Reg Prentice, I presume,' Ikey said and saw the

surprise in her eyes. 'Yes, I set a few inquiries in hand myself when Archie told me his suspicions. The man is a bully and a lecher. Three other women at that firm have complained of his unwanted attentions, and I have every reason to believe one of them is about to give evidence concerning a stolen cheque that has been cashed since Mrs Miller was sent to prison . . .'

'How do you know all this?'

Ikey smiled. 'I believe the original instructions came from a Mr Edward Hendry, a country solicitor?'

'You're the man the London police officer uses to do his undercover work?' Beatrice was disbelieving. 'Is that why you rescued Archie – and took it upon yourself to snatch June from her foster home?'

'As it happened, Archie was already under my wing when I was asked to make inquiries about his mother – and of course I knew all my friend Jonathan Carter had to tell me. Jon kept faith in me even when I lost my own, Sister Beatrice, and he saved me from drinking myself to death. He told me he needed help with a case concerning a down-and-out, and I was instrumental in proving that the man was not a murderer, even though he had fallen into a life of degradation. I've had a lot of experience in these kinds of cases since then, believe me – and I suspected something was wrong when I learned that you claimed not to have been kept informed of the order for fostering. Although even before that I was determined to help Archie fight the injustice he believed had been handed out to him . . . I do not like injustice or the way the law can be such an ass . . .'

'I knew there was something about you when you first came here,' Beatrice said and nodded her satisfaction. 'You didn't seem to me typical of the majority of down-and-outs that sleep rough on our streets . . .'

'I've done enough of that,' Ikey said and offered her his softest smile. 'Sometimes even now I sleep out under the arches, just to remind myself why I no longer practise the law as a police officer . . .'

'Ah . . .' Beatrice smiled. 'Yes, of course. You were in the force yourself. May I ask what happened to you?'

'You may ask but I reserve the right not to tell you at the present time . . .'

'Very well. We are all entitled to our secrets,' Beatrice said. 'What do you suggest we do now?'

'If I bring the children here, can I rely on you to keep them here until we get things sorted out?' Ikey frowned as she hesitated. 'You think there will be trouble because Archie and I snatched his sister from the foster parents?'

'If I were ordered to hand them over . . .' Sister Beatrice shook her head. 'Nothing will make me give them up, short of a court order – and your arrest for assault . . .'

Ikey laughed, throwing back his head in delight. 'You may set your mind to rest on that one, Sister. I don't think Mr and Mrs Bailey will be reporting me to the police. In fact, the local police will be receiving a visit from a friend of mine about now with the details of their abuse. June will give evidence if need be but both Archie and I heard her sorry story and I'll risk going to prison if it means getting that pair behind bars . . .'

'Then I hope you succeed and I shall of course do my very best for the children.' Beatrice rose to her feet and offered her hand. 'You have my word that I shall not allow them to be parted again if I can prevent it, more I cannot say. However, I think after our joint evidence is presented, we may be sure that the Miller children will remain here for the foreseeable future.'

'Archie is no longer a child,' Ikey said. 'He has been helping me by working with me on the Docks, but I believe his heart is set on a career in market trading and I think it might be as well to encourage it for the future.'

'Perhaps that decision will be his mother's rather than ours,' Beatrice said. 'However, I shall make no attempt to force him to do anything in the meantime – and June will clearly need special treatment . . .'

'Yes, she will, and that's why I wanted to bring her here. If you had not agreed to do your best for them I should have spirited them away somewhere and you would not have seen them again . . .'

'So, Archie, what have you to say to me?' Beatrice asked when the children had been bathed, fed, and June had been seen to bed in the sick ward to be fussed over by Nurse Wendy Beatrice and Archie were in her office. 'I understand from your friend that you feel you wish to leave school as soon as you're able – is that so?'

'I want to work on the market with Mr Hastings on Saturdays and holidays,' Archie said, raising his head to look her in the eyes. 'I'm not sure if he'll take me, because you sent me away without giving me time to tell him – and I daren't go and see him in case he told you or Billy Baggins. I saw them talkin' and I daren't go near . . .'

'Yes, well, I must apologise to you and your sister for what happened that day. I assure you that it was not my intention to part you like that and I am doing all I can to set things straight as far as I can – though I know nothing will ever make up for what happened to June.'

'No, it can't,' Archie said and glared at her. 'But I'm sorry I hurt you that day. I thought you would help me but you didn't – and that's why we took the letter from your folder . . .'

'Which Ikey has now returned,' Beatrice said and smiled. 'You need not feel too badly about that, Archie. It was in my mind that you and your friend might decide to take matters into your own hands . . . Try the cabinet now, if you like . . .'

Archie eyed her doubtfully as he went to the cabinet and discovered it was locked. 'You've locked it . . .'

'I normally lock it when I'm not using it, apart from a few days when it was deliberately left open . . .'

Seeing the twinkle in her normally stern eyes, Archie gasped. 'You knew what we intended to do . . .'

'I thought you might and though I could not give you the address, I had no reason to obstruct you, though I must admit that your subsequent actions were rather more . . . shall we say decisive than I had imagined?'

'June begged us not to leave her,' Archie said. 'She ran out of the door and Ikey backed across the garden to get her. That old witch threw herself at the car but he wouldn't stop and she fell into the road . . . but he didn't run over her.'

'Yes, that was sensible of him, even though we might wish it otherwise . . .'

Archie stared at her suspiciously. 'Sister! You don't mean that . . .'

'Well, perhaps that might be rather too brutal, but one fears that her punishment may not fit her crime, and physical retribution is satisfying, even though in a civilised world we must not condone it.'

Archie grinned. 'You're all right, Sister B . . .'

'I feel very angry at the way we've both been treated, Archie.' She smiled at him. 'Now, I have some good news for you. I intend to visit your mother in prison tomorrow. Your friend Ikey is to accompany me – and you may send anything you wish for her. I can give you some money if you wish to purchase anything?'

'I've got a bit saved from working with Ikey,' Archie said and blinked hard as he tried to keep back his tears. 'I'll get her some fudge, but I wish they'd let me and June see her . . .'

'If the various efforts being made on her behalf succeed, she may be home sooner than you believe. However, this is not certain yet so it's best to keep it to yourself. June is too fragile to be disappointed. You, Archie, are a young man, and I'm sure you understand that while we have hope nothing is certain until the release papers are signed.'

Archie nodded, although his throat was tight and he didn't feel grown up at that moment. He wanted his mum so badly, but he had to be strong for June's sake. He looked at Sister Beatrice and saw her for what she truly was for the first time, an understanding, compassionate woman who combined discipline with a compelling desire to protect the children in her care. She'd spoken to him as if he were an adult, joking over serious things, because she knew he needed help to adjust to what had happened to his sister.

'Thank you,' he choked. 'I know you didn't mean some of that stuff about running that old witch over, but you knew how I felt and you wanted to help me. I reckon you're a good woman, Sister B – and I'm glad we're back here with you . . .'

CHAPTER 20

'Sam wants to see you,' Mary Ellen told Billy that evening. 'He says he's got a favour to ask of you. I'm not sure what, but he wouldn't ask if it weren't important . . .'

'All right, I'll call in tomorrow before I set up my stall,' Billy said. 'Are you coming to the club tonight?'

'Just for an hour,' Mary Ellen sighed. 'I've got to revise, Billy. My first exam is coming up soon.'

'All right,' he said but she could hear the note of annoyance in his tone. 'I suppose I can find something to do . . .'

'I'm sorry. You do know I want to be with you?'

Billy nodded and bent to kiss her softly on the lips. 'It's all right. I just get a bit fed up sometimes – you know I'll help if I can . . .'

'I knew you'd say that,' she smiled up at him. 'I told you we'd had more stuff pinched despite the mirrors, didn't I? Sam's nailed them to brackets now so they can't be swung round. I didn't think people could be so rotten. What has Sam done that people think they can just pinch his stuff?'

'I suppose most wholesalers get a few things pinched. Mr Connolly warned me about keeping an eye out for thieves on the market; people crowd round the stall and then nick something when you're not looking . . . at least that's what he says.'

'Have you lost anything?'

'Nah,' Billy grinned at her. 'I reckon they know I'd knock their blocks off if they touched my stuff . . .'

Mary Ellen nodded and gave him a quick hug, remembering that when they first went to St Saviour's he'd been shorter than her, but now he was several inches taller, and very strong. Billy's arms closed about her, his lips caressing hers in the softest of kisses.

'Where is Rose?' he asked, realising that there was no sign of her sister.

'She's been out three nights this week,' Mary Ellen said. 'Marion thinks she's got a man, but Rose isn't that sort; she doesn't often go out with men – at least I've never known her to talk about a boyfriend. She always seems to think only about her nursing . . .'

'Well, maybe she's realised she's gettin' older,' Billy winked. 'Is Marion out as well?'

'Yes, she's gone to the pictures with some friends . . .' Mary Ellen laughed and moved closer. 'Are you thinking we've got the place to ourselves?'

'I was . . .' Billy looked down at her, his eyes quizzing her. 'Did you want to go to the club tonight?'

'I think we could give it a miss for once in favour of a night in on the sofa . . .' she gurgled with laughter. 'Oh, Billy, let's . . .'

'I love you so much,' he said and sat down, pulling her on his lap and proceeding to kiss her with more passion than he usually allowed himself. 'It's the first time we've had a chance to be alone like this . . .'

Mary Ellen snuggled closer, her hands moving at the back of his neck, fingers reaching into his hair, caressing. They went for walks by the river sometimes, trying for a space of their own where they could kiss and cuddle, but there were usually others about. Even in the back of the pictures, it wasn't really like being alone, although they snatched a kiss in the dark now and then.

'It's really nice being here on our own,' she said as Billy's kisses trailed down her neck right to the opening of her blouse. He undid a couple of buttons and teased gently with his tongue at the valley between her breasts just discernible above her bra. 'Do you want to take it off?' she asked, trembling slightly, because she was both excited and yet afraid of going further than they ever had. 'Do you want to . . . ?'

Billy turned her so that she was lying back against the cushions, pushing down her bra and kissing and caressing her breasts. His hand slid down the side of her thigh and then he inched her skirt up, his hand slipping underneath to caress her inner thigh and then slip beneath her knickers to touch her. She felt a shiver of anticipation and parted her legs for him to stroke her there, where he'd never touched her before, something inside her begging for him to do more – to make her his own – and a soft mewing sound escaped her.

Groaning, Billy buried his face in her neck and then she felt him tense as he jerked away and sat up, giving her a rueful look.

'This wasn't such a good idea, Ellie love,' he said and gave her his hand, pulling her to her feet. 'Come on, if we stay here I shall do things I promised myself I wouldn't until we're married . . .'

'You can if you want,' Mary Ellen said, looking at him trustingly. 'I love you, Billy – don't think I don't want to as much as you do . . .'

'I'm not going to give Rose the satisfaction of proving I'm what she thought I was,' he said and laughed wryly. 'I'm better than that, Ellie, and so are you. We'll wait until Rose relents and lets us get married. We're goin' to the club and you're goin' to pass your exams and take that teaching course . . .'

Billy was thoughtful as he walked home after seeing Mary Ellen safely in her door after their time at the club. It was still early and he didn't feel like going to bed. He would rather have been out with Mary Ellen somewhere having a lovely time, but lately all she seemed to do was spend a short time with him and then get back to her studies.

Something drew his attention to the girl leaning up against the wall just ahead of him. He was sure he knew her and when he got closer he saw it was Marion. She was crying and her pretty blouse had been torn.

'What's wrong?' he asked, stopping to put his hand out to her. She shrank back but then, seeing it was him, she threw herself against him and started weeping into his chest. Billy held her carefully. 'Did someone hurt you?'

'He beat me 'cos I wouldn't do it with another bloke who paid for me . . .' Marion wept. 'I ain't a whore, Billy, you know I ain't – and I won't go with men for money . . .'

'I know you're not,' he replied and frowned. 'Who

266

did this to you, Marion? What's his name? Tell me and I'll give him a good hidin' . . .'

'Oh, Billy . . .' Marion looked at him with tears on her cheeks. 'I wish you loved me. I'd never have got involved with him then . . .' She pressed close to Billy, reached up and kissed him hungrily on the mouth. 'Please, Billy . . .'

He pushed her gently back, looking at her sadly. 'I can't do that, Marion, you know I love Mary Ellen – but I'm your friend and if you tell me the name of the brute that did this to you, I'll give him a thrashin' . . .'

'No – he'd stick a knife in your back,' Marion said and looked over her shoulder. 'Leave me alone, Billy. You can't help me.'

'You should tell Sergeant Sallis, he'll arrest him.'

'No! I shouldn't 'ave told you . . .'

She started to run down the street. Billy stared after her, shaking his head. There was nothing he could do if she wouldn't either tell him the name of her tormentor or go to the police.

'Thanks for coming to see me, Billy,' Sam said when he visited the showroom the next morning. 'Mary Ellen told you I wanted to ask a favour of you?'

'Yeah, anything I can do,' Billy said. 'You know I'm working for Mr Connolly most of the time, but I can do any job you want in my own time . . .'

'I was going to ask you for two things,' Sam said and hesitated, then, 'I want you to take a good look at our stuff and keep your eye out for anything you think might have come from here when you're round the markets. A lot of it will be legit of course, but you never know what you might see when you're travelling round the various areas.'

'I'm already doing that,' Billy said. 'Mary Ellen told me about that stolen blouse she saw being unloaded. I think I know whose stall it is, Sam, but I'll make a few more inquiries and be certain before I say – and I'll let you know if I see more of your stuff in suspicious circumstances. Now, what was the second thing?'

'Have you found somewhere to live yet?' Billy shook his head. 'Well, I've got a few rooms above this place. I lived there myself when I started out, until some years ago when I bought my cottage. The rooms need a bit of repair and I'm going to set it in hand straight away, but it will be a couple of weeks before it's all done – I wondered if you'd take the rooms on, Billy. I'll have the plumbing and electric seen to, but you do them up yourself, paint them a bit . . .'

'What rent are you lookin' for?'

'I don't want rent – at least not money,' Sam said. 'I want you living on the premises, Billy. I don't like this place bein' empty every night. If I stop the rogues pinching from the showroom when they come in, the next thing will be a break-in. If you're on the premises it should deter some of them from smashing their way in . . . you see there's more to this than meets the eye, lad. I'm being threatened, because I won't pay protection money to someone. The pilfering is just to let me know that they're watching me – and I know it's just the first step. I've been told I've got one last chance and if I don't do as I'm told . . .'

'They'll beat you up and then they'll smash this place up . . . is that it?'

Sam nodded, his gaze very intent. 'Would you take on the job of night watchman, Billy? Be here and stop them breaking in and smashing it to pieces?'

Billy stared at him in amazement, thinking he was dreaming. 'You mean I can have it rent free just for keepin' an eye on the place?'

'If you're willing?' Sam arched his brows. 'I know you've been lookin' for somewhere to live and I'll feel much better if I know you're here a lot. I'll put the phone on for you and you can telephone me if you think there's something fishy goin' on – and I'll get some mates of mine round. The police are worse than useless. Call 'em out tonight and they'll arrive three days later and take notes. What I need is to warn the buggers orf!'

'That's why Mr Connolly hired me,' Billy said and grinned. 'I don't mind doin' the same for you – I'll be glad to move in tonight.'

'There's no electric yet . . .'

'I'll manage with oil lamps and a couple of torches until we get it put right,' Billy said. 'I don't mind camping out for a bit . . . even though I'll need to go back to St Saviour's to wash and eat for a while.'

'No need for that, you can come round the corner to me,' Sam said. 'It's time you left there, lad. I'm sure Sister will be glad to get rid of you . . .'

'Yeah,' Billy laughed. 'I'll bring my stuff round later when I've finished work. I'm not sure what Mr Connolly wants me to do for the rest of the day, but it's not often much on Saturday.'

'Don't let anyone know what you're doing yet,' Sam said. 'Oh, you can tell Sister Beatrice, of course, but no one else . . .'

'All right,' Billy agreed. 'We'll keep this between us, Sam – but I'm very grateful and it will make all the difference to Mary Ellen and me. Once I've got the place fixed up, Rose will have no reason to say we can't afford a place of our own . . .'

'So you're leaving us for your own home at last, Billy,' Sister Beatrice said when he told her his news. 'Well, I'm very pleased for you. I think it's an excellent opportunity for you – effectively, you'll be doing two jobs. Working for Mr Connolly and acting as night watchman for Sam. Yes, that sounds very satisfactory – providing you're not placing yourself in danger?'

'Oh no, Sister, I'm sure it will be fine,' Billy said. 'Sam's had too much pilferin' lately and he's putting a stop to it so he's afraid the rogues may try to break in at night, but if I'm there on the premises they'll think twice about trying it on . . .' Billy knew better than to tell Sister what Sam had told him or what he planned to do if the rogues did break in, because she certainly wouldn't approve of any rough stuff.

'Well, I'm sorry to see you go, Billy, but as you know, I have two more children staying here on a longer-term basis now and your room will come in useful. However, if you ever need advice or help please feel free to come to me. I stand in place of a parent to you and I am always here . . .'

'Yeah, I know,' Billy said. 'I heard Archie Miller and his sister were back. You could tell Archie Ted Hastings was asking after him this morning. He might give him a job if he asks . . .'

'Yes, I shall speak to him,' she smiled and nodded

approvingly. 'You are one of our success stories, Billy Baggins. I am proud to know you . . .'

Billy stared in surprise and then reached out and gave her a quick bear hug, from which she emerged looking flustered and unsure. 'I reckon you've done us proud, Sister,' he said. 'Yeah, I'm proud to know you an' all.'

CHAPTER 21

The woman entered the prison meeting room, looking round nervously. When she saw Beatrice she came towards her, some of her apprehension disappearing as she responded to the female prison officer's order to sit down. Drawing out a chair from the small table, she looked at Beatrice in inquiry.

'It's lovely of you to come and see me, Sister, but I'm not sure why . . . ?'

'I should have come long before this,' Beatrice admitted. 'Forgive me, Mrs Miller, but like many others I assumed there was no smoke without fire and now I am ashamed that I did not immediately take steps to offer you my assistance. However there were reasons why I delayed . . .'

'Why should you bother about me? We've never met, have we?'

'No, but your children were brought to me a short time after your unfortunate arrest . . .' Beatrice took a deep breath. 'I have more than one piece of news for you, some of it is unpleasant, and I fear that I hold some small blame in it, though others are more culpable.'

'You'd better tell me the worst,' Sandra Miller said and her hands were tight with tension on the table in front of her, her face pale and strained, and yet there was strength there too.

'Firstly, I think I should give you hope,' Beatrice said. 'I have been reliably informed that an action I and some others put in motion has seen some positive results. I believe it will not be too long before you are released – and another is tried for the crime of which you were accused.'

'Someone else told me that . . .' Her eyes closed for a moment, and Beatrice saw a tear roll from the corner of her right eye, and then she was looking at her. 'I must thank you for your efforts, Sister Beatrice, though I still do not know why you should have gone to so much trouble on my behalf.'

'Archie convinced me that you are innocent, and though at first I thought it just the words of a loving son, I have since learned to understand him – and therefore I am certain that his mother is not a thief.'

A smile touched Sandra's lips briefly. 'He's just like his father . . .'

'A good man, I am sure, and much missed.'

'Yes.' Sandra's eyelashes were wet with unashamed tears. 'Do you know when I am likely to be released?'

'The lawyers are working on it, but I cannot give you precise details. The person who has done most to help you was to have accompanied me today, but was unable to do so, but he assured me your release would be soon. It could even be within a few days, or it may be longer – but Mr Hendry assured me that I might pass the news on as he believes it definite.'

'Thank God . . .' Sandra smiled through her tears. 'You are extremely kind, Sister Beatrice.'

'I did only what I thought right, but I fear what else I have to tell you will not be pleasant hearing. Indeed, it will hurt you and you may blame me for not trying harder to prevent it, but I can only apologise and say that it was not my choice.'

'Has something happened to Archie?'

'Archie is well. I fear his sister, although now safely back in my care, has suffered in a way I wish she had not.'

Sandra gripped the edge of the table between them, her knuckles white with tension. 'What happened?'

'She was taken into foster care despite my doubts and against my advice – and I fear they were not good people. It was this that made me delay visiting you for I hoped she would be back safe with me before I saw you, and she is now. Unfortunately, June has been badly treated . . . violently molested, and she is suffering. She needs her mother and cries for you constantly, though Staff Nurse Wendy does her best to comfort her, as does Archie himself . . .'

Sandra stared at her, dismay, anger and bewilderment chasing themselves through her expressive eyes. 'How could such a thing happen?' she asked at last. 'I thought foster parents were rigorously checked?'

'And so they should have been, and were, I dare say,' Beatrice agreed. 'However, mistakes were made, and I believe the whole affair was rushed and botched. I have already put in an application to have the order for fostering rescinded and June placed legally in my care until you are able to take her back into your own loving arms.'

Sandra stared at her, tears trickling silently down her cheeks. She brushed them away impatiently. 'It must have been hard for you to come here and tell me this,' she said. 'What is being done about these people? Have the police been informed?'

'Yes, that was set in motion immediately by the man who took it upon himself to rescue her from those people, Mrs Miller. I have not yet heard the outcome but I imagine Mr Bailey and his wife will be arrested . . .'

'This man . . . the one that rescued June,' Sandra said. 'You're talking about Ikey, aren't you? He visited me a couple of days ago.'

'I didn't know Ikey had visited,' Beatrice replied and frowned. 'Did he tell you about June and how he rescued her?'

'No, he didn't,' Sandra said, a glint of anger in her eyes now. 'What sort of a man is he exactly?'

'He declined to tell me his story, but I believe he has known suffering of his own. All I can tell you is that he has been a good friend to Archie and June – he was the one that snatched her from her foster parents' house . . .'

'Snatched her?' Sandra frowned. 'Are you sure he is to be trusted?'

A little smile touched Beatrice's mouth. 'As sure as I am of anything in this life. They say you should not judge a book by its cover, Mrs Miller, and it is certain that you should not judge a man by his clothes . . .'

Sandra joined the other women at the work benches sewing mail sacks. She was seething with anger as she stitched at the coarse material, which roughened her hands and tore her nails, resenting every second she

275

was forced to spend in this place. Her anger was directed at the people who had believed a liar and ruined her life, the way she'd been treated as if she were a thief and her story disbelieved, and at the woman who had taken her daughter away from the safety of Sister Beatrice's care and given her to those wicked foster parents.

If she'd thought there was a chance of getting out of that place she would have fought her way free, but the sound of keys in locks haunted her sleep and she knew she was trapped until they let her out. It didn't stop the bitterness frothing inside her to know that people were working to get her free – she shouldn't have been in there and if she'd been home with her daughter June would not have suffered physical abuse.

Tears burned in her throat as she remembered the happy glow she'd felt after Ikey's visit. He'd told her that he was working to get her free – why hadn't he told her about June instead of letting her think her children were both safe? She wanted to shout at him, to hit him and vent her frustration and fury on him for not telling her – because how could she trust a man who had lied to her? How could she believe that he would really do what he'd promised?

Archie hovered at the edge of the market. Billy had told him to accompany him that morning and use his time to speak to Ted Hastings about getting his job back.

'Where shall I meet you afterwards?'

'If Ted isn't pleased to see you, just wander about the market and look at the stalls selling clothes. I'll ask you to look at some things at Sam's place later and you can tell me if you noticed anything similar while you were lookin' round.'

Archie decided he'd mooched about long enough and walked through the covered market. Ted was serving a customer and didn't see him immediately, but then he frowned.

'What are you doin' here, lad?'

'Billy Baggins brought me with 'im,' Archie said. 'He's doin' his job and said I should ask if you had a job for me . . .'

'I gave you a job before but you let me down.' Ted looked at him hard.

'They sent me away and I didn't know what to do. I wanted to come and ask for a job as soon as I got back to London, but I couldn't . . . you were talkin' to Billy and I thought you would turn me in . . .'

'Did you do something bad?'

'Not wicked,' Archie said. 'They sent my sister some-where else and I had to find her so I ran away and came back to London, but at first Sister Beatrice wouldn't help us . . . but then Ikey found the address and we went and fetched June from them rotten devils.'

'I think I need to hear more of this, lad,' Ted said, turning away as someone came to his stall and asked for a bag of onions. 'Look, come and see me at home this evening, and we'll talk.'

'I don't know where you live . . .'

'Go across to me daughter and she'll tell you,' Ted said. 'You come round for yer tea tonight – half past six – and we'll sort things out . . .'

Archie nodded and left Ted to get on with his work. His hands shoved in his pockets, he was thoughtful, because although Ted had seemed friendly enough, he wasn't sure he would trust him to work for him again. As he approached Ted's daughter's stall, he saw that she appeared to be angry and he heard her tell the man standing there to clear off or she would have the market warden after him.

'You're a fool, Maggie Hastings. You and your father both – it isn't wise to upset my boss . . .' he countered before turning to slouch off, a scowl on his face.

'Who was that, Maggie?' Archie asked.

'Just a slimy toad I want nothing to do with,' Maggie said and glared at him, then, as she recognised him, her expression cleared. 'Well then, Archie, where have you been these past weeks? Shame on you for lettin' me dad down – and after he took to you right off.'

'It wasn't my fault, Maggie,' Archie said, giving her a rueful look. 'I wanted to work for you Saturdays and when I leave school and I've asked Mr Hastings if I can – he told me to have supper with you this evening, and said you'll tell me where to come . . .'

'We're not far off Commercial Street,' she said. '5 Cheney Walk, down a little alley. What are you doin' the rest of the day?'

'Helping Billy Baggins,' Archie said. 'He'll be back for me in a minute . . .'

Maggie's smile left her eyes. 'I used to think Billy was a good lad, but he's got in with that Mr Connolly now . . .'

'Billy's all right,' Archie stood up for his friend. 'He's straight, is Billy – and he's my friend.'

'Well, I hope you're right,' Maggie said, 'but he wants to be careful workin' for that man . . . he's a bad 'un.'

278

'Who is Mr Connolly then?' Archie asked, puzzled. 'I thought he was respectable – owns a lot of market stalls, like your dad . . .'

'He does but he's not like my dad and don't you think it,' Maggie looked cross. 'Billy wants to watch what he does or he'll be tarred with the same brush . . .'

Archie was about to ask her what she meant, but Billy was walking towards them, and Maggie shoved a scrap of paper in his hand. 'That's where you come, but just be careful of that rogue and tell Billy to be the same.'

Archie shoved the scrap of paper in his pocket and nodded to her. He was thoughtful as he ran up to Billy.

'All right, young 'un?' Billy asked. 'Ted treat you OK, did he?'

'Yeah, I've got to go to tea tonight and tell him me story and then he might give me a job . . .'

'You'll do well with him and Maggie. I would have liked to work with them when I left school but Sister Beatrice thought I needed to learn a trade and now I've got a good job.'

Archie hesitated, wondering whether to tell Billy what Maggie had said about his boss. She had a fiery tongue and she'd soon told the man she didn't want hanging round her stall to clear off . . . perhaps she'd got a grudge against Mr Connolly. Archie didn't want to upset Billy, who'd been a good mate to him so he kept his thoughts to himself.

'Did you have a look round the clothes stalls, Archie?'

'Yeah, I got told to shove off twice,' Archie said and grinned. 'I think they thought I wanted to pinch somethin' but what good would a woman's dress or coat be to me?'

'Someone had coats for sale this morning? Winter ones?'

'Yeah. Only a couple but they looked good cloth . . .'

'Right, you've done well,' Billy said. 'Now I'm going to take you to look at some stuff where my girlfriend works and I want you to tell me if you see anything that looks like things you saw this morning – I mean stuff that could be from the same rail, do you understand?'

'Yeah, I reckon you're lookin' for pinched stuff,' Archie said. 'The bloke what had the coats were a shifty-lookin' sort . . .'

'Well, I only want to know if you saw anything you think might have been the same as things I'm goin' to show you now . . .'

'Archie said the coats were like the ones on our rails?' Sam said later that morning. 'What colour?'

'One was red and the other was grey.'

Sam opened his stock book and checked, then nodded, 'Yes, it says here that four grey coats were completed on Thursday last and four red . . . We've sold three red so there should be one left, and we've sold two grey coats.'

'You've got one of the grey, no red and six of purplish tweed,' Billy said and frowned. 'That's not a coincidence, Sam. Two coats gone and two coats on the same stall in the market . . .'

'But who owns the stall?'

'From what Archie told me, I think it must be Dick Wright . . . ugly little devil and quick with his tongue as well as his fists . . .'

280

'I know him,' Sam nodded and then frowned. 'He just runs the stall for someone else . . . I've seen someone there collectin' money off him.'

'What's the matter, Sam?' Billy asked. 'Why are you lookin' at me like that?'

'Because you're not goin' to like this,' Sam said. 'I'm sorry, Billy, but I'm afraid it all points to one man . . .'

'I'm sorry, Anna,' Mary Ellen said when the girl came back from her interview with Sam that lunchtime. 'We've had too many thefts recently, and you were the only one that had the opportunity to remove those coats . . .'

'You're always in there,' Anna said in a sulky voice, but her eyes didn't quite meet Mary Ellen's. 'It could've been anyone. How could I have smuggled them out?'

'Why don't you tell me?' Mary Ellen invited. 'If you told us how it was worked Sam might give you a reference.'

'To hell with you and your job,' Anna sparked to life suddenly. 'You can't prove nuthin' so don't think I'm goin' ter tell you.'

Mary Ellen shook her head as the girl walked out of the workshop. It was disappointing to discover that she'd been a part of the conspiracy to steal from Sam. They'd taken her on because she'd spun a tale of having a mother and four younger sisters at home to support, but now it seemed it was all lies; Anna had come here to deliberately help take their stock.

'I knew it had to be her,' Yolande muttered as the door shut behind Anna. 'It only started after she came here. Sam gave her a decent job but she didn't have the sense to know how lucky she was . . .'

'I wonder why she got involved,' Mary Ellen said. 'I mean she couldn't do it on her own, could she? She has to have an accomplice . . .'

'I saw her in the café with a bloke the other day,' Jilly said, looking up from her machine. 'Good lookin' . . . wears a Teddy boy suit. She looked frightened . . . as if he'd been threatenin' her . . .'

'You think he forced her to help?'

'I saw him grip her arm . . . vicious, he was. I wouldn't go out with a bloke like that however good lookin'.' Jilly frowned. 'I think I heard her say his name was Stevie something . . .'

'Stevie?' Mary Ellen frowned. She remembered seeing a bruise on Marion's arm, but when she'd asked her where it came from, she said she'd knocked herself at work. She'd refused to look at her when she made the excuse and Mary Ellen had wondered, but she'd thought Marion had too much sense to go out with a man who hit her. Yet some men could be very persuasive. 'You think this bloke was forcing her to steal for him?'

'Yes.' Yolande nodded, then, 'It's likely. I'm not sure how she did it, but she must've moved things when no one was lookin' . . .'

'All I can think is that she slipped things in with the rails of cabbage stuff that one of the customers had bought, so when they collected it no one noticed the odd extra garment amid the armfuls . . .'

Mary Ellen inclined her head. She thought Yolande was right; Sam and Billy had worked out it was the only way that it could be done, but how Anna had slipped in there at just the right moment no one could guess. Wandering over to Anna's station, she looked toward the window and saw that it looked out into the back yard. A man was working, stacking crates. Of course, it was a communal yard shared with the small leather workshops next door, and that meant anyone could enter. Someone could signal to Anna that now was the time and she could slip into the showroom on the pretext of visiting the toilets, quickly moving the articles to be stolen while someone kept Mrs Baxter or Sam busy . . . It had to be the way, the only way she could work with an accomplice. Anna would move the things she'd been told to steal and then, before anyone was aware, the customer would take his goods and no one would realise that hidden in the great pile of cabbage were two good winter coats.

Returning to her own station, Mary Ellen picked up the work she wanted to complete and carried it to Anna's place.

'Why are you doing that?' Yolande asked, because, as one of the senior seamstresses, Mary Ellen's bench was at the front of the workshop, while Anna's was at the back.

'Lots of light here,' Mary Ellen said. 'I'll try it for a couple of days, if you don't mind, Yolande?'

'It's up to you, but we shall be employing another girl as soon as we can find someone decent . . .'

'Yes, well, we'll see what happens then,' Mary Ellen said.

Whoever Anna's contact had been, he wouldn't come once he knew that she'd been sacked, so it was going to happen in the next day or so or not at all . . .

CHAPTER 22

'Well, that's a rare tale and no mistake,' Ted Hastings said and sipped the strong hot tea his daughter had poured to go with the meal of hot meat pie, chips and mushy peas she'd fetched from the shop. 'Had enough to eat, lad?'

'Yes, thank you, sir,' Archie said and smiled. 'It was great . . .'

'Yeah, well, if you work for me you can look forward to pie and chips or fish and chips twice a week. I'll employ you on Saturday mornings until you leave school, and then you can come with me every day. I reckon it would be best if you stay with me 'ere once you start full time, Archie. We 'ave to be up early mornings to get set up in time for when the eager beavers arrive – and then we have to go to the wholesale markets two or three times a week, pick up fresh supplies for the veg stall . . .'

'You've got several stalls, sir?'

'Yeah, I own six, but I rent four of 'em out to mates of mine, blokes I trust. Jimmy's gettin' a bit long in the tooth though. I'm thinkin' of keepin' it myself when he packs it in – and I'll need a good strong lad to run it, but that won't be for a couple of years: long enough for you to learn the trade. In time I might even let you 'ave one of 'em fer yerself . . .'

'I thought you might not want me when you knew it all,' Archie said, a flush in his cheeks, because he'd told Ted that he'd borrowed money from Halfpenny House, but intended to pay it back. 'I know some of what I did wasn't right – but I had to. Sister Beatrice said it was a mercy we did because June might have been hurt worse if she'd been left with them lot . . .' Archie scowled. 'I reckon what he did do was bad enough – the filthy beast.'

'You're right there,' Ted said. 'If I could get my hands on him I'd thrash the bugger to an inch of his life . . .'

'Now then, Dad,' Maggie chided. 'You mustn't say things like that – let the law deal with those people. You'll only end up in prison yourself . . .'

'It's just a figure of speech,' Ted said and looked a bit sheepish. 'But I should like to see that bugger squirm.'

'Language, Dad,' Maggie said and got up to clear the plates. She smiled as Archie sprang up to help her. 'You're a guest, Archie. Sit and talk to Dad for a while. I can manage the washing up.'

Archie nodded and followed Ted to his chair by the fire, pulling up a tattered leather pouffe to sit at his side. The cottage was of a comfortable size with a large kitchen in which they lived and a room of similar size across the hall, which was the parlour, but usually contained boxes of stuff Maggie sold on her stall. She'd told him to use the toilet upstairs before they ate, and Archie had seen there was an old-fashioned bathroom with a Victorian rolled-edge bath and big brass taps, also a toilet and basin, and a towel rail that was warm to the touch and probably heated by the closed stove in the kitchen. There were three bedrooms, but Maggie had told him that one of them was tiny and at the moment used to hold stock.

'If you stay with us when you leave school, as Dad wants, I shall have to put it all in the front room,' she said and grimaced. 'Not that it matters. I've no time for polishing a fancy parlour and I'm certainly not about to start courtin' . . .' She burst into laughter and Archie smiled with her, although he didn't see why it was funny. Maggie was no older than his ma and she could probably find a husband if she wanted one.

The kitchen was one of the cosiest rooms Archie remembered seeing, despite its size, because it was so warm and homely; at one end there was a huge dark oak dresser that Archie thought might be what people called a Welsh dresser; a big scrubbed-pine table dominated the centre of the floor and there were two comfortable armchairs, a rocking chair and a wooden grandfather's chair grouped near to the stove. Above the blackened stove was a shelf on which were arranged a rack of pipes, some tapers, a couple of blue-and-white vases, with bits of paper tucked behind them, and a brass box that looked as if it had come from the First World War. Archie's father had shown him his grandfather's box once and it was just like the one Ted had.

'They were sent out to the troops in the first big war,' his father had said. 'They had a few cigarettes, a bar of chocolate and a message inside. Your grandfather ate his chocolate and shared the fags with his mates, but he kept the box with him all through the war and it saved his life.' He'd shown Archie where a bullet had lodged in the lid, which had stopped it penetrating Grandfather Miller's chest.

'Now, tell me a bit about your ma,' Ted said as he filled a pipe with tobacco and lit it with a taper from the fire. 'What happened to her – and why are they going to let her out soon?'

Billy had decided the first thing he would do was to repair some of the window frames. Wind was blowing in through the cracks, and although it was still summer it would soon start to turn cooler and he wanted this place warm and cosy – and safe – before he brought Mary Ellen here to see his new home.

He spent several hours replacing rotten wood and fixing broken catches, because the last thing he wanted was someone climbing in during the night and catching him unawares. By the time he'd finished he was tired and ready for sleep. The rooms had a kitchen of sorts, but no way of heating a drink before he went to bed so he opened a bottle of beer and took a few swigs. Perhaps it would've been better to wait until Sam had got the electric and a few things fixed before he moved in, but he'd been impatient to get started.

Tomorrow, he would buy some paint and make a start on the ceilings. The kitchen had a sink, but it was stained and Billy thought he might buy a new one. He could buy some old cabinets from one of the many second-hand shops in the district, strip them down to the wood and repaint them – make the kitchen look modern and clean for Mary Ellen. She was used to that nice modern flat Rose rented from the council so he couldn't expect her to move into a dump like this . . .

What was that? Billy stiffened as he heard a noise from outside . . . in the back yard. It might be nothing, but he knew the leather workshop had packed up for the night long ago. Putting out his oil lamp, he went to stand at the window of the bedroom which over-looked the yard. At first it was too dark to see anything, but then he caught sight of a shadowy shape that moved cautiously towards the back door of their premises; another followed a second or two later, and then another. He waited a few minutes longer, but no one else followed. Three of them, then, but he could probably manage that many if he was armed. He heard a splin-tering sound and knew they'd attacked the back door. Sam had spent money on reinforcing that recently with several extra bolts and locks and they wouldn't get in that way so he had time to surprise them.

Billy reached for the club he'd placed near the door leading out to the landing where he could easily find it. His hand clasped the smooth surface and he bared his teeth in anger as he heard glass shattering. The bastards had given up on the door and were now attacking the windows. Sam had started to put metal bars across them, but the job was only half finished; they'd thought they had a little time, time for Sam to put the phone in so that Billy could call for aid if an attempt was made to break in, but it looked as if he was on his own . . .

He walked softly down the stairs, hesitating for a moment before he went through the hall to the stockroom at the back where the raw materials were kept. He could hear muttering, a raucous laugh as they discovered bales of material, sewing cottons, buttons, zips and all the other bits and pieces the girls needed for their work.

Billy swore softly. Not content with their pilfering, they were determined to strip Sam's place of as much as they could. He paused then threw open the door, snapping on the light. Three startled faces turned to look at him and ugly great brutes two of them were too, but it was the third one that shocked him.

'Stevie Baker – what the hell are you doin' here?'

'What does it look like?' Stevie sneered. 'We've come to teach Sam a lesson – so get lost and we'll finish the job.'

'I can't let you do that, Stevie. Sam is a good mate – 'sides, I'm his night watchman.'

'You bloody fool!' Stevie looked genuinely shocked. 'Connolly will do his nut when I tell him you've gone over to the enemy . . .'

'I took the job of collectin' rents,' Billy said, 'but I was a mug. I've been collectin' protection money and I've had enough of bein' taken for a fool . . .'

'If you think Connolly will let you get away with this, you're a bigger fool than I thought,' Stevie said. 'Now just get out of the way – unless you want to get hurt?'

'Why don't you and your thugs leave before you get hurt?'

'He needs teachin' a lesson, Stevie,' one of the burly men said. 'I'll soon deal wiv 'im . . .'

Billy took stock. He could handle Stevie easily enough but the other two were muscled, rough types and he would get the worst of any fight.

'I think you should leave before my boss and his friends arrive,' he said, deciding to bluff it out. 'Not that I need much help to persuade you to go, gentlemen . . .'

'Bloody gents, are we?' one of the thugs laughed and

spat in Billy's direction. 'You must be orf your bleedin' 'ead, mate. We're 'ere to do a job and we ain't leavin' until we've got what we want.'

'No, I don't think so,' Billy said, clasping his club firmly as he moved towards them. 'You can go nice and quiet or you can put up a fight – but you're goin' one way or the other . . . Sam and me are fed up with bein' ripped off by your lot . . .'

'Who's goin' ter make me leave then?' the first man said and moved forward aggressively.

'That would be me,' Billy glared at him. 'You're goin' to be very sorry if you don't just turn round and leave nicely . . .'

'Who the bleedin' 'ell do yer think yer are?'

'I'm the bloke who is goin' to teach you a lesson . . .'

'Try me . . .' the man invited furiously, squaring up, an iron jemmy clutched in his hand. 'Come on, you bleeder, I'll show you who's goin' ter get a lesson, and it ain't me.'

'Nah, Ricky.' Stevie laid a hand on his arm. 'Don't yer know who he is? We'd better do as he says and leave.'

'I ain't lettin' 'im push me around. He's only one and there're three of us . . . What are yer, bleedin' cowards?'

'He's Connolly's minder . . .' Stevie spoke in a low voice. 'We can come back if *he* says so but I ain't goin' against the boss.'

The man addressed as Ricky froze, his face a picture of indecision. Billy thought it might have been funny if he hadn't been in such a dangerous situation. He clutched his wooden club, lifting his arm suggestively as if to invite the intruders to come on to him.

'Are you Connolly's bleedin' man?' Ricky demanded.

'I don't see what it has to do with you,' Billy said, 'but as it happens I do work for him . . .'

'What you bleedin' doin' 'ere then?'

'I live here,' Billy said and grinned, 'and you disturbed my beauty sleep, mate – so are you leavin'?'

At that moment they heard voices outside and then a police whistle a little distance away. The intruders looked at each other uneasily and then Stevie bolted for the window and scrambled through; a second followed sharply, but Ricky lingered, clearly unwilling to retreat.

He took a step forward as if he would fight, but Billy squared up to him and his mates called to him to hurry. He hesitated and then retreated to the window, still looking threateningly at Billy.

'This ain't the bleedin' finish,' he muttered. 'We'll be back and next time you'll be wishin' you'd never been born . . .'

Billy lunged at him then, but he shot through the window and after that all hell seemed to let loose, shouting, police whistles and then banging at the back door.

'You in there! You'd better come out quietly or we'll come in and get you . . .'

Billy hesitated and then unbolted the door and let the police enter. Three burst in and another two climbed through the broken window. Billy dropped his club and one of the police constables approached him, a look of glee on his face.

'Caught you in the act, did we? Two of yer mates got away, but we'll have the rest of yer behind bars before we're finished – and the charge won't just be breakin' and enterin'. One of our officers has been hurt . . .'

'Not by me, Officer,' Billy protested as his arm was grabbed. 'I'm the night watchman here and I was trying to stop them stealing Sam's goods. It was lucky that you turned up – how did you know?'

'Likely tale,' the police constable said. 'Think up a better one for the magistrate in the mornin', mate, or you'll be facin' a long stretch behind bars . . .'

'What's goin' on here?' a voice Billy recognised with relief asked. 'Billy, are you all right, lad?'

'Sam, thank goodness you're here,' Billy said. 'This officer was just about to arrest me. They scared some rogues off though – three of them broke in a short time ago and I was tryin' to persuade them to leave when suddenly whistles started blowing and they scarpered.'

'Are you the owner here?' the police constable asked. 'This man claims he's your night watchman.'

'Yes, he is; he started tonight. He's goin' to live over the top and try to keep us safe from thieves breakin' in . . .'

'Started tonight, did he? That explains it,' the police officer said. 'We got a telephone call to say there was a light on upstairs in empty rooms and we thought we'd investigate, and then we saw a light down here and a broken window . . .' He removed his hand from Billy's shoulder. 'Apologies, but it seemed odd to us seeing as no one knew you were living here.'

'I'm just doing it up,' Billy said, 'but I shall be living here in future – and once Sam gets the phone on we'll be able to ring you ourselves.' He paused, then, 'I might have been in a spot of bother if you hadn't turned up – so thanks for your help.'

'Everything all right here then?'

'Yes thank you, Officer,' Sam said and drew a sigh of relief as the police constable withdrew. 'You're sure you're not hurt, Billy?'

'I'm fine,' Billy assured him, 'but the man they called Ricky says he'll be back and we can't rely on the coppers turning up next time. It was only because someone in the street became suspicious over my light that they were here when I needed a bit of help . . .'

'Nosy neighbours?' Sam grinned wryly and nodded. 'We'll fix something up, Billy; we'll be ready next time . . .'

'Good idea,' Billy said but didn't smile. 'One of them said something . . . he told Ricky not to fight me because I was Connolly's man . . .' He left Stevie's name out of it, though he wasn't sure why – maybe because they'd been mates at school, or because Stevie had got the thugs to leave when the police arrived.

'I knew it,' Sam said. 'I thought it had to be him. Oh, Connolly would never get his hands dirty, but he has a lot of men working for him who would . . .'

'Why didn't you tell me?'

'Don't worry, Billy. I knew you weren't involved and I wasn't sure . . . but I'm sure now.'

'Yes, they called him "the boss" – at least one of them did, and I'm sure the fact that I worked for him is the only reason that Ricky didn't go for me before the police got here.'

'I'm sorry, Billy. I know it was a good job for you.'

'No!' Billy said and his mouth had gone hard. 'I'm not my brother. I don't steal and I don't work for a crook . . . even if he does get other people to do his dirty work . . .'

'What are you goin' to do then?' Sam asked, looking thoughtful.

'I'll give in my notice. I've got a bit of savings so I'll manage until I can find something else.'

'What will you tell Connolly?' Sam frowned. 'If he thinks you're suspicious of him, he won't let you just walk off . . .'

'I'll think of somethin',' Billy said. 'I'm not sure what yet but I'll come up with some excuse . . .'

'Why not just tell him you've found a better job?' Sam said and smiled. 'I could do with someone like you about the place, Billy . . . I'll find some work for you, in the showroom and deliverin' . . . You can help Herbie and Bert and be around when you're needed, because I don't think we've seen the end of this rotten lot yet . . .'

In the end Billy didn't need to find an excuse for leaving Mr Connolly. When he turned up the next day, his boss gave him a look that would have sent shivers down the spine of a lesser man.

'So you weren't satisfied with the wage I paid you,' he said coldly. 'I don't like traitors, Billy, and I don't employ men I can't trust.'

Billy was about to retort angrily but thought better of it. 'I've done what you asked of me, Mr Connolly, but Sam offered me somewhere to live and in return I look after his place. I didn't think it would bother you, sir. I'm sorry if you think I let you down, but I'm gettin' married soon and my girlfriend didn't much like the idea of me bein' out at nights . . .'

'You owe me twenty quid for the stuff I let you have

on the market,' Connolly said. 'I'll give you a week to find the money . . . now get out. I don't want to see you again, unless you've got my money.'

'I can pay you now, sir,' Billy said and took a small bundle of notes from inside his jacket. He placed the money on Mr Connolly's desk. 'I'd still like to say thank you for the offer of work. Goodbye . . .'

As he walked away, Billy was conscious of Connolly's eyes on his back and he knew that next time he came face to face with the infamous Ricky, he wouldn't stay his hand. In Connolly's mind he'd chosen the wrong side and he wouldn't be forgiven.

He was glad to have broken away from a man he'd thought respectable, if a bit on the hard side, but now knew to be a rogue and a bully. Billy wasn't sure why Mr Connolly had been attacked that night, but in his business he must make enemies and no doubt they'd thought to find him vulnerable. He'd taken Billy on not out of the kindness of his heart, but because he knew he might be attacked again – and he would need another protector, but he already had a suitable man in his employ. Ricky would step into Billy's shoes easily enough.

He was thoughtful as he made his way home; pausing to purchase paint and various bits he needed to use for restoring the rooms above the workshop. Most of Billy's hard-earned savings had gone on paying Mr Connolly the money he owed and now he was stuck with a load of market goods he had no way of shifting, unless . . . A smile touched his mouth as he thought about an idea that had just come to him. Sam might not agree, but to Billy's mind it would tackle two problems in one throw . . .

*

295

Mary Ellen walked into Rose's bathroom and stopped in surprise as she saw Marion standing there in just her petticoat. She had blood on her mouth and bruises all over her upper arms, and was obviously crying. Seeing Mary Ellen, she turned away quickly and applied a flannel to her mouth.

'What happened?' Mary Ellen said. 'Who did this to you, love?'

Marion shook her head, but when Mary Ellen put her arm round her she started to sob, and it gradually came out. Stevie had started hitting her a few weeks back, because she wouldn't do what he wanted.

'What do you mean?' Mary Ellen stared at her in horror as the story came out bit by bit. Stevie had bought Marion lots of little presents and she'd slept with him at his flat, but then he'd started demanding that she slept with other men in return for all he'd given her. Marion had refused and told him she didn't want to see him again, and so he'd beaten her and left her lying on the street hurt.

'He's evil,' Mary Ellen cried and ran some cold water into the basin. She took the flannel from Marion and began to bathe her arms in the cooling water and then gently dried her flesh. 'Why don't you go to the police? I'll come with you . . .'

'I care about him,' Marion said brokenly. 'Oh, I know I flirt with Billy, but that was only to annoy you. I was envious because he's so good to you – but I loved Stevie.'

'You can't love him now,' Mary Ellen told her. 'You're not the only girl he's hurt, Marion. He's been forcing a girl at work to steal things for him . . .' She saw the look in her friend's eyes. 'What?'

'He was always askin' me things about you and Sam, how much stuff you sold and whether Sam kept his money at the workshops . . .'

'You didn't tell him?'

'I didn't know anything, except that you were busy. I told him you'd had some pilferin' and you'd put mirrors up . . . but that's all . . .'

'You would've though, if you'd known . . .' Mary Ellen looked at her sadly. 'I thought we were friends.'

'You only care about Billy,' Marion said and looked at her, eyes brilliant with spite. 'Well, he kissed me the other night after the youth club when you went home early because you were too busy. You think Billy's yours and you neglect him – but one of these days you'll lose him, even if it isn't to me . . . and I've had enough of you poking your nose in my business. You can tell Rose I'm leavin'. I've got somewhere else to stay . . .'

Marion pushed past her and went running into her bedroom, slamming the door shut and locking it. Mary Ellen stared after her, her throat tight. Had Billy really met Marion and kissed her the night they'd had a bit of a tiff because she couldn't stay late at the club? She didn't want to believe her, but Billy had been a bit odd with her the next day. She thought they'd made it up . . . but was he getting fed up because she had so much studying to do?

'Buy a market stall so that you can sell the cabbage for us and stop selling it in the workshops?' Sam stared at him for several seconds in silence and Billy thought he was going to dismiss the idea out of hand. 'We could certainly cut out the pilfering that way . . .' he said at last. 'And how are you going to run the stall? I'll need you here for at least part of the day.'

'I've got some ideas,' Billy smiled. 'It's only a Saturday site. Ted Hastings was telling me that the pitch next to him was being sold and he has first offer, but I think he might let us go in partnership with him. I'd take on young Archie Miller and there's another boy I know who used to be at St Saviour's. He's looking for work and I could give him a few hours. I'd oversee the stall, get set up and make sure they were settled for the day and then come back here. Ted would keep an eye on them . . . and if he's gettin' a share and exclusive rights to your cabbage, I reckon it will go like a bomb.'

Sam thought about it and then nodded, 'I think it could work, Billy. We don't get that much cabbage really, and I could cut out some of the traders and make it easier to serve the best ones. I've thought for a long time that I'd prefer to work for our better-class customers full time . . .'

'Yeah, why not?' Billy grinned. 'Why not make your customers ring to gain entrance, Sam? Like the jewellery manufacturers do? That shop across the road where they make gold chains, rings and stuff – you don't see people just walking in and out there. They make them ring a bell and only admit the customers they want . . .'

Sam nodded, looking thoughtful again. 'Nolly Rivers is an old friend of mine. He had to tighten his security a year or so back when raiders broke in during opening hours and threatened them all with guns and knives. He lost thousands that day and says he'd rather pack it up than have it happen again, so now he only deals with the customers he trusts.'

'He told me the same when I asked if he would design a wedding ring set for Mary Ellen.' Billy sighed. 'I can't afford it now for a while, because I had to pay Connolly twenty pounds for the stuff he told me to sell on his stall . . . and I have no way of selling it now . . .'

Sam frowned, then, 'Show me what he sold you, Billy?'

'Oh, I've got it in boxes upstairs; there's a few bits and pieces, but nothing from here . . . at least I don't think so . . .'

'It wouldn't matter if there was, because it will all go on the stall and get sold over time. No, don't you see, Billy? If he made his stallholders sell the stuff his rogues stole from here, he probably sold you stolen stuff from somewhere else – and if we could trace it and prove it was stolen . . .'

'We might be able to prove Connolly is behind the thefts . . .'

Sam nodded approvingly. 'I know most of the workshops round here, Billy, and I'll recognise their labels or their style.'

'You'd better come and have a look then,' Billy said. 'Because the last thing I need is to be selling stolen goods . . .'

'I'm sorry, Mary Ellen,' Billy said when he saw her on that Friday evening. 'You remember the jumper I sold you that you were going to give Rose for her birthday?' She nodded, her eyes widening. 'Well, it was stolen, along with about two hundred more . . .'

'Oh no,' Mary Ellen said. 'It was Rose's birthday yesterday and I've already given the jumper to her as well as a skirt I bought from Sam's – she's wearing them to go out in this evening. I shall have to tell her and get her another one . . .'

'No, it's all right,' Billy said. 'I've returned what I had left to their rightful owner and he was grateful, said it didn't matter about the few I'd sold – and thanked me for being so honest. He'd had his suspicions about who had broken in and stolen his stuff, but he's had more locks put on since then and says there's not much he can do about it, except be more careful in future.'

'So I don't have to tell Rose she's wearing a pinched jumper,' Mary Ellen said and gave a sigh of relief. 'Thank goodness . . . but you've lost money, Billy. It's a rotten shame.'

'It doesn't matter, because I'm working for Sam now and soon I'll have a nice surprise for you,' Billy smiled and kissed her. 'I'd much rather lose a few quid than be labelled a thief like my brother . . .'

'You're not a bit like Arthur,' she said and seemed hesitant, then, 'You know, I think Rose is softening up a bit. I asked her if we could get engaged on my birthday and she sort of said maybe. She's been in a much better mood lately.'

'She must have a new man,' Billy teased and Mary Ellen looked thoughtful. 'I may not be able to afford the ring I was going to get you by your birthday . . .'

'I don't have to have an expensive ring. One of those little silver ones with the clasped hands would be fine.'

'They're friendship rings, aren't they?' Billy frowned. 'Maybe I'll get that then if it's all I can afford, but it isn't what I'd planned for us.'

'Are you sure you still want to marry me?'

'What do you mean?' Billy was puzzled. 'Is something wrong, Ellie? What've I done?'

She looked at the ground as she answered, 'Marion was crying last night. Stevie beat her up because she wouldn't go on the game for him – and I told her she should go to the police. She got spiteful and told me you kissed her . . . she said you were fed up with me studying all the time . . .'

Billy took a deep breath. 'It was the night you said you had to leave the youth club early. I found Marion crying on the street when I walked home. She'd had a row with her boyfriend and I tried to comfort her, because she was frightened . . . and she threw her arms around me and kissed me . . .'

'You didn't kiss her?'

'You've got to believe me, Ellie,' Billy said. 'I wish you had more time sometimes – but I've got too much to think about over this business with Sam to be running after other girls. It's you I want . . . you must know it?' He frowned. 'You've got to trust me, Mary Ellen. If you don't we'll break up one of these days . . .'

'No!' Tears were running down her cheeks now. 'Marion says you'll get tired of me.'

'What does she know?' Billy's tone was gentle. 'Surely you know all I want is to be with you, Ellie?'

'All I want is to be with you,' she said and lifted her face for his kiss. 'You know I love you, Billy?'

'Yeah,' he grinned as the old confidence returned. 'I've got some good news for you – me and Sam and Ted Hastings are goin' into partnership on the market selling all Sam's cabbage stuff – and Jimbo says I can have his cabbage cheap when he gets any; I've just got to cut the labels out . . .'

'Who is Jimbo?' Mary Ellen was puzzled, but she clung to his arm, glad to see how excited he was and to realise that she'd been silly to let Marion's spite upset her. Billy had big plans for the future, just as she had.

'Jim Platter – he's the one I took the stolen stuff back to. They were all perfect stock, Mary Ellen. No wonder they sold quick for fifteen bob on the market. He was so impressed by me botherin' to give them back that he says we can have all his seconds in future – so we'll have exclusive rights to his seconds knitwear and Sam's cabbage as well. Archie and Nipper are goin' to run the stall between them . . . do you remember Nipper from St Saviour's? Well, he went on the ships for a couple of trips when he left, but he's got a bit of a weak chest. The doc told him it was a legacy from the days when they used to go hungry for weeks on end . . . in fact he didn't know what it was like to eat a decent meal until he came to us at Halfpenny Street.'

'Nipper always followed you about like you were his hero,' Mary Ellen said, remembering how they'd made friends with Nipper and his brother Jimmy.

'Yeah, we were all good mates . . .' Billy frowned. 'Did you know that Jimmy was killed about a year ago working on the Docks?'

'Oh no!' Mary Ellen's eyes stung with sudden tears as she remembered the cheerful lad who had been bruised and battered and half-starved when he was brought into St Saviour's. 'Jimmy always looked out for Nipper . . . he must miss him terribly.'

'He does,' Billy said. 'He's been living in a mission down near the East India Docks, taking whatever jobs he can, but he's going to find himself a room somewhere now that he's been offered a steady job . . .'

'You can trust him, Billy.'

'Nipper and Archie both; they've both had a rotten time, but maybe things will get better now. I popped in to see Sister and tell her what I was doing and she says that Mrs Miller is going to be released very soon . . .'

'If what you told me is true she should never have been sent to prison. They ought to give her a lot of money to compensate her for what she's suffered – and her family.'

'There're some things money can't make better,' Billy said, 'but I agree that she's owed. I doubt if anyone in authority will see it like that though . . .'

Mary Ellen nodded, looking grim. 'Things aren't always fair, Billy – but if Archie has a proper job that's something at least. Let's hope his mum can find them a home and a job for herself.'

'Archie has told me all about his mate Ikey; he's the one that found out a lot of stuff about Mrs Miller. I reckon he's a useful bloke to know. He might be able to help me and Sam . . .'

CHAPTER 23

'Sister Beatrice . . .' Sandra Miller sat down in the chair indicated across the desk in Sister Beatrice's office. 'Mr Hendry insisted on bringing me here after I was released this morning . . .' She glanced at the man standing in front of the empty fire grate. The weather was still mild even though it was autumn now and fires were not needed as yet. 'He says you have something to say to me?'

'Yes, Sandra, I do . . . I may call you by your name?'

'Of course.' Sandra smiled. 'After what you've done for me I think we must count as friends . . .'

'Yes, I would like to think so,' Beatrice said. 'Mr Hendry brought you here at my request. You have learned by now that your home has been boarded over and although some of your possessions were removed to safety by your friends, much has been lost . . . another injustice I fear.'

'I intend to approach the landlord and demand some sort of recompense,' Edward Hendry said. 'However, at the moment he's offering a derisory sum . . . twenty-five pounds. I've told him it isn't adequate but he claims the contents were fit only for the bonfire they had in the garden.'

'I dare say much of it was,' Sandra admitted. 'After my husband died I couldn't afford new carpets or curtains and the furniture was second-hand at the start. We were saving for a new home but . . .'

'Yes, well, it isn't just the value of the goods, it is the way it was all taken from you without reference to your feelings or the law,' Mr Hendry said. 'I doubt we shall get true justice, Mrs Miller – there is no fund from the state for reimbursing victims of false accusations and false imprisonment at present. However, I have spoken to your firm and they are willing to offer you your old job back – or one hundred pounds and a reference . . .'

'A hundred pounds . . .' Sandra gasped and her face was pale. 'That is a lot of money . . .'

'Hardly enough to compensate for all you suffered. However, it would be costly to bring an action against them and I can't guarantee that we should end up with more at the finish.'

'Oh no, I'm grateful for the money offered and the reference. I must have a reference or I shan't find work.'

'Well, that is not strictly true,' Sister Beatrice interceded. 'Since Angela retired to care for her twins we have not had a permanent secretary here. What I wondered was whether you might consider doing part-time secretarial work and combining it with some care for the children . . .'

'My children are here?' Sandra looked at her anxiously.

'Archie is out, but June is in the sick ward. We haven't put her back in the dorms yet, because Mr Adderbury says she needs a little time to recover from her ordeal.'

'Who is he?'

'A very respectable and clever psychiatrist, who gives us his services for free,' Beatrice said with a smile at the lawyer. 'Your children are here and I wondered if you would like to stay too – just until you can find a house that will suit you? In return you will help the carers and act as my secretary, and we shall pay you, of course.'

'You are extremely kind but . . .' Sandra drew a shuddering breath. 'Yes, perhaps it would be best for a while, until I have time to adjust.'

'Exactly,' Beatrice smiled at her. 'People can be extremely cruel, Sandra, and until everyone knows the truth you may find yourself shunned. However, you would be accepted here and even if you stayed with us for just a short time, you would have a chance to come to terms with your life and decide where you wish to go . . .'

'Yes . . .' Sandra looked from Beatrice to Mr Hendry. 'Perhaps you would let me stay here then – and Mr Hendry, perhaps you will get that reference and the money for me please?'

'I certainly shall, though I am not satisfied with the amount, but I fear it is the best we can do, and I hope for a similar sum from your careless landlord.'

'I can only thank you for all the time and effort you've put in on my behalf.'

'Most of the work has been done by Ikey,' Edward Hendry said and smiled. 'He persuaded that secretary at your old firm to come forward with her evidence and that led to the arrest of Mr Prentice, who when he was presented with the proof that he'd handled the stolen cheque, confessed that you were entirely innocent. Ikey told him he would get a lesser sentence if he made a full confession – and after that you were in the clear. Ikey is a most unusual man, Mrs Miller, but your son likes him and trusts him and I must say I do too . . .'

'Where is my son please? You said he was out . . .'

Beatrice frowned. 'He is working on the market with some more friends of his . . .'

'That has to stop,' Sandra said and frowned. 'He should still be in school!'

'Archie works Saturdays and holidays, but he's made up his mind to leave as soon as he's old enough.'

'Well, I am his mother and I want him at school until he's passed all his exams,' Sandra said and stood up. 'You've all been very kind and I cannot thank you enough for helping me to prove my innocence, but I am rather tired . . . and I need the stink of the prison off me before I go to June.'

'Of course.' Beatrice rose to her feet at once. 'Come with me, and I shall show you where you can rest and sleep. We have a kitchen here and the staff will provide you with a meal and a pot of tea if you ask – but we do request that you do not help yourself. Cook doesn't like people in her kitchen unless she tells them what to do . . .'

'I should not dream of it,' Sandra said. 'I shall feel better in a few hours and then perhaps we can discuss your kind offer again?'

'Yes, certainly,' Beatrice said and led the way out into the hall and into the lift. 'I will give you a brief tour downstairs and then take you to the nurses' home, where I've had a room prepared for you . . .'

'Ah, Archie,' Sister Beatrice smiled at him as he entered her office and he felt relief wash over him. When he'd been told to go straight to her office, Archie had thought he was in trouble, but he could see immediately that it wasn't the case. 'I wanted to tell you that your mother is here – she's with June in the sick room at the moment.'

'Mum's here?' Archie felt a rush of joy and he grinned at the nun. 'When did she arrive?'

'Just before noon,' Sister Beatrice replied. 'Sandra was tired and she wanted to wash and rest, but she's been with your sister for more than two hours now. I am sure she is anxious to see you too.'

'I'd have come sooner if I'd known,' Archie said. 'Can I go to see her now – I'm not in trouble, am I?'

'Not with me, but your mother is not happy about your having taken employment on the market . . .'

Archie's glow of pleasure faded for a moment. 'No, she wanted me to stay on and take all me exams . . . but I ain't goin' to use them fancy things. I like workin' on the market and Ted says I'm doing well and I'll be rich one day just like he is . . .'

Sister looked amused, but she didn't seem angry. She just told him to go and find his mother and sort things out with her. Archie wanted to run to his mother; he wanted to hug her and kiss her and tell her how much he loved her, and how much he'd missed her, but he walked slowly, dragging his feet because he knew she would be angry. Sandra Miller had big plans for her children and Archie had let her down; he'd promised to take what she would think was just a dead-end job on the market – but worse than that, he'd let them send June away and it was his fault that those bad things had happened to her.

He opened the door of the sick ward and immediately

308

saw that his mother was sitting on June's bed, holding his sister as she leaned against her, eyes closed, a look of peace on her face. His mother was talking to her, kissing her head and soothing her, but then she looked up and saw Archie. For a moment her eyes lit up with love, but then her look of welcome faded and she wasn't smiling as she held out her hand to him.

'Come here, Archie,' she said. 'I've been waiting for you . . .'

Archie went to her, took her hand and bent down to kiss her cheek. She turned her head and kissed him back on the side of his head, but still she wasn't smiling.

'I'm sorry, Mum. I know I shouldn't have let them take June away . . .'

'That wasn't your fault,' she said and now there was a faint smile in her eyes. 'I've been told what you and your friend did to help June. I'm proud of you for what you did then, Archie . . .'

There was a *but* lurking and Archie waited for the blow to fall. He loved his mum and he was sorry if he'd upset her, but he couldn't give up his dreams and his new life to please her.

'You know why I'm upset, Archie. I want you to stay at school, take your exams and make something of your life – like your father would've wanted for you, love.'

'I can do all the sums I need and I can keep books and write a letter – Ikey says I don't need all the rest if I want to be a market trader and earn a good living . . .'

'And who is this man to advise my son?' Sandra felt a surge of irritation. Ikey had by all accounts done most to get her name cleared, but he'd kept the truth from her in prison and he was telling her son it was all right to work on the market when Sandra wanted him to do something worthwhile with his life. She wasn't sure what yet, but she would like him to go on to college and seek a better life than she'd managed to give him.

'Ikey rescued June from those people. He's the one that's done it all, Mum – he got the truth out of Reg Prentice and made him confess it to your old boss . . . and he saved me from life on the streets. He's the best friend I've got, even better than Billy and Ted and his daughter and Nipper . . .' Archie's words trailed away as he saw that his mother was unmoved. 'He's a real good friend, Mum. You would like him if you knew him, just like I do . . .'

'Perhaps I should,' she conceded, remembering that she had thought him attractive when he'd visited her in prison, 'but he still has no right to tell you what you should do with your life. I'm your mother and I'm the one who decides what happens in this family.'

'You weren't here when we needed you,' Archie said truculently. 'When I was starvin' on the streets and attacked – and you weren't here when June needed you . . .' His voice trailed away as he saw the pain in her eyes and he was immediately sorry, because he hadn't wanted to hurt her. 'Ikey was here for us, Mum, and Ted and Billy, and Sister and Ted's daughter. They're me friends and I want to work with them; I want to make a good life for us and I'll make good money one day soon and then you won't even have to work. You can just stay home and look after June . . . as you should . . .'

Tears filled his mother's eyes and Archie felt her pain strike deep into his heart, but he couldn't relent and tell her he would do what she wanted. He wasn't ever going to be treated as just a kid again; as soon as the law allowed, he was going to work with people who treated him as if he belonged, respected him and looked out for him – but he didn't want to cause her pain.

'June will go to school again soon and she'll be all the things you want, Mum,' he said. 'I'm sorry but I've made up my mind. It's my life and you can't make me take exams if I don't want to.'

'We'll talk about this later,' his mother said in a voice Archie remembered from the past; back then it had made him resigned to giving in and letting her have her way, but he was older now – much older than the few months she'd been in prison should have made him. He might still be a youth in the eyes of the law but Archie felt like a man and he was determined he would never go back to school again . . .

'I'm goin' out later,' Archie said. 'I've promised Billy I'll do something for him. Don't worry about me, Mum. I'll be perfectly all right – and I'll probably stay with Billy or Ted tonight.'

'I forbid you to stay out all night! How long has this been going on? I'm quite sure Sister Beatrice doesn't know you don't sleep here . . .'

'It's the first time,' Archie said. 'Billy and Sam need a bit of help, so we're all going to be there – Ted and Ikey and a few friends . . .'

'Archie . . .' his mother's gaze narrowed. 'I'm your mother and I forbid you to do this . . . whatever it is.'

'I'm sorry, Mum,' Archie said, 'but I'm goin' as soon as I've had me tea. You're not to worry or be upset. I'll see you in the mornin' and when you've met me friends you'll understand . . .'

'Archie . . . Archie, come back here,' Sandra said and then realised she was talking to an empty room, empty apart from her and her daughter. Poor little June, her darling child, who was clinging to her as if she would never let go again. Tears filled Sandra's eyes and she bent to kiss her daughter's head, whispering of her love.

'I'm so sorry,' she whispered. 'I promise I shan't leave you again.'

'Mummy,' June whimpered and clung to her even tighter. 'Archie's friend Ikey is brave and nice. I liked him . . . he got me away . . .' Tears caught at her throat, and Sandra forgot her rebellious son as she cuddled her little girl. 'Don't go away again, will you?'

'No, I shan't go,' Sandra said. 'I'll stay here with you until you're ready and then you can come to my room and sleep in my bed . . .'

Archie ate his meal quickly; he was half fearful that his mother would come after him and demand that he went to bed immediately, as she would have if he'd defied her in the past. Yet things were different now, even though she hadn't accepted it yet. Too much had happened for Archie to give up his plans and become a child again. He wanted to please his mum, to make her smile and enable her to live in a home that he helped to provide, but he wasn't willing to give in all the way down the line. Archie wasn't a child any longer – and the part he was to play that evening was surely proof that his friends thought him a man now.

Ten days had passed since the last break-in at Sam's place. Customers had to ring to be admitted now, and they'd managed to stop the pilfering that had been going on for far longer than Sam had realised. Sam told them he'd been worried that he might lose some of his good customers, but they'd praised his efforts to ensure the goods were more secure and all he'd lost was the lower end of the market traders – and Mr Connolly.

'Connolly hasn't been in since that night,' Sam had told Billy earlier. 'I think he knows we suspect him and that's why he's stayed away. With three of us in the showroom his rogues wouldn't be able to smuggle anything out – and now Anna has gone it isn't easy to take something from the better rails and hide it amongst the faulty goods. Besides, we don't have that on the showroom rails now and every item has to be written down on an invoice and checked.'

'He'll turn his attention elsewhere now,' Billy said. 'I think you've stopped the pilferin', Sam – but I don't think he or his bully boys will give in that easily. Connolly is determined to teach you a lesson and one of these nights they're going to try a break-in again . . .'

'We'll be ready for them,' Sam said, 'but I'm not sure how long I can ask friends to be on high alert . . .'

It was Ikey who had come to the market stall just before they started to pack up for the night. He'd heard a whisper on the streets that a break-in was planned for that night, and he'd come to warn them.

'Are you sure?' Billy frowned. 'They're fools if they talk about it – it might just be a sprat to catch a mackerel . . .'

'I wasn't given the tip-off, I just happened to hear them whispering about what they planned, and I'm not sure but I think they intend to do harm once they get what they're after . . .'

313

Billy frowned. 'What kind of harm?'

'I'm not sure, but I imagine it was pretty evil, because the one they call Ricky was gloating, saying it would serve that cocky little bastard right . . . and I'm assuming they meant you, Billy.'

'He threatened to give me a good hiding next time.'

'I doubt if his intentions stop there,' Ikey looked thoughtful. 'I think it would be a good idea if we all kept an eye out tonight just in case . . .'

Everyone agreed and Archie had volunteered to help. At first Ikey and Ted had said he would be better off out of it, but Billy had taken his side and put his hand on his shoulder.

'Are you prepared to hide out in the yard and get really cold?' he asked. 'If you see anything, nip round the corner and telephone me and then the police . . . then just stay out of the way until it's over . . .'

'Thanks, Billy,' Archie said, feeling proud that Billy thought he was capable of playing a part in their plans. He'd listened to them talking about how much force it would be lawful to use, and Ikey had told them to keep it to a minimum.

'I'll be outside keeping watch like Archie,' he'd said. 'There's a few friends I can call on for help and they will be loitering on the streets somewhere – no one takes any notice of a drunk sitting on the pavement and they'll be discreet, but we're going to need numbers, if we want to finish this once and for all . . .'

They were all in agreement, and Archie had listened enthralled. This was the spirit of the old East End he'd heard so much about from his father, everyone willing to help and stand up to bullies. Yeah, he might be just a

314

young lad, but he had a useful job and these people trusted him. He had no intention of letting them down . . .

Taking up his place in a dark corner of the yard, Archie determinedly shut out the fact that he was cold and tried to ignore thoughts of the warm bed waiting for him at St Saviour's. He wasn't there, he was here and of his own free will, and he knew he wouldn't fall asleep, because he was too tense, too excited. Some of the others suspected that it would all be for nothing, but Archie trusted in Ikey. When Ikey told you he'd heard a rumour he wasn't making it up; he was an expert at lurking in shadows and Archie hadn't been able to spot him, even though he knew that he was here somewhere.

Ikey had spent years on the street watching, listening, helping others like him who'd fallen out of the everyday world into a kind of underworld and doing what he could to restore the balance. He couldn't help them all, all his brothers who slept rough night after night, and many of them didn't want to be helped; they drank because they wanted to and they couldn't change, but Ikey helped those he could and did the occasional under-cover job for his friend, the posh lawyer that Archie had seen once or twice – and Archie didn't know what his friend was planning, but he was sure he knew more than he'd let on, even to Billy and the others . . .

CHAPTER 24

Sister Beatrice replaced the receiver on her telephone. The Children's Department was struggling to find a place for a brother and sister who had recently lost their parents. Miss Sampson had asked if she could help out for a while and Sister Beatrice felt very virtuous for having handled the situation without showing even a hint of her personal satisfaction. Perhaps at last they were beginning to understand that they needed St Saviour's to carry on with its work.

Well, she considered her restraint deserved a nice pot of tea and since they were short of help these days, she would go down and make it herself. When she got to the kitchens she discovered that Sandra Miller was there and appeared to be making a tray of cocoa. She looked a little awkward when she saw Beatrice, her cheeks flushed.

'Staff Nurse Wendy was busy with one of the children. A little boy came to her complaining of stomach pains and he was vomiting when I left them. Wendy asked if I would make cocoa for the children and her and I thought as you'd offered me a job here it would be all right . . .'

'Muriel is a little jealous of her kitchen,' Beatrice said and smiled. 'It's best to ask during the day when she's here, but at night we have to look after ourselves. During the war we had to be so careful with the rations, because things were in such short supply, but now it's not as difficult, though I'm afraid that we still have to be careful because of our limited budget, but that doesn't apply to cocoa or tea and biscuits . . .'

'I should have thought a place like this would be government-funded these days?'

'Under the state umbrella there is presently a mixture of state-run and independent institutions for the care of children, because they simply do not have the funds to cope without the independents. St Saviour's is still an independently run charitable organisation. However, we are regulated by the Children's Act, as is every other orphanage in the country, and quite frequently suffer impertinent supervision visits, and ridiculous memos, telling us things we already know. I think the council people see us as a thorn in their sides, because they would prefer to run everything themselves. However, because of public opinion, we still have a place here in the East End and the care of the children is down to us. We often have difficult cases referred to us through the Children's Department, but the local police more often than not come to us first when children are in need of immediate help, because the council just doesn't have the right facilities. If we were not here, it would be a choice between a police cell and hospital until the Children's Department organised a place for them.'

Sandra nodded her head as she stirred the sugar into the drinks. 'Both Archie and June speak well of you, and I've decided that I should like to take your offer up, at least for a while, until I can manage to get a house where we can all live together . . .'

'Archie hasn't told you that he wants to go and live with Mr Hastings then?' Beatrice arched her brows. 'Your son has grown up, Sandra. You will find him changed a great deal. He knows what he wants to do with his life and I fear he will prove difficult if you try to impose your will.'

Sandra frowned, seeming as if she would say something rash or angry, but then she sighed and inclined her head. 'He is so like his father – my husband knew what he wanted and you couldn't change him whatever you said or did . . .' She shook her head and looked sad. 'What happened to my son while I was in prison, Sister Beatrice?'

'I don't believe he was abused or harmed himself, but he saw things and he felt responsible for his sister and what happened to her. He's made up his mind that he's a man now and won't be told what to do or used . . . eventually, he may ask your advice again, if you're patient. He will come back to you, if you have the strength to let him go.'

'Is that what it takes?' Sandra asked, her face pale and her eyes dark with emotion. 'I want to hold him and comfort him and tell him I love him, as I have June, but there's a barrier. I'm not sure that he trusts me now . . .'

'Archie trusts very few people,' Beatrice said. 'I let him down but I redeemed myself in his eyes – but I know that he loves you and he believes in you. He was so angry about what happened to you.'

'Archie is a good son, he always was,' Sandra said. 'Sometimes I was a bit hard on him, because I was so afraid of losing him. After I lost my husband he was all the more precious, you see.'

'Absolutely. A son is the most precious thing a woman can ever have . . .' Beatrice's voice was steady though it carried such pain that Sandra felt it in her breast. 'And to lose that son is the worst thing that can ever happen . . .'

'You lost a son?' Sandra said and reached out to touch her arm. 'I'm so sorry.'

'It was a long time ago, and time makes it easier to accept, though the pain never goes,' Beatrice said. 'Take my advice, Sandra. Be loving towards him and try to understand that Archie needs freedom to grow.'

'Yes, I'll try,' Sandra smiled at her. 'I'm not sure I can let go but I will try . . .'

Archie was so cold and tired that he wasn't sure he could keep his eyes open much longer. Surely it was too late now? No one was coming, because it was morning now and the church clock had struck two ages ago. Perhaps it wouldn't matter if he went home to bed . . .

Even as he was about to leave his vantage point, he sensed something beside him and then a firm hand slid over his mouth and a voice whispered in his ear.

'Don't move, lad; they've just arrived . . .'

Archie nodded and Ikey removed his hand. He hadn't heard his friend move behind him, hadn't been aware that he was close at hand, and he certainly hadn't seen the dark shadows that now appeared in the yard. He calculated there were six or seven of them . . . no, eight. A shiver went through him as he watched their stealthy movements.

'Go now, walk behind those crates and ring Billy,'

Ikey's voice hissed in his ear. 'He may be aware but we want him alerted, and then wait ten minutes before you ring the police.'

Archie didn't answer, just inclined his head. He moved carefully, slowly, always keeping behind the crates, which were stored in the leather manufacturer's half of the yard. His nerves were jangling and he could scarcely breathe as he heard the tapping sounds; the thieves were doing something but he wasn't sure what, because he'd expected them to use force to break down the door or smash windows.

Out in the street, Archie sprinted to the red telephone box at the end of the street and pulled open the door. He halted in disgust as he saw it had been trashed by vandals and was unusable. What was he going to do now? Several people in the area had phones for their businesses, but he was uneasy about knocking them up in the early hours of the morning. He had to do something! Suddenly remembering there was another box two streets away, Archie started to run.

He'd never run as hard in his life. His chest was heaving and he was terrified. Supposing this box was out of use as well? What happened if he couldn't let Billy know or the police?

By the time he reached the next phone box he was panting and his chest hurt. Everywhere was so dark and the light in the box was like a beacon; he'd never felt so relieved when he saw the phone was still in use. With hands that wouldn't stop shaking, he felt for his pennies and dialled the number he'd memorised. Billy's phone rang but there was no answer. Archie let it go on ringing for a while, but still no answer.

How long had it taken him to run here? He didn't have a watch and he'd lost all sense of time. Those men could have got in and attacked Billy. Supposing he was lying hurt inside? Supposing Ikey and the others weren't enough to stop them?

Billy dialled 999 and asked to speak to the police as an emergency.

'Police, how can I help you, caller?'

'There's a gang of men breaking into the clothing factory at the corner of Folgate Street . . .'

'Right, can you give your name, caller? Please tell me who you are and what exactly you saw.'

'About eight of them attacking the back of the clothing factory, next door to the leather manufacturer's . . . You want to get there quick or they'll hurt Billy the night watchman.'

'We need more details, sir. Please, can you give us your name and exactly what you saw?'

'Tell Sergeant Sallis Archie Miller rang and said Sam's place is being attacked again . . .'

Archie replaced the receiver as he'd been instructed to do and left the phone box, running back the way he'd come at a slightly slower pace. He was thinking hard, trying to decide what to do next. Should he just hang around at the front or go to the back and see if he could help? He'd been told not to return after he'd made his call, because they didn't want him involved in the rough stuff, but Archie was uneasy. Billy hadn't answered and he wondered if he'd been too late to warn him. Supposing Billy had fallen asleep and they'd caught him unawares . . . ?

Deciding to go round the back, Archie was shocked

at what he saw. Several fights were going on in the yard, fists and batons being wielded by a crowd of angry men and there was a lot of shouting and yelling as well as a few screams; some men were already lying on the ground, moaning and obviously injured.

Archie wasn't sure who was who so he couldn't join in the fighting, because he didn't want to hinder Sam's friends, but he saw that one of the windows had been completely smashed in and decided to go inside and investigate.

There was jagged glass still in the frame, so Archie took off the overcoat he'd been given at St Saviour's and pulled it up over his face and head as he climbed in. At first it was very dark but he could see light ahead of him and he crept out into the passage, listening for what was going on. Some of the rogues had got in here, that much was clear, and he could hear loud voices coming from the stockroom.

'That's it, smash everything, and rip the clothes,' he heard a man say. 'We'll destroy the whole place . . . and that cocky bugger Baggins an' all.'

'This stuff is worth good money. We ought to get some of it out . . .' another voice objected.

'Nah, Connolly said to trash the lot and get out – teach the buggers who's the boss around here . . .'

Archie froze in his tracks as he heard the sound of breaking glass and rails being overturned. There was nothing he could do to stop what was happening here, but he had to find Billy, to warn him they were out to get him . . .

He turned back and went up the stairs as swiftly as he could. There was no light on up here and it was a while before he could adjust to the darkness, but he stumbled up the stairs to the landing, and called out, hoping that Billy might hear him.

'Where are you, mate? Billy, can you hear me?'

No one answered. Archie felt for the switch at the top of the stairs and clicked it, bringing light to the landing immediately. He'd known that the work of restoration had been completed but he wasn't sure that the electric was on yet. Relief rushed through him as he ran from room to room, switching on lights and calling Billy's name. After searching each room, he was satisfied that Billy wasn't here and he went back to the head of the stairs, running down them and straight into the arms of a huge man he'd never seen before.

'What the bloody hell are you doing here?' the man demanded and gave him a rough shake.

'Looking for Billy,' Archie answered defiantly. 'I know you bastards have smashed everything up and I wanted to make sure he wasn't lying hurt up here . . .'

'He's all right,' the man answered and gave him a grin in which most of the teeth were missing. 'Get out of 'ere, lad, and leave this to the men . . .'

'Are you on our side?' Archie said and grinned back.

'Git afore I give you a thick ear,' his captor said and thrust him towards the back door, which now stood open. 'I've got work to do.'

Archie ran into the yard and saw that the fighting seemed to be over here, though from the screams and shouts inside, it was still going on there. Ikey was directing events from what he could see and a couple of bewildered-looking police constables had turned up.

Several men were lying on the ground and some of them were groaning. Seeing Sam, he went up to him.

'They're smashing up your stuff,' he said. 'I heard them say Mr Connolly told them to do it to teach you and Billy a lesson . . .'

'You heard them say it?' Sam's gaze narrowed. 'You'd better tell the police.'

'Yeah, all right . . .' Archie went with Sam to the constables, one of whom was busily writing in his notebook.

'What are you doing here?' Ikey said. 'You were told to go home as soon as you'd phoned for the police.'

'I had to go to the next box, two streets up because they'd broken this one,' Archie told him. 'Billy didn't answer and I thought they must have caught him . . .'

'Billy is all right. He was downstairs when the phone rang and it's due to him that we managed to get in in time to stop them completely trashing this place.'

Archie was relieved. 'He's all right then?'

'Well, he's got some bruises and a black eye. He's here somewhere . . . trying to sort this lot out . . .'

'Archie heard them talking as they were throwing the stuff about,' Sam said. 'Tell Ikey and the constable what you heard, son.'

Archie repeated what he'd heard and the constable duly wrote it down. Billy came up to them, frowning as he saw Archie standing there.

'I thought we told you not to come back when you'd done your job?'

'Archie was worried because you didn't answer the phone,' Ikey said. 'He went back in to look for you – that's why all the lights are on upstairs . . .'

324

'I forgot to put them off,' Archie said guiltily and Billy laughed.

'Cost me a fortune in electric bills you will,' he said and ruffled Archie's hair. 'You're a brave lad . . .'

Sam was talking to Ikey and the police constables. A Black Maria had arrived and half a dozen more police officers came rushing out of it, and after some consultation with their colleagues, started putting handcuffs on the men Ikey pointed out and bundling them into the back of their van. One of the police officers was Sergeant Sallis and he came over to where Archie was standing with Billy.

'You rang the emergency number,' he said to Archie. 'They sent a couple of officers but thought it might be a hoax until someone else rang the station and reported a disturbance here and then the night officer said you'd asked for me so we thought we'd take a look.'

'You're just in time to take these buggers in,' Sam said, 'and to hear what Archie overheard in there. Go on, tell him, lad . . .'

Archie repeated his story and Sergeant Sallis looked grim. 'I believe you, Archie; the trouble is Mr Connolly is a much-respected man in these parts and we'll have difficulty in building a case against him. We know what he's been up to, but everyone is too scared to give evidence against him . . .'

'I'm not,' Sam said, 'but I've only dealt with the messenger boy. He sent Stevie Baker to tell me what would happen if I didn't pay up. He and that other one . . . Ricky something . . . they gave me a taste of what I'd get by slapping me about a bit, but I refused to pay.'

325

'But I heard them . . . and I'll say so in court,' Archie offered bravely.

'I'll testify that Stevie told me Connolly was behind it all,' Billy said. 'Surely between us we have enough evidence to convict him?'

Ikey came to stand beside him. 'The sergeant is right, Archie. We need more than your say so, even though we all know you're speaking the truth . . . Our only chance is if one of these rogues decides to talk . . .'

'They're probably more afraid of Mr Connolly than us or going to prison,' Sergeant Sallis said. 'I'll do what I can but men like that escape the law too often . . .'

He went off to talk to the constables who had been busy rounding up all the rogues, most of whom had been thoroughly chastened and looked sorry for themselves.

'Is that the lot?' he asked. 'Which one is Stevie Baker?'

'Haven't seen him,' Billy said. 'I reckon he just sent the thugs in and kept clear himself.'

'So we've got them all?'

'Apart from the one that got away,' Billy said, a scowl on his face. 'His name is Ricky, but I don't know his second name. This is not my first encounter with that particular gentleman and I doubt it will be the last . . .'

'I imagine the man you're speaking of is possibly Ricky Martin, works for Connolly. I'll go round his house and have a word with him first thing in the morning.'

Billy nodded, watching as the police van drove off and the other men who had helped stop the raid began to melt away, returning to their homes and families. They nodded grimly to each other, because they were all traders themselves, hardened by necessity to the facts of life in London's East End. Mostly, they were law-abiding citizens, but there were times when it was necessary to stick together and stand up for your rights.

'You'd best come home with me,' Ted Hastings said, coming up to Archie and laying a firm hand on his shoulder. He had a red mark on his cheek and a cut lip, but otherwise seemed unhurt. 'Sam and Billy have a tough night ahead of them, getting that mess cleared up . . .' he jerked his head at the workrooms.

'Can't I stay and help?'

'Best not, lad,' Ted said. 'We've got to be up early in the morning. You'll have to keep the stall going until Billy can see to things again . . . Are you up to playin' truant for a couple of days until things get straight?'

'Mum says I have to go back to school now, but don't have to this week, we've got half-term holidays and I can work every day if I'm needed. OK, let's go then,' Archie gave in with a grin, though he was sure he could have helped with the clearing up, but Ted was right, someone had to keep the market stalls running, and he wanted to help in any way he could, even though his mother didn't like the idea of him working on the market.

'Sam's lost a lot of money, hasn't he?'

'Yeah, must be several hundred quid, but it's not as bad as it might have been if no one had been here. Never know what they might have done. If they'd started a fire the whole row could've gone up. Sam doesn't know if his insurance will cover him for the spoiled goods, but he'll recover, Archie. He's known tough times before, believe me.'

Archie nodded; silent for a moment, he asked the question that had been in his mind for a while. 'Why do you think Mr Connolly has got it in for him?'

'Sam wouldn't give in and pay a huge chunk of his profit. They had to make an example of him, because once this gets round a lot more of his victims are going to resist. Once the police have enough evidence to arrest him, there could be a rush of folk coming forward to accuse him and his bullies.'

'It's like what happened to Mum,' Archie said. 'That rotten Reg Prentice had it in for her because she wouldn't give in to him – and I reckon that's what this is all about.'

'Yeah, Connolly is warning us that he's top dog,' Ted said. 'It's all about marking out his territory, showing everyone what they'll get if they defy him. Trouble is, we might end up with a gang war before we're finished.' He sighed deeply as he unlocked his van and indicated that Archie should get in. 'I wish we'd got them all tonight, though. That Ricky Martin is vicious and I wouldn't trust Stevie Baker as far as I could throw him . . .'

CHAPTER 25

Mary Ellen looked about her at the scene of destruction from the previous evening and shook her head. Sam turned and saw her and walked to greet her with his usual cheery smile.

'It could've been a lot worse. If your Billy hadn't been so quick-thinking we might have lost all the stock instead of one rail.'

'Everywhere is such a mess . . .'

'Yes, I know,' Sam said and looked frustrated. 'We worked all night but all we could do was to board up the windows and clear out the glass counter. I'll get a wooden one next time – they're harder to smash . . .'

'Do you think they will come back?' Mary Ellen asked anxiously.

Sam shrugged. 'Not for a while, because we gave them more than they bargained for, but things won't settle down until Connolly is under lock and key. His kind is scum but too clever for the police. He's never involved in any of the dirty stuff himself . . .'

'Well, we'll help you get straight in here,' Mary Ellen said. 'We can sort through that stuff on the floor and see if anything can be saved – even if it only goes as cabbage. We might be able to salvage a few garments.'

'Make sure you shake them out, because there may be shards of glass,' Sam said, 'but don't worry too much. They didn't get any of the special orders, because I put them in the van and took them home.'

'Well that's a relief . . .' Mary Ellen smiled at him. 'We'll do what we can and then get started on the new orders.'

'Good girl,' Sam said. 'I'll get those boxes of broken glass into the yard.'

'Where are Herbie and Bert – and Billy?'

'I told Billy to have a wash and change, get himself something to eat – and the others are late in. I told them not to come in before lunch; they were both here last night . . .'

'I think you should take your own advice, Sam,' Mary Ellen said and took off her jacket. 'Me and the girls will hoover the carpet up and then we'll sort the rails out.'

Sam picked up a cardboard box filled with broken glass and headed towards the yard door.

'Go home when you've dumped that, get some rest, have a wash and your breakfast, and then come back,' Mary Ellen ordered. 'Leave this to us, Sam. We can manage for now.'

Sam nodded and yawned. 'Yeah, mebbe you're right, lass. I'm bushed and I could do with a sit down . . .'

Mary Ellen had the showroom almost back to normal when the men arrived to fit new glass in the windows. She surveyed the finished job with satisfaction, about to return to her work station and start machining when

Billy walked in, yawning and stretching. She gave a little cry of distress as she saw his face, which was badly bruised and cut.

'Oh, Billy, you're hurt,' she said. 'Your face is so sore . . .'

'Yeah, a bit,' he said, 'but we saw them off, Ellie, and most of them are in worse shape than we are . . .'

'I don't like you fighting the way you do . . .'

'There are always bullies out there,' Billy said. 'You have to stand up to them, love, otherwise they would just walk all over you.'

'I know, but you're hurt and Sam has lost so much money . . .'

'He knows it, but says it won't stop him carrying on. He does have insurance for the broken windows and counter, but he's not sure how he stands as far as malicious damage to the stock is concerned.'

'I hate that Mr Connolly,' she said crossly. 'I hope they make him pay for what he's done.'

'Yeah, me too, but he'll probably get off scot-free,' Billy said. 'It's no use, love. Sam just has to take the loss and think himself lucky he didn't lose the lot . . .'

He smiled and reached out for her. 'We're all still alive, love, and that's all that matters, isn't it?'

'Yes, it is,' she said and moved towards him, smiling as he reached out and took her in his arms. 'As long as you're all right, Billy, that's all I care about . . .'

'Archie . . . are you all right?' Sandra asked as he entered the room in the nurses' home, where she was sitting with June on her bed, reading to her from an Enid Blyton storybook. 'I was worried when I heard what

331

happened at that place . . . It was lucky you didn't get yourself killed . . .'

'Who told you?'

'Sergeant Sallis came to see Sister Beatrice and told us that it was you that alerted the police.' Her anxious gaze went over him. 'He said you were very brave, but we were concerned . . . You are all right?'

'Yes, Mum, I'm fine. I went home with Ted, because we had an early start. I've got to help keep the stall goin' until Billy sorts things out at Sam's place . . . and you can't say I should be at school, because it's the half-term holidays next week . . .'

'Yes, I do see that your friends need you,' she said and Archie felt the tension leave him. She was smiling. He'd been thinking he would get a flea in his ear when he eventually got home and here she was understanding how he felt and listening. 'It was a terrible thing to happen. Sergeant Sallis told us that you overheard something important and they are hoping to catch a criminal because of it . . .'

'Well, it ain't that easy 'cos he's respectable, only he ain't – it's just that he sits in the background and gets others to do his dirty work for him . . .'

'A most unpleasant sort,' she replied and hesitated. 'I hope you won't be involved in any more dangerous stuff, Archie? I rely on you to look after us, you know. I can't work full time yet, because of . . .' She gave him a look that told Archie she was thinking of June but didn't want to say. 'I'm going to do a few hours here and we'll all stay here for now, but as soon as I can manage it I want to get us a house of our own . . . like we used to have . . .'

'I'm goin' to stay with Ted for a bit,' Archie said. 'I came to tell you and to fetch my stuff, Mum. You and June should stay here for as long as you can – and mebbe we can find a house near Ted or somethin' . . .'

'Why near Ted?'

'Because when I work for him I have to be up early and go with him mornings – sometimes outside of London; it's a good job, Mum, and I want to keep it . . . I believe I can make something of myself on the market in time.'

'Yes, but . . .' Sandra stopped, as if sensing that Archie wasn't going to be swayed. 'Well, I shan't stop you staying with him in the holidays if it's what you want, but if we're going to be a family again we need a house of our own . . . and you have to finish school.'

'So that me and June can go back to lettin' ourselves in with the latchkey?' Archie asked bluntly. 'We didn't have a proper home after Dad died, Mum. I know you did your best and I love you, and I was frantic when they took you away, but that's no good for me now – and it wouldn't be much good to June either. You don't want her hanging around the streets or running off with people you don't know – and that's what she'll do if I'm not there to look out for her.'

His mother's face had gone white and he knew he'd hurt her again, but he had to make her understand. 'If you find a place near Ted it would be better. I can live with you and I'll be around more . . . but I've had enough of comin' home to an empty house. You've got to be home for us, Mum, especially for June. Why don't you stay here for now? Once I'm established and earning decent money, you won't need to work all the time; you can be there when June gets home and have our tea ready – and then we'll truly have a home.'

Tears were trickling down his mother's face. June sat up straight and looked at him. 'Don't be horrid to Mum,' she said. 'It's not her fault she had to work to keep us . . .'

'No, it wasn't and I'm not blaming her,' Archie said. 'It's a bloody awful world where kids like us with no father have to go home to an empty house every night . . .'

'I didn't know how much you resented it,' his mother said and brushed her tears away. 'I was just trying to make a better life for us . . . get us away from the slums . . .'

'We'd rather have holes in our shoes and live in a dump and have you around, Mum,' Archie said and went to put his arms about her. He kissed the top of her head and thought she smelled nice. It was a smell he'd missed and he felt rotten for having hurt her, but he'd had to tell her; he'd had to stand up for himself. 'I need to be near Ted so I can be ready to go with him in the van in the mornings – but we can find some rooms near there and you can make sure you're home for June at night.'

'Yes, Archie,' his mother was looking at him oddly. 'You've grown up, haven't you? You're really the man of the house now . . .' She gave him a wobbly smile. 'All right, you take your things and go to stay with your friend, but no missing school until you leave, do you hear? June and I will stay here for now – but I'd like to meet these new friends of yours, Archie.'

'Sure. Come down the market on Saturday and you'll

find Ted and the others there . . . all except Ikey. He don't work on the market. He comes and goes as he pleases, but when I see him I'll tell him you'd like to see him . . . I'll tell him you'd like to thank him for all he's done for us, shall I?'

'Yes,' she said. 'You tell him that, Archie . . .'

CHAPTER 26

Sandra was thoughtful as she walked into the kitchen to fetch hot drinks for June and herself later that evening. She saw Staff Nurse Wendy was there, and one of the carers. The nurse was trying to comfort the carer, who was in tears.

'Oh, I'm so sorry,' she said. 'I can come back later if I'm intruding . . .'

'Kelly has just had some very bad news,' Wendy said and looked sad. 'I'm sure she doesn't mind you knowing – her father sent word that her mother has just died . . .'

'Oh, I'm so very sorry,' Sandra said, immediately sympathetic. 'Is there anything I can do to help, Kelly?'

Kelly shook her head and then looked up, eyes brimming with tears. 'She's been unwell a long time and we were expecting it, but it's still a terrible shock . . .'

'Yes, of course it must be. I remember when my parents died and it was an awful time.'

'My sister Cate has left school and she's courtin' strong,' Kelly said. 'I've just got the one brother still at school and he'll be leavin' soon so we'll manage . . . but it will be an empty house without her . . .'

'Yes, of course. I meant it when I said I would help if I could.'

'You're very kind,' Kelly said. She stood up and wiped her face. 'I'd better go home and see to things. Wendy says Sister will understand, but it's leavin' her short-handed for this evening . . .'

'I'll do your shift,' Sandra offered. 'I'm here and I don't mind what I do – just tell me what you're meant to be doing, Kelly, and go home to your family. After all, family is what it's all about – isn't it?'

'Yes.' Kelly smiled through her tears. 'I suppose it's a blessing because she's suffered enough – but I'll miss her . . .'

She took a pad out of her apron pocket and wrote down a list of duties and Sandra took it, noting that it was mainly making hot drinks, keeping an eye on the dorms while the children were getting ready for bed and then checking on them every so often.

'There isn't much to do at nights, unless we get a new arrival or one of the kids gets sick,' Kelly said. 'We used to have more to do, but we're only half the size we used to be. I'll get off home now. If you need any help just ask Sister Beatrice or Wendy – Wendy often helps out if we are busy for some reason . . .'

'Well, I'll start making drinks then,' Sandra said after Kelly had gone. 'Poor Kelly was very upset.'

'Years,' Wendy said and looked sad. 'Kelly has been tied to her and she's had to look after the children and her father. She does have a very patient boyfriend, but I don't know what she'll do now – perhaps they'll go and live with her father . . .'

'These things are always so difficult,' Sandra said.

337

'Well, I'll make the first batch of cocoa – would you like one?'

'Not until later,' Wendy said and nodded. 'If you're not sure of anything, Sandra, just come to me. I've been here ages too and it's my home, although I have a small flat not too far away, just a short bus journey, or a longish walk on a pleasant evening.'

'I'll take drinks up to the sick ward first, because the children there all wanted some cocoa and then I'll see to the others . . .'

Sandra was thoughtful as she began to mix the first batch of creamy sweet drinks for the children. Wendy thought of St Saviour's as her home and both Tilly and Kelly had been here a long time. Perhaps she could find a life here for June and herself. Archie seemed determined to live his own life and she couldn't force him to go back to the arrangement they'd had before she went to prison, so it might be for the best. Sandra had never wanted her children to be latchkey kids, but she hadn't had a lot of choice. What else could a widow with two young children do?

'I can't tell you how pleased I am that you've finally decided to stay with us,' Sister Beatrice said when Sandra told her of her decision the next day. 'You can have June to sleep with you in your room, if you wish – or she can go back to her old dorm . . .'

'For the moment she wants to sleep with me,' Sandra replied. 'I enjoyed doing Kelly's work last night, Sister, and I think June and I will be very happy here with you for the time being. Archie has decided to live at his friend's house in the holidays and to sleep there on

Friday and Saturday nights, and since they seem respectable pleasant people, I cannot forbid it . . . though I should have liked to have a home for us all again . . .'

'Perhaps you will one day. These things have a habit of working themselves out, my dear.'

'Yes, and you've been such a good friend to me, Sister. I feel I shall be helping you out by working here for a while.'

'Your typing is excellent and I do find writing those reports such a chore. With you combining your duties it will be so much better for us all . . .'

'Yes,' Sandra looked at her thoughtfully. 'Kelly was so distressed last night. I wonder what she will do now?'

'She came to see me early this morning. It seems that her father has urged her to marry her young man – and that is only fair, because he's been patient for several years. Now that his siblings are grown up, he's going to live at Mr Mason's house, and Kelly will be cutting her hours so that she can keep house for them both, but she is happy to give us a few hours a week for the moment . . .'

'So you will be losing Tilly when she has the baby, and Kelly will be working less hours . . . you are going to need some more help soon, Sister.'

'Yes, a new girl,' Sister Beatrice sighed. 'I've been spoiled. At one time the staff was always changing, but we've had a settled period for some years. I suppose I shall have to look for someone . . .'

'Would you like me to visit the employment offices and ask if they have anyone suitable they could send along?'

'Oh yes, would you? I've recently had the offer of

another good nurse, but carers . . .' Another deep sigh, then, 'Ah well, I shall have to interview them in person, Sandra, but I'd value your opinion as a woman of the world . . .'

'I'm sure you have far more experience, Sister, but I should be pleased to help. I've arranged to visit Ted Hastings and his daughter this weekend for Sunday tea – and Archie is most insistent that I meet his friend Ikey this evening . . . though I'm not sure about him . . .'

Sister Beatrice laughed. 'You must not be prejudiced, Sandra. Ikey is remarkable in his own way. I jumped to the wrong conclusions at first – but since then I've realised he is intelligent, brave and resourceful, even if his methods are somewhat unorthodox.'

'To say the least . . . it was a wonder he wasn't arrested for what he did . . .' Sandra frowned. 'You haven't heard anything more about those vile people?'

'Mr and Mrs Bailey have not been found, but Mr Hendry told me the police think they used false names to leave the country. Had Ikey not acted promptly, as he did, June might have disappeared, never to be found again . . . and I dread to think of the life she would then have had . . .'

'Oh, my God!' Sandra's heart caught and her eyes stung with tears. 'She is still having bad dreams over what happened and Mr Adderbury told me it may take years of consultations to help her come to terms with her experiences, though he says because she was so innocent she doesn't truly know what that foul man did to her . . .'

'It may hit her harder when she is older and under-stands, but you understand, Sandra, my dear – and you suffer for her. I never push my faith on anyone, but God is always there for us, you know. You may find help and consolation in prayer . . .'

'I can't pray,' Sandra said. She knew the nun meant well, but her throat was tight with emotion, little shudders taking her as she remembered the despair she'd so recently experienced. 'I was branded a thief and a liar; they put me in prison for a crime I didn't commit, subjected me to humiliation and left me vulnerable to abuse, and they took my child into care – except that she was abused instead. What kind of a god does that, Sister Beatrice? I know you believe and you are a good woman. I honour you for your work and your compassion, and I'm grateful to you and all those that helped me . . . but I cannot pray or believe in a loving god . . .'

'Then I shall pray for you,' Sister Beatrice said gently. 'Archie will make his own life, but I shall pray that you find peace and that both you and June will be happy again . . .'

'I'm pleased to meet you again, Mrs Miller,' Ikey said and offered his hand. Sandra shook it, feeling hesitant, because although he looked respectable his clothes were clearly old and much worn, though his shirt looked clean and he'd shaved, but his dark, ash-blond hair was too long. Something irritated her about his calm air of authority when she knew he spent his life living rough. 'I'm only sorry I couldn't manage it before but I've been working on something important . . .'

'More important than my son's welfare,' she said feeling hostile, though quite without reason. She saw his greyish-blue eyes narrow and realised that he'd picked up her mood. 'Forgive me, that wasn't fair. I know you helped Archie a great deal.'

'Ikey doesn't need to bother about me now, Mum. You're out of prison and I've got a good job and lots of friends . . .'

'Your mum has a right to be anxious, Archie.' Ikey's calm voice sent little prickles down Sandra's spine. He was obviously a very thoughtful man and she didn't know why she felt so uneasy in his presence. 'It's all right, Mrs Miller, I'm not offended, but as it happens, what I'm working on now could still affect your son's future . . .'

'What do you mean? How could it affect my son's future – I thought Mr Hastings was a respectable man.'

'Ted is one of the best, everyone will vouch for that,' Ikey said, a smile lurking about a mouth that Sandra had just realised was distinctly sensual. 'Unfortunately, there is some unease brewing in the East End, Mrs Miller. I do not want to alarm you or Archie or his friends unnecessarily – but I believe a certain unpleasant person is intent on trouble.'

'You mean Billy's old boss,' Archie said, eyes bright with excitement. 'Ted said Connolly's itching for a fight. He owns a lot of market stalls and he hates the independents, wants to take them all over . . . or make them pay protection money . . .'

'Archie!' Sandra said sharply. 'Please don't interrupt. I want to hear about this – because if you're in danger I'm not sure I can allow you to live and work with Mr Hastings . . .'

'Mum! We've had all this over.' Archie threw her an agonised look.

'I don't think you should panic or go back on your

word, Mrs Miller. I assure you that if Mr Connolly does decide to make trouble, the police – and a few others – can manage it . . .'

'That is your considered opinion?' Sandra's gaze narrowed. 'Give me one good reason why I should believe in you, sir?'

'There isn't one,' Ikey said and his eyes were cool now, like an icy mountain pool, she thought irrelevantly. 'On the face of it I am the last one you should listen to, Mrs Miller. However, there are people who do trust me and if my friends are in trouble I will risk everything to help and protect them – and I consider Archie to be my friend.'

'Ikey's done more for me than anyone,' Archie said but was quelled by a look from those cool eyes. Sandra thought ruefully that this man who stirred her hostility without cause could control her son without lifting a finger while she had no influence over him whatsoever. 'Mum, please listen . . . remember that you've only got June back because of Ikey . . .'

'Yes . . .' Archie's words were so true and Sandra realised that she was behaving like a schoolgirl rather than a grown woman. Her cheeks burned and she knew she had to apologise. 'Forgive me, Mr . . . is it Ikey? I know what you did and I am grateful, but I love my children and I don't want them to be hurt – Archie is still very young, even though he's had to grow up too soon since his father died . . .'

'You don't have to apologise to me ever,' Ikey said and now his calm voice had warmth again and his eyes smiled. 'I promise you that I shall look after Archie as if he were the son I never had . . .'

Sandra's eyes met his then, and something started to

343

melt inside . . . the ring of ice around her heart eased a little and her eyes pricked. 'Thank you . . . I don't know what to call you? Ikey isn't your real name, is it?'

'It's Ikey these days, Sandra,' he said. 'I used to be someone called Nathaniel Blake, and I was a police officer, an inspector – my friend Jonathan is also a police officer, of higher rank than me, and he took up your case because Edward Hendry asked him to help.'

'And why aren't you still in the force, Mr Blake?'

'Ikey please,' he said and looked straight into her eyes. 'My wife died in a terrible car accident – and I drank myself half to death. I had to resign for the sake of the force and only friendship brought me back from the brink of despair.'

Sandra saw echoes of that despair in his eyes and her heart caught as she felt some of the pain he must have endured. 'I could say I'm sorry, but I will just say thank you for telling me, Ikey.'

'You needed to know,' he said simply and suddenly Sandra was ashamed of having doubted the man who had done so much for her and her children.

'I should have trusted you,' she admitted. 'You've proved yourself and I am grateful for all you've done . . . Can you forgive me?'

'Friends don't need to be forgiven,' he said and the smile on his lips made her heart leap and everything was suddenly so much brighter. 'Archie tells me that you're living and working here at St Saviour's for the moment, Sandra. Are you content with that?'

'Until I can find a home for us all,' Sandra said. 'I don't want a dump like we had before, but eventually I hope to be offered a council flat . . .'

Ikey nodded but looked thoughtful. 'If I were you I should stay here until June has settled again. She couldn't be left alone in a council flat or anywhere else. Wait and see what happens when you've got the compensation Mr Hendry is trying to get for you . . . and then, well, I may be able to help . . .'

'Yes, I shall stay here for a while,' Sandra agreed, because she knew he was right. June was too fragile to go to school alone and let herself in at night. When she was able to go to school again, it would be better if she came back to St Saviour's with the other kids. Sandra could give June tea and spend a little time with her before getting on with her work again. 'A woman alone is vulnerable, Mr Blake . . . I mean, Ikey. Without a husband it's hard not to neglect your children. Archie was right when he complained that I had to work all hours and put June's care on his shoulders, and I'm going to make things better for my daughter in future.'

'Remember that if you need help, I'm your friend,' Ikey told her with a smile. 'And now, I have to go to work . . .'

Sandra watched him leave, wondering why she felt disappointed that he'd had to go. She hadn't expected to like him but she did.

'I told you Ikey is all right, didn't I?'

Archie's voice brought her gaze round to him. 'Yes, love, you did,' she said, 'and you were right.'

CHAPTER 27

'I'm sorry it's not a gold ring with diamonds,' Billy said as he slid the little silver friendship ring on the third finger of Mary Ellen's left hand. 'I promise I'll get you one as soon as I've got a bit of money saved again.'

'I love this, Billy,' she assured him and kissed his lips. 'Keep your money for the time being and spend it on making our home nice . . . I can wait for a fancy ring.'

'You're a special girl, Ellie,' he said and held her close. They were in the rooms over the workshops, and Billy had almost finished painting the walls in the colours they'd chosen together. He still had all the white gloss to do, which would take weeks, because he didn't get much time these days, and Mary Ellen was going to make their curtains, but she could only do half an hour or so in the evenings, because she was either working for Sam or reading up for her exams. She'd already taken one lot and was waiting for the results; if she got the marks her tutor said she ought, she needed to take one more and then she could apply to take a post as a pupil teacher and attend college two or three days a week. 'I love you more every day . . .'

346

'Oh, so you didn't love me as much yesterday as today,' she pouted at him. 'I'm not sure I like that, Billy Baggins. Why didn't you love me as much yesterday – and did you only like me a week ago?'

'You're a right minx with your teasin',' Billy said and responded by giving her such a burning passionate kiss that she was left breathless and consumed with longing. 'My Ellie . . . I can't wait until you're all mine . . .'

'It's what I want too,' Mary Ellen said and looked at him with love. 'Now that we've got our own place and you've got a good job it isn't fair of Rose to stop us getting married. I'm going to tell her tonight that I want to be married on Christmas Eve.'

'Oh, Ellie,' Billy grinned. 'I just wish I thought she would say yes – but you know what our Rose is . . .'

Mary Ellen stroked his cheek with her fingertips. She liked the way that he tolerated her sister, who was often rude to him, calling her 'our Rose' and not being nasty or impatient. Billy was such a lovely lad, and Rose must be blind if she couldn't see it. She made up her mind that she was going to tell Rose tonight that if she didn't let them get married, she'd just move in with him and let people gossip all they liked . . .

Rose glared at the man facing her across her desk in the office at the hospital. She'd been such a fool to fall for the registrar in the first place, because she'd known what a philanderer he was and she had only herself to blame, but he was refusing to take no for an answer.

'You know you want to . . .' Mike Bonner said, coming round the desk to pin her against the wall. He

347

slid his hand down her thigh and began to edge her skirt up. 'Come on, Rosie, just a quick one . . .'

She brought her hand up sharply and slapped him hard across the face. 'Don't you dare talk to me like that – and don't call me Rosie,' she said. 'I'm Sister Rose to you and don't you forget it . . . and keep your hands to yourself.'

'You weren't like this in the back seat of my car,' he reminded her with a sneer. 'You just pretend to be a prude; underneath you're a dirty little whore like all the rest.'

Rose brought her knee up sharply and made him yell with pain as she connected with his private parts. His face twisted with anger and he slapped her back, making her gasp.

'You'll pay for that,' he said, turning away to bend over as he felt the pain. 'I'll get you sacked, you little bitch . . .'

'It's all right, I'm leaving anyway. I can't wait to get away from you.'

She picked up her jacket and bag and walked away, leaving him staring after her in anger. Rose knew that she'd burned her boats as far as this hospital was concerned and it was very likely she would be blacklisted at other hospitals too. Her only hope was that Sister Beatrice still wanted her at St Saviour's . . .

'Don't quarrel with Rose, love,' Billy said and kissed the end of Mary Ellen's nose as they stood outside the door of the flat she shared with her sister. 'Tell her we're engaged and we've got a place to live and say we'd like to be wed as soon as possible . . . but don't fall out with her. She's all the family you've got . . .'

'I know.' Mary Ellen sighed. 'You know I'm fond of her in my own way, Billy, but I've had enough of her saying things about you and she's always bossing me about. I know what I want . . . and that's to be your wife and to learn to be a teacher. Why can't she accept that I know my own mind?'

'Maybe she will,' Billy said, ever the optimist. 'In you go then, love, and I'll see you tomorrow in your break at work.'

'Yes.' Mary Ellen was warmed by the thought. Now that Billy worked full time at Sam's they saw quite a bit more of each other during working hours, which was lovely, because neither of them had a lot of spare time otherwise. She was working hard for her final exam and Billy wanted their home to be as perfect as he could make it. 'I'll be careful, Billy. Don't worry . . .'

'You'd better go in then,' he said and kissed her slowly, sweetly, letting her go with a sigh as she clung to him, her body clamouring with all the impetuosity of youth for more. 'I'll be dreamin' of you, Ellie love . . .'

Mary Ellen gave him one last hug and turned away, letting herself into the flat. Immediately, she heard the sound of crying and entered the living room tentatively, because she wasn't sure what she would find. She saw Rose sitting on the sofa, her head bent and her hands covering her face as she wept. She looked up as she became aware of Mary Ellen and there was such despair in her eyes that Mary Ellen ran to her and flung her arms about her.

'What is it, Rose love?' she asked. 'Are you ill? Has something terrible happened?'

'Yes, I've been stupid . . .' Rose wiped her face on her

handkerchief. 'I've assaulted the registrar for making a pass at me and he'll get me sacked, because he's a selfish pig.'

'Oh, Rose, as long as you're not ill . . .' Mary Ellen smiled. 'You'll find another job – and if he upset you, he deserved it. Surely Matron will understand that?'

'Even if she did they would still sack me and keep him, because I'm only a nurse. I feel such a fool – after all the years I've worked and now I shall probably have to leave London to get a job . . .'

'No, you won't,' Mary Ellen said. 'Sister Beatrice needs a good nurse and I know she'd love to have you. You're just the sort she can trust.'

'Yes, I did have a word with her, but it's not as much money. I couldn't afford to keep this flat. I'd probably have to live in – and then where would you go?'

'I'll get married at Christmas and live with Billy in his place,' Mary Ellen said. 'Oh, don't look like that, Rose. I love Billy and he's done the rooms up lovely – he wants you to come to a meal one night and see what he's done.'

'Really?' Rose looked at her oddly. 'I haven't been fair to him, have I?'

'No, but Billy doesn't hold grudges. He really isn't like that, Rose. Please believe us and let me get married – I don't want to wait until I'm twenty-one . . .'

'What about your teaching?'

'I can study at home with Billy, and do my college training a couple of days a week . . .'

'Supposing you have a baby?'

'We shan't,' Mary Ellen said. 'Billy said we'll take care – he wants me to be happy, Rose, and he'll take care of me, I promise . . .'

'Well, I suppose I'll have to say yes,' Rose agreed reluctantly. 'I'll keep the flat until after the wedding – and then I'll move into St Saviour's . . . that's if Sister Beatrice wants me when she hears the whole sorry story . . .'

'She will,' Mary Ellen said and hugged her. 'Don't worry, Rose. She'll be thrilled to get you, and I know you'll like it there.' She stood up and did a little twirl of delight. 'Oh thank you, dearest Rose. I'm going to be so happy – and I can't wait to tell Billy the wonderful news!'

She danced off into her bedroom, leaving Rose to watch her with a wistful smile on her lips.

After leaving Mary Ellen at her door, Billy walked home. It was past ten and this part of the commercial area was ill-lit, because several of the streetlamps were out of action. Feeling uneasy, Billy glanced over his shoulder. He was aware that someone was following him and he tensed, waiting for the attack, but he couldn't see anyone and stood for a moment or two looking about him. He could feel a tingling sensation at the nape of his neck and was almost sure that he was being shadowed, but no dark figure came rushing at him out of the darkness and he shrugged off his feeling of unease. Billy never let on to Mary Ellen, but both he and Sam were waiting for the next move against them.

'Connolly isn't the sort to just give up,' Sam had said. 'I didn't think anything of it at first, just took it for granted the pilfering and the attack on the workshops was petty revenge for my refusing to pay up – but what Ikey told us makes all the difference. Connolly is making trouble for us because he wants us out.'

351

'You reckon it's true then? They want to build a large supermarket and a shopping centre where we and the leather manufacturers are?'

'Well, the boss came round to see me, told me he'd received an offer for his premises, which he has refused, same as I did . . . but I just don't see where Connolly comes into it . . .'

'Ikey thinks he's the one that wants to build the supermarket. He's like a greedy fat spider, sitting there, gradually taking over as much of the East End as he can . . . He wants to own us all, have us dancing like puppets on his string.'

'Ikey heard a rumour that he's getting out of the market business and buying more property; probably thinks there's more money in it, and he's right. If it weren't for you, Billy lad, I'd probably have taken the money and run, even though my workshops are worth more than they're offerin' . . .'

'I thought he was all right once, but he's a nasty piece of work,' Billy had told him. 'Trying to intimidate you so that you sell to him. I should like to sort him out, but he's an old man and I can't give him a good hidin' . . .'

'Ikey said to just ignore any provocation. Connolly is treadin' on thin ice and Ikey is waitin' for the right moment . . . best to leave it to him, lad. I don't want you banged up in prison. You can't do either of us any good in there.'

Prison was the last thing Billy wanted so he'd taken the advice of his boss and Ikey and stayed clear of Connolly and his bully boys, but he was pretty certain it wouldn't end there. Connolly wasn't going to let things stay as they were. Sam and Billy had thwarted him when he'd ordered the workshops to be burned down; he would be planning something nasty and Billy just had to be careful and stay out of trouble if he could.

He looked round carefully as he unlocked the back door of the workshops and went in, relocking it and putting the bolt over immediately. The nape of his neck was prickling again. Surely no one had broken in through all the new security? He snapped on the light and called out, but no one answered. Grinning, Billy put the downstairs light off and went up to his rooms. No one had got in and he was letting his imagination play tricks on him and yet . . . he was sure he'd been followed home after leaving Mary Ellen.

The man stood in the darkness outside and watched the lights go on in the upstairs rooms, his face a mask of hatred and meanness. His hands clenched at his sides, because he'd itched to grab that cocky bastard and throttle the life out of him as he followed him home. If bloody Connolly would let him, he'd kill that one and then the fool that owned the workshop would fall over himself to sell. But Connolly said wait and he was the boss. Not many would dare go against him, though there were rival gangs that would just love to take over Connolly's patch. It was one of them that had been attacking him that time when Billy Baggins had happened along and saved him. He'd acted like a hero and Connolly would've treated him all right if he'd been content to work for him, but he'd changed sides, gone over to bloody Sam Parker, and that had made Connolly spittin' mad. He'd ordered the raid but that hadn't worked out either and they weren't sure who had betrayed them.

Someone had got wind of it, and Connolly wanted to know who; it was the only reason he was lettin' things run on for a while – to discover who was protecting bloody Baggins' back, because someone was.

Ricky knew that he'd been shadowed, just as he'd shadowed Baggins. If he could get rid of that bugger . . . Feeling a deep coldness down his spine, Ricky was suddenly very afraid. He wasn't sure why, because Connolly didn't scare him, even though he knew that the slightest hint of treachery would mean his boss would make sure he disappeared for good, but something or someone was out there in the shadows watching him, and Ricky felt as if he were the one being hunted . . .

He swore and lit a cigarette and slouched off, all thoughts of breaking in and murdering Baggins in his own home gone in an instant. London was gettin' uncomfortable. He'd got some mates in Birmingham and he thought it might be time to take a little holiday from The Smoke. Yeah, let Connolly do his own dirty work for a change.

He quickened his steps, aware that the menacing presence was behind him, close enough for him to hear the heavy breathing and yet he was too scared to turn and look. Breaking into a sweat, he started running . . .

CHAPTER 28

Sandra realised that she was singing as she made beds and swept floors, and she hadn't done that for a long time; even before she was falsely imprisoned she'd found housework a chore that had to be got through so that she could get off and go to her work, the work that kept her and her children from starving. She was feeling much better these past few days, and she loved working here in this friendly atmosphere where everyone seemed ready to lend a hand.

Her chores finished, she took the cleaning materials back to the scullery and washed her hands at the sink and then went into the large kitchen, where Muriel was busy baking.

'Oh, that smells good,' Sandra said as the cook took a tray of buns from the oven. 'Almond, I think?'

'Yes, almond buns and coconut tart today,' Muriel said. 'Wendy and Sister Beatrice are partial to the buns, and Kelly loves them too. The children love the jam and coconut tart. We couldn't make it in the war; it was plain jam tart then and occasionally treacle if we were lucky enough to get a big tin. I remember Mr

Adderbury used to get some parcels from friends in Canada and he always gave them to us . . .'

Sandra nodded and smiled. She'd heard a lot about Mr Adderbury the psychiatrist who gave his time to St Saviour's free of charge and was one of the founding members of the charity. He'd already given some of his time to June and he'd telephoned Sandra at St Saviour's to suggest a meeting with her presence required so that he could help June further.

'You must have had a hard time keeping this place going during the war?'

'It wasn't easy, believe you me, but we had a lot of stuff given to us. People were so kind then, always sharing what they had.'

'Yes, I remember what it was like when I was at home; in those days my mother never locked her back door and the neighbours used to come in and out as they pleased, and everyone shared what they had.'

'Times are changing,' Muriel looked thoughtful. 'I'm not sure that all this progress is for the better . . . the National Health Service is a good thing, I'll give you that, but I'm not sure I like all the new rules and regulations . . . and folks are not as friendly or trusting as they were . . . at least it seems that way to me. People used to look out for their neighbours, but since the Social took over it's all left to them . . . and they want to know the ins and outs of a cat's behind!'

'I suppose we all suffered too much in the last war for things to be the same.'

'Yes, I expect so, but I thank God for Sister Beatrice. She doesn't change and St Saviour's goes on in the same way despite them lot next door . . .' Muriel frowned.

'I don't approve of what goes on there and that's the truth.'

'No, I don't either, though Sister told me they sent the girl that got my June into trouble to a remand home . . . but the woman, Ruby Saunders, her that had June fostered, is still there.'

'If you want my opinion they should sack her after what happened. ' Muriel banged the used cooking trays in the sink.

'She couldn't have known what those people would do . . . and she did apologise to me in person soon after I came here, said she'd been taken in and thought they were good people . . . She seemed subdued and I think the experience must have put the wind up her. Sister said she was severely taken to task by Miss Sampson after she was told she should have run more checks on the couple – who have a murky record.'

'And you know who made her do that. Sister told her she must apologise and so she should . . .'

'June is a lot better since Mr Adderbury saw her last week. She wants to start school, but not where she used to go – there's a small church school she could go to quite near here, and Ikey said he would speak to the headmistress for me . . . arrange an interview . . .'

'Ikey?' Muriel sniffed her disapproval. 'He's quite a charmer, Sandra, but I'm not sure what he would know about the headmistress of a church-run school.'

'No, I wondered, but I didn't like to ask him.'

'Well, there's a bit of mystery about a man like that if you ask me . . .'

'Yes . . .' Sandra turned as June entered the kitchen. She was surprised to see animation in her daughter's face. 'Hello, darling. Have you come for one of Muriel's buns and a glass of squash?'

'Archie brought me some sweets,' June said and for the first time since Sandra had been to prison her eyes were alight with pleasure. 'He said Mimi came to his stall on the market and asked about me . . . She wants to see me and her mum told Archie I could go to tea at her house tomorrow. Can I, Mum? Mimi's mum said you can come too if you want?'

'Well, that was nice of her,' Sandra said. She'd planned to spend a quiet day washing and ironing in the kitchen of the nurses' home, but the pleading look on her child's face touched her. 'I don't see why not. Yes, we'll go – I'll ask Archie to take a note round for us. He is still here?'

'Yes, he's having fish and chips with us tonight – and Ikey is taking us to the chip shop where we can sit down and have it, don't you remember?'

'Yes, I remember,' Sandra said and a lovely warm feeling spread through her. 'We shall be spoiled, shan't we, love?'

'I'm going to play with Babs now, Mum,' June said. 'Her mum died last month and she's new here and she asked me to be her friend . . .' The serious expression on June's face caught at Sandra's heart then. 'She's had a horrid time, Mum, and I think she needs lookin' after . . .'

'So you're going to look after her?' June nodded solemnly and Sandra's heart jerked, because her innocent little girl had gone forever but gradually there was a new, more thoughtful June emerging, and she loved her so much that it almost broke her heart. 'That's all right then; run along, my love.'

'I'll share my sweets with her,' June said. 'Her father used to hit her but he's in prison now and she hasn't got anyone but me . . .'

'Well, she can share me if you don't mind, June. We'll take her to have fish and chips tonight if you like?'

June's face lit up like a candle. 'Can I ask her, Mum? Thanks ever so . . .' She rushed at her mother and hugged her. 'I'm so glad you're back. You won't go away again, will you?'

'No, I won't,' Sandra promised, crossing her fingers behind her back. No one could make such promises in a world that could be so unjust, but she would never leave her beloved child unless she was forced.

'Well, it's lovely to see her looking better,' Muriel said as June ran off to find her friend and tell her the news. 'Poor little mite . . . after what she went through . . .' Muriel hadn't been told all the details but it was generally known that June had been mistreated by her foster parents.

'Yes, thanks to Ikey and Mr Adderbury.' Sandra smiled and went over to the kitchen sink. 'Let me wash these for you, Muriel. I've finished my work and I've nothing to do until I get ready to go out for a fish and chip supper.'

'Are you going anywhere nice this evening?' Sister Beatrice asked Wendy as she saw her preparing to leave at the end of her shift. 'You've got the whole weekend off I think?'

'Yes. I haven't had a weekend off for ages, but with Rose O'Hanran joining us, it will make things a lot easier.'

'Yes, Rose is leaving her hospital next week. She decided to take the job I offered and will live here with us.'

'Well, I shall be glad of her help. It has been difficult since we lost Michelle, because none of the others has stayed more than a year . . .'

'I think Rose will settle with us for a while,' Sister Beatrice said and looked thoughtful. 'She seems to have had quite a change of heart . . . You will never credit this, Wendy – but Billy Baggins and Mary Ellen are getting married on Christmas Eve.'

'Good gracious!' Wendy was astonished. 'She's only eighteen – I thought she was studying to be a teacher?'

'Yes, she is,' Sister replied, 'but she told me she can study better if Billy is with her.'

'Young love . . .'

'I very much fear so, but we can only hope it lasts . . .' Sister moved towards the desk as the phone rang and picked up the receiver. 'Sergeant Sallis, good evening. How may I help you? Two young lads of seven and eight . . . you'll bring them in yourself? Yes, I see. Nothing much the matter except they're filthy, crawling with lice and half starved. Yes, well, we've had worse. I'll alert my staff and we'll expect you in half an hour.' She replaced the receiver and shook her head. 'It never stops, does it? Everything was going to be so different when that Labour government took over from Mr Churchill after the war, but if you want my opinion all the politicians do is sit around and talk, whichever party they belong to . . .'

'Ah, here comes Nurse Paula,' Wendy said. 'I would offer to stay and help you out, Sister, but I'm going to a show up West this evening . . .'

'That's nice. Are you going with Nan and Eddie?'

'Not this time,' Wendy smiled, her cheeks a little pink. 'Jon is a friend of my late mother's – a lovely person and we met by chance when he was shopping for himself in that new supermarket down the road. His wife died and I think he's lonely so when he asked I said yes . . .'

'And why not?' Sister Beatrice smiled at her. 'Enjoy your weekend, Wendy.'

Wendy heard Sister telling Paula to expect the two street urchins as she left and smiled to herself. Sister Beatrice was probably imagining the beginning of a romance, but Jon Higgins was twenty years her senior and the only reason Wendy had accepted his invitation was because there was no hint of anything like that. He was just a very nice gentleman and she enjoyed a musical show . . .

'You didn't mind my asking Babs to come with us, did you?' Sandra said to Ikey as they were being shown to a table large enough for them all, the excited children running ahead of them, eager to find their table first. 'June has made friends with her and the poor child has no one to take her out – I'll pay for her supper, of course.'

'No, you will not. I invited you all and I'll pay. I may look as if I'm broke, Sandra, but appearances are deceptive. I can afford a fish and chip supper for one extra.'

'Oh, you mustn't be offended,' Sandra said. 'I didn't want to take advantage, that's all . . .'

'You couldn't,' he said. 'I'm not a rich man but I earn enough to get by – and all I have is yours and your family's . . .'

'Ikey, how generous, but you can't take on the responsibility for all of us.'

'Can I not?' he said and there was a smile lurking in his eyes that made her want to smile too. 'I've been thinking the nights are too cold to sleep under the arches, Sandra. If I found a small house, big enough to take you, Archie and two little girls sharing a bedroom, and me, would you consider keeping house for me? You could still give Sister Beatrice a few hours when the kids are at school if you wish, but be there for them when they get home . . .'

Sandra stared at him, not quite sure what he was saying. 'You're offering me a home where I can bring up my daughter and have her friend to stay if she wants it and the authorities agree . . . why?'

'Because I'm getting older and if I don't do something with my life now I never shall,' Ikey said and laughed softly. 'You're a very attractive lady, Sandra Miller. I would ask you to change your name to Blake, but I doubt you would agree. You haven't known me long enough. I had the advantage, because I knew you through Archie months ago . . . and when I saw you I realised that the impossible had happened. I felt happy again. I shan't talk of love yet, because love grows over time – but you made me want to be happy, Sandra. I'm offering you separate bedrooms but in every other way it will be your home – and perhaps one day . . . but that's up to you . . .'

'Thank you,' she said. 'You've taken my breath away, Ikey. I hardly know what to say.'

'Yes would do . . .'

'I never expected anything like this would ever happen . . .' Sandra's mind was whirling. She knew that he was offering her a chance of real happiness and a way of keeping her family together. 'Why am I dithering? It's a wonderful offer – thank you. When can we move in?' She laughed. 'Oh dear, how impatient of me . . .'

'I'm hoping very shortly,' Ikey said. 'Let's keep it to ourselves for the moment, and then we'll tell the kids when things are more settled.'

'Yes, yes, and yes,' Sandra said and laughed for pleasure. This extraordinary man had changed her life so much in such a short space of time. She would take his offer of a home for herself and the children and perhaps one day she would be more than his house-keeper, but for now it was enough.

It was more than enough. Tears burned at the back of Sandra's eyes and the bitterness of the last few months was washed away by the kindness of others – Sister Beatrice and the friends she'd made at St Saviour's, and now this mysterious man she hardly knew.

Ikey had told her the reason why he no longer worked as a uniformed police officer, though she knew he did undercover work for his friend who was a police inspector. He worked in a wood yard, did odd jobs for his friends and lived a very unconventional life.

Was she a fool to throw in her lot with such a man? She sensed a mystery about him still, and yet she trusted him – and nothing would make her give up the chance to live in a nice little house, and care for her children and him . . .

CHAPTER 29

Ikey frowned as he followed the man shadowing Billy Baggins, as he walked home late that evening. It was late November now and the nights were cold. This was a part of his work that Ikey didn't relish, the hanging about dark streets in all weathers, but he'd chosen it after his wife died and Jonathan asked him to go under cover. He'd been at rock bottom, empty and despairing until his friend made him pull back from the brink, asking if he would help stamp out the corruption they'd known was at work in the force.

'If you take on the work no one must ever guess,' he'd said. 'You will need to ruin your reputation, lose your friends and go against all your principles – but if we're to wipe out this corruption I need your help to do it.'

At first Ikey had declined, saying that he couldn't do it, but his drinking had brought him down and he'd discovered that his friends looked the other way; he was no longer invited to official functions and he felt shut out – and, worse than all the rest, he couldn't stand being at home alone after Catherine had died in that terrible motor accident. She'd been driving his car and the brakes had failed; the collision with a brewery lorry had resulted in her death in hospital three days later. His darling Catherine had never regained consciousness, never smiled at him or spoken to him again. After her funeral he'd embarked on a drinking spree that ended only when he woke in a prison cell in a filthy state and his friend had taken him home, provided him with a bath, a hot meal and clean clothes.

'If you're going to spend your life on the streets drinking until you're out of your head, you may as well do the job I asked you to . . . unless you're determined to kill yourself?' Jon gave him a straight look.

'What is there left for me? I might as well be dead.'

'I thought you might want to nail a man who is hiding behind his uniform to get rich on the corruption of others?'

'Who would believe anything I said these days?'

'This time we'll play it clever. I want you to go undercover, live in the shadows and watch one of our officers. He's in league with Connolly, I'm certain of it – but unless we can find concrete proof, we'll never prove it. I'm not sure how many of my men are taking bribes – you're the only one I can trust, Nat . . .'

'Call me Ikey?'

'Why?'

'It's a corruption of my middle name and more suitable for a down-and-out than Nathaniel Blake.'

'Good man, I knew I could trust you – we'll get them, Ikey. And I'll be there to back you up every step of the way . . .'

That conversation had changed everything. Ikey had

pulled himself up, even though he let others believe he was still drinking, still living rough. Now he had a mission in life, a purpose that helped him forget the pain of losing his wife.

What he'd learned on the streets had led to the arrest of several lesser criminals, but as yet he hadn't found the link between a certain police inspector and Connolly. He already knew a lot about the affairs of Billy's old boss; where certain goods were stored – and a flat Connolly visited alone and in secret. It was here that any tangible evidence was likely to be found, and Ikey was waiting for clearance to go in but they had to be careful, because if word was leaked anything incriminating would be destroyed. Ikey wanted Jon to let him go in alone but so far his friend was being cautious.

Connolly knew someone was poking their nose into his affairs. It had taken patience to piece all the threads together, because on the face of it the man was perfectly respectable, but Ikey had watched and waited and now he was certain. Connolly was handling stolen goods. Not just the petty thefts, like the clothes from Sam's place. No, he was buying stolen jewellery, gold and silver, and if Ikey was right, he was telling the thieves where to steal from – persuading them to steal to order.

Ikey had got most of the information from contacts he'd made on the street, men who lived on the fringes of society, hearing whispers, taking risks to get him the evidence he needed, and in return he gave them friendship, small amounts of money and help when they needed it. He knew where the stolen goods were hidden, where they had come from, and who had taken them, but they needed to catch Connolly actually in possession of the stuff, and that wasn't so easy. When he'd discovered the secret hideout and with the last piece in place, he'd given all the evidence to his friend in the force and now Ikey was following Billy, protecting him as he did night after night from the menacing shadow that trailed him . . .

Ikey was lost in thoughts of the future and failed to notice the shadow looming behind him. Hearing something at the last moment, he turned just as the cosh was brought down on the side of his head. He knew when he saw the man's face that he was finished; Stevie Baker was the kind of coward that crept up from behind; this was a murder to order and Ikey was the victim. He'd upset Connolly a little too much. Even as Ikey lost consciousness he heard a shout and pounding feet, but he had no idea what happened next, because he was lost in the blackness . . .

'Billy?' Sister Beatrice looked at him in horror as she saw that he was covered in blood. 'What have you been doing? Are you hurt?'

'Most of it is his blood – Ikey's,' Billy told her, looking grim. 'I drove him off – Stevie Baker. He's Connolly's man and he tried to murder Ikey. I knew I was being followed tonight and then I heard the shouting and I went back to see what was going on. I saw Ikey fall, Sister, and that made me see red. So I went for Stevie and took him by surprise. He'd got an iron bar as a weapon and I hadn't so that's why I look like this . . . but he never was much good in a fair fight and he's looking worse – and he's in prison tonight. Sergeant Sallis saw what was going on. He blew his whistle and charged in and then two more coppers came and overpowered Stevie. It seems they were on the watch for him . . . He's wanted for running prostitutes and beating women up – and they'd had a tip-off that he was in the area . . .'

'Billy! Billy Baggins, do you always have to be a hero?' Sister asked crossly. 'What am I going to do with you? Why haven't you gone to the hospital?'

'I went with Ikey, but he's in a bad way, Sister – and then I came to tell you and Mrs Miller. I thought you should both know . . . he's going to need your prayers, Sister Beatrice, and she'll want to know.'

'Yes, she will,' Sister agreed. 'I understand Sandra has consented to be his housekeeper and this may alter things for her . . .'

'Well, I'd best get back home then.'

'You mostly certainly will not,' Sister Beatrice said. 'You have cuts on your face that need attention and you will not leave here until you allow me to bathe them for you. Come into the isolation ward. There are no patients in at the moment. Be sensible, Billy. If you wander round the streets like that you'll be arrested for breaking the peace.'

'Yes, Sister, thank you, Sister.' Billy attempted a grin and winced, becoming aware that he hurt all over. 'If you don't mind I might have a lie down for a bit. I feel odd . . .' He swayed and felt her hand steadying him, her voice telling him what to do, just as if he were back in the dorm and one of her boys again.

'I am sorry to wake you so early,' Sister Beatrice said as Sandra opened her door, wearing her night things. 'But Billy brought the news about an hour ago and he's now sleeping in my ward – and I thought you would want to know . . .'

Sandra clutched at her robe, an icy feeling at her nape. 'Is it Ikey? Is he hurt?'

'Yes, I'm afraid he is, quite badly, Sandra. Billy told me the news and a few moments ago Sergeant Sallis rang me – he says that Ikey's condition is critical. He's had an operation and they think it is touch and go whether he lives through the next twenty-four hours . . .'

'Oh no!' The blood drained from Sandra's face. 'Where is he?'

'He was taken into the London,' Sister Beatrice replied. 'I am so very sorry, my dear. I know he offered you a home and a job, but you are still welcome here – though that is not much consolation when a friend is ill . . .'

'No,' Sandra said, unable to say more, because her throat felt as if it were closing and she thought she might die of the agony seeping through her. 'I'm grateful but . . .'

'Yes, I understand,' Sister Beatrice said. 'Is there anything I can do for you, Sandra? Anything at all?'

'I'll get dressed and call a taxi. Would you look after June if she wakes and worries about me?'

'I'll wake her and take her into my office,' Sister said. 'She can have some cocoa and biscuits with me, and I'll explain where you are and why.'

'Thank you,' Sandra said and went back into her bedroom to quickly pull on her clothes. June stirred and Sister Beatrice woke her, helping her dress and taking her to the door. June ran back and hugged Sandra.

'You will come back, Mum?'

'Yes, of course,' Sandra said. 'Go with Sister please.

369

She will look after you. I'm not leaving you, I just have to go to the hospital and sit with Ikey for a while, but I promise I'll come back. You do believe me, sweetheart?'

'Yes, Mum. I'll be all right with Sister Beatrice . . .'

Sandra was thoughtful as she dressed. June was still afraid of losing her mother again, but she was past the stage of clinging to her all the time. She was so grateful that June was getting better, albeit slowly, and she knew it was due to Ikey that she had her back at all. If he hadn't risked everything to snatch June that day she might have been taken out of the country and lost to her family forever. A sob rose in her throat. She owed so much to Ikey and if he died . . . if he died she didn't think she could bear it . . .

'Mum, I came as soon as Billy told me,' Archie said as he sat down beside her on the hard seats in the hospital corridor. The walls were painted dark cream and the only windows were high up, making it seem very dark. 'Have you seen him? Have they told you how he is?'

'They say he came through the operation all right, but there is still some swelling over his brain and they don't know what will happen . . . If it goes down within a few hours he'll be all right with not too much damage done except for a few scars and some cuts and bruises . . .' Sandra gave a little sob. 'Oh, Archie, he's such a good man, a kind generous man – and he didn't deserve this . . .'

'No, he didn't,' Archie said and looked upset. 'I knew what he was doin' was dangerous, but he wouldn't tell me and he wouldn't let me help.'

'I should think not. If I lost you, too . . .' Tears slipped down her cheeks and she reached for his hand. 'I would've lost June if it hadn't been for him . . .'

'He saved me from being abused,' Archie said. 'He's my best friend – I love him, Mum. I care about him the way I did Dad – and I don't want him to die . . .'

'I care about him too,' Sandra admitted. 'I don't know what I'll do if he leaves me. I thought after your dad died I'd never be loved again, but he did love me, Archie and I . . . I love him.'

'Then he won't die, he can't,' Archie said and scrubbed at his face because he was crying. 'Sister Beatrice says she's praying for him – and I am too.'

'And me,' Sandra whispered, reaching for his hand to hold it. 'God has to listen to us, doesn't he? He can't let him die when we all love him . . .' She caught her breath as a doctor in a long white coat walked towards them, looking up at him with more appeal in her eyes than she knew. 'Is he . . .?' her voice broke on a sob.

'Mr Blake is through the worst of it,' the doctor said and smiled. 'I'm pleased to tell you that the swelling has reduced considerably and we have every hope that he will pull through. He's going to be ill for some time, of course, but we are fairly confident that there will be no serious damage to his brain.'

'You mean you still don't know?' Sandra was aghast.

'We think because the swelling has reduced he will be fine, but we can't be sure until he wakes up. However, he is through the dangerous stage, Mrs Miller. I suggest you go home. We'll telephone you at St Saviour's and let you know the moment you can visit him.'

'I want to stay here . . .' Sandra protested but Archie took hold of her arm.

'June needs you, Mum.'

'Yes . . .' Sandra's eyes pricked with tears. 'Yes, I must go – but you will ring as soon as he's awake?'

'Someone will notify you of any change in his condition,' was the answer she was given.

Sandra felt like screaming that it wasn't good enough. She wanted to be with him, to tell Ikey he was loved and needed, but knew they weren't going to let her near him until he was conscious and they knew more about how he was.

Reluctantly, she let Archie take her out of the hospital and on to a bus. It was so unfair. If she'd been Ikey's wife, she could have sat with him for as long as she liked, but because she was just a friend she had to wait until they allowed visitors.

'It's going to be all right, Mum,' Archie said as he paid their bus fares back to Halfpenny Street. 'Ikey will come through. Sister told me she believed it and I believe her. I don't reckon God would dare to let Ikey die after she prayed for him.'

'You shouldn't say such things, it's irreverent,' his mother rebuked him, but somehow she felt better. Surely with all Ikey's friends praying for him it would be a hard-hearted god that would let him die . . .

CHAPTER 30

'Oh, Billy, why do you always go charging in?' Mary Ellen said as she saw the way his face had swelled on one side and the black ring around his eye that was gradually turning purple. 'I don't want you mixed up in things like that . . .'

'I had to help Ikey. He was there because he was following me, protecting me, like he did most nights. Ikey thought I was in danger from Connolly, but it was him they were out to get – because he knew what they were and he found the proof . . . even though he probably doesn't realise it . . .'

'What do you mean?'

'Sergeant Sallis told me that they'd found all the evidence they needed at Connolly's secret hide-out: letters, registers of payments made and received and a lot more paperwork. Connolly, Stevie Baker, Ricky Martin and half a dozen others are behind bars awaiting trial for robbery, grievous bodily harm and attempted murder. He said that the Birmingham police picked up Ricky Martin and sent him back to London and now he's singing like a canary telling them everything. According to him,

Connolly is the master criminal round here, worse than the Krays, and they all had to do what he said or . . .' He chopped his hand across his throat and Mary Ellen gasped in horror.

'Oh, Billy, they might have killed you . . .'

'They might but they didn't – and Ikey played his part keeping me safe. He'd warned me what was going on when I told him I was being followed and when I saw him go down I had to help him, didn't I?'

'Yes, you did,' Mary Ellen agreed and smiled. Billy was still the impetuous brave lad he'd been when they were first at St Saviour's together and he always would be – and she loved him so much. 'But I'm glad you're not the one lying in the hospital.'

'He's woken up,' Billy told her. 'I went and asked this morning but they wouldn't let me see him. They said Sandra Miller was there and only one visitor is allowed in a day at the moment. He's still very ill, Ellie, and it will be a while before he can leave hospital.'

'Give him my regards when you do see him and tell him we want him at the wedding.'

'Yeah, I hope he'll be better in time, but I'm not puttin' it off even for Ikey.'

'He wouldn't want you to,' Mary Ellen said and hugged him, feeling emotional. 'I wish all this horrid business was over.'

'Well it is, all bar the trials and the stuff in the papers, but now they've got Connolly in a cell there will be plenty of people willing to testify. Besides, Ikey traced him to a flat in Wapping that no one knew he had – apparently, they found all kinds of incriminating stuff there: a list of police officers, MPs and business people, who were either

374

on his payroll or in debt to him, and details of blackmail as well. Enough to put him away for a few years, so Sergeant Sallis told me. Once it gets out that Connolly's finished, a lot more victims will come forward. They were afraid of him, but his power has gone now and they'll all come crawling out of the woodwork like worms . . .'

'Billy, that's horrid.'

'I know but it's true. Stevie Baker is the one that knew most of his dirty little secrets – and Sergeant Sallis said that Ikey's been working for the police secretly, gathering evidence, and it's not only the criminals that will be going down – half a dozen coppers are in for it too.'

'Police officers?' Mary Ellen stared at him. 'I thought they were supposed to be on the public's side?'

'Most of them are, but some are corrupt. Money is behind it, Ellie. A man like Connolly infects all those he comes in contact with. I'm only glad Sam told me the truth in time . . .' He hesitated, then, 'I know Marion isn't living with you now – but she's the one who told the police where to find Stevie last night. He hit her again because she wouldn't do what he wanted – so she went to the police and told Sergeant Sallis loads of stuff about him, including that he'd been talking on the phone to his boss and he'd been ordered to murder someone. She thought it might be me . . . but it was Ikey that Connolly wanted dead.'

'That wicked, evil man!' A shiver went through her. 'If you'd kept working for him, you might have been arrested too.'

'I should've been,' Billy said and shuddered at the thought. 'It could've ruined everything, love.'

'I'm glad you left in time . . .' she said and caught

back a sob. 'Poor Ikey – and Sandra Miller. You said she's sweet on him, didn't you?'

'Well, she seems to like him and they've let her sit with him so he must have asked for her, don't you think?'

'Yes, I do,' she said and hugged him, feeling so grateful that he was here and alive. 'Oh, Billy, please don't fight any more. I don't want to lose you . . .'

'You won't,' he said confidently. 'I'm going to wed you and then I'm going to look after you while you study to be a teacher – and I'll be with you when you're old and grey.'

Mary Ellen looked at him and then went into a peal of laughter. 'I can just see you with your walking stick, bringing me tea in bed . . .'

'I'll give you walking stick,' Billy said and made a threatening lunge at her. 'You little devil . . .'

'Now then, Billy,' Sam said, entering the workshop. 'No molesting my employees. Let the girl get on with her work, there's a good lad.'

'We were just talkin' about Ikey . . .' Billy said.

'Yeah, that was rotten luck. It's a good thing you were there – and Sergeant Sallis and his colleagues. Otherwise you might have been laid up as well, and I need you here. I've got a big order needs to go to the West End and I want you on your way in five minutes.'

'Right you are, Sam,' Billy said and winked at Mary Ellen as he left.

'Well, that's got him on his way,' Sam said. 'Get on now, Mary Ellen, there's a good girl. We need to catch up on our orders, because after losing all that stuff when they raided the place we're a bit short of stock . . .'

*

'Poor Sandra, she's that upset, sitting by his bed for as long as they would let her, but now she's had to come away, because they say he's got to rest . . .'

'It is very sad for her,' Mary Ellen said, a little surprised by her sister's concern for a woman she hardly knew. 'Billy says Ikey has been working undercover for the police all this time – he's a hero in their eyes, because they've caught a criminal who has been controlling a lot of the robberies in London.'

'Yes, so Sister Beatrice says. She thinks a lot of Ikey – and of Billy. It seems Ikey might have been hurt worse if Billy hadn't gone to his aid; he's a bit of a hero too.'

What had happened to Rose? Mary Ellen wanted to laugh, because her sister's sunny mood was so unusual. She seemed really happy and she was clearly enjoying her new job at St Saviour's. It had seemed a charmed place to Mary Ellen after she'd come to trust Sister Beatrice and the nurses and carers at Halfpenny Street, and perhaps a little of that magic was rubbing off on Rose.

'How are you getting on at Sam's now?' Rose asked. 'Does he know you're hoping to be a teacher one day?'

'He knows I'm studying and that one day I'll leave, but it's a long way off, Rose. I've got exams to do and then college work. I might get a few days here and there as a pupil teacher, but there aren't many places going so it may be ages before I actually take a class – and I need to get some experience at college first anyway. In the meantime, I can carry on working at Sam's.'

'What will Billy think if you're reading every night when he gets home and wants his tea?'

'We'll manage,' Mary Ellen said. 'Billy understands

377

and he wants me to do it, Rose. I'll keep the house tidy and cook simple meals . . . it will be fine . . .'

'Men say it's all right, but they want more attention than you think,' Rose said. 'You should consider Billy, love. Once you're married, it isn't just what you want any more . . .'

Mary Ellen turned away. For once she didn't think Rose was being mean, but speaking out of concern. It made her thoughtful for a while, but she was too busy with her studies and making her wedding dress to worry about it. Billy loved her and she loved him, nothing else mattered. She could hardly wait for Christmas Eve and their wedding.

CHAPTER 31

'What time is Ikey coming home?' Archie asked his mother that Sunday morning. 'Where will he stay – or will he go straight to the nursing home?'

'The nurses said he would probably be sent down in an ambulance to save him the stress of a journey by train. He couldn't drive himself, though he has friends who would take him. His chief constable has visited him several times. He wants Ikey to go back to the force now that they've rooted out all this corruption. I don't know if he will, because he wasn't feeling up to talking about it . . .'

'What about you?' Archie said, looking at her anxiously. 'Are you going to marry him, Mum? Supposing he's an invalid for the rest of his life?'

'In that case I shall be both wife and nurse,' she replied, sounding cross. 'Really, Archie, you wouldn't want me to let him down?'

'No, I didn't mean it that way. I'll never forget what Ikey did for us, Mum. We've got our June back because of him, and he's my friend. I love him – but I love you, too, and I want you to be happy, to have a good life . . .'

'Thank you, my darling. You're so like your father – that is exactly what he would have said to me, but you know I do love Ikey. It's a different love from the love I gave your father, but it's just as strong – and if Ikey is ill I want to care for him for as long as it takes.'

'Good, I'm glad,' Archie said. 'I'm off now then . . .'

'Where are you going?'

'Nipper and me are takin' June to the circus this afternoon and I've got to do a little errand for Ted first. There's some stock we need to sort out for one of his stalls. I'll have a snack with him and Maggie and I'll be back by one thirty to collect June.' He grinned at her. 'We've got to get Ted a Father Christmas suit. Sister was worried we hadn't got anyone to hand the presents out this year, because Mr Adderbury was doing it at Halfpenny House, so I asked Ted and he said yes . . . though I think he's getting the collywobbles now over it.'

'All right, love,' Sandra said. 'I've got a bit of washing to do and then I'm going to the hospital to see Ikey off before he goes.'

She smiled as her son went off whistling. He seemed to have become a young man all at once, and there was little left of the boy she'd known before she was sent to prison. Glancing at the clock beside her bed, she calculated that she just had time to wash the things she needed to before tidying up and catching a bus to the hospital . . .

Sandra's heart caught as she scanned the ward for Ikey and discovered he was not there. His bed at the far end had a new occupant and there was no sign of him. Was he waiting for her somewhere, expecting her to come and say goodbye? She'd arranged to be here by two o'clock and there were still twenty minutes to go but Ikey was not here.

'Are you looking for Mr Blake?' a pretty young nurse asked as she turned away.

'Yes, I am. He was supposed to be leaving for the nursing home at two and it's only twenty to . . .'

'Oh, but he hasn't gone to the nursing home. He declined the offer and left this morning – about half past eleven I think it was . . .'

'He left?' Sandra was stunned. 'Did he leave a message for me – his address where I could find him?'

'I'm sorry, I don't know. You could ask Sister. She's at the desk . . .'

Sandra thanked her and walked slowly towards the desk. If Ikey had left the hospital some hours ago he could have come to St Saviour's or telephoned and left a message. She felt apprehensive as she approached the senior nurse and asked when Mr Blake had been discharged.

'Ah yes, Mrs Miller, isn't it?' Sister said, nodding. 'Mr Blake left at just after eleven this morning. He decided that he did not wish to take up the place at the nursing home as he felt well enough to look after himself – I understand that a friend has invited him to stay and he has gone there for the Christmas period.'

'Oh, I see . . . thank you so much.' Sandra's throat caught with emotion. She was not quite sure how she felt as she turned away. It was good that Ikey felt well enough not to need the extra time in the nursing home, but she couldn't help wondering why he hadn't let her know his intentions. He'd changed his mind about one thing, was it possible that he'd changed his mind about the way he wanted to live in the future? A great well of hurt rose up in her breast, because she'd thought he really cared for her – but perhaps his near brush with death had made him see things in another light?

Catching the bus to take her back to St Saviour's, Sandra stared blindly out of the window. It was damp and unseasonably warm, not a bit like Christmas, and she felt close to tears. Had she given her heart too soon? Perhaps she'd mistaken Ikey's intentions – perhaps all he'd really wanted was a housekeeper and when she'd told him she loved him in a burst of emotion that first morning after he woke up, he'd felt obliged to smile and say they would be married. Or had he said that at all? Had he murmured something about wanting her to be happy?

Sandra couldn't recall. She only knew that she loved him and she was anxious that he'd refused the offer of two weeks at a nursing home. Was he really strong enough to stay with his bachelor friend? Who would look after him if he had a relapse or became suddenly ill? If he didn't want to go to the nursing home, Sandra was sure Sister Beatrice would have let him have one of the spare rooms in the nurses' home for a few days and she could have looked after him . . .

Tears stung her eyes but she refused to give in to them. Perhaps he would be waiting for her here, or he might have telephoned . . .

'Here it is then, old fellow.' His friend handed Ikey a thick envelope. 'I gave your instructions to the lawyer and he has done everything you asked – though I couldn't quite see why you wanted it to be that way . . .'

'Trust me, I know what I'm doing,' Ikey smiled oddly. He had a nagging headache but the doctors had told him he must expect them for some weeks to come. He had some pills that helped but was trying not to take them too often because he didn't want to become dependent. 'I want her to be secure if anything happens to me . . .'

'Why should it? You're all right, aren't you?' Jon's gaze narrowed. 'Is there something you haven't told me – is your head all right?'

'I have awful headaches at times, but I'm told they will gradually go.' Ikey touched the scar on the side of his head and felt the tiny bristles of hair where they'd had to shave his head for the operation. 'I look much worse than I feel.' He smiled self-deprecatingly. 'No, the doc seemed to think I'd been lucky and there will be no lasting damage – but there is always a possibility of a blood clot developing after an operation like mine and . . .'

'What?' Jon frowned. 'It's more than that – isn't it?'

Ikey sighed and confessed what was on his mind. 'Connolly is behind bars and some of his associates, but they know that I put them there and even from prison he could arrange for another assassination attempt. I'm not sure it would be fair of me to marry her, Jon. She's lost one husband – it could break her to lose two. I think if I give her the house and just live there with her acting as my housekeeper . . .'

'Connolly's power is broken. He'll be more worried about protecting his own back when he gets inside than sticking a knife in yours. Is making Sandra Miller your housekeeper what you really want? Is it because of Catherine?'

'No, no, it isn't. I wanted to marry Sandra, I really did, but I feel it would be unfair to her . . .'

'You're a fool, man,' his friend told him. 'There are times when you take honour that bit too far. Think of yourself for once. As for you working for us again, I'm not going to take no for an answer. You can take a month or so to get over it, but then I want you back at the station – do you hear me?'

'Yes, me lud,' Ikey said and pulled an imaginary forelock. 'As your lordship demands . . .'

'Give her the house if that's what you want, my friend, but please do not throw away your chance of being happy again. Love comes along too rarely; you should grab it with both hands.'

'Well, I'll let her choose,' Ikey said. 'If you wouldn't mind my using your phone I'd like to ring St Saviour's and ask her if she will come here. I really don't feel like getting a taxi there.'

'You should've had that extra time in the nursing home . . .'

'I'm sick and tired of hospitals and nurses,' Ikey said. 'I'd far rather stay here – unless I'm in your way.'

'Don't be a bloody fool!'

Ikey laughed and then winced. 'My damned head. It feels as if a thousand hammers are at work.'

'Did they give you anything to help?' Ikey nodded. 'Then take the bloody things and don't be a martyr. You're lucky to be alive, my friend, and even luckier to have a beautiful and loving woman waiting for you. Grab what has been offered and stop worrying about what might happen. I could walk across the road and get knocked down and killed by a bus – any of us could.

384

Tell that conscience of yours to get lost and marry the woman . . .'

'Only if you'll support me to the altar?'

'Damned right I will, and drag you there if I have to,' Jonathan smiled. 'Now make that telephone call and I'll see what my housekeeper has left us for lunch.'

Sandra was nervous as the taxi pulled up outside the lovely old building in Kensington. She'd been told to come in a taxi and that the fare would be paid; it was all arranged for half past five and she only had to get in when it arrived. She got out and looked uneasily at the names on the bell at the side of the door, pressing the one that belonged to Jonathan Carter. A few moments later it was opened and he appeared, wearing a thick overcoat.

'Ah, Mrs Miller, we were expecting you, and here you are. Please go straight up the stairs and turn left; it's the first one and I've wedged it open. Ikey would have come down, but I was just leaving. He's had a headache ever since he got here so if he's a bit grouchy just ignore it. He's a really good fellow you know – though at the moment he looks more like one of the criminal fraternity with that shaved head . . .'

Chuckling to himself, Jon went out and the door closed after him. Sandra ran up the stairs, her heart beating wildly. She saw the door as he'd described it and went towards it, pushing it open and moving the wedge with her foot so that it closed after her. She was in a small hall with a polished wood floor and an antique side table with a bowl of flowers on top, and a mahogany chair standing to either side.

'Sandra, is that you?' Ikey came to the door of the sitting room. He looked pale and anxious and any feelings of annoyance she might have had at the way he'd behaved vanished in her anxiety for him. 'Please come in. Jonathan's gone out like the good soul he is to let us have some time alone . . .'

'Ikey . . . I've been so worried. When you'd gone . . .'

'Yes, I know. I should've let you know, but I made up my mind to leave on the spur of the moment and just got a taxi and came here. It was too much trouble to bother with a public phone . . .'

'Jonathan said your head aches?'

'Yes, it's quite bloody sometimes, but the pills help and they told me it will get better in time – but until it does I have to put up with it, I'm afraid.'

'I suppose after what happened you're lucky it isn't worse . . .'

'Yes, that's what Jon tells me. He's given me quite a lecture this afternoon . . . Sit down, Sandra. I'd rather like to myself . . .'

Sandra sat on the sofa and he took the armchair opposite. She glanced about her. It was a smart flat, with leather chairs and sofa, small tables, all antique and expensive, a few pieces of silver and one or two pictures on the wall. The home of a professional man, but not the kind of home Sandra liked or felt comfortable in.

'Are you feeling terrible?'

'Not brilliant,' he admitted. 'I suppose I should've gone to bed, but I've had enough of hospitals and beds.'

'Yes, I expect so,' Sandra smiled. 'You don't like being the patient, do you?'

'Not much . . .' His smile was just the same and Sandra's heart caught. 'I shall rest though, I promise. Will you forgive me for not letting you know – but I didn't decide until this morning.'

'Of course. You don't owe me an explanation, Ikey.'

'I think I do.' He gave her an odd look. 'I still want all those things we talked of, Sandra. I have secured the lease of a house for us and I want you to go there and get it ready for us; it is yours and I want you to make it your home – whether you wish me to live in it as your husband is up to you . . .'

'Ikey, I told you . . .'

'In the heat of the moment. I'd been badly hurt; you were afraid I might die . . . perhaps you've thought differently since?'

'No – have you?'

'I have realised that it might be selfish for me to marry you. No, hear me out, Sandra. I do love you and I do want you as my wife – but have you thought that I might suffer a relapse that could kill me, and there is a possibility that Connolly will try to have me murdered in the future?'

'Billy told me that Sergeant Sallis says Mr Connolly is denying that he ordered your murder. He says that it was all Stevie Baker's idea – but the police are disinclined to believe him. Stevie thought he would get lenient treatment if he gave evidence against his old boss, so he may escape a charge for attempted murder, but Billy says the police are going to charge him with grievous bodily harm and running prostitutes. Someone came forward and gave evidence concerning him and she'd been badly beaten up.'

'I see . . .' Ikey frowned. 'Connolly is going down for a long time. He'd kept records of money paid to police officers and MPs on his payroll so he'll be charged with corruption, and interfering with the due course of the law – but the biggest thing they found was his set of private accounts. It seems that our friend has been cheating the Revenue for years, and Jon thinks that is enough to put him away for twenty years. He might be able to wriggle out of some things, but once the tax inspector gets his claws in, he's had it . . .'

Ignoring this, Sandra went straight to what was worrying her. 'Did the doctor say a relapse was likely?'

Ikey saw the anxiety in her eyes and met them steadily. 'Only a possibility – but I wanted to be fair to you, Sandra . . .'

'Do you think it's fair to break my heart?' she said and got up, going to kneel by his chair, looking up at him. 'If I lost you now it would break my heart, Ikey, because I love you – but none of us knows how long we may have. I could die before you . . . but if the worst happened and one day you were suddenly gone, at least I should have had some happiness . . .'

'You're so brave,' Ikey said and leaned forward to touch her cheek. 'You've known the bitterness of loss once and yet you're willing to try again. I wasn't as brave as you – when Catherine died I went to pieces.'

'You're a very brave man,' Sandra said, 'but we all have our weaknesses and perhaps Catherine was yours.'

'She was young, lovely, and she didn't deserve to die,' Ikey said, 'but I've come back from the brink – and I am ready to try again, if you can put up with me?'

'I don't think I could not marry you now,' she said and reached up to kiss him. 'I know you're still not well, my dearest, but I'll prepare our home and, when you're well again, we can marry . . .'

CHAPTER 32

'Well, that's a sight I never believed I'd see when that young tearaway was running through the corridors at St Saviour's.' Sister Beatrice turned to smile at Angela who had come up to London for the wedding. 'Who would have believed that a rebellious lad like Billy Baggins would turn out so well?'

'Oh, I always thought they would get married one day,' Angela said and laughed. 'Mary Ellen was a good influence on him from the start and I think it's wonderful the way he's supporting her so that she can better herself and become a teacher.'

'Rose should have let her stay on at school, of course,' Sister Beatrice said. 'But it has turned out quite nicely after all . . .'

'Who is that rather odd-looking man sitting on Billy's side next to his best man?'

'That is Ikey. That shaved head is rather off-putting, but I dare say his hair will grow. He was the victim of a nasty beating, and Billy helped drive the rogues off, assisted by Sergeant Sallis.'

'Ah, he's Ikey and the very attractive lady next to him

must be Mrs Miller. Mary Ellen did tell me some of it when I popped in to see her before we came to church. She was always one of my favourites, you know . . .'

'I remember very well. You took her to see *Bambi* when I had forbidden her to go to the pantomime with the others.'

'Yes, I could never forget. How arrogant I was at the start . . .'

'I wouldn't say that – we both needed to learn, if you ask me.'

'I was sorry I could only get twenty tickets for you this year. Mark told me to buy tickets for all the children, but they just weren't available.'

'We offered a choice of the pictures or the pantomime and it turned out very well,' Sister Beatrice said and sighed as the happy couple went through to sign the register. 'Can you stop for the party this afternoon, Angela? Archie's friend Ted Hastings is playing Father Christmas and we have presents as usual. We may have a few carols, but this year we joined in the concert at the church hall. Several schools sent choirs and St Saviour's was invited to attend and pick a few of our children to sing with them. It turns out that Archie has a rather good voice, though he had to be persuaded to sing solo . . .'

'Well, I could drive down a bit later . . . but no, perhaps I'd better not. I believe Mark has asked some friends for midnight mass and drinks, so I'd better be there to make sure everything is ready. Perhaps next year . . .'

'If we're still here.'

'What do you mean?'

'Shush now, the bride and groom are leaving . . .'

Everyone watched the happy couple leave the church

and then stood to file out and follow them into the crisp cold air. Thankfully, it was not raining, which was an improvement on the weather of the past few days.

Sister Beatrice threw some confetti and smiled as Billy and Mary Ellen posed for photos and then left in a car for the reception.

'Ah well, I must return to St Saviour's.'

'You're not coming to the reception?'

'Oh no. I wanted to see them wed, but I have work to do . . .'

'What did you mean when you said if you were there next year?' Angela persisted. 'You're not thinking of leaving?'

'No, not unless I'm asked. I simply wondered if the Board considered it worthwhile keeping St Saviour's open – and, of course, there's always the possibility that the Welfare Department might decide to take us over completely; in which case I do not think I should care to stay on. Besides, you have your big new home, which I know is very modern, clean and efficient . . .'

'Yes, it is all those things, but I'm not sure we've got it right yet. I've heard one or two disturbing stories about one of the male carers. Mark has been investigating . . .'

'Is that Mr Gerald Smith – the one who shut Archie in a cupboard and left him there for an hour?'

'Amongst other things, some of them rather more serious,' Angela said. 'He had such excellent references, came from a good private school – a headmaster, retired because it was too much for him. Unfortunately, it appears that he lied to us. He was asked to resign because of a disagreement with their board over matters of discipline. Now that he's leaving it that means we're looking for someone to take his place, and it's not easy. The children either run rings round the staff or they're scared because they're ill-treated. I so often think of you and wish that you could be there as well as here. You always seem to know how to appeal to the children, to make them behave as they ought. If we were ever to close St Saviour's I should press for you to be invited to take over at Halfpenny House . . .'

'Well, that is a compliment,' Sister Beatrice said and smiled. 'Thank you so much, Angela, for the vote of confidence. I hope to stay on here for as long as the Board allows, but I know that the trend is towards moving the children out to the country. The air must be better for them, of course, but I'm not sure some of them would settle, you know.'

'I am very sure we need you where you are for the time being. I only wish I had you in Harlow as well . . .'

'An impossibility, I fear.' Sister Beatrice raised her brows. 'Why don't you take it on, Angela? The twins will be in school before long and I can't see you being happy stuck at home for ever. I know you fundraise and that dance you organised in the country this summer raised several hundred pounds – but I think you would make an excellent Warden for Halfpenny House.'

'We call her a Superintendent there,' Angela said. 'It's more modern, they say, and in keeping with the way things are moving, but sometimes I think it was so much better here . . .'

'You are being sentimental and nostalgic,' Sister Beatrice said with a shake of her head. 'Life moves forward, my dear. When St Saviour's was begun in the

393

war years there was a desperate need for it; the need is still there to a certain extent and there will always be children in need of care – but whether Halfpenny Street is as relevant now as it was then I'm not sure. I believe that the Board was more farsighted than I was willing to admit at the time. One day things will be done in a more formal manner. Sergeant Sallis will not ring me in the middle of the night to admit a child found wandering, but the Children's Department, and they will take over more and more. We shall be completely state-run, though whether it will be better for it I can't say. Homes like ours must move with the times or be ignored and forgotten . . .'

'How sad,' Angela said. 'I didn't think I would ever hear you say that, Sister.'

'Neither did I,' Sister Beatrice admitted. 'Whatever happens, you will keep in touch?'

'Yes, of course.' Angela pressed her hand. 'I must go to congratulate the bride and groom. You're sure you won't come?'

'No, I have things to do . . . our children are looking forward to their Christmas as always . . .'

'I wasn't sure you would come,' Mary Ellen said and kissed Angela's cheek. 'I'm so glad you did. Billy and me think of you as part of our family. I shall never forget what you did for us that Christmas when Billy hid in the attic and I was in trouble for helping him . . .'

'That is a long time ago,' Angela said and shook Billy's hand. 'I wanted to wish you both all the luck in the world. I'm very happy for you – and if there's ever anything I can do for you, let me know.'

'You're so kind and thank you for the lovely tea-set you gave us. I shall keep it for best . . .'

'I'm glad you liked it,' Angela said and moved on into the hall to mingle with the other guests.

'It was lovely of her to come all the way up for our wedding,' Billy said after she'd gone to stand with Staff Nurse Wendy. 'She was always all right – but she must have loads to do at home as it's Christmas . . .'

'Yes, but she was always special to me,' Mary Ellen said. 'I felt so miserable that year, with Mum ill and then dying – and Sister was so horrid at the start.'

'She's not now though,' Billy said. 'Did you see that lovely lace she sent for us? I reckon that's handmade . . .'

'Her mother used to make it,' Mary Ellen said. 'We've been lucky and had a lot of nice things, Billy. Ikey gave us a cheque for a hundred pounds. I don't know if we ought to take so much . . .'

'He can afford it,' Billy said. 'I know he acted as though he was broke when we met but he's got enough. He's not rich, just comfortable, and he'll have a decent job again when he's able to work – but he's got Sandra Miller now and she'll look after him.'

'Just like I've got you,' she said and looked at him lovingly. 'Only you're the one that looks after me, Billy . . .'

'I promised I would, didn't I?' he said and bent his head to kiss her softly on the mouth. A little cheer went up from Nipper and some of Billy's mates and Mary Ellen blushed fiery red. 'Take no notice of that daft lot. What do you say we pop in to St Saviour's after this has finished and show them your dress and bouquet?'

'Oh, could we?' Mary Ellen asked. 'Haven't we got a train to catch to Southend?'

'It doesn't go until half past six. I didn't want to leave too soon, because if there's one thing they know how to do in the East End, it's celebrate. I think we should have a real good knees-up, and then pop into the old place before we go home to change.'

'Yes. Rose is going to be there, because they've asked her to help with the children's tea.' Mary Ellen glowed as she looked up at him. 'We couldn't ask them all to the wedding, but they are family, aren't they? All the staff and kids . . . we're all part of one big family really . . .'

'Come on, Ellie love,' he said and took her hand. 'I reckon they're all here now – let's cut the cake and then they can start on the beer . . .'

'Ooh, that's pretty,' June Miller said, touching the soft white silk of Mary Ellen's wedding dress as the children gathered round excitedly. 'Did you really make it yourself?'

'Yes, I had some help cutting it out, but I sewed it myself,' she said and smiled at the young girl. 'It's my job to make clothes.'

'I should like a pretty dress like this one day,' June said and looked at her mother. 'Mum is going to marry Ikey, you know. She's picked a nice cream dress and jacket with a red hat and gloves and cream shoes, but I wish she would wear a dress like yours . . .'

'Well, I tell you what, if there's time when I get back from my honeymoon, I'll make you a dress similar to this for your mum's wedding. When is she getting married?'

'Not until the spring, so the house is ready and Ikey feels better.'

'That's a promise then. I'll come round and measure you and then I'll make it for you – as a present . . .'

'You're nice,' June said and touched the dress reverently.

'I was lucky when I came here. I made friends and I had people do nice things for me – so why shouldn't I do nice things for others?'

'I'm going to tell Mum,' June said and ran off to find her mother. Mary Ellen turned to her husband as he touched her arm.

'We don't want to miss the train . . .'

'I'll just say goodbye to Sister and Rose – and Mrs Miller,' Mary Ellen said. 'I shan't be two minutes . . .'

Billy nodded, watching as she kissed a few people and received hugs in return from most. Sister Beatrice just smiled, but that was enough. He was just about to hurry his new wife when Ikey came up to him.

'Billy, you can drive, can't you?'

'Yes – did you want me to drive you somewhere?'

'No, but I shan't be needing these for a while.' Ikey held out the keys to a Morris car. 'You'll find it outside in the street. Save you bothering with the train, lad. Have a good time and give our love to Mary Ellen . . .'

Billy thanked him but Ikey had gone and he saw he was talking to Archie Miller. Smiling, he watched as Mary Ellen was surrounded by the children, all of them clutching at her, giving her small tributes, not wanting her to leave. She was as popular with them as she always had been, and that was because she still visited, brought them a few sweets, and read to the little ones when she could. It had been a good thing to come here, because these people were their family, and now that Ikey had loaned him his car, Billy knew there was no hurry to leave . . .

CHAPTER 33

'Oh, Billy, this is lovely,' Mary Ellen said as she glanced round their room with delight. 'Look, there's a balcony looking over the sea and everything . . .'

'Well, I asked them special for the best,' Billy said and smiled down at her, seeing the excitement in her eyes. 'We've never had a real holiday, Ellie, just a day at the seaside or a trip to the zoo – but this is our wedding and we're having a proper honeymoon . . .'

'It's wonderful,' she said and put her arms about him. 'I'm so happy, Billy. I never thought I would ever have all this . . . you and a lovely room at the sea and our own home to go back to.'

'Sam gave me a wad of notes before we left,' Billy told her. 'He didn't know what to buy as a present and I told him we'd got a lot of the stuff we needed so he gave me money – and it's as much as Ikey gave us. It will set us up proper, love. If you wanted, you could give up work and concentrate on your studies . . .'

'I'm happy going on as we are,' she said and pressed closer to him, looking at him with love. 'It will be there when we need it – when we have a family or something.'

'I like the sound of that,' Billy said, 'but we're not going to start one just yet, love. I made you a promise and I shall keep it.'

'You're so lovely,' she murmured dreamily as he held her tight, and then suddenly bent down to sweep her up behind the knees and carry her to the bed. 'Billy, you wicked man! I do love you . . .'

'I know, but I love you more,' he said, 'and I'm going to show you just how much, my little angel . . .'

Mary Ellen gave a gurgle of laughter as he pounced and then she was being kissed in such a way that she could hardly breathe let alone think, her panting in rhythm with his own as their clothes were stripped off and they delighted in the feel of bare flesh, of being close in a way they never had before. As Billy touched his lips and tongue to her breasts, delicately flicking them and then moving slowly downward over her flat belly, making her cry out in pleasure, she was glad they had waited, glad he'd been strong enough for them both, because it was so lovely, so wonderful that their first time was as a newly married couple.

'Billy, Billy,' she whispered, her hands in his hair, stroking his nape and then down his smooth back and over his hips. 'Oh, it's so nice. I didn't know . . . I didn't know it could be so lovely . . .'

'Nor did I,' he said hoarsely. 'I've wanted you so much but there's been no one else for me, Ellie love. I never want to lose you or have anyone else. You've always been my love, even before we went to St Saviour's.'

'I didn't always know,' she confessed, 'but then I did and now . . .' She arched as he touched her between her thighs and she trembled with desire, her breathing fast and excited as he moved on top of her, and then he was inside her and she cried out with pleasure, feeling the joy of being his, of being one with the man she'd loved for so long. 'I love you so much, Billy, and I love this . . .'

'You're all I ever wanted,' Billy panted and then felt the climax as he came inside the protective sheath he'd used. 'Oh, hell, I'm sure it's not supposed to be that quick . . .'

Mary Ellen clutched at him and giggled, kissing him because he looked so disappointed. 'Never mind, we're only learning,' she said. 'You and me together as it should be, Billy. I don't want you to be all practised and clever at it – I want to know you've never been anyone else's.'

'Oh, Ellie love,' he whispered. 'You make everything right, you always do – even when my ma died, you made it better. We'll learn how to do it proper and make it good for you . . .'

'I'll enjoy practising so don't get good too soon, Billy,' she teased and started to tickle him, laughing as he retaliated and then started kissing her again and touching her, before leaving her abruptly to go to the bathroom. When he came back, Mary Ellen knew he wanted to do it again and she smiled up at him, welcoming him back to her arms, feeling the joy of loving and being loved.

And this time it was wonderful . . .

Rose bent to lay Mary Ellen's wedding flowers on the double grave of her mother and father. Mary Ellen had given them to her and asked her to do it rather than toss the bouquet as was often the custom.

'I want Ma and Pa to have them,' she'd said, her eyes

moist. 'They couldn't be with us, but this way they can share.'

'You're a lovely girl, Mary Ellen,' Rose had said and smiled. 'I'm glad we're friends, love. Be happy – it's all I've ever wanted for you.'

'Thanks, Rose – and you be happy too. It's what they would have wanted for us both . . .'

Rose straightened up and walked away. She felt a bit lonely and couldn't face going back to the council flat now that both Mary Ellen and Marion had gone. Sister Beatrice had offered her a room in the nurses' home and she intended to move in as soon as she could pack her things.

She was thoughtful as she left the gloomy churchyard behind. She wasn't on duty that evening, but perhaps she would call in and see how things were for an hour or so before she went home.

She walked the last few yards up Halfpenny Street, studying the rather grim exterior of St Saviour's; from the outside it looked forbidding, but inside it was a happy place, a place of hope and renewal. Rose enjoyed working here; she liked her fellow nurses and the carers, and she respected Sister Beatrice, even though there had been times when she disliked her, but now that was all forgotten.

'Ah, Staff Nurse Rose,' Sister said, coming along the landing towards her. 'You're not on duty this evening?'

'No, but I just thought I would come in and see if there was anything that needed to be done.'

'Feeling a bit lost without Mary Ellen? You've looked after her since your own mother died, haven't you?'

'I tried, even though she lived here. I tried to do what I could . . .'

'And I'm sure you succeeded. Mary Ellen shows a good example to all our children and I believe she will make an excellent teacher. I am sure you must be proud of her?'

'Yes . . .' Rose smiled and the clouds fell away. 'I am proud of her, Sister.'

'As am I – of her and Billy,' Sister Beatrice said. 'Well, we're quiet for the moment, but that's usually the way it is before the storm breaks. Shall we have a nice cup of tea and a biscuit before the deluge as it were?'

'Yes, why not,' Rose agreed, suddenly feeling content as never before. 'I'll go down and fetch a tray . . .'

St Saviour's
will give them hope...

When there is nowhere to turn...

One place will give them hope.

The Orphans of Halfpenny Street

CATHY SHARP

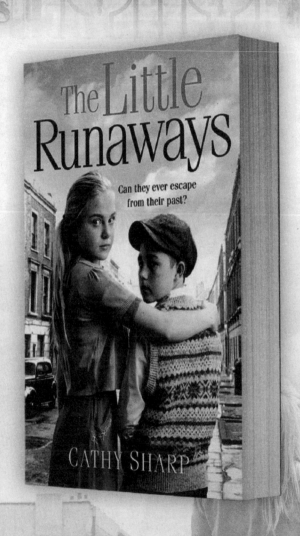

Christmas for the Halfpenny Orphans

The third instalment in this **compelling** saga